METAL AND BONE

A Steampunk Cinderella Story

C.I. CHEVRON

CYPRESS KNOLL PRESS

Cypress Knoll Press
Cookville, TX

This book is a work of fiction. Names, characters, businesses, organizations, places, events and incidents either are the product of the author's imagination or are used fictitiously. Any resemblance to actual persons, living or dead, events, or locales is entirely coincidental.

For information contact; address www.CIChevron.com

Cover design by Steven Novak
ISBN: 978-1-7335913-1-7
LCCN : 2019936227

First Edition: April 2019

Acknowledgements

This book could not have happened without the patience of my family, thank you for understanding when I head off into my own little world.

I also want to thank my critique partners who are so diligent about catching plot holes and those pesky overused words.

OTHER BOOKS BY C.I. CHEVRON

Cogs and Fur (Book 2 Mutants and Modifieds)
Tooth and Nail (Book 3 Mutants and Modifieds) (2021)
Four Days to Fusion
Unsealed
Beyond the Stars

Visit www.CIChevron.com for more information and offers into
the World of Metal and Bone.

Chapter One

A Thief

G as mask or goggles?
That became the most pressing question when she considered an outing in London's night. Cinder worked mostly by tactile memory, one eye on the ink smudged darkness, the other on the deceptively gentle waves of the Thames.

Very little moved this time of night, the wise fearful of those lurking in doorways and the mists rising without warning from the waters. Both could strangle and rob the unsuspecting in a heartbeat. One of gold, the other of life. However, circumstances did not make Cinder timid. She raised her face to the sky, testing the direction of the wind.

The journey by heliobike from Iron Crest had been easy enough, the wind pushing her all the way with only the minimal amount of pedalling required to keep her slight weight aloft. But the winds had turned fickle since the chemical rain and often changed on a whim. She hated to be caught in a delicate situation.

Gas mask it is.

Mask in place, she turned her spyglass from the waters to her evening's target. A fairly new townhouse by the late Mr. Hatchet, owner of the aptly named Hatchet Shipping—a veritable eye sore since its upgrade several years ago. She couldn't help shuddering as she studied the gargoyles perched at each corner, Notre Dame imitations by some aspiring artist with absolutely no talent for sculpting. She watched a long moment to ensure they weren't some sort of sentry automaton.

The Franco-Prussian conflict and the loss of the Victorian royal lineage jump-started the use of mechanical soldiers. The metal encased mechanicals, though slow and programed to certain behaviours, could make her life difficult. Especially if they looked up, which they rarely did.

Cinder cared little for the particulars of the Hatchet estate, or even about the automatons. All that mattered was that the unfortunate man's rise in fortunes made him a board member of the prestigious Academy of Medical Advances. As a result, he had access to the latest experiments conducted in the little-known division of legal human modifications. She flexed her left arm, state of the art pistons sliding soundlessly, unlike her *illegal* modifications.

The metal appendage trembled a bit and rather than risk a fatal error, she pulled a hypodermic from the case at her belt. Next to the syringe loop hung three glass vials. She chose one and injected the nerve rejuvenator in the shoulder stump. A quick study of the hand revealed the tremor gone and she could focus on the evening's goal.

The deceased's family planned to hold the watch in town and bury the chap quickly. Fresh body parts were at premium with the explosion of medical entrepreneurs, or Body Snatchers, looking for ways to profit from the war. Besides, the funeral party presented the perfect opportunity for the young Lady Hatchet to convince her friends of her sorrow.

Cinder *did* give her some credit for the sort of skill required to convince a gentleman forty years her senior of true love and even more to get him to marry her. Then again, it could be the family's jewels she planned to inherit over the objections of the stepchildren—all older than herself.

Cinder scoffed. *Mere baubles.*

Next to the papers that could give her and other inventors insight into helping people in dire circumstances, they were nothing.

The shadow of an airship moved across the moon, blotting the wan light filtering through the coal smoke and ash. Cinder crouched closer to the large chimney, eyeing the spectre suspiciously. Most airships declined to navigate the city at night, choosing to dock rather than risk a fatal collision in the dark. From her experience those who ventured out this time of night had nefarious plans, including herself.

And time to get to it.

Leaving the heliobike for another time, she pulled a baton from her pack. With two twists and a snap a vaulting pole materialised. She leaped to the next building, moving across the rooftops with a lightness born of many nights practice and necessity. Getting nicked by the police as a burglar would seriously kink her plans for the rest of the evening.

Target rooftop secured, she frowned to see the airship now moving her direction. The ship could be a younger son returning home from the wars on the continent, pushing his crew into danger in his rush back to the arms of his family.

Arrogant aristos. She conveniently forgot that, if not for her modification, she once might have fallen under that appellation herself.

Adjusting the mask, she drew three silver balls from her pocket and lifted them to the weak moonlight. They shivered and moved, uncurling into three mice the size of large rats. They stretched, made a few swipes at cleaning their metal whiskers, then sat up and looked for the fourth.

"There you are, my pets. Judith took your friend Clarence for assurance, so let's make this quick and get him back." Three sets of eyes stared back. She could never be sure they understood everything she said. The little mechanicals sensed when one of their number went missing and worked with urgency to ensure Ella returned from town before her absence inconvenienced her stepmother.

Stepmother! Jailer more like it. These tiny metal creatures had more warmth in their tiny claws than the arrogant witch who married her father just six months before his death.

Or murder.

Shaking off the morbid thoughts, Cinder released the mice and they scampered down the walls, diamond claws digging into brick, plaster, and ivy alike. The moonlight took on a green tinge as the mists rose, so she adjusted the oxygen tank before rummaging through her bag.

She released the catch on her left hand, twisting to detach the artificial limb, and replaced it with a grappling hook. It always paid to carry extra hands.

Though completely ambidextrous after all these years, a small part of her remained thankful the left arm was the one taken in the accident and not her right.

She coiled the rope into the compartment in the lower arm, secured the hook end to a billowing chimney, then followed the mice off the roof.

Despite the early morning hour, lights blazed from the lower level of the three-story structure. One or two candles sputtered in the upper windows, servant's quarters, no doubt, and unlikely to be occupied for a good many more hours.

However, from the second story window where the mice came to rest, a soft glow emanated, making its occupancy unclear. She halted two windows away, feet light on the sill, except for the boot made extra heavy by the packing required to make up for her lack of toes.

Next, she sidled across two dark windows, the rope a valuable aid to her left side clumsiness.

She rested her cheek against the ivy and prepared to risk a glance into the room indicated by the mice. "Of course, why would it be easy?" Her pets merely stared at her. "In there? Are you sure?"

Flora flicked an ear.

"What is that supposed to mean?" Cinder hissed but got no response. She looked towards the window at the left, the one where her informants told her the vault rested.

Phillipe rustled the ivy.

"Shh. Alright, alright. I'll look." She leaned over the sash and peered into the fire lit room.

Chapter Two

A Prince

A lone man sat in front of a glowing fire, eyes staring into the crimson depths, head bowed. One long leg stretched out before him and, despite the youth in his face, a cane rested against the armrest.

Close by sat a silent tea service, the clock ticking steadily the count down to the automated tea refill.

The chap's profile revealed a strong chin and hawkish nose, but both with a refinement and thoughtful set that suggested good breeding. His handsomeness set her heart beating against her chest with a flux of painful memories.

Her father often sat thus. Long hours near the foot of her bed as she healed. She pulled back and leaned against the building, agony rushing through her blood with every heartbeat.

Her body healed eventually, slowly, however, her father's mental health never did. The loss of his wife in the same accident that took Cinder's limbs left him devastated. The depth of both his love and misery tortured her dreams. Once she fantasised of having such a love—one whose strength surrounded and protected her. Later, she cursed the idea of it when that same love left her bereft.

Focus, Cinder.

She felt better calling herself that name. Her stepmother thought it amusing she was often covered in the marks of her chosen trade and called her Cinder with derision. Lately, those she helped took to calling her that and she liked it. It made her feel strong.

With this thought she shrugged off the melancholy feelings.

It mattered not whether the stranger be handsome or not, son or visitor. A time of mourning in a house full of strangers coming and going presented the perfect time to strike. In times like this, blame often shifted to the more destitute relatives before common sense could prevail and an outsider considered. By that time any trail left would have turned cold and any evidence corrupted.

Perfect.

A familiar coldness stole over her and she grasped at it, steadying herself. Besides, who would miss a satchel of papers when jewels occupied the same shelf of the same safe? What thief took papers of no obvious value anyway? Hatchet had deposited them into the dark recess with barely a glance.

Or thus said his secretary.

A weaselly fellow to be sure, but one who owed her for the nice left pointer finger which, when covered by a glove, looked perfectly normal, and when exposed doubled as an ink pen.

An ingenious creation even if she did say so herself.

The creak of a rope above caused her to dive into the ivy. Peering upwards she cursed. In her moment of inattention, the airship from before had stopped overhead. A ladder swung empty in the night, a passenger already disembarked.

Through the leaded glass the sound of a door opening drew her attention back to the room. She couldn't help herself, she leaned over to watch, then caught her breath.

The man entering was of a completely different calibre than the brooding gentleman. Although his arrival was quiet, his presence filled the chamber. The fire flared in the grate at the gust of air from the swinging door. A touch of wildness entered the staid room as shadows danced. A piecemeal English naval uniform and dreadlocks, along with an eye patch gave the man the look of a privateer.

Two firearm belts crossed his hips, leather ties securing them to his thighs. Bandoliers of ammunition bumped against the buttons of his jacket, a knife and a rapier—one high one low—graced each hip. Even from her disadvantaged view point, she could be sure the fellow concealed more weapons, though to wear such armaments into a gentleman's home would have made several of the ladies downstairs swoon.

Were she the one alone in the room no doubt the urge to leap to defend herself would be overwhelming. Even the most naive child could see the newcomer dangerous in the extreme.

As it were, the chap slumped in the chair started forward, pulling his cane close and half drawing a blade from the handle before relaxing. He drew his leg under him slowly, closed the cane and used it to stand. "Your highness!" He barked in a sand on glass voice.

The armed man stepped across the distance before the other gained his feet. He clapped the injured fellow on the shoulder gently but with enough force to seat him again. "Basil, Ol' Chap, it is terribly good to see you, but if you don't sit yourself back in that chair, I will kick you in the good leg."

The gentleman settled back with a laugh. "Can't stop with the orders now can you, Aerysleigh."

The other grinned, an expression that promised trouble. "Aye, can't let my best set of eyes be out of commission for too long. What say the streets?"

Cinder trembled and threw her back against the ivy. *The Prince!* How different he looked! Hard and fierce now, scared and changed. Then again, weren't they all.

Her scalp tingled with a terrible premonition. Of all the jewels in London, no, in all of England, none were as valuable as this information. Prince Aerysleigh *here.* Basil Traverson, not only a police commissioner, but apparently a friend.

Many speculated on how the rogue royal kept tabs on the country while he fought in the wars on the continent, and it seemed clear he had his own way of doing things. Nothing of this appearance had appeared in the papers. No whisper of rumour on the streets or among the servants. Nothing.

A horn sounded from the river, a warning of the rising mists.

The prince cursed and footsteps thumped towards the window. "The devil, Basil? What are you doing with your window open this time of night? Injury I understand, stupidity, however, is not like you."

Cinder tugged on the spring in her arm and dropped below the sill. The gentle *shhhh* of the line filled the night and she held her breath. But the only reaction above was Basil's ungracious scoff and the snick of the window latch. Drapes snapped shut.

Well, that was that. Mind still whirling, she gave a double jerk on the rope and ascended, the spring mechanism winding more silently now that the danger had passed.

Unbidden her mind drifted as it often did when life got too intense. She let herself disappear into an unbelievable fantasy, one that blended with the memory of her mother at the Steelhaugh annual ball, but this time it was herself in the iridescent dress covered in sapphires. She pressed her forehead against the sash, fighting the tears. Always in Ella's memory her father stepped into her mother's arms, but tonight it was the braided stranger. The evening would continue imbued with magic, until she stumbled and revealed her modification that is.

And that would be the end of it.

In her mind, fans covered scowls and fingers pointed. A monster. A stirring in her pocket brought her attention to the present. A sharp nose jabbed her hand.

"I know, Flora. I'm going." The mouse leaped to the sill and scuttled across, diamond studded claws clinging to the brick, blue light from her heart stone blending into the snowflakes of moonlight poking holes in the cloud and soot cover. Dane and Phillipe followed their sister, only one quick glance back to ensure her compliance. At least they never lost focus, sensing the urgency of their mission and the requirement of stealth.

Shaking the last vestiges of the dream from her psyche, she determined to press on. *Focus, Ella, no time to mess up lost in a girlish daydream.* Such a thing might have been if her mother had not died, if the accident had not turned her into an illegally modified human, if the war had not taken everything.

Flora pressed her nose to the target room's leaded glass, cutting a small circle for her entrance. Her brothers used their combined weight to trigger the latch. Cinder pushed it open and paused behind the heavy curtain. She motioned for her three accomplices to scout and they slid down the drapes to the floor. Their small size would go unnoticed by roving servants or mechanised devices. In the span of twenty breaths they returned—luminescent blue eyes blinked up the all clear.

Surely, Father never intended these rodent companions to turn to a life of crime, but she couldn't help but be cheered by their company. Though mechanical, they were her only allies in a world run amok. She tapped the heel of her boot and extracted her lock picking tools. The vault sat evident behind a hinged family painting.

Mr. Hatchet, made trim by the artist's forgiving brush, rode a rearing charger, musket held high in the air, gas mask in place. Not that the portly merchant ever handled a weapon beyond those required for the occasional sport.

Resisting the urge to take a knife to the pretentious art, Cinder did draw the line at family heirlooms, she instead slid the weapon along the sides and back for booby traps. Hopefully the younger generation possessed more taste, though she highly doubted it.

The ting of metal on metal warned her of a trip wire. It may be attached to a siren or perhaps only to a bell in the housekeeper's room. She cut the wire and tied if off, then swung the painting outward to reveal an ironclad door. As with many of the furnishings in the room, the merchant had skimped on this as well.

"Draw the drapes, my friends."

Dane and Phillipe scampered to do as directed, Flora climbed to her shoulder to watch. Cinder drew the torch hand from her bag, snapped it into place on her stump and attached the gas lines to the small canisters. She pushed the handle of the spark maker, then adjusted the flow until a blue flame made shadows waltz.

The spare hand made for extra bulk to be sure, but it cut the time of breaking into more secure vaults in half. Two minutes and she had the papers in her satchel. Four and she stood on the sill, debating her options.

The roof was out now that the airship hovered above, the streets had a greenish tinge warning of the gases that would make people desperate and dangerous.

The kite it is then. She scanned the surrounding buildings and patted the pocket where the mice rested. Just need a little height is all and the billowing steel factory near the docks offered the perfect launch site.

At the chime of the church bells that marked the hour, she took to the air and floated towards her next destination.

CHAPTER THREE

A RESCUE

Pistols and boilers, couldn't anything go right?
Cinder tugged on her left line to turn away from the bridge, but the fickle wind, stirred by the unstable gasses, pushed back.
This is going to hurt.

She braced for the impact, her head turned to protect the mask. A cable jerked the kite's flimsy material holding her aloft, like a child's spinning top she whirled around the pivot point and slammed into a support. She scrabbled for purchase on the brick, one set of toes obeying her command, the other set, the metal ones, acted as more weight to pull her down.

Disturbed birds scattered from the high refuge. Wings obscured her eyesight for the precious moments needed to plan her defence and landing. The elements mocked every attempt to find a secure hold. The wind buffeted her, first shoving her away and then gleefully slamming her back into the brick.

The outer lenses on her gas mask cracked, further blinding her along with the flashing sparks from the head blow. Again, the wind pushed, treating her more as smoke on the breeze than a full-grown woman. As a last resort, she faced the brick and slammed her left hand into the support. Metal gleamed, iron tipped nails scrabbled against the mortar until her feet found purchase.

She took a steadying breath and looked around. Fate had landed her near the centre of the bridge on the tallest most spire. She spied a nest the size of three men lying side by side several feet above her.

She shuddered. *Of course.*

Of all the bridges across the Thames, of all the supports to strike, she found herself just below the Valkryie's nest.

With diabolical timing, a face contorted by a frightening mix of mutant and modified, peered over the edge. Its metal beak snapped, and the form disappeared only to begin clambering down the other side of the support, metal claws scaling the brick with no problem.

Cinder reached for her knife with a sigh. She liked the Valkryie. He protected London's dwindling bird population, particularly pigeons. His calling and obsession both. He nursed those broken by careless machines and people and provided a safe haven from the mists and predators. More than once she had run into him at the Machine Shop and liked the gentle way he handled the birds.

However, more like an arachnid than avian, he considered unwelcome guests fair game. She didn't blame him, food grew scarce everywhere, but she did resent the fact that tonight she happened to be *le repas de jour.*

A pigeon tumbled from its perch, wings beating at her head. She slapped it away, aiming for maximum damage and hoping to distract the Valkyrie with the bird's squawks.

She turned in time to parry a vicious strike of the metal beak. "Don't," she warned, lashing at the air in front of her and at the same time striking one of the lines that held her fast.

The Valkyrie scrabbled away then climbed upwards and grabbed the strings to her kite, pulling her closer while staying safely out of reach. She slashed at the lines. A fall into the tainted Thames would kill her for sure, but it would be on her terms. As though sensing her resolve, the birdman looped one of the loosened ropes around her neck and pulled. Cinder flailed away from the support, the metal rim of the gas mask the only thing saving her neck from snapping.

Anger, or perhaps lack of air, clouded her vision once more. The Valkyrie gave a heave and she rose quickly to one of the guide wires leading to the next support. She reached up with her modification and clamped her fingers down, locking them. With her right hand she sawed the ropes.

The birdman walked along the line, perfectly balanced. She

jumped, hoping to throw him off. Her weight did nothing to the heavy cable. He grinned and snapped his beak. She tried to pull herself up, but where her arm may be inhumanly strong, her shoulders were not.

She stilled, waiting.

He dropped suddenly, the bounce nearly unlocking her knuckles. She twisted at the last minute, driving her knife into his beak, forcing it open. "I'll take it off, I swear it."

He jerked away then snapped out a reply in Morse code. "P-R-E-T-T-Y C-I-N-D-E-R M-A-K-E N-I-C-E T-R-E-A-T F-O-R B-I-R-D-S."

"Oh, I will, will I?" She forced the knife upwards, wishing for the strength of her left hand to drive the blade straight through and into his brain, but one had to work with what one had.

She kicked, fighting the tearing claws. Oxygen hissed, the line torn from its fitting. If only she could rid herself of him, she could slide down the wire to the next support and be gone. She swung, bouncing him against the support as the wind had her, each time feeling a slight slip of her hand on the cable. The claws loosened, the damaged man flinging himself opposite her perch.

They eyed each other for a long moment, the tense peace bringing the birds back to roost. Several within reach. She ripped the mask off, sobbing for unrestricted breath. She grabbed a pigeon that cooed then struggled, covering the cry as her knuckles slipping became the least of her concerns. The buckles holding her modification to the stump of her arm stretched. Pain screamed through her. If something didn't change soon it looked as though a final swim in the poisoned waters below would be her end.

The Valkyrie stilled, eyes riveted on the bird in her grip.

"I'll kill it," she said.

He nodded, backing off even more, raising his eyes to where a shadow loomed.

What now?

She followed his gaze, the sleek form of the airship that dogged her all evening appeared above, a ladder dropping even with the danger of the winds crashing it into the bridge. Despite the pain screaming up her arm she couldn't help but admire how steady the pilot held the slim ship, a skilled airman for sure. A figure slid down the ladder, braids flying, and she gulped. She knew that silhouette.

"Need some help?" asked a deep voice with a trace of humour.

If she hadn't been in such desperate straits, she would have kicked him for the salacious comment. Instead, she gave the bird a good shake and let it fall. A scrabbling on the other side of the support indicated the Valkyrie followed. She sheathed her knife and finally reached for the cable with her human arm, releasing the strain on the buckles cutting into her flesh. Scarred though it was, it still hurt.

"No, thank you. I'm just hanging out here on the bridge this evening. Lovely night for gymnastic exercise, is it not?"

The prince chuckled, swinging the ladder close with his weight, hand outstretched. She didn't hesitate, grasping his palm and pulling herself onto the twirling ladder. For the first time ever, she found herself face to chest with a man, actually standing on his boots with her own leather and metal footwear. Immediately she lightened her left foot, unwilling to hurt him, hoping the darkness and her clothing hid her modification. He smelled of strong Bohea tea and boiler smoke.

Up close he proved as handsome as the swooning ninnies at the tea parties her stepmother attended attested to. The braids hung to just past his shoulders, jingling faintly with charms and beads. One coco dark eye smiled down at her, the other covered by a patch with a white line of a scar running from nose to temple.

"Gymnastic exercise, is it?" He tugged on the ladder and it began to rise. Lanterns appeared, men peered over the edge, soft calls in the night noted the position of the ship in relation to the bridge.

Cinder turned her face towards the London skyline. Hopefully the darkness hid the remains of her disguise. Blood trickled down her shoulder where the Birdman's beak had lacerated her garments. Conscious of her bare shoulder, she clutched at the overcoat, surreptitious about pulling extra material over her face.

Prince Aerysleigh's gaze followed her movement. "And here I thought I was rescuing a damsel in distress."

She lifted her chin. "Do that often, do you?"

"At least once while in town. However, usually it involves fainting spells and dropped kerchiefs." He seemed to ponder. "No, I am definitely sure I never saved a woman from the clutches of the Valkyrie."

"You will recall that when you dropped your ladder, The Birdman had already retreated. So, saving me as a damsel is truly a moot point."

His teeth gleamed white in the darkness. "Indeed. Regardless, though I know independence to be the fashion for young women these days, I will venture an admonition to be more careful this time of night." He gestured to the hissing oxygen tube. "Besides the obvious danger of the mists, there are disreputable characters out and about."

"Including the both of us?"

He chuckled. "*Touche.*"

"You do not need to warn *me* of the dangers of London."

She looked up at him as they once again fell into the quick repartee that marked their first meeting beyond memory, beyond war. This camaraderie came too easily. Her breath hitched. She needed to get away, put distance between them. Besides, in no way could he recognise her as that mouthy Baron's daughter. They were no longer the same people as those eager children meeting for a brief moment on the aeroport.

One thing could separate them forever.

She motioned to the dark spire shrouded in onyx mists. "If you would be so kind as to deposit me at the cathedral."

"All Saints? They offer sanctuary for those caught from home when the mists rise."

She shook her head. "No. The Catholic's St. Drogo."

Although his body did not pull away, she sensed an increasing distance gaping suddenly between them.

"They also offer sanctuary." She added and dropped her gaze, all confidence lent by the anonymity of the dark dissipating like a spark of flame in a gale.

St. Drogo offered shelter for a pitiful, but swelling number of people. Only those no longer considered human by the Houses of Parliament dared seek refuge there. Though many of those who found themselves on the Saint's doorstep had been changed by fighting in the wars that kept the aristocrats safe in their perfect world.

The prince leaned away, as far as he could with her feet atop his own and motioned to the men aloft. The ship changed course as though words had been exchanged instead of a few hand signals. The silence stretched, an uneasiness between them growing.

Words failed her on how to explain she consorted with monsters.

She ducked her head when nothing came to mind. She swung out a bit, straining to catch a glimpse of the small landing dock that would relieve this now very uncomfortable situation.

Her gloved hand covered his for the briefest instant as she moved to prepare. She ignored his deep intake of breath and removed from her satchel a perfectly normal grappling hook and rope—no need to show off things that would only disgust the Prince further.

The ship slowed.

"Thank you," she murmured. "Sometimes even monsters need a little help."

"But I don't—"

She didn't wait to hear his painful response. Flexing her metal fingers round the rope, she dropped quickly. She well knew what the Peerage thought of those like her.

There were laws after all.

Chapter Four

A Trap

Aerysleigh couldn't help but breathe in the unique scent of the woman standing so lightly upon his toes—ashes and jasmine. The comforting homey smell of boiler and forge as well as the exotic.

Mysterious and beautiful.

His mother once had a valuable ittar given as a gift by a visiting rajah. He cringed at the memory. The crystal itardans met a sad end at his curious hands. His mother's rooms smelled of the precious oil ever after.

The young lady gave him an evil glare. He couldn't help but stare, trying to make out her features under the mass of tangled hair, so light it shimmered in the darkness. Then it struck him, she thought him recoiling from her.

What few words of their conversation made her think herself hideous to him? Despite her torn clothing with the enticing flash of pale skin, her only request was to be taken to St. Drogo. His eyes widened.

Oh.

She tossed and hooked a grappler with impressive precision—one of the flukes jabbing the air dangerously close to his hand. The marines would be looking to recruit her with those sorts of skills if she didn't watch it.

"Thank you," she had murmured, the words dragged from her as though by torture. "Sometimes even monsters need a little help."

His tongue tripped over words of denial. Did she think him such an insensitive cad? By what standard could she hold him in such low esteem?

Many former soldiers found themselves at the doors of the least judgemental cathedral in town. He had not the opportunity to visit the place himself. He softened and considered the words to explain how her presence made him feel like an obtuse schoolboy beholding his first beautiful woman—and failed.

She gave him no chance. Wrapping a heavily gloved hand around the rope, she skimmed away from the ladder and disappeared among the shadows.

Sky Serpent pitched sharply, driving towards the Thames and the open water of the channel beyond. Aerysleigh climbed and grasped the hands of the nearest soldier.

First mate, Beth Wickersham, looked behind him as though for another passenger. "Trouble?"

He shook his head, unwilling to share the entrancing lady with anyone. "No, just some poor sot needing a lift."

Despite the darkness he could just imagine the raised eyebrow of the hardened soldier. "The Birdman usually makes short work of fools."

Aerysleigh strode swiftly along the darkened deck, dodging the ropes, soldiers, and crew that went about their business without words.

Though the hour late, his crew operated with silence and efficiency—hallmarks he insisted on. He took a great risk coming to London, if the missives from his mother were any indication, the marriage hunters were closing in. Despite the war, despite a married older brother, despite his prior commitment to the military, matrimony loomed on his horizon.

He surveyed the rising moon, admiring the white light clashing with the green of the poisons. He always did find beauty in the oddest things. He felt the gaze of his first mate like a dart between his shoulder blades.

"St. Drogo's?"

He waved off her questions. "I didn't ask." Not like she gave him the chance. He scanned the horizon. "Warn the crew to stay sharp and get us out of here." His mother had spies everywhere. She'd not miss a chance to hold him here if the slightest inkling of his presence shivered up her spine.

His meeting with Basil, though under the sad occasion of Mr. Hatchet's passing, revealed nothing indicating Prussian infiltration of his beloved country.

And he trusted Basil. Though one of the aristocrats and a third son, he served in the army honourably until his injury. His new occupation as commissioner of police gave Basil a unique perspective from the streets the army did not enjoy.

Such a wasted, dangerous trip. Too much time spent away from the front lines. He slammed fist into palm. "It's been too quiet."

"Your highness?"

He shook his head. "The front has become a stalemate of patrolling airships and messages from a besieged France. The clashes are becoming less frequent."

Beth raised an enquiring brow. She opened the door to his cabin. "And this is a bad thing?"

He strode to the bolted down table covered by a large map. "The enemy never rests. The only quiet on the front comes before a major storm."

Beth nodded and moved to the other side of him, hands braced on the wood against the roll of the ship. Aerysleigh took up his pencil and erased the two grey circles added a month before. An interrogation of a Prussian spy told him a new faction of the Prussian army was on the move. Their objective no less than London herself with a covert scientific operation.

He rubbed a hole in the map and shook his head at his carelessness. "Nothing. Basil has heard nothing about this supposed Prussian scientist infiltration."

"A lure perhaps?"

Aerysleigh lifted his head and stared at his first mate. "Get Sergeant Gant in here immediately."

He didn't have to give the order—at that moment young ensign Kate Worsham rushed through the door with hardly a knock. "Captain, sir. The watch reports a communication from across the channel."

Aerysleigh raced to the poop deck, Beth breathing down his neck.

A lure!

He should have known. He climbed the lines without gloves, dropping into the crow's nest next to the young watch. He jerked the spyglass from its sheath and aimed it to where *Cloud Spirit* patrolled the French coastline. Reading the flashes, his mouth flattened into a tight line. Thunder rolled across the choppy waves, the cumulus clouds flashing with the explosions of the cannon fire.

Too late.

A lure it was, and he had fallen for it like a first-year novice. The Prussians set a fine trap, betting on the Prince's need to investigate the Prussian infiltration rumour and leaving *Cloud Spirit* at the mercy of the Prussia's greatest warship, *The Sieg.* The must have sneaked up the coast, bolstered by allies in Spain.

He swung to the decks below. "Get us over there!" he bellowed, all thoughts of circumspection flying in the face of his guilt. Beth gave the orders. The boilers roared. The airship knifed through the crisp night with renewed speed.

The Sergeant called the marines to quarters. Cannons rumbled below decks as the gun crews brought down the partitions and loaded their weapons. The crew moved in grim determination, all eyes cutting towards the prow and the battle just out of reach. *Sky Serpent* shuddered, the fickle wind rising and pushing against the hull.

Moisture beaded and dripped signalling a storm, most likely seeded with rainmakers by the enemy. Though invented by one of the finest military minds of British history, Lady Captain Steelhaugh along with her husband, BaronSteelhaugh, Prussian spies stole the plans upon her tragic death and now used them to their advantage whenever possible.

Beth stood near, her breath at his shoulder. "We won't make it, Captain," she said under her breath.

He clenched his fists at his side. A ball of fire, so large as to be seen with the naked eye, began a downward drift. The flaming ship moved gently, like a feather on a spring breeze, rocking first this way and that. The white envelope, now lit with the orange of a sunset, flared as pockets of gas ignited. Left, then right, the ship swayed as though she may yet right herself and make a stand or flee.

Yet the fire would win. Once meeting with the boilers, flames would engulf the entire vessel. He couldn't tear his eyes away, barely hearing the call of the mate as she expertly directed the aeronaughts to pull the most from the bucking ship, holding his breath each time *Cloud Spirit* brought her prow upward.

Captain Heardsly would fight to the end, but the end was assured. The enemy ship, now unseen in the gathering gloom, fired one last volley. *Cloud Spirit* yanked left, then plummeted, no longer a feather on the breeze, but a pelican in free fall.

"She's gone, Sir," Beth whispered.

Aerysleigh fought to restrain himself from grabbing his pistols and firing at *The Seig* while it slunk away victorious. Biting his lip against obscenities unbecoming of a gentleman and captain, all the while berating himself for his stupidity. He fell for the oldest trick in the book—a rumour planted just for him.

"I know," he finally answered.

Chapter Five

The Fence

Her footsteps echoed loud in the seldom used stairwell. Cobwebs blocked her way and she had to duck and sidle around the thick nets. The spinners of such monstrosities were not the normal arachnids peering from dark corners.

No, these mutants of the soot, mists, and maybe a few illegal experiments guarded the rooftop entrance of the cathedral. One, the size of her palm and big enough to consider the odds of making her a meal, skittered close at her imprudent touch to a sticky web. At another blockage, she freed the mice again to take it down from the walls. A mutant spider stalked Flora.

"Dane!" Cinder hissed.

The brother hurried to his sister's aid and tugged at the legs from the would-be-attacker with an expression akin to curiosity. The last of the spiders behind, she stepped into the shadows of the first level.

A shrouded woman lit a candle in a quiet alcove. The large bank of candles gutted and smoked, sending shadows dancing. The war caused a great need for intercession and few wax tapers remained unlit. Wreaths of smoke hugged the shoulders of every saint like ghostly arms.

Cinder lit her own with a taper and knelt, crossing herself. Though not particularly religious, she figured such a simple gesture couldn't hurt. She adjusted a covering for her lower face and stood.

On a pew near the confessionals a cowled figure lounged. Snores that seemed just a little too forced set a soft rhythm for the murmured conversation of a novitiate offering sanctuary to a wide-eyed youth. At last the petitioner slipped out a side door, and the candles swayed in the sudden draft.

The sleeper raised a brass hand polished to a high shine. "'Ere's your coin, doll?"

Cinder ignored the question, gliding towards the narrow booth confessional in the shadow of a thick pillar. As Cinder, a special friend to St. Drogo, she enjoyed the ability to move freely.

However, some people were either ignorant or disagreed.

A knife hissed through the air, swirling the cloying air without warning. She stepped to the side, allowing the knife to clang harmlessly against the wall. This guard must be new.

The novitiate motioned for silence. "This is a holy place. No brawling here."

The guard bowed his head. "Yes, Father."

Because he showed such good manners, and the fact he didn't make a terrible night worse, she decided not to report his slip in protocol. Besides, between heliobiking from Iron Crest, the burglary, the scuffle with the Valkyrie, and then the emotional drain of revealing to Prince Aerysleigh her monster status, the black flower of exhaustion feathered her vision.

But the guard would not be satisfied, moving to block her path. "I mean it, Doll, only those with the coin are welcome here." As if her covered metal arm and mechanical hand weren't enough.

She removed her gloves and turned both hands. "This is my coin." On the back of the left a cog, cut in half and shaped like a crescent moon, had been soldered. Across the mechanical knuckles 'metal' appeared in an elegant script.

The guard stared, then swallowed hard. "C—Cin—Cinder. I'm sorry. Please go ahead."

She lowered her arms, tugging at the cloth self-consciously. Her head knew she was among friends. However, the necessity of hiding her illegal modification became so ingrained, the discomfort of revealing the gleaming metal—even some of it—to others who understood, never went away. Of course, she knew no one with such extensive modifications joining metal and spine—in fact, admitting to this illegal modification could get her arrested.

The guard hadn't moved. She peered closer and caught a glimpse of mustard chin fuzz and a full lower lip. Just a boy.

She offered him a smile to show she held no grudges and headed to the Saint's Chapel. Gas torches flickered in the windowless room creating an unnatural closeness. Metal glinted in the shadow of the furtherest pillar, another guard, but one who knew her. She turned the back of her hand and fitted the half cog into the crypt key. Magnets caught, a boiler hissed, and pistons sighed. Silently a circular section beneath the crypt turned, exposing a stairway lit by a single gas lamp.

Cinder didn't hesitate. She could have walked the path blindfolded. A circular room with another guard greeted her. Tombs lined the wall, but not those one might expect beneath a consecrated church. Visages of the modified departed stood guard against any grave robbers who found their way there. These were the first to have lived and died as exiles when they chose to undergo the surgeries to make them whole once more.

The statues varied. Perhaps her favourite was Sir Jeter Abijah Bacon. She touched the outstretched metal hand. His funds allowed the rapid advancement in mechanical hardware such as the exquisite piece sported by Cinder herself. Next to him lay Max Barman-Cartwright, a gentleman of as many professions as modified body parts.

Not one to tarry when the night grew short, Cinder hurried down the passage to her immediate left.

Adjacent to St. Drogo stood a respectable pawnbroker catering to the gentry. Its proprietor, the thin, bespectacled Mr. Flavian Wright waited on a steady flow of patrons. Nattily dressed in a subtle fashion which neither offended the prickly rich by being too poor nor above his station. He counted among his clients aristocrats on hard times, ladies wishing a bit a freedom hard coin could buy, and young gentlemen whose vices outstripped their income.

Two rooms were filled with the usual weekly assortment of garments hocked by the less wealthy. Most of those would be redeemed on Saturday before church. Other items such as the workman's tools and the like were in constant flux. The Modfair Pawn enjoyed a respectable reputation though perched under the shadow of St. Drogo.

The Fence, the business run by his co-joined twin, Proximus, dealt in a different sort of product entirely. She climbed the stairs and pushed into the large room backing the respectable establishment in to one that was…not.

As in business, the stark physical differences between the twins was as that of gold compared to clay. Unless one considered they both wore glasses.

Proximus hulked at one end of a wooden counter reading a newspaper through thick lenses perched on a bulbous, oft time broke, nose. A woman leaned close, nearly spilling out of a corset. She pulled a hat pin from her tumble of curls and placed it under the magnifying glass mounted on the far side.

The broker pushed the item back without glance. "I tol' you, Winnie. That pin ain't worth nothing except to stick into some gent with roamin' 'ands."

Winnie turned her face to the light, smiling at him through a metal mask hiding a mouthful of dental rot. She pressed forward, ample wares on display. "Come on, Dearie, just a copper. It's been four nights of the gases and business been's slow."

"Give her its worth, Proximus," Cinder said from the doorway.

The story on page five so engrossed the hulking chap that he merely pushed a copper over to the woman.

It disappeared down her bodice in a blink. "Thank ye, miss." She darted out the door leading to the Potter's field and the streets.

The paper rustled and the big fellow eyed Cinder, bald pate gleaming with a brass skull cap. "That's coming out of whatever you've got for me."

Cinder shrugged. "You know you'll have Mr. Wright sell that pin in The Modfair for three times as much."

"Ain't much demand for hat pins."

"Only the rich have the luxury of demand," she rejoined. She nodded to the array of limbs arranged on the wall. "Is that Harcourt's hand I made him?" The beggar seemed to be always losing his hands—or pawning them.

"'E loaned it to Bobby Linkpin for a day on the docks. Bobby's wife needed a dress for church, a cousin's baptism or something, so we traded for a spell."

Cinder gritted her teeth. "And Harcourt is wearing?"

"His pincher of course."

"Most likely frightening little children and pinching purses while mothers tend to their fussy babies."

Proximus shrugged. "It is what it is." He folded his paper. "What do you have today?"

Cinder dug in her satchel yet again and placed two diamond earrings on the counter top.

She had Proximus' full attention now. "That's more like it." He swung the glass over the items and Cinder hardened herself as the jewelry winked in the dim like as only true jewels could.

Her mother donned the baubles during the last ball thrown before the war, and they were one last memories of her parent. Bartering was the most common form of exchange in the underworld of the poor, though hard coin came in handy.

She nodded at the paper. "What's the news?" She hungered for tidbits of information. Sometimes weeks stretched between the times she could obtain release Iron Crest. Seeing the Prince this night when he was supposed to be well away on the front lines also spurred her curiosity,

"The usual. Prussian ground troops are on the move. Napoleon has won several battles. Spain is playing both sides. But don't worry, we are on the right side." His dry tone indicated how much he believed the rubbish. A good look around showed the losses suffered by England. Every day the numbers of the maimed and emotionally damaged made their way from the continent to St. Drogo or like places. Most ended up in the Thames, victims of the unpredictable gases, or in the potter's field behind the church. "Nothing in this paper. Want some news." He pushed another paper towards her. She barely caught the name *The Dinted Draper* and a headline declaring "Protest for Modified Rights" by Molly Mayhem, before looking away. She did not need to know that sort of news. In the wrong hands it could be dangerous.

"Umm...anything on the prince?" she asked as casually as she could.

Proximus flipped to the third page of *The Londoner's Weekly*. "Prince Robert will be at a luncheon of the Concerned Ladies for Better Sanitation tomorrow." He tipped the paper to display a drawing of a thin gentleman who looked nothing like the dashing prince who had swept from the sky that evening.

She shook her head. "The other prince."

"Prince Aerysleigh? Well now, he's a different story, isn't 'e, but not one that makes the papers. Bloke in 'ere the other night says hows the fellow cut through a whole Prussian Fleet to rescue a downed floundering crew. Snatched them right out of the ocean."

Yes, she could see him doing that.

The pawnbroker scoffed. "'Course it's all stories and lies. No aristocrat is going to risk his life for the common sailor."

She shrugged. But he *had* risked his ship to help a stranger stuck on the Valkyrie's bridge. "You're most likely correct."

Proximus slid the payment across the counter. Not a twitch rumpled the curtain separating the pawn shops. Cinder took the coin without counting. No one quibbled with The Fence.

A desperate chap with little sense once pulled a knife in dispute of his payment. Proximus stood and half turned, allowing his co-joined twin, Mr. Wright, to join the fray—the other held a pistol aimed at the heart of the dissenter.

The smaller twin attached to the back of his brother waved the pistol towards the door. "Leave," he ordered.

The irate man left without further ado, but two nights later his body turned up face down in a gutter from a gunshot wound. There could have been any number of reasons for his death, but the fact that he'd threatened The Fence was not lost on the rumour mongers. The twins never denied or confirmed them, adding to their reputation.

Proximus gave her a look. "Rough night?"

She deposited the purse in her satchel and tried not to smooth the tumble of curls. Taming the waist length locks proved difficult on good days, add wearing a gas mask half the night, a fight with an insane modified, and she could imagine the nightmare she appeared.

"I've had better." She gave him a quick look. "Why?"

"Just saying you ain't going to catch no prince."

She couldn't help but chuckle while she made her way to the door. "No, but modified women don't get the princes anyway."

Not even in the fairy tales.

CHAPTER SIX

ST. DROGO

The passage to the hospital from the First Tombs was much larger, longer, and well-lit than the path to the Fence. But it was also occupied. The niches built for tombs of the faithful were occupied here and there by those seeking shelter. It served as an overflow when the hospital and poor house could take no more.

Cinder walked quickly, making no eye contact. Her disguise was nearly gone, and with it the certain brashness that possessed her while wearing the mask and going incognito.

Still a hand reached out. "Please." A woman nestled her young child in one of the many niches along the hall. One or even both patients at the hospital no doubt. The demand for the services of the doctors who tended the body and engineers who installed modifications, grew daily.

She handed her a coin and moved on.

A soft "bless you" followed.

Gaining the stairs, Cinder forced her feet to take them one at a time. Her body protested the rigours of the night, while her mind disapproved of her slowness. Dawn approached, and she must be away before full light. She could not be spotted in the city by any who might possibly recognise her. Years of hiding away at Iron Crest as an illegally modified person deeply ingrained her fear of being seen.

Eliana Graceling Steelhaugh, Baron's daughter and apprentice forger, disappeared from all society that fateful day her father chose to make her a monster instead of letting her die with his wife. But with her father's passing, the whole family was to be in mourning. A convenient excuse to hide the questionable activities at Iron Crest.

As she walked, she rearranged her clothing, shedding the Cinder persona to one more appropriate for a lady. She stopped in an alcove and slipped a skirt over the breeches. Her hair, a tangled mess on a good day, she twisted tight and wrapped it into a ball a few pins from her bag held in place. Transformation complete, Ella, volunteer smith and all-around carry about stepped from the shadows.

The scent of blood, lots of it, tinged with burned skin heralded her arrival. Now she stepped lightly over the legs and bodies stretched in long lines—all waiting for the kind of help only offered in the shadow of St. Drogo and during the hours of darkness.

Here there was precious little metal on display, and those with stumps for arms and legs eyed her gleaming modification with envy and fear. She let the sleeve hang in tatters. Let them look, for if this is the path they chose, this is what they would become, never to see the light of day.

If misfortune revealed them a monster, they could be jailed or, if the bill before the House of Lords passed, be declared property of the state and turned over to the School of Medicine for dissection and experimentation.

However, the desperate hope for a useful limb drove people to desperate measures. A hand which could steady a crate in turn earned money to feed a family. A leg would make a sailor seaworthy again.

She passed out coins freely. Heaven knew she had no use for money. Her bags would be searched when she returned and anything that did not belong, confiscated.

Two men shoved one another in the beginning of an argument. She pushed between them, using the weight of her body and arm to muscle a burly dock worker against the wall. "Stop it, Drax, you're scaring people and I am not in the mood tonight."

Drax, a fellow made huge by heavy manual labour, often took hits of opium to relieve various aches and pains. The drug, however, had an opposite effect on the man, often sending him into fits of berserk rage. She hoped tonight was one of his saner nights. "Sorry, Miss. I don't know what come over me."

She pointed to the tall security automatons called WARs against the far wall which kept order.

A metal head turned left and right, attention caught by the commotion. The other, both ancient models whose reliability was quirky at best, slumbered still.

"Well, sit down and think about it. You don't want to wake the guards." Her statement drew the crowd's attention to the metal machines and most shied away. St. Drogo engineers scavenged these particular models from the wars on the continent, however, lack of time to reprogramme and service the machines made them unpredictable at maintaining peace.

Ella turned to the Harcourt, the amputee she discussed with Proximus earlier now wearing a lobster-like pincher in place of a hand. "And you need not antagonise him, Harcourt, you know how he is."

The instigator of the fight, a skeletal chap with a slight hunchback, who also happened to be Drax's best friend, waved his appendage negligently. "Just having a bit of fun, Sweets. He's got such a pretty bald pate."

Drax jerked forward, big fist curled in an unspoke threat. She shook her finger at him. "I said sit down." She turned back to Harcourt, a well-known piece of beggar work, knife appearing in her human hand to emphasise her point. She tapped his pincher and metal clanged. It got his attention. "You can call me Miss Ella—not Sweets—and if you cause any more trouble, I will get a WAR to toss you out on your bum then get you banned. Is that understood?"

He gulped and nodded. A ban was the last thing someone could want. St. Drogo was a last stop. The streets became a death trap when the gases got heavy and a ban meant no door welcoming mutants or modifies would open. Good luck appealing to the more genteel folk to help. Folks like those lining the halls of the cathedral were second class citizens—if considered human at all.

In her years at the hospital, very few were banned. Most disappeared. One for sure killed himself.

"Ella!" A weary woman in a nurse's uniform of black broad cloth and crimson speckled apron, stood in a doorway. "'Tis good to see you, lass."

She smiled and hugged the nurse despite the blood. "Sukie! Good to see me or the gifts I bring?" The Irish nurse with flaming hair turned grey had been a fixture at St. Drogo since Ella's first day. In fact, she gave Ella her first assignment of passing out bread before the soup kitchen began an organised affair.

The sharp panes of nurse's face softened. "You, my dear, always you. How is Myrtle? It has been so long."

Ella's face froze and she tried to keep her smile. How *was* Myrtle? She shook her head. Her good and faithful servant could even now be suffering for her tardiness. "She sends her love, as always. It's difficult to get away."

A scream turned her focus to the room on the right.

"Hold her still," a voice grunted. "Sukie, are you going to be helping me out any time soon?"

A woman in a red speckled white apron stood beside a table with a small girl of six or seven strapped tightly to a chair built for larger, stronger patients. A pinched faced fellow knelt on the floor, gripping the youngster's hand. The child's head, shoulder, and chest were covered in blood, and she squirmed and screamed in her father's grasp. The doctor tightened a band on the girl's arm, thumped a vein and held a hand out. "Morphine."

The nurse who greeted Ella brushed by with a syringe. Eliana turned away. Heat rushed to her face and she leaned against the wall for support. She hated needles, even if she had to use them almost daily.

"Hold the ear like so, Sukie, and move over a bit so I can see. Now, Euda, sit still please, this might pinch a bit." The child wearing frock made from a man's shirt, slumped as the drug took effect. "Aristocrats," the doctor scoffed over the little one's dark curls. "Ran the girl plumb over, nearly took off her head, but only took the ear." A wet *splosh* and the remains of a tiny, mutilated ear dropped to the floor.

Dr. Bon Hamlet's dark skinned marred with large patches of white shown with sweat. She cursed and moved her head to find the best light. Ella quelled her queasiness and adjusted the lamp. "Does that work better?"

"I know the sound of that voice. Get over here and help." She glanced up and squinted through tiny, round glasses. One pupil widened, unequally magnified to distorted proportions by the lens positioned over the right eye. It did nothing to detract from the lady's unusual beauty, marred, or maybe enhanced, by the patch of white skin pieced against the dark on her cheek like a patchwork quilt. "Hold the skin here, Ella."

The surgery finished, Sukie led the patients from the room. The doctor caught Eliana's mechanical hand. "Ahh. I'd love to make a study and drawing of this appendage, you know. The magnificent, though somewhat elusive, Dr. Bihari deigned to grace England with one of her majestic appearances for this one, eh?"

Ella slowly withdrew her arm, neither confirming or denying such a rumour, despite Dr. Bon Hamlet's prying. "I wasn't much myself when the surgery took place."

"No, of course not. But it's a wonder to behold. Why are you bleeding?"

Eliana touched her cheek. "Rough night."

"Must have been. You certainly look the fright."

"So, I've been told."

"Won't catch any beaus looking like that."

What was with everyone tonight?

"Beaus aren't exactly my cup of tea." Nor would they ever be.

"There's plenty of men who would look past—" the doctor waved her hand, "certain issues. You need to give it a chance."

Ella flushed, thinking back to the prince that evening, then shook her head. First time in the presence of a man and she goes all doe-eyed. She dug in her satchel for the reason for her late-night visit to the home of the deceased. "I brought the file you requested from Mr. Hatchet's."

The doctor washed in well used water and reached for the papers with red stained hands. "The research proposals?"

Eliana shrugged. "I didn't have time to check, but they t'were the only papers in the safe." Sukie returned to the room and proceeded to clean up. Ella caught the nurse's attention, she still had a final delivery. She removed a packet from her satchel and handed it over.

The nurse took the package with eager hands. A sheet, thin and shiny as the sea on a clear day, winked from the dull brown paper with another package filled with weeds.

"Oh, you good woman," the tired looking nurse breathed, holding the dried greenery to her face. A sweet smell filled the small space between them. "Cannabis and silver." She kept unwrapping, "Opium. The drugs are good, but the silver—how did you manage such a feat. Never mind, I don't want to know. Wait! Mr. Forsythe, bring Euda back."

The doctor stayed in her corner at a small table, seeming totally absorbed in the file. While she waited for the patient's return, Sukie took a pair scissors to the silver and cut a tiny piece. "Without this to fight infection, the child would be dead before we can remove the stitches."

The father returned with the sleeping girl, skin now cleaned of blood and Sukie tucked the silver infused cloth behind the ear then nodded to an attendant. "You may bandage it now." Once again, the patients left.

"You knew," Ella said.

"What?"

"That Euda would die when you sent her out the first time."

Sukie sighed. "I hoped for once the odds would play in my favour, that the parents would keep it clean, and they would give her the medicine I prescribe, not sell it. I hope against hope, which is why I even work here. Few doctors will, and it is always with hope at the last moment a benefactor, such as yourself, will send something to tip the balance. Today—it worked."

The doctor still ignored them, flipped a few papers and held one to the light. Her breath caught in a pained gasp. "Do you have any idea what was in this file, Ella?" Cinder and Sukie hurried to her side.

Ella peered over her shoulder, but the words swam, the letters changing places before she could catch the words. She looked away. Diagrams, schematics, mathematics all came easier than reading. "You told me to get the proposals given to Mr. Hatchet. Is that not what they are?"

"Yes, but there also a sealed addendum to a bill being submitted to The House of Lords." Her eyes scanned the contents quickly. Ella suppressed a spurt of envy but listened carefully when the doctor spoke. "Someone wants modifieds with over a certain percentage of modification, or any mutant, to be detained and taken to the medical School for research. Somehow this got tucked between all the proposals." The doctor shook her head. "If it isn't the Prussian army, the mists, we have our own people turning on us. However, I believe you came by this paper for a reason and I will ensure it gets into the right hands."

Ella slumped against the wall, too tired to dwell on the ramifications of a single paper or how it might affect her. More pressing matters waited at home. "I need a ride to Iron Crest."

Dr. Bon Hamlet nodded absently as the next patient shuffled in. "Of course. Just let me attend to this patient and I will see what I can do. In the meantime, see if you can find places for some of these people to sleep. The body snatchers aren't waiting for the homeless to die any more. People are disappearing right off the street."

Ella knew the danger of those sleeping exposed. Body Snatchers did a brisk business. "It's urgent."

"Everything is urgent, Eliana, you are in an illegal hospital with sick people next to a church which shelters as many destitute they can."

"I know, but—"

"Valkyrie! You can't bring birds in here!"

All exhaustion fled. Ella whirled towards the door and narrowed her eyes at the metal beaked man. "You! You attacked me."

The Birdman shied away from the loud exclamation, shielding a tiny form against his wraith-thin body. He moved his lower jaw, clacking a coded message

"I don't care if I was on your bridge. You just can't go about eating people."

"Calm down, Ella," the doctor soothed. "Valkyrie isn't always in his right mind. What were you doing on his bridge?"

"Long story, but it doesn't matter." She jabbed a finger at her attacker. "You ever bite me again I will wring the neck of a pigeon every single day, do you understand?"

The fellow clacked his beak then scooted closer, holding out one of his birds, most likely the pigeon she had savaged earlier.

"This is not a veterinary, Valkyrie." The doctor shook her coat at him. "Get that filthy thing out of here before it makes people sick."

Eliana laughed, "Or someone makes it a meal."

Valkyrie lurched back, for the first time a whiny sound escaping his throat. The doctor and she exchanged glances and Ella sighed. She couldn't hold his earlier actions against him. The gases made them all a little crazy, particularly those under constant exposure. Before the rain fell, he'd been a regular chap who loved to sit in the park and feed the birds during his lunch hour. He'd been a banker, a respectable person moving up in the world. But then again, hadn't they all.

She reached for the pigeon. "Let me see it."

He cowered, snapping at her hand.

She shrugged. "Last chance." It wouldn't hurt her feelings if the thing died—it was his fault after all—*he'd bitten her!*

The Valkyrie hesitated, then laid the bird gently in her hand.

She glared at him. "And I am serious about the others. Don't try to eat people."

He nodded eagerly.

"Ella," Dr. Bon Hamlet sighed, "I don't have the time."

"Neither do I, but we have to try." She nodded at the emaciated modified pacing before the door, head bobbing like one of his pigeons. His twisted mind so far gone he didn't even realize how his actions mirrored those he protected. Birds died daily, the life of a pigeon not all tea and crumpets, but when a man such as the Valkyrie reached out for help, they had to try.

The Thames' gases were changing them, turning them iron hard like the metal used to repair their bodies. The insidious vapors robbed the poor of London of all softness, leaving the hallmarks of humanity for the pampered rich. The aristocrats sat in their halls of marble and light with no thought for those who clean them. Those clutching at the tattered rags of humanity, with metal and bone, even if it meant helping a bird while others waited.

"For all our sakes," she said softly.

Chapter Seven

Iron Crest

Ella slid down the chimney of the forge, her body hitting the hearth with a bone jarring thud when her strength failed. A puff of ash heralded her arrival, cinders lifting on the still air and fluttering in a breeze from a crack in the window.

Her father added this large, brick room to Iron Crest Manor when just a young man. He loved to tinker with new inventions, the automatons throughout the house were a testament to his innovation. However, upon the Baron's marriage to the airship captain Octavia Feathermote, the forge became a hub where the two brilliant minds connected and created. By the time Eliana arrived, their routine had become so firmly set it was just a matter of Nursey bringing the baby to the room to visit her parents.

Though the poor lady, and several nannies afterwards, tried to teach her proper manners and ladylike deportment, her earliest memories were of leaning over the fire with her mother watching metal change from winter grey to blazing scarlet. Of building dolls with nuts, bolts, and a soldering iron. Of joining in a family celebration when a particular fine piece of workmanship tested true. Oh, how she missed that.

Her mother first showed her the iron rungs built into the chimney. 'Just in case' Mother said as though letting her eager daughter in on a great secret. And Eliana couldn't thank her enough for both the memory of closeness and the ladder. Just as Father gave her the loyal mice which cheered her darkest hour, so had this ladder allowed her egress when all other avenues had been bolted to her.

She yawned. Besides, entering this way she could pretend she arrived earlier than she truly had and cry exhaustion for sending her into a deep sleep.

Though coating her entire being in noxious filth, the warmth of the embers seeped into her chilled bones. The hot plate made a hard pillow, the flue a slight draft, but she lay her cheek on her hands and relaxed into the soot.

Her struggle with the Valkyrie damaged one of the pigeon's legs. Whether he or she were the cause, it mattered not, her heart ached over the little creature's unnecessary pain. She and Dr. Bon Hamlet made it comfortable within a crate hidden in a dusty corner. Neither held out hope for its survival. If the innate fragility of birds didn't kill it, one of the more ambitious of the patients may see the poor thing as the means to feed a family.

Comfortable in the heap of ashes, her mind wandered over the night's disastrous events. Such a cursed evening! At least her stepmother did not suspect her penchant for coming and going by the chimney. If she had she surely would have lit the fires and even now Ella would be roasting in the flames.

A puff of ash from an exhausted sigh made her sneeze. She smiled at the arching motes and drifted into sleep.

"So good of you to finally grace us with your presence, Cinder." *Discovered!*

She tumbled from her warm bed to the frost cold stone below. Even so, her lip beaded with perspiration at the autocratic, slightly nasal tones of her stepmother's voice.

"Look at you, all covered in soot. Make yourself presentable and come to the drawing room. We need to speak about your responsibilities." The lithe form paused on the iron threshold, teeth gleaming in a predatory smile. "As well as the consequences of not fulfilling your duties."

Ella hurried to the cooling barrel next to the hearth and splashed a few drops of water on her face. She struggled out of her rough breeches and loosened her corset to shrug out of the shredded shirt. Peering in the polished brass plate which served as a mirror, she fought with her hair.

The comb refused to detangle the clumps of dried blood from the fresh scratches on her face. Instead, she covered the mess with a maid's cap and slid into a black day dress. Every painful movement reminded her of the tussle with the Valkryie and her muscles cried for her to slow down.

Still, she had no choice but to follow her stepmother into the green and gold room. She couldn't help the words wrenched from her soul at the changes which greeted her. "What have you done?"

Her favourite floral paper of twisted vines, her mother's choice when she married The Baron, hung in half torn tatters from the walls. All the furniture except for one chair and a low footstool were now stacked haphazardly in one corner. Several cherished pieces— her mother's brocade chaise, the dainty writing desk, the coveted water colour 'The Girl and the Automaton' by Thomas Fowler in its gold frame—sat outside the double doors where the moisture beaded on varnish and canvas.

Only a month since her father's passing, and this woman had the nerve to destroy everything. Eliana fought back tears. Next to the forge, this drawing room held some of her happiest memories. But she refused to cry. She would not give this evil fiend *that* pleasure.

The new Lady Steelhaugh made a sweeping gesture. "A little remodelling is all. Guests will be received here from now on and the drab paper from years ago did little to make this room appropriate for such functions."

"Drab?" Cinder echoed, unable to comprehend the devastation around her.

Her stepmother clucked her tongue and sat on the chair, arranged the fall of dark skirt, and finally folded her hands in her lap. "Your parents really didn't have a sense of fashion or decor, did they? At the very least they could have hired a decorator. Green and gilt? Trees and vines? Hopelessly outdated." She sighed dramatically, placing a hand on the stiff folds of organza covering the decolletage of her dangerously low-cut *mourning* dress.

Where had she found the time to purchase yet another new dress?

However, the detested woman continued. "But that's to be expected when a man marries beneath himself. Imagine, an airship captain and a baron. So cliche." She shook her head, each word a dagger in Ella's heart. "And the scandal! Besides, you will see. Bold colours in brown and red will liven this room up, make it a conversation piece." She pointed to a stool. "Sit."

"Brown and Red?" Eliana repeated. "But those are Prussia's national colours." Even the most ardent advocate against the war stayed well away from any combination of those colours in both dress and decorating. "Why would you do that?"

Lady Steelhaugh turned swiftly from a false cheerfulness she used around Eli's father to the cold witch-like one she knew from the moment he turned his back. "I said *sit.*"

Ella dropped, the weight of the changes in the room on top of the evening's escapades stealing all the strength from her. Her knees buckled and she folded gracelessly onto the little seat designed for feet rather than a grown woman of eighteen. She balled the black, crepe mourning dress in her fist. Thankfully, the heavy fabric withstood the shredding of her mechanical hand.

"There now—" A knock caused Lady Steelhaugh's head to swivel to the door in annoyance. For the first time, Ella noticed a tiny mark behind her stepmother's left ear. A brown dot with a red centre. From the distance it looked like a mole, but the pattern seemed too deliberate.

"What is it?" Lady Steelhaugh demanded.

Myrtle stuck her head in and frowned at the mess of the room. "Begging your pardon, m'lady." She purposefully avoided eye contact with Lady Steelhaugh, choosing, rather, to address Ella. Her metallic voice skirted the edge of disrespect. "Ye called fer me?"

Lady Steelhaugh rose with a rustle. "Come here, Myrtle."

The old gunner turned maid and general help, opened the door the rest of the way. "Yes, ma'am." She moved with a peculiar gait. Pistons sighed with each step, the glow of her circuits illuminating her in a blue aura despite the bulky mourning cloth.

Dr. Bon Hamlet may marvel over the exquisite workmanship of Ella's nerve and mechanical fused arm, words would have failed her had she seen the complete modification of Myrtle's body. During her service on *The Lady Peril* under Ella's mother, the human gunner lost her life saving her Lady's. For her devotion, Lady Octavia moved mountain and sea, some whispered even made a bargain with the devil, to save her. A fact Myrtle made light of when her joints required oiling after a bout of wet weather.

"You *know* you are not to address a fellow servant as a Lady. The terrible poverty pushed upon us by her father's unfortunate death and the suspicious circumstances surrounding it, has made her responsible for paying off his debts. She has become a common servant." With a toss of her ebony tresses, Lady Steelhaugh glared at

Ella. "No different from yourself."

The gunner stiffened. "She 'as worked 'ard enough for you. This is 'er house."

Ella closed her eyes. *This could only end badly for the both of us.* "Please, Myrtle."

The old servant glared and muttered under her breath. Sometimes Ella wondered about Myrtle's programming. She seemed so human at times. But Dr. Bihari had not been heard from in years and her secrets were gone with her.

However, Ella's stepmother did not seem to mind the automaton's unpredicted outburst. A fact more frightening than if she had reacted. "Finished?" the Lady enquired.

Myrtle lifted her chin.

"Very well. You will remember this is my house now. If I had full say in the matter, you would both be turned out on the street. Lucky for you, I have found a way to make the best of an untenable situation."

Lady Steelhaugh rose and dug into the folds of her skirt, pulling out some sort of mechanical device. Sparks ignited as she wound the metal object. It whirred in her hand, and Myrtle spun to escape.

Too late.

With a savage thrust, the Baroness touched her metal arm. Lightning arced from plate to plate. Myrtle's mouth opened and closed reflexively.

Ella jumped up and leaped towards the pair. "Stop! What are you doing?" she cried, but she already knew. The price of defiance was pain. If not to her, then her friend.

Lady Steelhaugh jerked the electrical device from Myrtle and stepped back. The modified servant crumpled to the floor. Ella knelt beside her faithful friend, feeling for a heartbeat. The blue glow faded, systems shut down with a type of overload Ella did not understand.

"No," Ella screamed. She flipped open the compartment on her metal hand where she kept her screwdriver, then wrestled the servant to her back and ripped at the buttons of the maid's dress to access the special compartment built in her torso.

"Hold on, Myrtle...just a quick restart." She fumbled, metal scrapping against metal. Two shadows caught the corner of her left eye.

My stepsisters.

They stood like quiet lurkers in the corner between the bookcases, shoulder-to-shoulder, partly turned towards one another for comfort and strength, watchful gazes on their mother.

Ella pleaded with them through the tears. "Help me."

Neither moved. Ella did not understand their relationship with their mother, but by the way they watched her, they feared their mother too much to help her.

Lady Steelhaugh leaned close and touched Ella's shoulder.

Pain ricocheted through her body, lancing down her limbs and sending them into uncontrollable twitching. She vomited and clutched at her middle, trying to stop the throbbing pain. Her lungs constricted. Her chest froze. All the air forced from her body in one gasping exhale.

"There. Now that I have your attention. We can have a proper talk." The Lady sat back down and arranged her skirt once more.

Ella squirmed on the carpet. She tried to roll away from the pool of vomit, still attempting to help Myrtle, but couldn't stop the twitching. She sobbed in a breath, air starved lungs wheezing. Her mechanical hand refused to move at all, while the nerves attached to the appendage overloaded, the fingers glaciated into a claw. The compartments sprung open. Tools and her precious stash of coins tumbled haphazardly with every jerk of her body.

Tears leaked into the carpet. She hated them. Hated this woman who could bring them to her eyes after everything she endured.

"Come now and sit. Like I said, we need to have a talk."

Ella spied the screwdriver and reached for it. A weapon. She would ram the sharp end into that cold heart for what she did to Myrtle.

"Yes, I see what you are thinking, but let me warn you, in defying me you will never have the chance to revive that disgusting creature. I will have her torn apart bolt by bolt and each piece melted down."

Ella's hand stopped its quest.

The Lady leaned forward and winked. "Don't think I wouldn't do it. You both have experienced enough of my resolve to know that resistance is futile."

"What have we ever done to you?" Ella managed to keep a sob from escaping.

"You?" the Lady laughed. "Why nothing." Her brows lowered. "Your mother on the other hand, now that is a different matter entirely."

CHAPER EIGHT

STEPMOTHER

E lla's stepmother wrinkled her nose and motioned to the stool. "Now sit up and let us have a proper conversation. I doubt your earnestness in listening while you loll about on the floor." A small movement in the corner drew her attention to her children.

They accompanied their evil mother to the house seven months ago. Locked in the forge more often than not, Ella did not know them well. Like one person they sidled towards the double doors and escape, growing completely still when their mother's eyes landed on them.

"Ah yes, you are still here. Be about your lessons. I am finished with you two. As you can see, I have business to attend to."

The girls bolted, but Isabeau, the eldest and taller of the two, risked a glance back at Ella struggling to seat herself with a look bordering on pity.

The Lady stared after them and sighed with a shake of her head. "Such disappointments."

Ella tried to maintain her perch on the tiny stool, the world spun and rocked, and she nearly slipped to the ground again.

"You may look like your mother, but you only have half of her strength. Still, for me to keep this house, you must be alive. If you die, the house goes to charity." She sniffed, "A home for war veterans...such a romantic fool."

Ella took a deep breath and willed her body to sit on the stool. "You spoke with Mr. Hanafin?"

"Many times. But my hands are tied. I did intend to dispose of you in a respectable matter in time, but I have an arrangement in mind that may work out better than expected."

"Dispose of me? Why?"

"Because you are Octavia's daughter, of course. It would have been better if you were male. A son for a son. A husband for a husband. But the traitorous witch never did anything properly."

"I don't understand. How could any of this be related to my mother? She died years ago."

"Yes. The day of your accident, the day the rains began. And they were all her fault, weren't they?"

Ella froze. Lady Octavia led the assault against a poisonous gas cloud buffeting across the channel. Her weapon of choice, silver nitrate missiles with which she hoped to wash the gases down into the channel before they hit England. She accomplished her goal...with disastrous results.

Instead of dissipating in the water the chemicals remained, carried by the currents to shore and poisoning the Thames where it met the sea. In theory, the idea should have worked, if some bizarre chemical reaction didn't keep refreshing itself where fresh and saltwater met. All her mother's commendations, battles won, strategic mastery, all forgotten in the rain.

His wife's ignoble death, the maiming and subsequent modification of his daughter, forced the withdrawal of Baron Steelhaugh from society. He took the time to throw himself into fighting the insidious Prussian infiltration with his wonderful mechanical creations, then married someone he thought as noble and true as his late wife.

Ella saw it clearly now, the mark on her stepmother's neck, hidden so well before now proudly displayed. The stamp of the enemy.

The evil woman seemed to come back to the present with a jerk. "Now, what do you think would happen to all of this if someone, perchance, reminded the King that the Baron married the woman who destroyed the Thames? Hmmmm? A woman who poisoned the waters and the people? What would happen if his daughter's illegal modifications were revealed? Not to mention all the good you do at the hospital in her name."

Ella couldn't help the way her mouth hung open at the cruelty of her stepmother.

"Octavia was an adept actress, she even had her handlers fooled until the very last. But I can see that you are just as in the dark as the rest of England." The Baroness leaned forward. "But here's a little secret—your mother was a secret agent for Prussia."

Ella nearly fell from her perch again. "You lie!"

"No. I knew your mother well. We grew up together. Many years ago, the Emperor foresaw the time when Prussia would take her place as the conqueror of Europe. He ordered orphans to be raised for this purpose."

She touched her ear where the tattoo lay hidden under a perfect curl. "We were marked here, educated thoroughly, then allowed to pursue careers befitting our temperaments. Your mother chose physical pursuits and soon became our most talented airship pilot. I followed a more intellectual path. When it became apparent Octavia caught the eye of the Baron, your father, she obtained permission to marry. It served Prussia's purpose well. She moved freely among our enemies, gathering information, reporting back. Meanwhile, I worked on chemical weapons to give us the advantage in the war, a set of viruses which could change the physiology of a man."

Despite the fact this fiend infiltrated her home, murdered her closest friend, and slandered her mother and father, Ella couldn't help but wonder after these weapons. They sounded hideous. "Change them?"

"Yes, some were designed to make soldiers stronger, faster. By combining the essence of beasts with man we had some great successes. Others were too weak and died. Gas seemed to be the best medium of dissemination, though many had to be passed via injection of some sort. It took numerous experiments on subjects both willing and unwilling before we found the right combinations but find them, we did!"

The woman's face closed off as she reminisced about her experiments.

A shudder ran down Ella's arms. Those poor people on whom the trials were carried out. Rumours abounded for years that Prussia carried out biological experimentation on their own people, but she never dreamed of receiving a firsthand account.

Her stepmother's cultured speech picked up an excited cadence and she leaned forward. "We planned to strike multiple countries at once, our airships were positioned around the globe, ready for the attack, when your mother turned traitor."

The Prussian agent's knuckles blanched, her iron grip on the arms of the chair tightened, the weapon on her palm whirred in response. When the device reached a shrill pitch, Lady Steelhaugh relaxed and smiled.

Ella looked quickly down, beginning to comprehend the terrible rage turning the fine patrician features into a mask devoid of humanity.

"Octavia led a strike force of airships against our secret lab, destroying years of work. She stole the research and ran like a cur coward."

Relief flooded Ella. Even in Lady Steelhaugh's twisted account, her mother's honour won out in the end. Never would she believe her mother to be a Prussian agent, let alone working for a secret scientific faction. She died a hero, the torpedoing of her ship the act which set Britain on its path to war.

"My husband pursued her. He commanded *Grey Spectre,* an airship on patrol near the lab. The storms were rising over the channel and her only avenue of escape was to fly through them. A risky proposition, but that was Octavia's way. It paid off for her that time. *Grey Spectre* went down with all hands, including my husband and son. The next day our agents found her trying to reach the English King in Bristol and gunned down her ship. A great victory for the Fatherland."

No pity stirred in Ella for this woman when, in the next breath, she celebrated her mother's death. She longed to thrust the screwdriver into her stepmother's frozen heart, but the sight of Myrtle's still body on the rug forced her attentiveness.

"Of course, her traitorous acts put us years behind. Everything was lost and France was already a pain in the side of the war effort. So, we started from scratch. The lab explosion killed many of our most brilliant scientists, and we have been unable to recreate precious little of their great work. Especially debilitating was the loss of Dr. Frankenstein's notes."

She replaced a wisp of ebony hair that dared to escape her hair dressing when her passion rose. "But now we have this facility to start fresh. It is old but secluded, with protocols already in place. People rarely visit. With your father chasing shadows planted by my people, you were never presented and rumours abound about your fate. It is perfect. My comrades and I can work in peace."

Focus on the problem, Ella. I just need to get away from here, go to the solicitor or one of Father's old friends then tell them about Judith, expose her for a Prussian agent, and win back my life. It would not bring back her parents, but she could rid the house of this filth.

She cursed her weakness when her voice trembled. "What do you want from me?"

The new Lady Steelhaugh's fine white teeth shone predator white in the gloom that seemed to creep from the shadows. "I am glad you asked. I knew if you were half as intelligent as your mother *and* inherited her flawed sensibilities, you could be reasoned with, or coerced, depending on the circumstance, of course. I see it took a little of both, which no doubt would have made her proud. It just makes you another tool for me. So...on to what I want. I need information. I need money. And I need the leaders to recall Britain's favourite son and to focus on something they care more about than the war."

"I don't understand," Ella said. "I've done everything you've asked. I have cooked and cleaned and scrubbed and done the work of the servants you dismissed. Where would I find the time?" She paused, then blurted, "Besides, don't you have spies for that kind of thing?"

"Of course, I do, but nothing is more satisfying to me than Octavia's daughter working for my own ends. The unusual talents fostered by your parents and your...*affliction* are the perfect combination. However, this staying out until past dawn working at the hospital or feeding the poor compromises all and I will not stand for it." She nodded towards Myrtle. "There will be consequences for your actions. And time? You will just have to find it."

No use explaining the horrible night she had. Her stepmother must in no way suspect the prince's presence. Of all the royal family, the soldier prince caused the most damage to Prussia in the war. While other royal family members passed out medical supplies or visited the hospitals, the prince fought. She looked away and remained silent, praying the woman interpreted her silence as acquiescence.

The lady stared at her intently then sighed as though disappointed. "Your mother really did teach you nothing, did she? She had the intelligence and might of the Prussian army at her disposal and yet threw it away. For what? Love? A corrupted nation?"

Judith replaced her heavy glove and reached over with her

charge device and prodded Myrtle. Sparks arched and the gunner's body jerked, while her inner clockwork started with a terrible clanging sound. Judith held it for half a second. When the servant did not respond to a solid kick, Judith prodded her again.

Finally, Myrtle blinked, struggling against the current arcing through her body. Her scream ripped across Ella's nerves. She rushed over to her old friend, and despite the servant being four times heavier and a head and half taller, Ella gathered the faithful servant into her arms.

"Shh, shh. Just rest and refresh your system."

Myrtle stopped struggling and touched Ella's face. "Are you alright?"

Ella stifled a sob. After being electrocuted three times, her friend still asked after her welfare. How did she deserve such loyalty? Ella hadn't even been able to come to her defence. Now the evil Prussian agent knew to use Myrtle along with the mice as hostages against Ella's good behaviour.

Any thought of escaping, of getting the word out, died before fully formed.

I can't risk them. To do so would mean abandoning Myrtle to the mercy of a monster devoid of gentler emotions. One who saw friendship and love as a means to an end. Weapons to be wielded, weaknesses to exploit. She could never do it.

Ella bowed her head. "I'm here, Myrtle. I'm fine."

Judith loomed over them. "Clean up this mess you made and get to making breakfast." She glanced at her pin watch. "I will expect to be served at exactly nine and no later. You have one hour."

If Ella could have concentrated all her loathing at that moment into a death beam of some sort, her stepmother would die instantly. But no matter how she stared, no matter how she hated, Judith returned her look second for second. But where Ella felt her passions boiling inside, her stepmother showed no feeling at all.

If possible, this made Ella despise her even more.

Chapter Nine

Sisters

hank you, Flora," Ella took the spoon from the helpful mouse and arranged it on the tray. A chain clinked as an egg rode a track from the small hen house in the kitchen garden. She winced as it tumbled and cracked on the flagstone.

Another mess.

She bent to clean up shell and yolk, but Myrtle shooed her away with a hiss and a clank. "I'll get that. You take the linens to the girls, I'll serve the devil woman."

Ella tried to frown at the old gunner's disrespectful tone. "You know she likes me to wait on her."

"She can do without." Obviously, the near-death experience did not leave the impression stepmother wanted. "You're about ready to hit the floor. No doubt she'll be wanting to send you out again tonight. Just to make her point."

Ella shook her head. "I can't. I haven't worked at the forge." People depended on her. Every day she delayed using her talent to work on the modifications was another day someone lived in misery.

Misery exacerbated by her mother bringing the rain.

Then there was that pigeon that needed a leg. If it still lived, of course.

Flora snatched the dish towel from her hand and delivered it to

Myrtle with a cheeky flick on her copper ear.

The antics of her pint-sized helper brought a reluctant smile. "Traitor."

Myrtle waved the rag at her. "Go. Then to bed with you. Work this evening, before you leave."

Knowing when to retreat, Ella turned to face the stairs, each riser on the steep servant stair a mountain to be conquered. The person who designed the manor house, or any Lord's residence for that matter, certainly did not have the servant's best interests in mind. As a child, she considered navigating the narrow halls and stairs an adventure. Now, after the hundredth time making her way to the second floor balancing a load of freshly cleaned linens, she heaped curses on the head of every architect that ever lived.

She stopped and hiked her black skirts, tying them into place with her apron strings. "That will take care of you." What did it matter? No one would observe her immodest behaviour.

Besides, the prince himself saw her in much worse. The thought of the gallant royal who took the time in the wee hours of the morning to rescue a damsel in distress lightened her heart— purposely forgetting his reaction to her request to be dropped at St. Drogo.

Her stepsisters shared a room on the second floor—all other rooms reserved for Judith's guests. As usual, Ella found their door tightly closed, against her or their mother she could only guess. They seemed to avoid contact with everyone. Indeed, in the months since Father first added them to their family, they remained as much strangers as when they first arrived. They spoke rarely—mostly to one another.

Finding herself unable to knock with the armload of sheets, she motioned for the largest mouse, Clarence, to get the door. He climbed the jamb and used his weight to pull the handle down. Ella slid her foot in the crack and entered the girls' room. At this hour she expected to find them napping as usual.

Raven haired Isabeau slammed an armoire shut, but not before Ella caught a glimpse of glass distilling apparatus assembled on a shelf. Aurelia, petite and blonde with wraith-like paleness of hair and skin, whirled, a syringe dropping from her startled grasp.

Odder still, Aurelia hissed at her. Not a sound of pain, though blood trickled down her arm where a bandeau plumped a vein, but one of anger. Isabeau stepped forward to block her entrance, hands extended and fingernails long and curved.

Ella had observed this type of aberrant behaviour before at St.

Drogo—never in a sophisticated lady ready for introduction into society. Ella moved slowly, placing the linens on a chest at the end of the nearest bed. Always, she kept one eye on the sisters. The hair on the back of her neck stood up and she prepared to defend herself at a moment's notice.

They tracked her every movement, green and violet eyes unblinking and wary.

With a deep breath Isabeau managed to gain control and straightened, the cornered-animal look receding. Her dressing gown gaped revealing bound breasts and padding under corset and chemise. It gave both a rounder and younger look. Though they often acted younger, they were seventeen and eighteen years old. Even more disturbing were the needle marks and fresh bruises which covered the arms of both.

Isabeau charged, ramming both hands into Ella's shoulders. "Get out!"

She stumbled back, muscles weak with fatigue. Ella grabbed the other girl's hands. Her stepsister winced under the metal grip. Ella loosened it but did not let go.

"What are you two about?" she demanded, deciding boldness may cower them. Instantly, their demeanour turned fearful, staring over Ella's shoulder at the open door.

Aurelia rushed by and shut the door swiftly yet quietly. The willowy blonde placed a finger on her lips. "*Shh.*" Together they stood frozen, the only sound their own agitated gasps as they listened for a call that indicated their mother heard.

Gambling her two stepsisters may become allies, Ella softened her gaze. "Judith is eating," she whispered.

Still her sisters remained spooked.

"Myrtle is with her and will thump on the servant's stairs if something changes."

Isabeau cocked her head, dark eyes taking on a greenish cast. "Yes. I have heard that signal before."

The tension in the bedchamber softened as the three took a deep breath and relaxed.

However, Ella was not about to let things go. "What are you two up to?"

Aurelia approached, hands up as though placating a wild animal and eyes pleading. "Please. You must not tell Mother."

"Why are you hiding your ages?" demanded Ella, with a sniff. "As if your own mother could forget. And what's that distilling equipment? And why are you bleeding?"

As though she forgot, Aurelia, covered her arm and swept up the syringe.

Isabeau once again put herself in front of Aurelia as though fearing Ella might attack. In fact, Ella witnessed her do this very thing many times on the occasion Judith lost her temper.

"Please," said the raven hair beauty. "There are things you don't know. Things you *can't* know."

"Obviously."

Ella turned to Aurelia. "Are you sick?"

The younger girl shot a glance at her older sister. "That depends on how you define sick. I am what I have been created to be. Please. Just trust us. We don't want to hurt you."

Ella flexed her hand. "As if you could."

She did not like the way the sisters' eyes communicated over her head. She tried to retreat and put her back against a wall.

The girls moved with her, faces desperate. "We could." They assured her in one voice. Shivers raced up Ella's flesh and bone arm.

"But all we want is to be left alone," added Aurelia, "Right, Isabeau?"

The other relaxed. "Right. Look, we saved something for you. Consider it a peace offering."

"What do you mean?"

Both girls walked to the wardrobe next to the window, away from the armoire. Isabeau climbed in, reaching to the back. "Did you know there's a compartment attached to the wardrobe?"

Ella snorted. "Of course, I did. My father used to lock me in there to see how long it took me to get out." One of the reasons she developed those skills useful to Dr. Bon Hamlet.

Aurelia stared a long moment. "Yes, I've heard of your unconventional upbringing."

"You have no idea," Ella said quietly. Tired of their games and knowing Judith's never-ending list of chores waited, Ella snapped. "What are you two about then?"

"The secret compartment has worked well for hiding certain things, so that is where we put it," Aurelia explained. "I know you don't trust us, but please, just..."

Ella gasped as Isabeau reappeared with one of her mother's favourite ball gowns.

"We sneaked into Lady Octavia's chamber when Mother ordered it cleaned out. We wanted to find something for you, but so much was already taken," explained Aurelia.

"Mother took the jewelry and smashed the perfumes," continued

Isabeau.

"But we knew if we could save something, we should," finished her sister.

Ella fingered the shimmery silk. Like the earrings she just pawned, Lady Octavia Steelhaugh wore the gown to the final ball before the rains. Too young to attend, Ella sat on the stairs in the company of Myrtle, admiring the beautiful women flitting hummingbird-like between the rooms.

However, when her mother entered, all others faded away. The dress moved as though imbued with life of its own, whispering to the other dresses. The trembling silk tossed blue sparks into her mother's eyes, blurred around the edges like a Monet painting. Her father never took his gaze from his wife, eschewing fashion and asking her to dance.

Ella sank to the floor and pressed the material to her cheek.

Like swans her parents floated across the gold hued wood. When her mother spun, the dress sparkled with the light of a thousand candles.

It was a time before people needed gas masks on hand. Before *Lady Peril* crashed into the sea with Mother and Ella's limbs. Before evil alchemists turned people into monsters. That one memory, despite the illness and pain plaguing her teen years, still contained the magic of youth.

"Thank you," she whispered. "Oh, thank you." She stood and handed the dress back to Isabeau. "Please, put it back."

The sisters shared a glance between themselves, disbelief maybe, she couldn't be sure. Ella explained. "If she knew that something of my mother's survived, she would surely destroy it." Evidence suggested the woman rifled through her papers in the forge when she travelled to the city. Ella could not stand to put the dress in jeopardy and the safest place would be with these two secretive sisters.

Aurelia nodded and Isabeau disappeared returned to the wardrobe. "We will keep it for as long as we can," she assured her. Something in her voice caused Ella to take a closer look. The other girl seemed sad.

"What do you mean? Surely she doesn't search *your* chamber."

"Of course, she does." Isabeau snapped, reappearing from between her own dresses. "If you haven't noticed, there are listening devices in everywhere—including our room. We search every night to discover them, but she moves them regularly, so we know she is in here often."

"What kind of listening devices?"

"Pipes," replied Aurelia, "leading to her room mostly. She's waiting…" The girl shivered and drew her dressing gown more tightly around her.

Isabeau put her arm around her sister. "Regardless, if you keep our secret, we'll keep yours."

Ella sighed. "Just like your mother then, holding my dress hostage like she holds Myrtle, so I'll go about her ungodly business."

The twins looked at each other, then Aurelia shook her head and placed her hand on Ella's mechanical one. "No, Ella. Of all things we do not want to be like her."

Isabeau joined their hands. "Like sisters." Ella smiled and hugged them both close.

She never wanted sisters, content with her parents' devotion and then survival, but for the first time it was as though she weren't facing Judith alone.

Chapter Ten

A Death

The silence of church bells told the sad tidings better than any clamour could. Both the King Redmond and the Crown Prince Robert languished with an illness that stymied the physicians.

Queen Constantina sent out a desperate call for British medics, shamans from the dark continent, snake oil salesmen from the Colonies, and an Obeah priestess from her homeland of Jamaica to attend the royal family. Ships sailed on water and air, bringing precious herbs, salts, and therapies from distant lands.

Nothing seemed to help.

Perched on the widow's walk of a dark town house, Cinder surveyed the silent streets. Big Ben struck ten, a time when parties should be in full swing. Instead, silence shrouded the houses, the city seemed to hold its breath as it waited for news.

Cinder's heart ached. Knowing, though unable to prove, somehow her stepmother had a hand in the misfortune plaguing the royal family. It could not be coincidence that just weeks after revealing Judith's penchant for creating poisons capable of changing men into monsters that the royal family fell ill.

She rappelled down the alley side of the building, pocket

burdened with Mrs. Morton's sapphire tiara. She recently wore the jewel studded hairpiece to a tea with Judith. Ella suspected that besides the impunity of wearing such a gaudy piece, the lady slighted Judith at some juncture. That seemed the case of many of targets assigned to Cinder, but once again, nothing in the way of proof.

She slipped into the darkness, avoiding the waste thrown from the windows and doors of the fancy house and headed for The Fence.

"Hey there, watch where you're walking."

Cinder leaped back with a very undignified screech. "Harcourt, you scared the life out of me. What are you doing lurking back here?"

The fellow chuckled and unwound himself from the inky shadows. "Maybe's same as you, Lady Eliana."

"Stop that," she hissed. "That girl doesn't exist anymore." The man was one of the few who met her long ago, when she first started visiting the hospital under a different name, under different circumstances. When she dreamed she could actually do some good.

"Besides, you're no thief," she added. *If one didn't count begging with one hand and pinching pockets with the other when a kind soul leaned in close to drop a penny into his cup.*

He clacked his pincher in response, and she groaned. "Why do you still wear that thing? I made you a hand."

He chuckled. "And a fine one it t'was. I fenced it. It's hanging on the wall over Proixmus. Besides, this here is museum stuff. The first made by the elusive Cinder. But I's know the truth, you know. Do you?"

"About what?"

"About the Lady Eliana."

Cinder looked both ways down the alley. Rats moved, but there could be others just as hidden as Harcourt had been. "I told you to stop that. She's dead, you hear me?" All that was left was a dishonoured thief. Despite what Dr. Bon Hamlet thought, there would be no future for her and the sooner those who remembered her as a Baron's daughter forgot it, the better chance of keeping her friends alive.

"Ahh, but the daughter of Octavia will fly again, this is what *I* know."

"You're talking nonsense." She walked down the alley, "And turn that pincher in for your hand, you hear?"

"Such pretty boots," the old man crooned. "They leave a special mark, you know, at the houses where you have been. But don't worry, I took care of those."

Cinder whirled, suddenly conscious of the special boot cradling her half foot. "What do you mean? Have you been following me?" His hacking and wheezing drew the worst of attention, perhaps even get her caught.

The beggar raised his hands and backed into the wall. "Just doing what I was told, is all. The marks in the flower beds, or the lawns. You must be careful to sweep them."

"Doing what you were told?" A sweat broke out on her lower lip. *Could he be a spy for Judith? Could he inform the Prussian agent of my movements? Those detours taken through St. Drogo especially so spies could not follow?*

But Harcourt could.

His presence at the cathedral was one of her very first memories. His comments about her boot turned her stomach sour. Most people in the underground knew about her modified arm. Not the special bio mechanics which made it a modern marvel, of course. The metal and bone arm opened minds where her accent may have gotten her locked out or even hurt in the places she went.

But her foot was another matter.

The same rope which removed her arm also took half of her foot. Her father created special boots to cradle the stump, allowing her to move almost normally—to handle a foil and grappling hook again with barely a hitch in her step. No one knew of it beyond her deceased father, the doctor who created her prosthesis, and Myrtle.

Possibly, a servant saw something during a change of bandages when she was laid low by infection all those years ago, but Ella doubted that. The Baron had been fiercely protective about her injuries, tending to them himself with Myrtle.

Harcourt's knowledge was just more leverage which could be used against her. An insane urge to throttle the chap blinded her and she nearly drew her rapier. At the last minutes, she shoved it back into its and leaped for him. She would check him for the brown dot with a red centre the German's marked all their people—then throttle him. As though sensing her murderous intent, the hunchback moved out of reach, scuttling down the alley with a wail certain to bring the police.

Cinder ran the opposite direction, ducking finally into welcoming doors on St. Drogo.

"Come, child," a priest beckoned. "It is an ill-omened time to be out."

"Have you heard news?" she asked.

The clergyman shook his head and barred the door. "Only that the death watch has begun."

"That's it then, they are giving up?"

"Maybe not giving up but hope fades with every hour. I have heard the heir suffers more. Queen Constantina has dispatched her airship to recall Prince Aerysleigh from the front."

Ella's heart leaped at the mention of her dark rescuer, then fell. "No!"

The priest regarded her quizzically at her outburst. "He must stay on the front. He is our most effective general in the war," she finished in a quieter tone.

"True. But the succession must continue. The royal family is our heart."

Cinder shook her head and stalked towards the passage way to The Fence.

Proximus would know the news. His sources were impeccable, and most owed him something or other. But as she moved the coffin, bells in the distance tolled. First one, then another, then a terrible clamour that could only mean one thing.

A royal had died.

Chapter Eleven

The Hunt

Though the moon hid its face, Aerysleigh still ran *The Sky Serpent* just below the clouds, far enough above enemy ground troops and low enough to avoid the watchful eyes of his quarry.

The hunt for this prize ran the length and breadth of Europe. From a secret dock in the Black Forest, through the Rhine Valley, to the Baltic Sea and back again yet she always gave him the slip. Only through careful planning, pouring over the maps and good-natured, though somewhat heated discussions among his lieutenants, would he finally have her by morning.

Aerysleigh tapped young Thad on the shoulder and flipped the goggles over his eyes. "Tell Lieutenant Burrows to bring her up so I can see above the bank...Carefully now...wait for my mark."

Thad turned to the telegraph and tapped out his message, the lines running directly to his second in command, Beth Wickersham, at the helm.

He turned his face to the sky. When the water vapours thinned, he double thumped the boy's shoulder. The telegraph clacked his orders below.

The ascent of the airship slowed until the crow's nest broke into the starry expanse, clouds trailing behind like a diaphanous train. He climbed the central mast to get even higher and wound the crank on the goggles. The night lit up green, allowing him to see in the darkness.

"There she is," he breathed.

The rope trembled and Thad joined him. They gazed in silence at the large ironclad. Armed with guns on nearly every deck, *The Sieg* was a beast. No matter that she handled like a naval ship wallowing in high seas, she could fire from any angle. Years ago, the vessel made her mark in history with the defeat of Lady Captain Steelhaugh's *Lady Peril* over the channel.

First the mammoth disabled her opponent with a combination broadside attack of 36, 24, and 12 pounders. Then the prow mounted six barrelled cannon could shred any airship if brought close enough.

However, on a spy mission to the secluded air dock in the Black Forest, Aerysleigh discovered her weakness. Only sharp shooters protected the stern. That is where he planned to attack. His own lithe *Sea Serpent* handled like a dream and his crew were the best and most well-trained crew in the air. They would not flinch, and they would take down the Prussia's prize once and for all.

Even better, take the decks with a boarding crew and claim the ironclad for king and country. The taking of her would be a major blow to Prussia and a boost in the development of Great Britain's own weapons. Aerysleigh grinned at the thought, ignoring the warning warmth at his brow until the goggles *sitzed* and nearly singed his eyebrow off.

He cursed and dropped back to the nest. He'd never been able to fix that glitch. Five minutes of use was all he could get before singing his skull. Though a most useful invention, it could be very irritating.

With a wide smile, Thad dropped down beside him. "Are we really gonna take her, sir?"

Aerysleigh rubbed his brow and grinned in return. "In the morning we should catch her. Then, aye, she will be ours." He nodded at the telegraph. "Tell them to take us down again and put on the speed. She seems to be pulling away."

Thad jumped to carry out the orders under Aerysleigh approving gaze. *A good lad.* Though only fourteen, he'd seen a good many battles on *The Sky Serpent*. Despite his youth, Aerysleigh already planned his promotion.

"Do you think she's made us, sir?"

"No. The winds are stronger up where she sails, but not to worry, Lieutenant Wickersham won't let the prize out of her sites this time."

Thad's teeth flashed feral in the dark. "No Sir, not after that fog over the Rhine."

Aerysleigh nodded back. Men need avenged. Two were lost when they followed *The Sieg* over the Rhine and a billowing pocket of poisonous gases caught them unawares. Lieutenant Wickersham manned the helm at the time and in the confusion of the moment their quarry slipped away. With the loss of the men it became personal for his second. She swore to amend her mistake next time the ship appeared in her sights. The whole crew swore to ground the massive ironclad.

Aerysleigh stuffed the goggles into the leather pocket strapped to his side. Not much of his uniform conformed to military standards anymore, but uniforms rarely contained the pockets necessary to hold important gear.

He buttoned on his gloves then grasped the rope and slid down, around the envelopes to the deck below. The rounded metal studs embedded in the leather protected both flesh and leather. It became one of his first inventions. After only a few days of climbing the ropes as a new recruit, he invented them—and never regretted it. Except maybe when his temple throbbed all day from a burn.

He nodded to Lieutenant Wickersham who passed off the wheel and hurried to his side. The change accomplished in absolute silence.

"Tell those men without duties to get some sleep," he ordered. No need to mention the additional speed, he could already feel the power as the ship surged. Men moved about in the pitch black—sure footed and quiet. He couldn't help the swell of pride at their efficiency. Where illumination was necessary, men kept the lamps carefully shielded. All cabin windows were blackened. No bells or whistles, no drums, or marching of feet oft heard on other military airships marred the silence.

"Are the men finished mounting the guns on the prow?" he asked.

"Almost, sir, they will be ready by morning."

Aerysleigh took a chance on reducing the strength of his broadside by moving the guns to the front of the ship. However, if they were to take the most terrifying of the airships in the sky, their surprise must be absolute.

"*The Sieg* will turn to the East in a few hours," Lieutenant Wickersham reminded him.

He gave a curt nod. "Yes. If their captain keeps the same patrol route as in the past. That is all we have to go on if we are to pull this off. Keep on course and turn as we've discussed." He nodded towards the prow. "Keep the men working. Hold her steady in the cloud bank."

Wickersham let out a sharp breath at his shoulder. "Risky."

"Yes, but we can't afford being seen by lookouts. We attack in three hours' time."

The second saluted and returned to her post. Aerysleigh retreated to his cabin to attempt a rest, but instead paced the floor. By the light of a single candle he went over his calculations and second guessed his plan of attack.

A tentative knock at the door broke his concentration. "Sir?"

"Come in, Julia."

Wickersham's cabin girl slipped through the portal with a tray. "Begging your pardon, sir, Mister Grey says you're to eat before you go to fighting scores of Prussians." She set down a cut of mutton and potatoes.

He nodded curtly. *Blasted cook was always trying to feed him.*

He appreciated the concern, but food was the last thing on his mind right now. He dismissed the girl and sat, staring at the dinner. It reminded him of his mother ordering him to sit still and eat. Now, as then, more important things occupied his mind than filling his stomach. Memories of his mother turned his thoughts towards home. By the time Sergeant Phipps knocked on his door to tell him the guns were in place, he was decidedly morose.

"What's the matter, sir?" asked the Sergeant.

Aerysleigh lit a new candle and stood. "Just thinking."

"Thinking that taking *The Sieg* will get us some leave time at home?"

He shuddered. *Home.* Once again, the last thing on his mind. Last time he attempted a short visit to the palace while his ship received much needed repairs, he regretted the choice immediately. His first mistake was thinking a quiet time catching up with his older brother even possible. His second was thinking his mother wouldn't hear of it. The queen packed his days with teas and the nights with card parties. Each engagement filled with mothers displaying dim witted daughters for his consideration.

"Maybe for some of you," he conceded. "I'd just as well prefer to fight until the Prussia crawls back to their borders and stays there."

The sergeant grinned. "Queen's got plans for you, does she?"

"How did you guess?"

The grizzled fellow shrugged. "Any time a man's on his own and happy for it, all the women in his life seem hell-bent to saddle him with a wife. I suppose for a prince it's no different."

"Worse," agreed Aerysleigh. "I prefer the Air Force and *The*

Serpent over a wife."

The Sergeant laughed. "That's what we all say when we are young, but given time, Captain, there are women out there worth giving up this life."

Aerysleigh raised his cup. "I will bow to your superior knowledge, sir." The Sergeant had outlived two wives and raised a fistful of daughters. But the man's words made him remember a blue-eyed girl who glared up at him whilst standing on his toes. He shook his head. There were less pleasanter things to think of tonight.

"Give the men a ration of ale and rest before the morning. Then let's go get that ship."

"Aye, Sir."

Chapter Twelve

A Battle

Once again in the crow's nest with Thad in the early morning hours, Aerysleigh scanned the tops of the clouds. He grinned at the flash of lights port side of the prow. The airship turned as predicted, the captain evidently bound by orders to adhere to a certain patrol route. But this made it perfect for an ambush.

"We did it, sir," crowed Thad.

Aerysleigh clapped the lad on the back. "We sure did. Let's give the order to pour on the steam and get this attack—" His voice broke off as light jumped across the tops of the clouds. "What the devil?" He whipped the telescope from his belt and stared behind.

Thad crawled up and balanced precariously on the edge of the protective railing. "It looks like one of those luxury airships," he said.

"Sure enough." The slim little liner sparkled with a myriad of lights, reflecting the pinking sun off unblackened windows. If it were later in the day, he could have heard the chink of tea cups and smell the starch in the butler's shirts.

"Perhaps she got lost," offered the lad.

That wasn't hard to imagine. At least once a year, some member of the aristocracy got himself killed by unpredictable gasses or boarded by privateers as he impressed his friends with a tour of the war zone. Most of the buffoons played it safe and stayed behind the heavily patrolled air on the border of France. However, being this early, there may be only one sleepy crew member at the helm.

And he was flying her flying straight into a battle.

The Serpent lurched. Aerysleigh prevented Thad from pitching over the edge by grabbing his coat tail. He turned back to where *The Sieg* had floated in blissful ignorance of their stalking just moments before. His heart raced. Men now manned its propellers; the great blades swiveling to slow the ship and begin its turn. *The Sky Serpent* had mere minutes to strike.

He slammed the telescope closed. "Rise, Rise, Rise! Begin the attack."

Thad dropped to the telegraph and tapped out the message. Aerysleigh grabbed the rope, cursing the precious seconds it took him to reach the upper deck.

"Battle stations! Prime the cannons. She's turning."

Julia jumped into the telegraph box just behind him and waited for the next set of commands. She managed the five tapping machines arrayed before her confidently. The click of outgoing and incoming messages added a strange beat to the war preparations.

Boilers roared and the ship surged upwards. A shadow loomed just above, the bottom of the *Sieg* blocking the waking sun. Aerysleigh gritted his teeth. Their manoeuvres, and the quarry slowing, made them overshoot their mark. The mast with the lookout groaned and then cracked. Ropes cracked like bull whips then loosened. The mast and crow's nest slapped against the envelope as it folded and hung suspended.

"Thad!"

"Here, sir." He whirled to find the white-faced lad at his shoulder, evidently having descended the same rope. He held up his hands, gloves smoking. "I sure like these gloves you invented, Sir. My hands wouldn't have made it."

Aerysleigh let out his breath and clapped the boy on the shoulder. "Battle stations!" He roared.

Silent no more, the crew flew to their posts. *The Sky Serpent* bolted upwards ending up poop to broadside with *The Sieg*. For a surreal moment no one breathed as they stared at the mighty shadow the enemy ship cast. The crew of *The Sieg*, their sights set on the smaller prize of the luxury ship, gaped in shock at the battleship appearing from right below them.

There would be no trying to capture *The Sieg* today.

"Higher!" He yelled again. "Get us above those cannons." Their main goal now was to survive. Thankfully *The Sieg* had the weakness shared by all airships—the envelope. It fluttered temptingly almost within reach.

Just a little more.

His gallant vessel rose and turned, much more quickly than the larger ship. For the hundredth time in as many seconds, he thanked the shipwrights for the slim lines and easy handling of his ship.

Today it may just save their lives.

The turn completed before the enemy crew could react. Aerysleigh gave the order as the prow mounted guns came to bear. "Fire!"

Seven cannons responded instantaneously to the order, breaking through the armoured panels designed to protect the envelope, but not yet damaging it enough to bring down the ship. Aerysleigh counted the beats of his heart as the broadside guns, weakened by seven guns fewer but still a considerable force, found their mark.

A man screamed and tumbled from the deck. Enemy snipers perched in advantageous positions and now picked off his crew.

"Fire!" He commanded, Lieutenant Wickersham's repeated command an echo before he finished. Again, *Sky Serpent*'s cannons barked, this time the larger guns made it past the armour and breeched the hull. Sergeant Phipps boomed below, counting down the seconds. The crew of *The Serpent* applied their daily practice to practical use, reloading the cannons from a minute for the smaller guns to three minutes for the larger.

Previous battles taught them that the Prussians could reload in three. The smaller ship could potentially get a fatal blow to the enemy before suffering their first hit.

The Sieg's cannons answered back, thundering without any synchronisation from the myriad of decks. Aerysleigh frowned. *Evidently, they've been practising as well.*

His ship shuddered as hits slammed into the lower decks. A cannonball skimmed over the poop deck shattering the railing. One passed so close it singed his jacket. Flying debris turned into miniature missiles. A piece of railing lodged in his arm with the sharp bite of hound.

He paid it no mind.

Others struck the rigging. Lines popped and snapped with the force of lightning. Men tumbled overboard.

"Marines! Take out some of those snipers." He spied Thad line up with the men, gun snugged tightly to his shoulder, firing even more rapidly than the seasoned soldiers. He'd grown up on the moors and with an Enfield could fell a bird at 500 meters.

Sergeant Phipps reached one minute in his count.

"Hold her steady. Fire when ready." Several cannons responded to his order and he felt a flush of pride. It took him half a second to realise no more tapping came from behind. He whirled. The telegraph station with Julia had been obliterated in the last volley. The cabin girl lay unmoving in a seeping scarlet pool.

"Fire!" he ground out. "Bring that beast to heel."

More cannons growled out their challenge. The prow of *The Sieg* dipped. Men fell into the clouds. Aerysleigh gripped the rail, entranced by the enemy's disgrace. Across the way another man stood on the poop deck returned his gaze. No doubt the captain, just realising the fatal wound of his ship.

He turned his gaze to the carnage on his own vessel. Tendrils of smoke seeped across the bodies of the wounded and dying. Moans filled the abrupt ear ringing silence. Slowly, slowly, *The Sieg* disappeared into the clouds.

The mighty Prussian ship defeated.

Chapter Thirteen

Recalled

Aerysleigh couldn't help but see death approach as the luxury yacht drew nearer. The death of his dreams, of the freedom to seek new horizons, of friendships bound in blood. This was no lost aristocrat who wandered into enemy territory. He could have almost lived with that.

The approaching ship signified something so much worse.

With the chiming of the hour bell the yacht's details grew clearer. Graceful lines he knew like his own face. Gaudy gold railing glinted in the rising sun. The hull and deck glistened a gleamed white, much different than his own black painted, crimson stained boards. The blue and red Union Jack all proclaimed the airship from whence his love affair with flying began. A swan of the air.

Queen's Pride, an anniversary gift from King Redmond to his bride, came with the promise should she ever wish, she could visit her family at any time. His mother never took advantage of the offer, rather, devoted herself to her new country, family, and royal duties without looking back.

Due to a little-known fact that Queen Constantina suffered from air sickness, short voyages of state on the airship were the only reasons the yacht left port. That and rentals to those currying favour.

He almost breathed a sigh of relief upon seeing the lack of the House of Highridge standard.

A recurring nightmare featured his mother hunting him down and taking him by the ear as she did when he hid from his lessons as a child. He could imagine her voice berating him for the bad example set for other boys and girls.

The few times he returned home, they circled each other warily. The fact that she believed his fascination with the Air Force a childish whim cast insult on his every belief. All the queen wished was that he return home to take on the proper mantle of a prince. Numerous times he thanked his lucky stars Robert assumed these stately duties with enough sobriety and self-importance to satisfy their mother.

Ignoring the heavy beat of his heart which had nothing to do with the battle, he turned his attention to *Sky Serpent's* deck. The moans of the soldiers filled his ears. He ignored what the approaching ship may bring and focused on immediate concerns.

He knelt beside Julia and gently closed the green eyes which heartbeats earlier snapped with intelligence and good nature. Though he fought in countless battles, the loss of young ones still hit especially hard.

A shadow blocked the sun. Thad stood at his shoulder, looking down at his friend, unabashed tears leaked down blood-splattered cheeks.

"I'll take care of her, sir."

Aerysleigh rose and nodded. He stepped down to where the masters and lieutenants waited with reports of damage and death. Medics moved quickly between soldiers. The able bodied of all ranks helped where they could.

Lieutenant Wickersham gestured towards the brightly lit, oncoming vessel.

He stopped any forthcoming observations with a raised hand. "Attend to matters at hand first." He nodded towards *Queen's Pride*. "We will deal with her later." The masters fired off their reports in a well-ordered manner. He gave directions as needed, however, after so many hard years, they knew their responsibilities well.

"Sir," ventured his second-in-command finally.

He tore his eyes from the ship where the aeronauts gave directions and threw lines to the arriving crew. "Yes?"

She pointed at his arm. "Perhaps you would like to get that looked at? Before you meet with the—"

"No," he snarled.

Already the lord to whom his mother lent the ship stood impatient to board, his manner filled with the self-importance of the aristocracy that drove him crazy. A bevy of minor officials waited. Collars starched. Cravats perfectly tied. Coats without a speck of lint or blood.

Two planks slithered between the decks. He glared across the way, meeting the eyes of the portly Lord berating the exhausted aeronauts struggling to secure the lines. Aerysleigh let his anger mount over the unnecessary dead and wounded caused by this posturing fool. The plan to take *The Sieg* was perfect! Except for the appearance of this aristocrat with a bureaucratic bumbling, he'd be in charge of the greatest Prussian warship and all her innovative marvels.

Not watching her fall.

By the time the Lord put his foot on the deck of *Sky Serpent*, his rage threatened to spill into actions unbecoming a gentleman.

The Lord raked Aerysleigh's bloodied and tattered uniform with a barely concealed sneer. "I am Lord Reginald Sydney Cholmondeley. I demand you take me to the captain, His Highness Aerysleigh Cole Highridge, immediately. I have business that cannot wait." He ran his gaze around the ship, blind to the misery he caused, only surprised that the captain had not hurried to meet him in his borrowed finery.

Aerysleigh ground his teeth together. "I am the Captain."

For once Lord Cholmondeley's superior facade faded and he eyed Aerysleigh in confusion. Granted, a year passed since his last visit home. Those few times he did see his family, he made sure the inconvenient times made social niceties impossible. Due to long hours stalking *The Sieg*, he lacked the polish of a proper gentleman with long hair woven into a hundred tiny braids contained by a ribbon and several days growth of beard.

However, no matter he be the lowliest pot scrubber, the bloke should grovel at his feet in thankfulness for saving his life. Instead the inflated peacock looked around him as though he found himself on a tugboat instead of in the presence of the most decorated crew of the war.

The Lord finally recovered himself and executed a court bow. "Forgive the mistake. Congratulations, your highness, on a well-deserved victory."

Aerysleigh fisted his hands in his breeches, trying desperately not to strike the flatterer. "What do you think you are doing here, sir?"

The queen's emissary glanced up, eyes wide and mouth agape in obvious confusion. "Your highness?"

"This is a war zone. Your gaudy parade into a carefully planned and near perfectly executed ambush cost me the lives of irreplaceable soldiers and experienced aeronauts. Not to mention the loss of a valuable prize. So, I ask you once more, *what is your purpose here?*"

Lord Cholmondeley straightened, gathering his wits. Aerysleigh clenched and unclenched his fists with the effort to not grab the Lord and throw him overboard. Queen Constantina had obviously chosen a lack-wit for her errand boy. What could it be now? A party to attend? Heaven forbid, found him a wife as she threatened every chance she got.

"I am sorry to be the bearer of unpleasantness, your highness. The queen undoubtedly wishes she could be here herself—"

"Knowing my mother's aversion to flying, I highly doubt that. I doubt you carry worse news than losing a quarter of my crew saving your worthless hide? Spit it out, Man, what does my mother want now?" Once, she tracked him down while he repaired *The Serpent* on the coast of Spain and ordered his return to England immediately. The purpose? To receive an award for a battle fought six months earlier.

In his shock at the forthright questions, Lord Cholmondeley lost all aplomb. "The Crown Prince, Prince Robert—"

"Yes, I know my brother's name, what is it?"

"Well, he's dead, sire. The King is weakened and not expected to live his natural span of years..." The man's words drivelled on, but Aerysleigh felt as though gut kicked by an iron shod draft horse.

Robert dead? How could this be?

Robert's disapproving countenance flashed before him, a reminder of their last argument.

At Robert's wedding to a shy Austrian princess, an occasion that required his presence despite the war, the elder prince cornered him after the reception, berating his disregard of his princely duties— words that fell directly from his mother's mouth.

"I am saving this country, Robert, so puppet princes can marry fairy tale princess', pretend Europe isn't soaked with blood as tyrants battle over mere miles of territory."

"Why you self-righteous blighter, you think so low of everyone except your high minded mates, as though all we do is party and visit the tailor. I'll have you know, the Royal family is the symbol of this—"

Aerysleigh flapped his hand, "heard it."

"We take stands against people like this Cinder thief—"

"Ahh, has someone been taking big brother's baubles?"

Robert tensed, then threw a quick jab—a move so unlike his brother it took Aerysleigh completely by surprise and he fell on his bum. Sure, he could blame the alcohol, they imbibed freely, him to suffer through tedious conversations around him, Robert in celebration. But it was more than drink.

The queen caught them rolling on the floor like children. Robert returned to his bride with a slight limp and bruises. Aerysleigh sported a shiner the next day from that sucker punch, his ears still ringing from the fierce scolding from his mother.

And now, no matter how annoying they found each other, there would never be another time. Aerysleigh shook his head to clear it of the memory, refocused on the Lord Cholmondeley.

How could he possibly be still be talking?

"With your father suffering so, the Queen requests your immediate return to England."

"Return? Now?"

How could she request such a thing? Although the Prussian airship now lay in the channel, he knew enough of the enemy to know they would not relent until the last soldier perished. They moved underground, shifting men and equipment to strategic points to threaten France while negotiating with Spain. English ground troops needed the air support he could provide to balance the power between the two. Napoleon may be a tyrant, but France was the only thing standing between the German Confederacy and Britain's interests.

Aerysleigh had an inkling the Queen's recall fell in line with the Prussian plans. Besides, he well knew, his mother had things firmly in hand.

"I see we came at a most opportune time," postulated the Lord, "The defeat of *The Sieg!* Such a wondrous feat. The largest Prussian dreadnaught. I am honoured to be a part of it."

Aerysleigh twitched an eyebrow at the absurd comment. Abruptly he turned to his second. "I think I should get this arm taken care of now" It was either that or kill the flattering sod.

As though sensing his mood, Lieutenant Wickersham motioned towards the stairwell leading below decks where he could cool off. "Of course, Captain."

"You are bleeding!" exclaimed the prig. "You must come immediately on board *The Queen's Pride.* My own personal physician is travelling with us and is entirely at your disposal."

Aerysleigh tried a polite smile, but by the way the Lord and his entourage retreated, he suspected it appeared more feral than he intended. "I have my own medics," he rasped, and turned away before he *did* strangle the man.

Chapter Fourteen

The Queen

"I'll not do it."

Queen Constantina regarded him stonily. Aerysleigh almost regretted his harshness of tone. *Almost.* Dark smudges beneath his mother's eyes and a shrillness of tone never there before revealed her fatigue, as though she teetered on the edge of hysteria and only her iron will kept her from tumbling over.

However, even his love and concern for her would not sway him. "I will *not* be your new Robert. I will *not* fill my time with parties and social niceties. There are people dying for England. And you are more than capable—"

"Your time of playing boy hero is over, Aerysleigh. You are needed here. Not only is Robert gone, your father's condition worsens daily—"

"Playing?" he interjected. "Is that what you think I have been doing these past ten years?" His heart dropped. "Do you truly not comprehend the utter devastation on the continent? The determination of the Kaiser and the Tsar to crush the Ottoman Empire and then our interest abroad? I may have defeated their warship, but ground armies have taken our allies. The Boars are rising in South Africa. The Empire is crumbling despite costly sortie attempts to penetrate those countries—"

His mother waved the facts away like a sour smell. "Enough. I get plenty of updates from the Lord Generals. All they do is request money, men, and supplies. Prime Minister Albany is meeting with Alexander's representatives and negotiations are underway."

"For what?"

She smirked at him. "If you came home more often, or even checked in with your superiors, you would have known negotiations have been ongoing. Your defeat of *The Scuttle*—"

"*The Sieg*—"

"Whatever—solidified our positions abroad and now the armistice papers are being signed."

Aerysleigh paced back and forth, wanting to throw himself from the second-floor window in his frustration. "You can't! They are evil, Mother, bent to destroy or take everything. Including England."

"Nonsense. They can have the areas they already conquered or annexed, including Alsace-Lorraine." She gave him a half smile. "You didn't think I was paying attention to such matters, did you."

He gaped at her, amazed at how seriously he underestimated his mother. While he fought to smash Prussia and to free the countries under its thumb, she meddled behind the scenes, pushing for a treaty that would end up threatening England more than outright war and gas clouds ever could. "You handed them everything they need to regroup. Prince Frederick and Prince Albert are in position to march on Paris. Napoleon's grip is slipping. If a treaty is signed, Britain gives them permission to continue the work Lady Steelhaugh destroyed years ago."

"Yes. Her devastating endeavour that cost our country dearly. The chain reaction poisoned the land and made England's coast a very dangerous place, I might add. It was the beginning of our misguided attempts to meddle where we do not belong."

"But—"

She held up her hand. "There are no 'buts'. The Houses have voted. The war will end. You will take up the mantle of crown prince." She turned to a gold laced table where sat a neat stack of invitations. "As for a wife, there are several attractive young ladies with expansive dowries." At his silence she glanced up. "There are also some young widows."

His face must have revealed his utter disgust at the sudden change of track in this conversation, for the queen thumped the stack back down. The steel seemed to melt from her spine for an instant.

"Really Aerysleigh, there is no other choice."

He waved away her protest and turned to gaze at the stretching palace gardens. "Once—" He broke off at her anguished look. Not the time to open old wounds. "I have cousins," he offered.

"Posh. Barbarians."

Aerysleigh frowned at his reflection in the window. His father's marriage to his Jamaican planter princess had been a hotly contested love match. She left the poverty-stricken country and invested herself in proving to the world her worth as a queen. She managed capably.

By the time she produced three children and lost one, his mother was firmly installed as a force in the palace. She argued behind closed doors for trade agreements and aid when hurricanes or disease struck her home nation—but never again set foot on its white beaches.

As a result, the royal children never met their cousins, only knew of their existence. So, what if he grasped at straws. If he thought taking on the role of crown prince onerous, marriage would kill him off where all the cannon shells of the enemy had not.

"I have made you an appointment with the tailor later this afternoon and of course, you must visit a barber." She motioned in his general direction. "I understand being locked on a ship for long period may inhibit personal hygiene, but Aerysleigh...really. There is no way you will catch a wife looking like that."

For the briefest instant he thought of blonde hair floating on the night air, then shook his head and crossed his arms over his chest. "I won't cut my hair."

She leaped to her feet, her smile bright enough to put shame to the sun rays which skimmed the clouds and could blind a bloke. The smile that once captured a king. She placed a hand on his arm, victory assured. "We'll deal with that later."

"No, we won't."

"Your old tutor, Mr. Hansley, will be here to bring you up to speed on the political landscape and—"

"Not Mr. Hansley." *How could the old goat still be alive?*

She handed Aerysleigh a piece of paper. "These are your engagements for the week."

Incredulous he flipped it over to find both sides covered in his mother's neat script. "Have you not heard a word I've said?" He waved the list. "Parlour parties and tree plantings. Airship christenings, hospital walk throughs, and what is this...?" He shook the list at her, "scheduled jaunts in the park? These are not the activities of a prince. Am I a prize horse to be auctioned off?"

"Now you are just being dramatic. There are also some dates for polo. Though I admit the schedule to be light. So many families have already left for the country." She flipped her fan. "Really, Aerysleigh. You are being childish. Parliament seizes more control every year. We must make ourselves useful if the monarchy is to survive."

His throat constricted as though caught in a noose. "All of these are appearances for appearance's sake. This is not who I am. This is Robert's forte. I am not he." He let the paper flutter to the floor.

He had not meant to talk of Robert in the present, as though the crown prince could enter at any moment. He closed his eyes and breathed deep, prepared to apologise for the breath of pain he caused his mother. If only he could speak to his father. They saw eye to eye more oft than nought.

"What about Ursula?" He said.

His mother's nose pinched. "The Princess Ursula is not on the table. Not only is she not blood, she failed to produce an heir." She hissed with ugliness unbecoming a queen, denying what they both knew. The arranged marriage of Robert to the Austrian princess had failed. The Princess rarely ventured from the palace before the loss of her husband. Now she devoted herself to the care of the King.

Once there had been another, a princess of light and fury. One that would have made a better King than any of the Highridge children. His twin, two minutes older and eons more mature than himself, even at fifteen when they lost her in a boiler explosion. Unconsciously he touched his eye patch.

"The people love her," he persisted, though in truth he forgot the gist of the conversation.

His mother's eyes grew wild. Her gaze followed the movement of his hand. "Stop it, do you hear?"

"What will you do, disown me?"

"England doesn't need a boy hero right now. This country can do without another dashing airship captain or a dabbling inventor." She just wouldn't let that time he blew up the fountain rest. "We don't need a beautiful face with foreign blood sitting on the throne. The people may love her, but in the end, she is just a foreigner."

Like yourself he neglected to point out. But then again, his mother did not have aspirations to rule. She preferred to stay in the background, the seat of true power.

"The best thing for this country now is a crown prince ready to be king. Though Robert fulfilled his familial duties, you are the one that makes the news." She said *that* with a sneer. "Despite all effort to the contrary, you are England's favoured son and you *will* take your destined place." She raked her gaze over him.

"If you feel like you need to have an occupation there are the trade agreements for the Colonies' helium that need to be renegotiated. The copper miners are restless and calling for more safety measures and higher wages."

He turned away. "None of that matters if Prussia achieves her goals."

Queen Constantina rose. "Always you were a wilful, insolent child. Now you've grown into a rebellious man. It is time to step up and you will."

Aerysleigh stopped himself from the self-conscious act of touching the hated braids or straightening his cravat. Although he knew she spoke in anger and pain, he still felt the bite of the words in his soul.

He inclined his head. "Your pardon, Mother, for not being the one who died. If I could change it, I would."

God knew he spoke the truth. Despite their differences and the fact they grew apart, he loved his elder brother. He couldn't always understand Robert's choice to toe the line and let his father and mother shape him to their will, but he would have traded places in an instant. It was Aerysleigh's destiny to die young, not the Crown Prince's. Death was the lot of a soldier, not a that of a beloved prince.

"Aerysleigh…"

With a sharp bow he quit the room before more harsh words could be exchanged.

CHAPTER FIFTEEN

A FRIEND

ontemplating the fate laid out for him by his mother, endless parties, scheming mothers, empty-headed socialites looking for a conquest to set them above their peers for the life time, left Aerysleigh considering a jump from the Hungerford bridge. Self-pity? More a mourning for the life he wished to live, one with meaning instead of a superfluous figurehead.

King Redmond's condition worsened. His muscles shrank and jerked in a way that completely flummoxed the physicians. The Princess Ursula only left his side when ordered by the Queen to her duties.

Aerysleigh wandered along the street in front of the House of Lords. A boy hawked newspapers on the corner, and he paid hard coin to find out the news in his own country.

He perused the headlines: *'Cinder Strikes Lord Cholmondeley'.* He chuckled at that one. Serves the bloke right for interrupting the battled with *The Sieg.* *'No one Safe* and *Third Body in Three Days discovered in the Thames—Cinder to blame?'* All written by a Molly Mayhem.

He groaned. "*Walking About Fashion Inspired by Cinder?* Honestly?" On the second page he found mention of several proposed bills being discussed in Parliament, a whole page dedicated to a list with description of bills before Parliament, and at the very end a small article titled '*Survivors Tell Human Experiments on the Continent*'. "What the devil?" He closed the paper and glanced at the name. "*The Dinted Draper?*" He glanced at the boy. "What paper is this?"

The boy blushed from his stained coat collar to the cap pulled tight over his ears. "Begging your pardon, sir. That's for…" He trailed off into a mumble while grubby took the paper and replaced it with another—*London's Weekly*. "There you be, sir. There's news for one sich as yerself."

Whatever did the boy mean?

Aerysleigh looked through this paper and did not find much of interest. He sighed and handed it back to the boy. "I'll take the other." He tossed him another three pence. "Keep the coin," he said, then continued on his aimless way, halfheartedly thumbing through ads. Most were aimed at the modified, but there were others. Belts for apothecaries, surgeons. Grease to keep parts quiet. Clockwork parts and the latest automated work carts.

Just months ago, his life had been perfect. Now he felt like a puppet. His network of spies which tracked Prussia's covert war effort disrupted by his sudden recall and a cease fire. He straightened.

Enough of this, Aerysleigh. She only said where you have to be at certain times. That leaves plenty of wiggle room for other activities.

He nodded in resolve. He would contact his crew, most reassigned while *Sky Serpent* got refitted for courier duty. Despite his mother's forced optimism, the tone of the world had changed.

There could be no peace on the continent. Though the front seemed quiet, London herself seethed. Just when he thought he might put a finger on it, the feeling shifted. In just a few short months he had lost touch, and it needled.

He recalled the girl on the bridge, her hard-eyed look and yet her vulnerability when she believed him to think her a monster. Yes, this restlessness seemed linked to the people in the shadow of St. Drogo. And where did this Cinder come into play? Was he merely a thief or something more sinister?

Aerysleigh rubbed his face. It seemed he saw conspiracy in everything.

Chanting pulled his attention to the road before him. A crowd carrying signs marched past, yelling for rights for modifieds. Yet another issue facing the country he seemed disconnected from.

Lost in thought, he did not notice the man coming down the steps until their shoulders met with a solid thud. The other fellow stumbled and Aerysleigh reached out to steady him.

"Pardon!" He cried at the same time as the other, then he recognised his old friend. *Just the chap he needed to see.*

"Basil, how are you?"

His friend's tired, green eyes lit up and he bowed. "Your servant, sir."

Aerysleigh clapped him on the shoulder, relieved at the escape from his turmoil. "None of that, now. We served on the same ship…" his words trailed off as he got a good look at the fellow. "I say, Basil, you look rotten."

Basil's sour expression lightened. "I could say the same for yourself." He stepped back and touched Aerysleigh's gut with his cane. "I see they've been feeding you well enough, but you look fatigued."

Aerysleigh shrugged. "Late nights…ship time is much different than that of the peers."

"Ah, I have heard. My cousin attended Lady Harrington's latest gala."

"She did?"

"She reported your official entrance to the marriage market."

Aerysleigh tried to remember any relatives of his friend and failed utterly. Although they spent many years serving on the same ship, photographs were rare. However, the other's auburn hair did stand out. He shuffled through the possibles in his memory and found they blurred together.

Basil laughed outright at his obvious struggle. "Never mind then. She's heard enough stories of you to steer clear—not that she has any plans to marry again. Zylpha observed you from afar."

Aerysleigh cleared his throat and changed the subject. "So how fares it with you? Catching criminals as we planned?" Once both of them planned to retire from the air force and seek a commission to the newly formed Scotland Yard. Basil landed a job after having his knee blown out and receiving an honourable discharge.

His friend stepped back to put a more than physical distance between them. The hair on the back of Aerysleigh's neck raised at the look in the man's eye, bringing his thoughts full circle to the unseen currents. They even seemed to affect this rock steady bloke.

"Are you asking as a friend or as my prince, sir." Basil asked.

Taking a moment to study his friend, Aerysleigh grew concerned with what he saw. He did not exaggerate when he said his old mate looked ill. A wariness hung about the once jovial visage he never observed before, even at the height of the war. What had happened in the months he allowed his mother's schedule to consume him? Now, this friend seemed a stranger.

"That bad, huh?" Aerysleigh asked in an attempt to lighten the mood.

Basil breathed deep and threw a glance over his shoulder at the House of Lords from which he came. "Indeed."

Aerysleigh bowed and pointed down the road. Time to make amends. "By your leave then, let me buy you lunch, and I will allow you to regal me with your tales of the criminal element lurking on the streets."

Basil finally allowed himself a smile and led the way towards the Red Lion Tavern. "Once again, your servant, Sir."

Chapter Sixteen

A Meeting

"There are odd goings on in London these days," Basil began as they chose a corner where they could have a modicum of privacy.

Aerysleigh nodded, ready to soak up the news.

"Bodies are turning up drained of blood," Basil continued, "some torn apart and half eaten, as though savaged by an animal."

"A repeat of Jack the Ripper? Dr. Frankenstein?"

"No. Different. At first, I thought it was the influx of veterans. Most have no place to go, wounded, without a shilling to their name after fulfilling their terms in the army. Too many end up on the street as beggars. Others turn to crime. I even investigated orphans and widows from the workhouses and the poor shelters. But few of these people turn to crimes such as I have witnessed. Evidence just doesn't add up and there is more."

"That sounds bad enough."

"Indeed. But even the criminal element is afraid. Copper Fingers Pernella and Knife 'Em Mic have warned their people off the streets and conduct their business in the light of day instead."

Despite the serious nature of the conversation, Aerysleigh couldn't help a smile at the underworld criminals name. "Good for the metro police then."

"Not really. The crimes occurring after dark now are the kind that give men nightmares. Three constables turned in their resignations just this week, the last after vomiting her dinner all over my shoes."

"Hard to keep a shine that way." Aerysleigh commented while his mind reeled. Certainly no one talked of these things at the parties he found himself attending lately.

His friend seemed not to hear. Warmed to the topic, he plunged on. "Indeed. I have spent the morning petitioning all who would listen in the House of Lords and Commons to issue a warning for the residents of London. I have met with iron ears at every turn. You caught me at an ill time just then and I beg your pardon for assuming that you would be the same."

"And how is that?" He asked.

Basil banged his cane on the floor in obvious frustration. "Believing that life is all garden parties and horse races! They take more umbrage at this Cinder fellow stealing their baubles than the blood running in the gutters."

Not the first time Aerysleigh heard the name by a long shot. He set *The Dinted Draper* on the table. "Mother spoke of this person. But even more, this paper is full of his exploits."

A faint smile touched Basil's lips. "Of course. And the fact that you have heard of this black-hearted thief and not the other crimes demonstrates the lack of interest in such things. It gives me little reason to hope for the Lords to listen." Basil took a deep breath and leaned back in his chair, however the tension still showed in the set of his shoulders and white knuckled grip on his cane. "I know your mother has kept you busy filling your brother's breeches for the gossip mongers." Basil blanched at his thoughtless joke. "Begging your pardon, my friend. I am truly sorry to hear of Prince Robby. He was a good chap."

A lump large enough to choke him, blocked Aerysleigh's throat at the sympathy. It reminded him of his musings in the minutes before he met Basil and the unending hopelessness he faced. "This ailment that struck down Robert and now ails my father defies all medical knowledge. It seems at times a wasting disease and then a palsy." He shook his head at his despairing tone. A dead prince heir, a weakened king, a throne he never thought to inherit and never wanted. "But let us talk of other things."

The commissioner snorted. "Certainly, you do not find the criminal element entertaining?"

Aerysleigh shook his head, "You know me better than that. It is diversion from my mother's latest schemes to get me married off and producing an heir as soon as possible."

"Ever an officer of the Society of Interfering Ladies?"

Drink nearly spewed over the table at his old friend's mention of the name they assigned to their mothers as boy's. "You do not jest. I think she has grown worse with the loss of..." he swallowed his words, not ready to turn his conversation back to the absence of Robert at the palace. "So, tell me the story of this Cinder person who has the lords and the ladies of the realm so concerned they cannot attend to the mundane matters of the city?"

Basil eyed him long and hard as though trying to determine if he asked in jest. It was hard to admit he attended the parties in the hope of pacifying his mother long enough to get some time to himself. He paid no attention to the talk flowing around him, all of it seeming so insipid and pointless after the war and the death that seemed not to have touched the peerage.

"I do not believe Cinder to be a part of the murders. He is a thief, and a very good one at that. However, his targets seemed to have changed lately."

"How so?"

"At first his thefts seemed harmless, papers and plans. Hints he may be an inventor or working for a black-market scientist. Maybe even an agent for the Kaiser. Thing is, he would steal plans and papers and leave the jewels. Then I noticed the beggars, night soil boys and prostitutes had a little coin. However, the thief came by his money he seemed to be a regular Robin Hood."

"Then?" Aerysleigh prompted.

"The fellow changes tactics and starts to steal jewels and money. A lot of it."

"How mysterious. And no clues as to his identity?"

"Very little. There is no determining where he will strike next, at a party, at a home, at a club. He seems to be a talented pickpocket, a master of disguise which allows him to get close to his targets, and then, if unsuccessful, he strikes at the home in the dark of night."

"So why the name Cinder?"

"That stems from one of the only observable clues. The presence of soot, sometimes smeared from glove or clothes."

"A blacksmith or labourer?"

Basil snorted. "Perhaps, but that accounts for nearly three quarters of the working class or even anyone living in or around Dorset Street. Not to mention those working the Smith's Quarter."

That street name turned a cog in Aerysleigh's brain. "The one backing the Catholic church, St. Drogo?" Thoughts of the cathedral brought to mind a midnight passenger he couldn't seem to forget.

"Yes." Basil allowed the server to deposit his plate, then leaned forward. "But there are a few other clues that make the case particularly befuddling. Small footprints—"

It was obvious to Aerysleigh that Basil found his vocation intriguing. Something Aerysleigh envied him. "Like a woman? It wouldn't be the first time," he asked.

Basil smiled. "No. More like a mouse."

Aerysleigh's confusion must have shown on his face because the bloke laughed, a truly amused sound that lightened the shadows under his eyes. Though happy to alleviate some of the other's dourness, he would rather be let in on the joke than the butt of it.

Basil ceased his merriment, obviously seeing his friend's distress, and leaned forward with a more serious air. "Mice. Several of them. Trained pets, I think. This is the way the thief gains access to the valuables. Lord Chillnaught has a steel vault located two stories up with several of the more unusual traps. Cinder evidently scaled the side of the building, cut a hole in the glass, disabled the traps, opened the vault, and took the jewels belonging to the honourable gentleman's wife."

"He sounds more like an ordinary thief."

"Perhaps, except for the fact this was all done while the fellow slept in the same room, a bed backed up against the door of the vault."

Interest piqued, Aerysleigh mused over the information, the darkness in his soul lifting as he latched on a way to do something useful. Not only would this keep his mind occupied, it would reconnect him with the people he missed. "Let me help you, Basil."

Suddenly once more the wary man on the steps of parliament, Basil eyed Aerysleigh as he would a stranger. "Chasing criminals is hardly the past-time of a gentleman, nor one likely to be condoned by Queen Constantina when she has other ideas for your time."

Aerysleigh frowned. "But *you* do it. A commission from my father, was it not?"

Basil laugh came out more as a sigh. "Oh, my friend, that is why men followed you to their deaths, and would multiple times over. I never understood it, despite your upbringing, you never saw the status of men."

Of course, Aerysleigh knew what his friend referred to. As a prince, he cut his teeth on aristocratic snobbery—every outing carefully monitored for the appropriateness of rank of his companions. Once he made friends with the nephew of a gardener, a boy of his own age, for which he had been roundly chastised. He later learned the gardener had been let go and regretted being the cause of his dismissal ever since.

He turned his signet ring on his finger. "In war there is no rank. It is only a fellow's ability to stay alive and command that matter."

"Rubbish," Basil snorted, "many a capable soldier lived and died at the boilers when suited for so much more. A man or woman's rank is where they are born, and most often they stay there. You are the only one who could never see that. Like that time you promoted Orson Coppersmith to lieutenant and Captain Grepnisk came aboard."

"Yes, I had to ask the prig to leave when he refused to dine with my officer." Aerysleigh smiled at the memory of the captain's outrage, a strange mottled red and purple colour.

"Others of your rank would have chosen the captain over the mate," Basil reminded him.

"Then they would be fools. Besides, supper was getting cold and the inflated poppycock was just there because his father..."

"Had a commission from the King, yes, I know," his friend finished with a penetrating gaze.

"Coppersmith was one of the best. Lost him in a skirmish over Paris."

They shared a moment of silence then Basil pressed his point. "I was commissioned by the king, Aerysleigh. However, I am not a first son, even a second, I am the third son of a gentleman. Working with me chasing common criminals would not be seen favourably by either your mother or her friends."

Aerysleigh flashed a mischievous grin. "All the better. I will help you catch this Cinder fellow, patrol with the constables, anything to keep me moving and my mind active." Regain a connection with the people grown so distant. He hated to beg, obviously Basil shied away from the prospect of having a prince of the realm poking about his business, maybe even getting hurt.

Despite Basil's spiel, it stung he might not want him due to his rank. After fighting the war for so long, shoulder to shoulder with brave men and women of all social levels, it hurt to think that it meant nothing when he came home. Basil might refuse him, the set of his eyes clued Aerysleigh to the gist of his thoughts. And they did not seem favourable for him.

Fine, beg he would. "Please, Basil."

His friend stared into his eyes and finally sensed his desperation. "Alright then. Come to the yard tomorrow and we'll take a look at what I have. It wouldn't hurt to have a fresh pair of eyes on it."

"I can't thank you enough."

Basil smiled and touched his hat. "As ever, at your service, your highness."

Chapter Seventeen

The Hospital

The bolt on the hinge joint squeaked in protest as Ella tightened it down. "Try it now," she said.

Delia, the woman over whose knee she bent, adjusted her skirt, reached down to throw the locking mechanism, and stood. "It works perfectly." Her tired face lit up with a smile that erased wrinkles and time. "Thank you. Climbing stairs with the laundry and my broken..." she trailed off. "I fell a few times and Mrs. Renot fired me for soiling the clothes." The care worn shoulders slumped.

Ella put a hand on her arm. "I know how you feel," she said gently.

The laundress lifted her chin, disbelief clear. Ella could just hear her thoughts. *How could a lady understand such things?* She refrained from rubbing her own aching back. How could she indeed.

"No matter, with this leg as good as new I can get a new job right away."

Sensing Delia's need for distance, Ella stepped away. "Of course, you will."

The laundress leaned closer, the smell of garlic and lye soap nearly overwhelming, and asked. "I'm still under the percentage, right? They're not going to take me and—" Her whisper faltered.

Used to this question by now, Ella patted her arm. "You're in no danger. The current bill stalled in the House of Commons so you're fine."

The laundress sighed and relaxed. "Thank ye, Miss."

Ella hated the fact the poor lady felt compelled to ask. Though closed for the summer, the threat loomed that someday, just because a person wore metal, they could be declared non-citizens. No voting rights.

Sometimes, when exhaustion did not carry her into sleep right away, Ella wondered who Dr. Bon Hamlet talked with about the papers and projects Cinder managed to steal. *Better yet, who passed on such sensitive information? Who petitioned for and represented these poor people?* There must be someone. Two of the last three proposed laws remained unpassed.

Delia's tow-headed toddler wrapped his arm around his mother's leg and popped a thumb in his mouth, bringing Ella back to the present.

"Mum's all fixed?" He mumbled around the appendage.

Ella tapped his nose. "She sure is, but no more playing with her leg like it's a toy. This is a valuable piece of equipment your mum needs. Understand?"

The boy nodded. His mother poked his shoulder and warned. "Mind your manners."

"Yes, miss."

Ella winked at him. "Good, lad. Let me see if I can find you something else to play with." She rummaged through a box of recently donated odds and ends. The ubiquitous concerned ladies' groups more oft than nought gave utterly useless things— mismatched boots, silk bonnets, pipes, and ceramic figurines. This particular box arrived by way of a servant with instructions to give it to the needy. However, Ella remembered seeing a certain object a young boy might like.

Flora climbed her skirts to peer over her shoulder, then leaped into the box to show her the flattened piece of stitched leather.

"Good girl." Ella pulled the ball from the box. "I think this will do." She detached a finger from her mechanical hand, replaced it with the pump needle, hooked up to an air canister, and gave the ball two quick puffs. As the ball grew, so did the boy's eyes. She handed him the toy. "Here you go. Much better than a locking clasp, don't you think?"

The boy's hair flopped as he nodded, but he didn't reach for the ball until his mother nudged him. "Go on then, thank the lady."

"Than' ya," the boy breathed.

Ella touched the woman's arm. "See the doctor about those bites on his arm, please." More and more people seemed to be turning up with rat bites. The lady nodded and pulled the boy from the closet sized room.

Alone, Ella pushed her knuckles into her back, watching the mice play with a large dust bunny in the corner, smiling at their antics. Her grin faded when the dust bunny opened its eyes and growled. The three mice leaped back, paused, then attacked. Soon nothing remained but dirt and dust.

Just another strange and unexplainable occurrence.

Last evening's assignment by Judith proved easy—a simple pick up of a stack of cash left in a vase filled with peacock feathers. A hand off to be sure, but Ella didn't dare risk finding out from whom. Both Myrtle and Clarence were held hostage to ensure her silence. Afterwards, she hurried to the hospital to help where she may—to make amends for her evil deeds and for her mother bringing the miserable rains.

Tonight, she also brought several prosthesis to fit on waiting patients. The little work she managed to do at Iron Crest included mostly drawing and figuring dimensions, perhaps forming heavy duty supports. Once she arrived at the hospital, she passed the plans to the machinists, smiths, and tinkers to create proto-types.

Tinker Maybelle never reported for her shift, so Ella filled her spot and tried to get other things done in the meanwhile. In the crush of bodies filling St. Drogo, she didn't mind being away from the forge or the sick in the Commons. She welcomed the cool breeze sifting through the ancient bricks.

A large fellow with a bald pate and crooked nose plunked down in the rickety chair before her. "Mistress?"

Ella sighed and smiled, examining the armoured shoulder which looked as though ravaged by rabid dogs. She removed the rivets and then the metal plate. "Good morrow, Drax. Looks like the rats are getting bigger down by the docks."

The dock worker and sometimes night guard nodded grimly. "The whole place be gone to the dogs. If it ain't body snatchers, it's the werewolves."

"Werewolves is it?" she asked. *How much opium had he inhaled today?*

Drax shrugged, letting the rest of the medieval looking metal encasing clatter to the floor. While Ella straightened the steel plates, the big fellow related his night on the docks. "I took night duty at Grey Shipping Wharf. The partner they give me, Daft Davy, jus' went mad. Attacked me, he did, bit clear up my arm and nearly made it to my neck."

Ella snorted and got a swift glare.

"Yah, no one believes me. But I see queer happenings at night on the docks. Thing is, Davy got bit hisself not two nights ago by something when he took a piss. He jus' yelped and jumped. I figured it a rat. Guess I knows different now."

After the dust bunny incident moments before who was she to question a bloke's story? His wasn't the first, though maybe the most coherent, she had heard. Dr. Bon Hamlet told her some of the stories people brought her to explain strange wounds or occurrences. Some of the tales were enough to turn blood to ice.

Ella bent to her task of reheating and patching the plate. "I added some reinforcement here and here," she said, hoping he could hear the contrition in her voice for her disbelief. She riveted the piece onto the strap of leather connecting the plates. "That should do it."

Drax stood and rolled his shoulder. "Thank-you, Miss. I am still under the percy law, right?"

She patted his coat of mail. "You're good. You don't have any metal actually attached to your body. Just armour."

He nodded. "That's right. You're a positive sage, Miss." He wandered out into the Common room, she hoped to find some rest.

With no one else in the tinker line, she entered the rectangular common room behind the big man. The miasma of sickness and hopelessness nearly slapped her to the ground. She took a shallow breath and plunged ahead.

Without the Cinder mask and clothing she was simply Ella, dedicated volunteer. Few could guess the guilt that drove her to sleepless hours tending the ill. She shook away the last image of Mother before she launched the rockets that caused the rains and bent to get a dipper of water from the common pail.

Beds lined the walls, some three high. A family of five set up house around one set. A group of veterans, mangled faces and bodies liberally enhanced with metal, took turns resting in another. One marine hacked as she passed, a deep, phlegm-filled cough signalling a near end while his mates hovered.

She drifted from bed to bed, calling a nurse at a blood-soaked bandage and adjusting modifications for those who could not make it to the tinker's door. One of the automatons that carried hot water down the central aisle, sputtered ineffectively, so she topped off its boiler, turned it round and gave it a push. She offered what words of encouragement she could, but most froze on her tongue. She kept her modification hidden in this crowd, the press of bodies making her timid.

There are so many, and there are always more. Every night St. Drogo filled with the poorest of the poor, not to mention a few of the relatively rare middle class. Rooms overflowed, men, women, children packed like fish in a net.

A body hurled into the room, rousing the automatons by the door. "It's the snatchers," the little boy screeched.

A woman screamed and multitude lunged for cover. The eyes of the iron soldiers gleamed red as they went into attack mode. Ella snapped into action. She jumped on the nearest bed frame and stripped the glove from her iron hand and used it as a megaphone to be heard above the chaos. "Calm yourselves," she yelled. "Snatchers cannot breech these walls and you know it." In the ebbing quiet that follow, she grabbed a nearby able-bodied fellow and shoved him towards the iron guards. "Pull the cards on those machines, quick now."

She collared the wayward child and peered towards the door, curious as to what set the tyke off. The fellow managed to shut down the guards just as the doors flung back a second time.

A young priest, hands tight against his robes in obvious distress, walked backwards into the room. "Please, sire, if I could just direct you towards the East Wing where the poor are housed—" His pleading stopped as he stumbled over a suddenly vacated wheeled chair which spun gently in a cleared semi-circle in the clearing path.

Ella's gaze, as well that everyone else, jerked towards the commotion. Despite the early hour, it had to be only 5 o'clock, a phalanx of suited men pushed through the double doors.

In front of them a gentleman stood next to the priest in a tall hat, surveying the room with piercing eye. "I came during the day and saw those quarters. It is a very good work you do there, but I wanted to see the rest of the hospital and it seems this is the time and the wing to do it."

All present froze. Even the bedside automatons, programed to alert nurses to medication schedules, seemed to pause their tick tocking, then there came a great fluster of movement.

Patients shuffled to clear a path down the congested centre aisle, but those behind shoved forward, resulting in little change to the amount of room. Some tried to hide their modifications. Others pushed to escape.

A handful remembered their manners despite their shock at the visit of royalty and tried to bow. Several ended up falling like a path of soot stained petals with not-so-gentle nudges from behind.

Standing on tiptoe to see above the heads in front of her, Ella gasped and ducked down. Though dressed to the nines in fawn trousers with buttons running from ankle to waist band and a silk, double breasted vest of bold green, a man at the front surveyed the room as though on the deck of his warship.

The Prince.

CHAPTER EIGHTEEN

THE TINKER

"This chamber is mostly reserved for those…" The priest attempting to slow the charge floundered for proper words, but the prince filled him in.

"Modified?"

"Yes. Though often the sick must also share the room."

Several of the prince's hangers-on paled, one retched and stumbled out of sight. The prince and two others, besides the hand wringing priest, managed to make it through the door.

Ella slunk towards the Tinker station and the exit beyond, trying to avoid detection. Who knew if Prince Aerysleigh remembered the girl he rescued from the bridge, but anonymity was one of her stepmother's requirements and she dared not expose herself further.

However, the patients, delighted to have a royal visit, made no effort to move out of her way. The prince walked down the narrow aisle. Shaking hands, making appropriate comments, but his eyes roved the crowd.

"There is a lot of fine metal work here, Father," he commented. Admiring the display of decommissioned war automatons prepared for salvaging. When a patient allowed, he examined a modification with the eye of an inventor.

Once again, the priest hesitated over his answer. "Yes. The Lord provides many caring people who give of their time and talents. You have already met Dr. Bon Hamlet and her staff, perhaps we should continue to the apothecary. This room is rather close."

"Nonsense. I see an exit just there, let us continue."

"That only leads to the machinists, engineers, and the forge," explained the clergyman. Ella groaned and peeked over the bobbing heads to glare at the young priest.

He caught her look and hedged. "Hot, uncomfortable places."

This evidently piqued Prince Aerysleigh's interest for he straightened and looked even more excited. "Your hospital has its ow engineers?"

Once again, the cleric paused, and Ella gritted her teeth. They should have found someone else to direct the prince on his tour, at this rate St. Drogo would have no secrets.

"Not exactly, your highness. St. Drogo backs Crowdott Street, where there are several shops of all trades."

"Lead on then," said Prince Aerysleigh. "A breath of air will do us all good, I think. And I wish to see the authors of some of this exquisite workmanship."

Ella grimaced. There would be no dissuading the prince.

The group turned to single file and moved closer. Sensing escape impossible, Ella grabbed her welding helmet and shoved it on her head then pulled on her welding gloves. Precautions against the slim chance the prince remembered her from that night several months ago.

Hands tugged at her skirt. "Please, Mistress, my ear fell off again."

Nearly jumping out of her skin, Ella whirled to confront the small form seated in the Tinker chair. Euda, the girl run over by the carriage the same night Ella met the prince, held out her metal ear. Instead of a blood-soaked face, she now sported a metal auricle of Ella's design. However, in the girl's rough and tumble world the ear often ended up knocked off.

Grateful for a task, Ella turned the ear over. One of the three tiny magnets designed to attach to metal studs embedded in the skin around the external auditory passage had come off.

Flora leaped to the desk and helped her find the drawer with magnets in Maybelle's workstation. The mouse climbed to her shoulder and observed through the thick pane of the protective helmet as Ella soldered one on.

"Just one minute and you will be set, doll. You tell those brothers of yours to play nice."

Euda reached up and rubbed the half cog on the ear that looked from afar like a tiny earring. "Georgie were playing Cinder, Miss, he needed my ear for his arm."

Ella frowned as she leaned close to align the ear. "You tell Georgie that if he doesn't leave your ear be, Cinder might pay him a visit," she whispered.

Euda grinned. "Yes, Miss."

With a click, the ear snapped into place.

"Fascinating."

Ella and Euda looked up to find the prince and entourage crowding the doorway of the Tinker's little room. Flora cuddled closer to her neck, hidden under hair and mask.

The prince stepped back, looked at the sign above the door, "Tinker, eh?" He knelt in front of Euda. "How is your ear?"

"I don't like toffs," the child blurted.

The entourage, hovering beyond Prince Aerysleigh's wide shoulders, huffed in a collective gasp like addicts in an opium den. The prince rocked back on his heels but did not lose his smile. "Why ever not?"

"A toff ran over my head. He smashed my dolly. You talk like a toff, so I don't like you."

The prince nodded. "Fair enough." He looked at Ella. "I guess her hearing works fine. My compliments..." His eyes raised to the Tinker's name created from cutlery above her work station. "Maybelle."

Euda giggled. "That ain't Maybelle." *Time to get the child out of there before the Prince's patience ran out.*

Ella pushed the girl out of her seat, "off with you, my cabbage, and curtsy to the prince afore you go," she copied the Cockney from the streets.

Performing her best cross between a bow and a bob, Euda skipped from the room, brother's boots slipping about her tiny feet.

"Will you not remove your helmet, not-the-tinker-Maybelle? I would like to meet the inventor behind such an ingenious device. Magnets was it?" asked the prince.

Ella took one look at the throng at the door, the judging eyes, and decided remaining anonymous best. Prince Aerysleigh glanced behind him and raised his voice, "Leave us."

"Sire," a fellow dressed as a guard protested.

"I am perfectly safe, Geoffry. Stand outside if you must but try not to gape." The guard shot her a warning glare—as though she were on the verge of attacking his ward, then stepped out of sight. The other obeyed as well, except the priest who waited for her leave. She nodded slightly and then he too disappeared.

Prince Aerysleigh's gaze sharpened at her, she should have none

Great, there went any reputation she may have. She kept her eyes downcast. "Help you, guv?" she asked.

"I'm curious, is all," he said.

"Not a trait encouraged at St. Drogo," she said dryly.

He cocked his head as her cockney slipped and she wanted to kick herself.

"Indeed. I have tried for days to get beyond the front vestibule."

Under the mask, Flora tapped Ella's cheek. Ella nudged back with her chin to get her to stop. Instead, the mouse reached up and pulled the lens release, conveniently rolling into a ball and slipping down her blouse.

Ella reached to catch the glass piece before it shattered on the floor, missed, and ended up head butting Prince Aerysleigh with the helmet as he lunged to do the same.

"*Ooph.*"

Ella jerked off the mask in time to grab the prince's arm before he fell. "I am so sorry, your highness." She guided him to the chair, into which he collapsed.

The abuse of Drax and then the prince was too much for the rickety thing. The legs flew to the four corners of the room. Over balanced by the sudden downward pull of the heavier body, Ella tumbled onto his lap, skirts flying.

"*Ommpp,*" he grunted.

She floundered for her feet, but found herself tangled in chair, skirts, and legs. Her metal hand flew back and struck the Prince another solid blow.

Strong arms locked around her and ceased her struggles. "Be still," the prince commanded.

She did as bidden, all too aware she lay sprawled across the Prince. Unable to raise her eyes, she mumbled. "I am so sorry, your highness."

His chuckle made her look up. Where facial hair was expected among men, he was clean shaven. Where hair trimmed close to the nape of the neck advertised a well-groomed man, he grew his long. He smelled like Iron Crest, like freshly trimmed trees on a fall day with the hint of smoke from the brush fires and a hint of Bohea tea. The eye not covered by the patch twinkled with good humour as he returned her regard.

After the space of five breaths, it could have been a life time for the track that Ella kept, he broke the silence. "There now. I think we can untangle..."

She tried to leap to her feet.

He held her tight. "Now, now, don't throw us down again." She flushed and allowed him to help her to a half standing position from which she stood easily.

Immediately she turned and offered her gloved hand. He clasped it tightly and allowed her to assist his own rise. "Thank you," he said graciously, "you have quite the grip there, Miss Tinker."

"Not a tinker," she corrected before she could think. "Just a volunteer, or all-around helper, if you please." She stepped forward, flushing as he took a defencive step back. "I really must apologise for my clumsiness."

"Not the first time I've taken a blow to the head." He laughed, putting a hand to his temple on the side of his eye patch. "Though I can't say it has ever been more unexpected or from a prettier source."

Ella fought another wave of warmth flushing her skin and tried to regain her composure. "Say that to all the girls, do you?" The conversation rang like the one they had the night he rescued her from the bridge.

His gaze jerked to her face. "Only those that bash me over the head." He finished. He paused a beat then motioned to the door. "I have this feeling that you may be a better tour guide than Father Francis. Would you do me the honour, Mistress Tinker Volunteer."

Relieved that he hadn't recognised her as the girl from the bridge, Ella bobbed a short curtsy, but hesitated. "Honestly?"

He grinned. "I would expect nothing less."

She nodded and stumbled about in her mind for the right words to phrase her thoughts. "The people in this wing of St. Drogo are..."

"Modified, yes, yes, I understand—"

She held up a hand to stop his words and his jaw clicked shut at the imperious gesture. Prince Aerysleigh's impatience and willingness to brush off the feelings of others, raising her ire. "I don't think you do. Body snatchers take people both alive and dead. Mutations are the norm instead of a rarity. There are bills before the Houses that measure the percentage of modification a person may have before being declared and automaton or second-class citizen, people are sensitive about their modifications and to have people like you—"

"Me?" The gentleman looked shocked. "What exactly are people like me?"

Ella shrugged, "Sight seer, do gooder, whatever. The people here are shy folk. Many of those that you walked by in the common area work very hard to keep a modification hidden to keep their jobs, make a living. Discretion could be the difference between bringing home bread or going hungry."

The prince nodded. "Alright then." He turned to leave then paused at the door. "But the ear. Could you show me how you created such a thing?'

Ella laughed, pleased to not have to send him away empty handed when he seemed so excited about the wonders he passed in the common room. "Certainly."

CHAPTER NINETEEN

THE TOUR

After a slow start to his tour, though he couldn't blame it entirely on the priest, he had appeared unannounced at a truly ungodly hour after all, Aerysleigh learned more about the perpetually downtrodden in an hour than in his whole life. The suffering and human misery surpassed the aftermath of even the worst battle.

His guide, a pleasant distraction from the wretchedness if ever there could be one, gave a much better, albeit abbreviated tour, than the overwhelmed priest. She marched along the echoing halls, refusing to allow him more than the briefest glimpse into any of the several rooms jutting from the brick hallway.

She merely gave a wave and explained each one's purpose. Her cockney slipped now and again, as it had in the Tinker's room when she lectured him, but he listened intently.

One of the chambers held women and children. Another a kitchen, though the scents emanating from the food clashing with the general air of rot and ruin, forced him to step away quickly. Still another cavernous room smelling of damp and close bodies, served as an overnight refuge when the mists were particularly aggressive, laundry, and on and on.

There was even a small lending library for those who could read. Though from the looks of the place it was little frequented.

Aside from the library, each and every room nearly burst with the press of hunched bodies and listless forms of patients. Even so, children darted here and there as they sought to make a little fun in such a dark place. Occasionally, laughter spilled from them, but not often. However, besides the rooms, people lined the halls. Overflow, the tinker explained, which would dissipate with the mists when people returned to their work.

His entourage no longer shadowed him after being forcibly ejected by the arrival of an elder priest claiming the activity did the patients ill. As a result, he travelled in relative anonymity.

The girl, however, did not.

Though she walked softly, gaze lowered demurely, people noticed her.

Hands reached out and clasped hers. "Bless you, Ella." "Thank you." Were just a few of the phrases he overheard.

Ella, he mused.

The name fit the shy creature before him, but only somewhat. The way she stood up to him hinted that the down trodden gaze hid a talented woman of strong ideas and sharp intelliegence.

At the door of the steaming kitchen a girl, face half black mottled with white, looked up from a four wheeled cart she tinkered with. "'Ere you go, Miss—" her speech halted and when she noticed Aerysleigh and she shrank against the wall.

Ella put a hand on the wooden handle. "Thank you, it looks wonderful," she said softly, giving the girl a squeeze on the shoulder.

The child straightened under praise. "There's a new punch card and bearings," she said quickly, "It will go to the end of the hall and back again." Lifting a pot smelling of ginger with several dippers hung on the side onto a small platform evidently designed for such use, the budding mechanic gave it an encouraging pat.

Ella let go of the cart and the conveyance steamed away. It moved at such a pace anyone could fill a dipper, take a drink, and replace the utensil within a few steps.

The patients, distracted by the steaming cauldron, allowed Ella to continue her tour with less stops. He kept looking behind him to watch the mechanical device. Of course, he had seen such things in taverns and tea houses, however, such devices seemed regulated to the working class—the rich preferring to rely on a bevy of servants to see to their needs. If found in the shops frequented by the aristocrats, such things were more of an oddity than the norm. His fingers itched to take it apart, to see its inner workings. Then he thought of Euda's ear and the other wonders filling this stretching cathedral and inevitably to the girl he rescued from a bridge months ago.

In a large, windowless chamber located at the very end of the massive hall and separated from the others by a good distance, the sour scent of unwashed bodies pushed like a fifth solid wall. A smell so foul Aerysleigh jerked his head away and his eyes watered.

The Tinker offered him a mask. Lavender filled his senses and he breathed deep with welcome relief. Priests and nuns moved among the sick in billowing robes and face masks of their own. Blood and death had their own particular gruesome smell, but this seemed worse than a three-day old battlefield.

"You get used to it after a while," advised his guide. She gazed into a room where the overpowering smell smacked him like a fist. "Or so I am told. The patients here suffer from various rotting diseases or the flux. Best to stay away. This was once part of the Sisters of Mercy little convent attached to the Cathedral. They moved over to the other side of the pauper's cemetery."

Besides the nuns, he spotted an occasional doctor or nurse, but they were few and far between. Some of the doctors wore beaked facial coverings left over from the medieval era. Even when the girl moved on, he stood at the door. No one noticed his presence. Patients, men, women, even children, lay naked and moaning in their own feces. Those with strength plucked at the skirts of the obviously overworked and exhausted nuns, begging for water—or an end to their misery. In all his years, even in the aftermath of battle, he never witnessed such suffering.

"Come. The forge and machinists' shops are close," his guide urged. Still he did not turn away until she pulled at his sleeve and then grabbed his arm. It took him the length of a long cloister to gather his wits. He desperately sucked the fresh air rushing through the arched colonnades. Though it seemed as though hours passed, dawn in no way brightened the fountain or herb garden in the quadrangle just outside.

The air warmed unnaturally quickly the further they walked. He recognised the crackle of smith's fires and the muted roar of torches used by metal workers of all trades. Just over those sounds came the clatter of striking iron, the pounding and shaping of hard metals.

He often walked the streets where the tradesmen plied their wares, enjoying their boisterous work. Even so, he suspected those products displayed in the light of day differed from those being worked on in the shops along the walls of St. Drogo. The sounds ahead seemed almost furtive, hushed as the night pressed down.

How could this be?

How could a whole, previously unknown, world exist here in the dark as those with money hid from the mists? Though much of the activities of peerage took place in the late hours, especially during the season, the aristocrats hid from the dark, protected by their high walls, servants, and patrolling police.

However, these people truly owned the night. The cathedral flung their doors open to those rejected by polite society, giving freely protection and aid against the evil happenings in the street. A sense of shame rose like bile in his throat and he found it difficult to swallow back down.

How could he be so far removed from the people he believed he knew? Here he prided himself on being a fair captain, giving each man or woman an equal shake to rise, yet now witnessing the depths from which some of those had risen, he realised how wrong he had been.

No matter how equally he treated people, they had to overcome so much more.

He tugged at his coat as the heat grew, though Ella seemed immune. She paused at wooden door crossed with iron and fastened by a series of complicated locks giving it the look of a large Japanese puzzle box.

When the lady placed her palm on the first, a shadow detached from one of the columns. "Where's your coin?" a fellow said gruffly. When Ella turned to face the boy, which could only be a guard of sorts, he paled and backed away. "I'm sorry, Mistress, won't 'appen again."

Despite the heavy welding clothes under which she had to be sweltering, the tinker inclined her head in a way that took Aerysleigh's breath away. No commoner knew how to bow so graciously. That arrogant mixture of condescension and entitlement. Not once before had she used it, so he suspected some sort of history with this young guard.

His mystery guide *had* to be a lady. Perhaps from a family fallen on hard times due to the war. Besides her clear speech, which she seemed to try to hide in a street accent occasionally, she had the air of good breeding. The look once again reminded him of the damsel from the bridge. Despite the similarity of pale hair, one of the only things he could see clearly both now and that dark night, the other had called herself a monster.

He saw no evidence of any modification on Ella.

"Let me help you, mistress." The reaction of the boy, both fearful and fawning, puzzled Aerysleigh.

The lady gave him no chance to ask anything of the young fellow. She motioned the boy away with a wave, her expression kind but firm. "No need. You do your job well. The smiths will be returning their drawings soon so keep up the good work."

She turned back to the door, spinning the four locks in an unfathomable pattern so quickly he could not follow, then lent her weight to the door.

It didn't budge.

Aerysleigh glanced at the guard, but the boy clasped a hand behind his neck and looked towards the ceiling as though he hadn't seen anything. Ella studied the locks for a moment and then pushed again. Nothing.

"Allow me," Aerysleigh leaned against the oak door, surprised at its heft. This portal belonged in the Queen's Bank at number four Oakes Abbey.

With a grate the door swung and, despite its size, revealed a short hall leading to a windowless room. Metal tubes covered every available wall space. Some entered from the ceiling, others from the floor. All seemed to congregate in a brass cylinder two meters high, with a number pad and a door. Two WARs stood at rigid attention— not like the slumbering half salvaged ones he's seen sitting in out of the way places in the halls. These were active and alert.

"Password," one demanded.

The tinker hurried over and whispered to the speaker. It fell silent but remained vigilant.

Aerysleigh nodded to the markings. "What is WAR-PR1?"

Ella rubbed a smudge from the automation. "War Automaton Revised Plan Room 1. SPA—I mean the cathedral, has scavenged and reprogrammed a good assortment of the decommissioned metal soldiers."

He nodded. "Smart."

"They are," she agreed. Though he wasn't necessarily referring to the automatons. "And good at what they do." She checked the clock works and punch cards in the automatons. Finally, she shut the door with a nod of satisfaction. "Everything looks good, Warp one." She turned to Aerysleigh. "Once they are reprogrammed from killing, of course."

Ella walked past him and pressed a series of buttons on a

number pad. The cylinder door sucked back with a hiss, pipes contracted and expanded.

"What did you do?" He asked.

"You wanted to see some of the other inventions without taking apart Nell's cart—" She gave him a teasing look which said she had noticed his itch to catch the steam cart earlier, "or getting attacked for getting too up close and personal with a modified's body part, so I requested several plans from the library."

"Why don't we just go there?"

She gave him an odd look, "security is paramount for these types of things."

He hearkened back to his conversation with Basil. "Oh right, the Cinder thefts. The Medical School and physicians are upset about those."

She gave dismissive shrug. "Those, I suppose, and others. I don't think Cinder is selling bodies, do you?"

"No. You think there is another element involved?" He couldn't keep the excitement from his voice. If there was a Prussian infiltration, these people would be in the know. The street people saw things, heard things that himself, and even Basil, would never. "What have you heard?"

Avoiding his question, she turned away when a tube thumped down in a nearby pipe. Opening the glass portal to withdraw the delivery, she turned towards a table in the centre of the small room. "I don't hear anything," she said. "In fact, I try to hear as little as possible. There is enough work here to do than worrying about simple thefts."

He studied her, trying to determine whether to push the issue or not. Evidently a favourite with the inhabitants of St. Drogo, she definitely had her secrets. But St. Drogo brimmed with secrets. Besides, he learned long ago pushing people rarely got the desired results—unless it involved an enemy prisoner. He turned his mind from that train of thought to a more appealing view.

Golden hair tumbled from beneath a simple maid's cap. Blue eyes sparkled with good humour. She removed her welding coat and laid it on the arm of a War. Her day dress was simple cotton, worn thin, but embracing a trim figure. She moved with grace and a businesslike mein.

Ella pointed to a list of numbers stretching across the wall. Beside each number, starting at one and going into the hundreds, were names. Some with one and others with several. "Inventions, patents pending the approval of Lord Stillingfleet, a benefactor of St.

Drogo, are kept in an impenetrable vault to which a select few are granted access."

"I have heard of the marquess. Somewhat of a recluse I understand."

She waved a hand. "In truth, I know nothing of him. He is just the inventor of the systems."

"But your process seems to bypass the Patent Office. After the designs for the metro were stolen, they increased their security tenfold."

She outright laughed at him as she upended the tube and a rolled paper slipped into her palm. "I had not heard of the pilfering of the metro plans or why anyone would want to steal them, though I doubt the thief had much trouble getting his prize."

"The theft does seem strange, but no more than any other performed by Cinder. Papers from the medical society, proposed bills, even the minutes from The Medical Academy's board meetings have gone missing."

She gave him another odd look and spread the plans out on the metal table, tacking each corner down with a magnet. "The police are blaming the thefts on Cinder?"

Aerysleigh leaned over the table. "It seems to fit his profile. Plus, the ease that the thief entered seems to indicate a level of expertise beyond the regular cat burglar."

The girl across from him laughed softly. "Trust me, no matter what went missing, the patent office is no more secure than before. Nothing will go missing from *this* vault, and besides, the things stored here have not been approved for release. Just experiments or thoughts which an inventor might produce with a collaboration. For example, this ear constructed with the help of Dr. Bon Hamlet."

He allowed himself to be distracted while she explained the insertion of a plate with metal studs embedded just below the flesh. The relatively simple process involved creating an ear piece, affixing the magnets, then attaching the magnets to the flesh.

He leaned over the plans. "So simple yet elegant."

She flushed under his praise and returned to the number pad to retrieve another tube. She spread this one out and this time he helped with the magnets.

"What is it?"

She grinned. "A prosthetic hand for a cook. Here we have magnetic compartments to hold knives, spoons, and then there are the extra fingers that can be detached for ladles and skewers. Even different sized forks."

She traced the lines of the arm. "This one was for a woman who lost an arm to a withering disease. The difficulty came in making it slim enough to hide under a uniform, yet useful as well. I have heard reports from reliable sources she is a much-prized asset under a very particular lady." She grinned, eyes sparkling in a truly captivating way. "And the best part is that the lady has no idea she enjoys the food from a modified person."

"Brilliant," Aerysleigh could not resist the urge to cover Ella's hand.

"Not that it should matter either way, but this is amazing. You are amazing. I certainly could have used this type of innovation on my ship, that's for sure." He did not know if it was the lateness of the hour, the fact that he should be exhausted, or the privacy of the quiet that made him maudlin, but he had no right to unburden himself on this lady.

She reminded him of himself many respects.

He tightened his grip on her fingers. Visions of advancements danced before his eyes. "Have you ever applied to the Academy of Metallurgy or the medical schools? The guild of the Honourable Master Engineers? These innovations would be the toast of the town. I will give you a recommendation myself."

Instead of excitement at his generous pronouncement, one certain to remove her from the dungeon-like atmosphere of St. Drogo, the girl slowly withdrew her hand from his.

The light in her eyes died and her face took on a particular closed off look. "You mistake my intent, your highness," she said coldly. "I did not bring you here in the hopes for some sort of advancement. I meant to simply keep you from causing an unnecessary commotion." She lifted her chin, the demure lady gone, a social warrior stood in her stead. "I am happy right here, helping the folk who need helping."

He considered her a moment, argument dying on his lips. "But these advances should be open to everyone," he finished lamely.

"They are. To all who need them that is. Are you forgetting about Bill 456 making the rounds in Parliament?"

He frowned and shook his head, totally at a loss. Talented with metal and knowledgeable of politics? His mother would positively swoon over such a woman. A very good reason to keep his fascination with the young miss as covert as possible. "What Bill? A law?"

She sighed in obvious frustration. "Yes, a law. The one that keeps getting amended about the percentage of metal one can use on their body before they are considered automatons and not represented citizens. It changes constantly, but the people here live in fear that one day they may be declared non-human." She motioned to the plans and then slowly began to re-roll one. "Besides all that. It matters not. I must stay here. This is where I am needed."

Aerysleigh moved around the table separating them. He gently removed schematics from her hands, slipped each into its tube, and put it in the delivery system. Before she could reach for another, he caught at her arm.

"I don't understand. Though your devotion is commendable, my lady."

"Don't call me that," she hissed. "I am merely a servant who uses her free time to help those less fortunate."

He laughed at that. "A servant you are not. Think of the good you can do, with the proper equipment, help from the best minds in the country...what could possibly be keeping you here?"

She snatched her hand away. "This *is* a proper medical facility. It works for those in need instead of those who can pay."

A small steam powered cart rolled into the room, at its helm one of the nurses he met on his first visit. Sukie, he thought, proud to have remembered her name, but the conveyance caught his attention.

He hurried over to study it. Another modern, mechanical marvel. The driver stood on a platform in front of a small boiling engine and behind that a two-wheeled cart. She steered with a simple handle attached to a single wheel. Tubes filled with engineering designs spilled out of the cart's basket, evidently returning from the cathedral's various work stations. Places he had been conveniently distracted from getting a tour of.

He stood up tall and rolled his shoulders, the long night finally catching up to him. From his vantage he caught sight of the sun streaming through the high, stained glass windows in the outside hall. *Good, more light to examine the cart.* He looked up to ask questions of the driver.

The nurse didn't spare him a glance, her gaze fastened on the tinker. "Ella! What are you still doing here?"

The girl's welcoming smile slowly faded, her eyes darting to the cart then beyond the darkened room to the dawn lit hall beyond. He straightened in defence as the girl turned fearful.

"You are returning the plans," Ella said. The statement seemed to echo in the stone chamber but worry overflowed the words.

"Yes." Sukie pulled on a handbrake and stepped from the cart.

"Ella, it is nearly 10 O'clock. The sun rose hours ago."

Whatever the significance of the time, Ella turned cloud white. Aerysleigh hurried to her side, thinking she may swoon. He placed an arm around her shoulder, but neither woman seemed to recognise his presence. A most unpleasant feeling after so long being the centre of attention.

"So late," Ella murmured, eyes riveted on the streaking light, "How did it get to be so late?"

"I will lend you my carriage." Aerysleigh offered, "it will get you wherever you need to be."

Now they noticed him, and it was not as he wished.

Ella pulled away from him. "What? No!"

Sukie grasped her hands. "Ella, your helio bike. The wind blows in a westerly direction this morning."

Ella nodded. "Yes, yes. I must be away."

Without a further comment she hurried from the room leaving Aerysleigh gaping after her.

Sukie whirled on him.

"As for you, your highness, you should not be here either."

He raised a brow at the tiny woman, ready to ooze the charm he had in spades.

The nurse held up a silencing finger. "I don't know what you are doing here, but it is past time for you to be gone. The next time you visit be sure to make an appointment with Lord Stillingfleet."

She added a smile that bore him no goodwill. "Please."

Chapter Twenty

Consequences

lla threw herself into the kitchen, fumbling at her apron
strings and cursing the thick fingers on her mechanical hand.
The mice leaped from her pocket and scurried to gather
utensils and cups on a tray. Ella cranked the chain to bring
the eggs from the chicken house and stoked the fire—all before
taking more than a few gasping breaths since pedalling the helio bike
from London.

An eerie silence descended in the kitchen. She wiped her hands
on a rag and set it down. Even the chickens, usually vocal protesters
when she turned the collector on, seemed subdued.

"Where is Myrtle, I wonder?" Ella muttered. Usually this time of
the morning Myrtle would be clanking about the garden, or in the
hall, or on the stairs. Needing little rest allowed Ella's stepmother to
use the metal enhanced servant mercilessly. Every morning, Lady
Steelhaugh supplied both of them with a long list of chores.
Sometimes Ella could not finish all her work, but for Myrtle it
became a point of pride and she worked until she checked
everything through with an insolent spray of oil.

Today, the only note hanging under the summoning bells was

Ella's.

"Judith must have sent her to fetch something," Ella reasoned. Though Myrtle, being a modified, could only venture to a few of the farmers who had served the Steelhaugh family for years.

A glint of light caught her eye. On the centre table lay a pile of metal. A blue stone sat on the top. Beside it a piece of her mother's stationary. The three mice climbed the table and gathered around. Though machines, they seemed sad. Something about their manner tipped Ella off to have a look. What she saw nearly stopped her heart.

"No."

All that remained of Clarence lay in the pile. His heartstone, usually a bright fire reflecting his mischievous personality through his eyes, lay cracked and dull. Ella slumped to the stool beside the table, a trembling hand reaching out to pull the scraps closer but not quite managing to touch them.

Ella stroked Flora's nickel alloy body. "How could she?"

Father never said how the heartstones powered the mice, however it was evident this one would never shine again.

Long ago, when the tiny creatures were presented to her, she thought them just silver balls. She nearly threw them to the ground when her father told her he would be leaving. Though several months after the accident, she still struggled to control the strange appendage attached to her upper arm, fevers came and went, people she had known all of her life thought her dead and still her father planned to leave her? In her heart she believed her father was leaving because she was damaged.

Then the silver orbs uncurled, pulsing blue through their joints. The smallest—Flora, Ella later named her—sat up and began the very mouse-like action of cleaning her whiskers, then she looked up at Ella and Ella found acceptance in the blue gaze.

Father had cupped his hands around hers and knelt. "They like you," he said softly. But Ella knew better—machines did not like people.

"How do they work?" she demanded. "What trick is this?"

"No one knows," he said simply. "They came from a secret tomb in Egypt your Godmother Bihari found. The sun seems to have something to do with it, but more, they sense the heart of the person who holds them. If it is good, they will open. Always keep them secret and safe, Eliana. They are special. Like you."

From that moment on, the mice and she were bound together. No matter what she did or was forced to do, they knew her heart. Even now, as they helped her steal for her stepmother, and before when Dr. Bon Hamlet asked certain things of her, the mice knew it was all in the effort to protect them and herself. To keep their secrets safe.

And she had failed.

She laid her head on her arms, ignoring the spasmodic jerking of the left. "I am so sorry," she whispered to the scrap pile.

What would her parents have to say about her failure?

So lost in the presence of the charming prince she forgot her duties. As a result, a friend paid the highest price. Judith had ensured Ella would never be able to piece Clarence back together. Never again would he scamper with his brothers and sister or tickle her awake in the morning. All because of her.

Phillipe picked up the stationary and brought the note to her. Tears welled as traced her family's crest decorating the creamy card. How had her stepmother come by this? Ella kept the precious paper hidden behind a rock in the chimney of the forge.

I hope we understand one another.

The trembling in Ella's limbs became an earthquake, she shuddered and fumbled at her belt for the nerve rejuvenator. The syringe teetered on her fingertips and tumbled to shatter on the flagstones.

Ella laid her head on her arms, too weary to care. Her father often stressed the importance of taking the medicine regularly and warned the success of the technique used by Dr. Bihari to attach her arm to her spine depended on it. Despite the wonderful evening in the presence of a too-good-to-be-true prince, the reality of her life overwhelmed her. The three mice shook her human arm, but the tremors dropped her to the floor where she shuddered uncontrollably.

Rough hands gripped her, and the prick of syringe sent a welcome calmness through her nerves. She looked up into Myrtle's enraged face.

"What do you think yer doin'?" The old gunner demanded, hauling Ella to her feet and setting her none too gently onto the stool. "What happened? Why didn't you take the potion? Did Judith hurt ye?"

Ella blushed and smoothed her rumbled skirt. "No. I—she killed Clarence." She motioned to the pile. "I just couldn't." She buried her face into her hands and sobbed, great gasping, heaving sobs.

Myrtle clomped to the side board. Moments later a dishrag slapped Ella in the face. She jerked her gaze to the woman who had been with her since childhood. "Pull yerself together," Myrtle growled. "Ain't nothing go'in get better with yer blubbering or killing yerself."

"But Clarence—Judith—"

Myrtle glared at her. " 'e's a mouse." Metal groaned as she returned to Ella's side and gripped her shoulder, steel fingers digging painfully through the thin fabric of her day dress. "No matter 'ere he came from, 'e's a mouse. Ye be Eliana Graceling Steelhaugh. Daughter of Baron Alsanger Victor Steelhaugh, genius and inventor. Daughter of Lady Octavia Grace Steelhaugh, greatest airship pilot to ever live. Yer the Lady of Iron Crest, the legacy of your parents flows through you every day and every night you give yer all at St. Drogo. You ain't some namby moll the likes of Judith or even those at the hospital."

She gave Ella a shake that made her teeth rattle. "You must be strong. You will get through this." The hopelessness threatening Ella receded, leaving her devoid of feeling but with a sense of purpose.

"Stay safe. Keep it hidden." Ella chanted. Her father's words every time he left her.

"Yes," confirmed Myrtle. She turned away and swung the tea kettle over the fire then stoked the stove. "When we were going down that time I became this, your mother stood at the helm, determined to hold *Pegasus* steady until the last moment to save as many lives as she could. Hold steady the course, Ella. Jus' like yer ma."

"I wish—I wish..." Ella wished her mother had not thrown her from the ship as she went down. She wished her father had not married Judith. She wished so many things she could not put into words. Above all, she wished for more nights like the one before, a future perhaps. One beyond slaving for Judith and working in atonement for her mother who poisoned the Thames. Accidental, yes, but still on the shoulders of the Steelhaugh family. Myrtle put an end to that line of reasoning.

"Defective boilers, Ella, ain't no wishing." Myrtle tossed a dead chicken scalded for plucking in front of her. "This is it."

There was no softness in the gunner, there never had been, but she raised Ella as best she could. Neither asked for this, yet here they were.

Ella dragged the poultry to her and began the messy job, the steel throughout her body hardening into resolve. She would not give Judith another chance to hurt her. She would do as told, maybe shorten her hours at the hospital. She had been too visible, pushing the boundaries of what was her life. Never again would a loved one pay the ultimate price due to her selfishness.

Even if it meant never seeing the prince again.

Chapter Twenty-One

A Deal

Once again Aerysleigh paced the parlour as his mother sat serenely wondering at his sanity. However, his visit with Basil and seeing the people at St. Drogo convinced him of the rightness and necessity of this path. His suspicions, even those as yet unfounded, of covert Prussian activity in England, could only be found among the common people, on the streets.

They held a wealth of information there. The advances in modifications alone, unseen past Dorset street, astounded him. He hadn't even been able to speak to the doctors about other advancements. What knowledge was being discovered out of necessity?

It brought a question to his mind which plagued him incessantly. Could any of it help his father?

He closed his eyes, thinking back to his last visit to the darkened sick room of the man he loved above all others.

His father lay under a pale sheet piled high with down comforters and wool blankets. The chamber felt close and hot. Violent, unpredictable tremors wracked King Redmond's body. His father's spare frame, once tall and lanky, had shrunk to the likeness of a cadaver. Large hands rested on his chest as though already in death's repose and if not for the shakes, Aerysleigh would have thought him already passed to Heaven's gate.

A phalanx of doctors, scientists, alchemists—even a priestess from his mother's home country—stood or sat within arm's reach. They took the royal blood or forced remedies down the monarch's throat, up his nostrils—anywhere. Each procedure another drain on the King's waning strength. When Aerysleigh gripped his father's long fingers, he barely had the strength to press back. Opening his eyes seemed beyond his effort. No doubt about it, he was slipping away.

If only he could speak. The king was never caught unprepared. Surely, he would have a contingency plan in the terrible event he lost his first born. One that did not include Aerysleigh. They both knew him ill-fitted to the task.

Indeed, if he were to get out of this terrible predicament of being crown prince and eventually king, he needed his father back. The king understood the temperament of his second son better than any. Ever since the accident that took Aerysleigh's eye and the life of his twin sister, his father seemed particularly sympathetic to the wild streak driving his son. The push to live life to the fullest, not just for him, but for the sister he once loved as himself.

The sister his mother seemed to have forgotten.

Even now she flipped through her messages, a triumphant grin on her lips. "I am so glad you have come to your senses, my dear." The smile nearly forced him to throw his hands into the air and leave without achieving his objective.

He steeled himself. "I said I would do these things on one condition."

She lifted her gaze to his, expression thoughtful if not wary.

Good. At least he still had the ability to keep her guessing despite the fact he had come into her presence to capitulate. But not entirely.

"I want to work with the constables. You remember my friend, Basil Traverson, of Wind Butte. Father gave him a commission and he is doing some very credible work."

Queen Constantina sat very still then took a deep breath. "I remember. His father is…"

"Is a gentleman, and Basil acquitted himself honourably in the military." Aerysleigh hated his wheedling tone, but once again he found himself begging.

"But the police, son, such a *low* profession." She drew out the word low with every ounce of dainty disdain she could muster.

"I am not giving in on this, Mother. I'll do everything you ask, but I need this for myself." Best not to delve into his true intentions, she would not understand. She expected any successful treatment for his father to come from the medical society, learned men, scientists with degrees from all over the world. She would never understand nor support his reasoning that perhaps the cure for his father lay closer to home.

The plans this Cinder fellow is stealing. Though Aerysleigh despised the dishonourable actions of the bloke, he could not help but wonder after his motives. Did he work for a scientist even now on the cusp of a great scientific breakthrough? A stretch? Perhaps, but one he was willing to explore to save his father. He may even retain some of his sanity after it was all through.

He waited, refusing to speak again until the queen came to her senses. Finally, his mother slapped down the papers he suspected she wasn't reading in the first place. "Very well then. And you will search for a wife?"

He took a deep breath. How long would his plan take? How long could he put off matrimony? The queen wanted this settled quickly. Six months maybe?

Not a lot of time, Aerysleigh.

The image of the blonde tinker made his heart smile, but at the same time it hurt. His proud mother would never allow such a union, despite her own slave heritage and love match. Since his infancy she emphasised marrying for advantage and would not allow her sons the same luxury that took her from the sugar plantation to the throne.

He attempted to read her expression, judge how much time he could extract. He studied the high cheekbones he inherited, the bronze skin which seemed kissed by the sun no matter the season. He even had her hair, though she kept hers carefully coiffed and covered to hide the black curls while he let his grow long and braided. His darker skin worked for him in the military, the men seeing him more as one of them than the pale upper crust ordering them to their deaths.

"Yes," he finally said. "I will look. But I will not be rushed."

"Six months," she said.

"Pardon?" Just as he figured, she chose his lower time limit.

Queen Constantina pinned him with a knowing look and he wondered why he believed he could ever get something by her. "Though you think I do not understand you, and at times I do confess you baffle me, I know your delaying tactics well, Aerysleigh. I will give you six months to find a suitable bride or I will find one for you. At the end of this time, we will hold a ball and an announcement will be made."

"You would set a time for love?" he demanded, mind whirling. Judging his father's condition today, he didn't have that long. He would either be cured by then, no matter the outcome of Aerysleigh's investigations, or in the grave. If the former, a bride would be off the negotiating table, if the later a bride would be the least of his concerns. While he struggled with himself, his mother rose and stood before him, taking his hands in her own.

Then she did something she hadn't since he was a boy. She removed his eye patch. His wounded eye blinked in the onslaught of light and instinct made him reach for the covering. His milk white eye and the scar crossing it made many people uncomfortable.

"Look at me, Aerysleigh," she said. "I know you think I am being unreasonable, but this is best for the family. For England." She stared up into his face, unflinching at his disfigurement.

He squeezed her hand. "Six months then."

CHAPTER TWENTY-TWO

THE MUSEUM

The garden reeked of the noxious fumes from the munition's factory and the stench of unwashed bodies packed in close. However, the ladies in attendance at the museum garden for the great sculpture reveal, seemed not to notice. Each wore a smile placed there by a misguided sense of social charity. Exclamations of 'oh it feels so uplifting to help those in need' and 'What a grand idea to allow art patrons to lift up the destitute' nearly shook Ella from her servant's perch.

How inappropriate were the gay linens and the high pitched chatter.

Ella wanted to scream at them, *we are in the middle of a war, you old hens! Can you not feel the suffering of your own people? Those upon whose backs your levity is bought?*

She held her tongue. The armistice was signed. Trade resumed across the oceans. Airships that once battled on the mainland now carried trade goods.

Her gaze slid to where her stepmother chatted with Lady

Dunsdale, probably eyeing her emerald bracelet for Cinder's next mark.

The enemy is right there.

Why couldn't they see how Baron Steelhaugh's widow, though gracious and beautiful on the outside, mocked them with every word, with every pretence of actually caring about their troubled bowels, or the next appointment with the proctologist?

Ella gripped the coats tightly and stood in the shadow of the columns. Uninvited. Her presence required. The Lady Steelhaugh needed a maid servant, and having dismissed all the others, Ella fit the bill nicely.

What would happen if I run to Princess Ursula and reveal Judith to be a conniving mad scientist and double agent? Would Her Highness laugh at me? Lock me up?

No one cared. The Society of the Concerned Ladies for Widows and Orphans only concerned themselves with one thing—the appearance of their goodness.

Ostentatiously the purpose of this gathering of tender-hearted matrons was to dedicate a monument memorialising those lost in the war. The mothers, fathers, sons, and daughters who gave all. Also, to raise money for the local food bank which would most likely funnel the funds to other uses.

Ella snorted, Prussia probably placed a double agent in their midst, just waiting for the influx of monies so more experiments could be conducted right on the streets of London.

The orphans would benefit more from some of the furs draped around the sloped shoulders. The poor would never see a penny of it anyway. In fact, the only concession all was not as gay as it seemed were the servants around the edges, all holding gas masks and protective outerwear for their mistresses in the event of an attack. Not that it had happened.

But it would, Ella mused, and by the activity of those coming and going from Iron Crest, it may be sooner than later.

An artist stood at the foot of the sheeted creation, keeping back those who urged her to reveal her creation before the designated time. However, only Princess Ursula had the honour of indicating when that would be.

After having seen some of this woman's earlier works at a showing sponsored by the princess several months before, Ella sincerely hoped it stayed covered. Grotesque did not even come close to describing the tortured metal sculptures presented by the artist. Though one looked suspiciously like Proximus—if stood on its head and viewed through a kaleidoscope. She assumed the art appealed to the princess at some level.

"Where is Prince Aerysleigh, I wonder?" asked the Lady Suthmeer to the Lady Connelly. "Was he not expected to escort Princess Ursula at this event?"

"Indeed," answered the other honourable lady, "I had my Tempie wear her rose coloured gown. Is she not lovely?"

Lady Suthmeer barely spared a glance for the girl, "Arline is just there in the green and Lenore in the lavender. It is so difficult to dress two girls to meet royalty, you know. It does no good, however, if he shirks his duties. After all, this is an important social function. We *are* raising money for the children."

More like trying to trap a prince.

Though having yet to attend a function where the prince actually put in an appearance, Ella was eternally grateful to dodge that particular painful experience, he garnered her complete sympathies. How could anyone stand to be paraded around like some prize stallion?

Unable to bear the farce of a party anymore, Ella turned away to stroll the walkway. Along with the ladies, she couldn't help her disappointment at the prince's actions since his return home. After the one visit to St. Drogo she had not heard of him returning.

Thank goodness.

Still, she hoped he would right the wrongs done to the war veterans and modifieds. Instead he ducked parties and shark-eyed mothers who saw him as raw meat for the marriage market. Rumours were he often worked with the constables.

But it did not help. People on the street grew more fearful of body snatchers. More laws were proposed, and some passed, to keep the modifieds as secondary citizens or worse, objects to be experimented on. Security had tightened everywhere and with her limited time, keeping up with politics and medical experimentation became difficult. Ella helped where she could, but nothing seemed to be enough.

She harrumphed.

Of everything, what burned her boilers most were veterans on the street, turned loose for having been injured in the line of duty, age, or a reduction of men at the front. No mattered how it angered her, she had no power to do anything.

Stay safe. Stay hidden.

Observing her stepmother deep in conversation, Ella turned to the neglected elegance of the museum. At least she might be able to glean some information from these hallowed halls to help with smithing.

Before the age of war, The National Museum of Metallurgy and Mineralogy had been one of the brightest hubs in all of England. The board of directors awarded scholarships to a worthy few, matched apprentices to masters, and interviewed cutting edge metal workers from all walks to showcase their skill. However, in the aftermath of war the interfering busybodies took over.

One whole wing lay dismantled. Plans to dedicate the wing to the fine arts, paintings and sculptures, were in the works while some of the engineering marvels were regulated to the basement.

Rage rose before she could squash it. *Button and bobsleds, this was a museum for Metallurgy.* If people wanted art, they could go to a gallery. Heaven knew there were plenty of those already.

She turned from the new wing and headed towards the area where she could find the history of the development of prosthetics. The progression began with hooks and peg legs, each with a plaque which documented the uses of the different alloys.

The dust in these parts hung heavy in the air and on the displays.

"Blast it all," Ella grumbled, unafraid of using her unladylike language in these uninhabited chambers. She used her stepmother's coat to wipe clean a particular piece on the homogenisation of iron-nickel-chromium alloys for heat resistance.

"I would ask that you keep your musings to yourself. There are some of us who are trying to study here."

Ella whirled at the voice behind her. A swift jerk triggered the compartment in her mechanised hand and she presented a dagger towards the one who surprised her. So caught up in her study, she failed to notice the presence of another student in a musty chair, a large tome resting in his lap.

"I say, sir, you might have made your presence known sooner. I might have gutted you on accident." But she already recognised the voice and the eye patch gave him away.

Prince Aerysleigh chuckled. "I highly doubt it, Tinker Lady, you were engrossed in your own little world." He closed the book and rose. "But now you intrigue me. I seem to find you in the oddest of places, but never when I am actively looking for you." He came and stood quite close, reminding her of both the rescue from the bridge and the night they had spent pouring over the projects. "You have not been to St. Drogo of late."

Ella dropped her eyes and stepped back.

He followed me.

"I had not heard that you made a habit of visiting the cathedral, sir." *Run away,* her brain begged, trying to bring up the image of Clarence's deconstructed metal parts. But her heart beat so hard it stole her breath. "There are many Anglican choices nearer to Kensington."

"True. Besides, a particular nurse, Sukie I think, made it clear that my presence may make some uncomfortable. However, I have tried to pass by with the constables almost daily."

As much as she longed to stay in his company, the need to escape pressed on her. She retreated again, but her backside brushed one of the plaques. He followed and stepped beside her.

"Why?" she breathed against her will.

He looked down at her, "I enjoyed myself that night, more than I have at any of these endless affairs." He waved his hands towards the ladies in the garden, bringing Ella back to her senses.

Ella stepped back and covertly replaced her knife while pretending to fiddle with her glove. "Excuse me, your highness." She made her feet head towards the door. She needed to escape before anyone came looking.

The prince caught her arm. "Please, don't run away again." She glanced at his hand. He dropped it and moved to a more proper distance, bending over the plague she perused just minutes earlier. "What, pray tell, caused such consternation that brought low language to these hallowed halls?" He teased, using his chin to motion her over.

Her father always chided her mother on the airship language she used around Ella and the fact that their daughter seemed to use it at the most inopportune times. Despite her misgiving, she longed to linger. "This wing happens to be a particular interest of mine," she said. "I was not expecting to find a lurker in the shadows listening to my private conversations."

The prince laughed a deep rusty sound as if not used to the act. It was a robust note which rang down her spine pleasantly. After two hours of high-pitched cackles, it was a sweet relief.

He peered at the plaque and rubbed at it in the same manner she had. His tightly braided braids, neatly tied back into a ponytail with a black ribbon, were covered in a top hat, as though to aid in disguising his identity. While he looked, she admired his strong jaw, clean-shaven where most men sported beards.

Finally, he gave up and shook his head and Ella looked elsewhere least caught gawking.

"The state of these older wings is such a shame. Every day the advances showcased in these halls are used in the war, from weapons to medicine, to better ships and war machines. But innovation in other areas, our foundations, are lost," he said.

She nodded, her own thoughts parallel with the deep mourning in his voice. "So, what do you study then?" she asked, "Some way to increase miner safety and increase copper production? Agriculture perhaps?"

He managed to make sheepish look good then showed her the title of his book. "The Metallurgy of Advanced Prosthesis."

She couldn't help but laugh. "I see. Are you a doctor then? A tinker, or machinist?"

"In truth, I met this lady quite adept at making such devices," he paused.

"And you hope to woo her with your knowledge of her craft?" she prompted, ducking her chin to hied the warmth rising to her cheeks. "I honestly could not recommend that book."

He glanced at the tome. "No?"

"No." Her gaze tightened. "Try perusing the latest advancements discovered during unsanctioned experiments at the Royal Medical School. I think you will find the dissection and experimentation taking place there enlightening."

"I..."

Her ire rose, humour fleeing. This man had been home for months with only one measly visit to St. Drogo to see the people who had bled for England. He christened a few retro-fitted ships, backed Parliament when they claimed the truce a success. Not that she read every bit of news she could find on him. Everyone did.

"Better yet, try the docks. See the innovative ways the veterans attempt to adapt to missing limbs. The homeless not only have to find their next meal but avoid being nicked by body snatchers. Chat with a modified just come from having his body measured to the nearest tenth of a percentile to be declared human. These people would give you greater insight than any book."

He took a step forward, dark eye slitting and brows furrowed. "Do you presume to take me to task for neglecting my princely duties?"

Forgetting the fact that Judith may appear at any minute, Ella put her hands on her hips. After years immersed in the suffering of the slums as London's industries boomed and more workers moved from country to city, she needed to get this terrible weight off her chest. Prince Aersyleigh could do so much more than her own small efforts.

For once she did not back down from the idea, he might suspect her to be modified. *What of it?*

He already knew of her work at St. Drogo. She stepped forward and puffed out a breath, glaring up into his face just inches away.

"Presume? How can the Lords *presume* to call humans automatons because of the percentage of metal they use? By what right do they *presume* to create a whole new class by taking away rights? It is bad enough the poor must fight for survival and have little representation. Then veterans return maimed and are no longer considered citizens. This after fighting for the very people who hate them. Where is the compassion for the man or woman disfigured in service?" She heaved a great sigh after her tirade, breath straining against corset as she gathered her arguments for another verbal charge.

"You seem to know a good deal about such things, Miss Ella. You do a great enough work with the downtrodden."

"What I do is a pittance. You, on the other hand, could change the course of all those things going wrong in Parliament."

He retreated a step and held up his hands—a sure sign of surrender. "I am merely looking for clues into a case I am working on with a friend."

She deflated instantly. Like everyone else he did not care. She eyed him up and down and played along though only halfheartedly. "Ah, truth comes out. You care more about petty crimes than the true issues right before your nose."

Prince Aerysleigh frowned and shook his head. "I have no idea what you are talking about."

She snorted. "London does not need another constable right now."

Besides, he couldn't play the part of a foot pad if he tried. His fawn trousers had buttons running from ankle to waist band and his silk, double breasted vest of bold green reeked of wealth. From his top hat to perfectly tied cravat, the fellow exuded class. And he smelled so good, like freshly trimmed trees on a fall day with the hint of smoke from the brush fires.

"I like to list my profession as other."

Sure, he did.

"But I do enjoy consulting Scotland Yard. Right now, they are focusing on an interesting case."

She raised a brow, pretending nonchalance as her stomach clenched. She knew what came next. "Let me guess, Cinder." She did not even try to hide her disappointment.

"You steal my thunder, my lady, I see you have heard of the reprobate."

Heart and hope plummeting to her toes, she waved a negligent hand. So, her stepmother was right after all. Aersyleigh fell like fresh game into the baited trap, his attention diverted by the vocal protests of a few rich slighted by Cinder rather than the plight of the destitute and maimed.

She willed him to look beyond the problems of the peerage to turmoil seething a mere block away. "There are so many other things more important that a petty thief."

"Hardly petty. He has stolen thousands of pounds worth of jewels, enough to..."

"Fund a small army?" She finished for him.

"Yes, actually."

What if he knew the truth? What the money actually went for? What would he do? The words trembled on her tongue.

Instead she said, "In reality, what harm does he do? We have veterans who return from the war mangled in both spirit and body. There are rumours of terrible things happening on the streets, but the ladies of the peerage are here at this worthless gathering to pay money which will never ease the plight of anyone but the enemy."

"Ella!"

Ella threw her hands across her mouth and stared wide eyed down the hall. Her stepmother searched for her. She must not be caught talking to anyone.

She curtsied. "I apologise, sir. Occasionally, I let my mouth run on before my brain."

Prince Aerysleigh stared at her as though thunderstruck. Perhaps she had overloaded his brain with new thoughts. He recovered himself quickly and returned the formality. "*Au contraire,* my lady, you are a breath of fresh air in a city filled with insanity."

"Ella!"

She turned. "I must go."

He reached for her and she winced as his softly gloved fingers touched the hard metal of her hand. "Wait."

But she did not, she turned and fled, nearly bowling over her stepmother in her hurry.

"Where have you been?" The lady demanded.

"Oh, just wandering." She motioned to the label of the hall, "an area of interest for me."

Judith lifted a lip. "Indeed. Come along. They unveiled the

monstrosity in the garden and the ladies are taking their leave. The girls have disappeared. You are teaching them bad habits, and I won't have it. Go along and tell the carriage we are ready."

Ella hurried to put as much possible distance between herself and the prince. A shadow caught her eye and Aerysleigh appeared in the doorway, she prayed her stepmother didn't see.

Isabeau and Aurelia stepped from an adjacent hall, drawing their mother's attention at that exact moment. The way their eyes met hers over Judith's shoulder, she suspected it was not an accident.

Chapter Twenty-Three

A Party

Throughout the month after the death of Crown Prince Robert, Lord Chamberlain issued the order that the court and all the people of England observe a deep mourning.

The general gloom dampened even the sturdiest of spirits. London's theatres suspended production until further notice, the police and military wore black crepe around their left arms, and women flooded the milliner with orders for dresses of a somber nature.

Despite the general depression of the city, the air at Iron Crest could be called far from restrained. The more Ella eavesdropped on the goings on in her own home, the more she suspected the malady which struck down the royal house might have been orchestrated by undercover agents.

Even so, Judith commanded Myrtle to bring champagne from the cellar, Isabeau and Aurelia into their party dresses, then ordered Ella to scrub the house from top to bottom.

Hot house flowers filled every corner in lavish arrangements. Candle in all the chandeliers shone like a thousand miniature forge fires, casting everything in a becoming glow. Brass gleamed, the silver sparkled, and nary a speck of dust, oil, or ash marred the oak floors.

Foreign staff scurried about under directions from a plump woman with mean eyes. Ella recognised none of the new servants, her stepmother refusing to draw on local help. A fact sure to alienate Iron Crest from the surrounding countryside even more.

The aroma of suckling pig, pheasant, and lamb prepared for a feast made Ella's stomach clench and rumble unbecomingly. However, when she eased into the kitchen for bite and a rest, the cook chased her out screaming obscenities in German and thumped her metal arm with a wooden spoon.

The disgust in her face needed no translation.

After being surrounded by modifieds both at home and at the hospital, Ella sometimes forgot the prejudice against people like her. Covered by her day dress, the arm stood out no more than the other. Evidently, Judith shared her stepdaughter's secret with everyone. She retreated to the forge, fighting another pain that made her hunger inconsequential.

Suddenly the mice rolled into their protective balls.

"What—?"

Judith's voice froze the words on her lips. "Good, you are where you belong."

Her stepmother stood resplendent in a scarlet gown at the door. No attempt at sobriety here. The black bodice sparkled with paste gems matching the red. Her shoulders were bare as was a generous amount of cleavage. The material clung seductively to every curve, tight in front and flaring over the bustle. Disgusted with her stepmother's lack of decorum, Ella pretended fascination with a new design on the drafting table.

"Do you know the Marquis Rothmundoth?"

Ella shook her head, something she would have done whether or not she knew. Just recently Dr. Bon Hamlet mentioned the Marquis' involvement in promoting a law to stop Modifieds from voting and a plan to stage a protest march when he travelled to Parliament. But she said none of this.

Judith gave her an exasperated look. "His townhouse is near Ladbroke Estate." Ella kept her eyes lowered. "He is in possession of a great many raw opals I would like you to relieve him of." Her stepmother walked to the table and grabbed one of the mice. Phillipe.

"Please—" Ella bit back the objection when Judith arched her brow—daring her stepdaughter to continue to protest. Daring her to question her place when Judith could crush everything Ella loved so easily. Ella sighed, resigned to her life as a thief. Aching to know that the money she stole was used against her own countrymen. Against the modifieds. Against the prince.

"Did you have something to say?"

Ella swallowed an impotent scream, but instead said what she had to. "No, ma'am."

"You will leave now, out the chimney. Stay away from the house." She gave Ella a disgusted look. "I do not want any metal monsters around for my guests to see."

"But, what have you done with Myrtle?"

"I have locked her in the basement where such things are kept. Pure people will wait on my guests. If I see any sign of you…" She held out her hand where Phillipe sat, his heartstone glowing faintly through the smallest cracks as he listened. "You will lose another of your friends." Judith grinned in a way that twisted her beautiful face with hate, "and you didn't have that many left."

Ella sat heavily on the high stool at the table. Over a week passed since she had visited the hospital and guilt ate at her, but exhaustion seemed to win out these days. She couldn't tell if it was because of the work or her spirits, but lately she noticed that she didn't care about that either.

"How—?"

"Figure it out. Dig a hole for all I care. But you will not be seen in this house by even the lowest servant. This evening is too important for—" Judith stopped herself. "Never mind. Just leave and do not return until late tomorrow *with* the opals."

Judith shut the door without another word. A moment later the lock clicked. Flora popped her head from Ella's pocket and twitched her whiskers at the portal with a decidedly cheeky bob of her head. Ella couldn't help but smile. "It is a good thing you can't talk, little friend, I think you could get me into plenty of trouble."

Flora leaped to the table and stared at her before looking towards the door then back again.

"No, I can't go that way." Dane joined his sister and sat atop a recently completed project plus another hand for Harcourt. Ella made it—not when she noticed his missing or in the glass cabinets of The Fence—but when a young boy rendered handless in a conveyor belt accident tried to sell her a paper with one of Harcourt's prosthesis. She wouldn't have noticed even then if not for the way people gave him a wide berth. Perhaps the old beggar wasn't as nasty as he made himself out to be.

She stood and straightened her shoulders. A new energy filled her. She might as well make a night of it. She would get the jewels then deliver the completed projects. People depended on her.

As she packed, she became aware of sounds indicating the arrival of the first guests. Boilers sounded overhead as airships docked and left, horses neighed and snorted, carriage wheels crunched. Everything indicated this would be one of the biggest parties ever held at Iron Crest by her stepmother. Definitely not a secret one either.

Why would Judith risk such a gathering at such a conspicuous time? An event this big would surely draw attention.

Curiosity aroused, Ella attempted to peer out the window and found a fresh board nailed to the outside sash.

"Conniving cuttlefish!" Slapping the pane, she turned and studied the room, ignoring the gnawing in her stomach. Her hand trembled, absently she injected the shoulder muscle. A diet of bread, water, and porridge brought the tremors more frequently.

She glanced into her pack, letting her mind assess the situation, when her questing fingers revealed how few injections remained. So low. Nearly two years had passed since Dr. Bihari sent a package with the precious medication. The longest stretch ever. Ella hoped she had not been forgotten, but it would not really surprise her.

Of a sudden, it became imperative she return to the city. She longed for the gentle acceptance of her friends, and even if the odds were against it, get a glimpse of the prince who seemed to appear in the most unexpected places. She glanced at the chimney, that would be the way out tonight—with a slight detour.

Ella determined to get a glimpse of these 'important' guests filling Iron Crest first. This party just seemed too conspicuous for a secret Prussian agent. What was her plotting stepmother up to?

Mind made up, Ella grabbed her gas mask and strapped gaffs to her boots. She tied her projects in a bundle attached to a rope and climbed the chimney. There, hidden in the lee of the stone was her pedal glider. Ella passed it by. Setting her hand into a grappling claw, she rappelled down the side of the building and flitted through the thyme and rosemary scented kitchen garden.

Ducking underneath the dining room window, she peered inside. The doors between the library and dining room stood open and nearly twenty-five people moved between the two rooms. Besides the men's dark evening coats, nary an article of mourning was in sight. The majority of the gathering were men with bright paisley vests and bold cravats. The women—ten in all—wore silk and taffeta. They resembled bright peafowl as they swept elegantly across the floors, long skirts swishing like tails. Aurelia and Isabeau blended into the corner furthest from her.

Isabeau's eyes were strained, Aurelia's calm hand tucked into the crook of her arm. Suddenly, the dark-haired sister sniffed the air, then turned her gaze straight to Ella's position. Ella ducked back quickly, her heart pounding. When no alarm came, she peeked back in. This time both girls stared at her. Aurelia shook her head. Ella ignored the warning and moved on.

The windows and the open doors to the patio allowed the cool, night air to move freely. Iron Crest, being five miles from London proper, rarely saw the poisonous gases of the Thames. Still, a few attendees cast wary glances out the door, watching the sky for the rise of the deadly fog.

Judith and three men took their ease near the window Ella chose to peek through. With a gasp, she pressed tight against the stone.

"I heard just today," her stepmother said, "that the prince's recall is permanent. He will take the place of his brother and of course the father in due time."

"But the question is, what sort of king will he be?" asked a nasal-voiced man.

"He is barely over mourning his brother and now he is thrust into the social circles by his mother," said another.

Judith chuckled. "My source at the palace seems to think Queen Constantina wants the line of succession secured immediately. Prince Aerysleigh is already on the way to assume both roles of king *and* husband."

Ella willed her heart not to miss a beat at the mention of the prince. It boded ill for him to be the subject of Judith's conversation.

"The queen takes much upon herself. Does she suspect Prussia's role in this recent outbreak?"

"She does not strike me as having the mental agility for simple addition, let alone unravel a trail as cunning as ours." Judith said in that scoffing tone used too often on Ella. "No, at the gatherings she is as witless as the rest of them. However, Prince Aerysleigh may be of a different ilk."

"I agree," volunteered the nasal-voice. "He is not some molly serving his time behind the lines in the safety zones. He is quite the war hero and has the scars to prove it."

Judith tittered her social laugh once again. "Scars only prove him slow."

"Still, we must not underestimate him," said the third who sounded worried about the prospect of the returned prince. "Don't you think this party premature?"

"Premature? *Nein.* My plan for Cinder to divert the attention of the aristocracy while they are under the false security of this armistice is working perfectly. I have already made plans for one of my daughters to marry the prince. Our agent at the palace has the ear of the queen and is already whispering—"

Another voice broke into the group's conversation. "Leave us."

A moment of silence and then the snick of a match before the smell of strawberries wafted by on a cloud of smoke. Ella cringed back, afraid to breathe for fear of discovery, her heart beating so loudly she felt sure it could be heard above the music.

"This is a lovely party, Jutta," said a voice devoid of any emotion to turn the words into a compliment.

"You are most gracious, *Herr Fisc—*"

"But need I remind you, this is your last chance. You were relocated at considerable expense, if you recall, and to celebrate before the ultimate victory is...unseemly."

"But, sir—"

"Enough. Your hate for Oktavia still drives you. It makes you blind and reckless. You risk too much. I want you to reassess your position and plan carefully."

"Yes, sir."

It did Ella good to hear her proud stepmother so contrite. She finally managed a breath. Surely, they would not talk so freely if they suspected someone eavesdropping.

"Oswin is frightened of the prince," observed the newcomer.

"He is frightened of everyone."

"*Ja*, however, he has good reason to be frightened. He and you both underestimated Oktavia and look at the damage we sustained because of it."

They must mean Mother. Ella cheered the cold man for digging at Judith's weakness again.

"He was also in love with her," her stepmother mocked, envy and loathing obvious.

"I suppose everyone was a little bit infatuated with her. She ruled the skies and played us all. A master of deception who managed to blind everyone. The culmination of all of our years of training." The stranger's voice sounded proud though Ella's mother escaped him.

"For what? To throw it all away over the love of a man? How low she sunk from the high ideals she was taught," said Judith.

Despite the fear of discovery, Ella smiled in the dark. Her mother loved Papa enough to the reject years of brainwashing which turned her into the ultimate spy. She loved that Lady Steelhaugh remained true throughout.

"Did she? She made you look the *dummkopf,* not the other way around. I would hate to see you lose this opportunity because you underestimate the prince as you did Oktavia."

"I understand," said Judith, actually managing to sound contrite.

"*Gut. Gut.* Now tell me how your experiments are coming."

"I am sorry to report I am still making up for what was lost so many years ago."

"The girls are growing well."

What did her stepsisters have to do with anything?

"Indeed."

"And the others?"

"Unstable."

The man harrumphed and Judith added quickly, "we *are* making headway, despite the loss of *Herr Frankenstein's* notes. But for now, I think that my Cinder idea is working well to keep suspicions from our clandestine activities. Perhaps they will distract the prince as well."

"Perhaps. However, your Cinder is also Oktavia's daughter, is she not? An inventor and talented blacksmith in her own right. Never forget that."

"I would hardly call what she produces the work of talent."

A long silence followed and Ella realised she had lingered too long. Any moment someone could choose to turn right when stepping out onto the patio for a breath of air or to wander the kitchen garden instead of the formal one. If she were caught the consequences would be dire.

Judith believed these conversations held in perfect safety. The servants all gone, Ella locked up, her own daughters frightened witless of her, and Myrtle most likely threatened somehow. Still, something kept her crouched in the dirt.

"Don't underestimate that one either. Or the prince."

"Yes, sir."

The shadows moved from the window, and Ella crept away.

Chapter Twenty-Four

The Stalker

The night closed around her, clasping at her like a desperate beggar. Cinder adjusted the oxygen flowing into her mask and took a deep breath.

Was it wrong for her to rebel at her sudden change in circumstances? From mistress to servant in her own home? Any time away from the drudgery of laundry and stove seemed like heaven, even if she was on one of Judith's errands. She embraced the soot laced darkness.

Munition and airship factories spewed ash, smudging the night like a a toppled inkwell on clean parchment. A gentle rain of fine powder coated the eaves and sills of rich and poor alike. She welcomed the smell of fire from the bellowing boilers driving belts and presses, so like her forge.

The streets were barren, a testament to the dangerous gases creeping wraith-like from the dark river water. But that was not what raised the hair on the back of her neck.

A sound scurried behind her. Too large to be a rat. "Who's there?" She demanded, hand on her sword.

Nothing answered, but she felt eyes track her every movement. A malevolence filled the void and for a brief moment all sound stopped. Nothing from the river, the factories, the docks, not ever the cough of a child or yell of a man.

Too quiet.

She stepped lightly towards the flickering halo of a street lamp, eschewing the alley's relative safety. But when she reached the main street, none of the usual night lurkers appeared. Again, the sound ticked behind her and she pressed the button on her new vambraces. A knife snicked out of each one. At least she learned something from her painful altercation with the birdman. Just as she began to relax the sound came again. She peered down the alley.

A shadow moved, large and hulking. Proximus lumbered into view. "Cinder!"

She tried to hide her surprise. "Proximus. Mr. Wright." She never saw the twins outside of The Fence.

The big fellow tipped a shoulder so his co-joined twin could join the conversation. "Young lady, this is not a night for your activities. Return home." Mr. Wright's voice echoed through a gas mask, distorted and disgruntled at her presence. As though she had interrupted something.

She could not tell him she had no choice. "I have business."

Proximus shook his head and glanced around warily. "It is dangerous."

She kicked at the mists. "No more than usual."

The ambulatory twin stepped closer, allowing Mr. Wright to bend near. How they communicated was anyone's guess, the larger twin seemed to sense the other's intentions. "Worse than usual. Go home, child."

She narrowed her eyes at the order, realising how close they now stood. She stepped away, drawing her sword. Proximus turned faster than a thought and nearly caught her. Instead, Mr. Wright snatched the rapier from her grasp. She crouched, pointing the knives at the two.

Mr. Wright sighed. "We are not the enemy, Cinder. There is something out here tonight. Betty..."

A howl crashed through the alleys so loud timbers shook and mortar pebbled from high up.

A wolf? In London?

Proximus drew a large axe from his side, Mr. Wright a pistol. "Quickly," said the little twin. "To St. Drogo."

Cinder didn't have to be told twice. She whirled and fled, Proximus on her heels.

They thrust themselves through the door at the moment something large hit the outside. Together they strained to close the portal against the unseen force. Metal scrapped on the outside, like a cat sharpening her claws. However, the force fighting them was much bigger than a sassy feline.

The door inched open.

The cathedral guards rushed to aid and threw their shoulders into the effort. The door suddenly snapped shut.

Ella threw the bolt and leaned against the wood. "What was that?" she gasped.

Father Mark hurried between the pews, crossing himself and murmuring a prayer.

"Prayers aren't going to help us against that," Mr. Wright chuckled at the clergyman. They all took a deep breath and the tension leaked from trembling muscles.

The priest shook his head. "Where is your faith, Mr. Wright?"

"Washed away in the rains, dear sir."

The priest *tsked*. "God will protect us." He pulled a lever in the stone beside the door. Metal clanged. The decorative spikes couched in flowers reversed suddenly, driving through the door. Something whimpered on the other side of the door.

"God, eh?" asked Mr. Wright.

"God ever favours the prepared," rejoined the cleric.

"But what *was* it?" asked Ella.

"We don't know." A new voice joined in. From the confessional stepped a cowled fellow with a metal mask covering half his face. It glinted in the light of the prayer candles. Lord Stillingfleet, Marquess of Wheelfell and stalwart advocate for all the modifieds.

Ella curtsied swiftly, "Your grace." She kept her head bowed, posture subservient.

The gentleman robbed her of all composure when he bowed in return. "Lady Steelhaugh."

"I—uh—sir." She snapped her jaw shut, hoping the others had not heard, but a quick glance at her friends near the door showed no surprise in any of them.

Had she no secrets?

Time to direct the conversation back to the monster at the door. "Pardon, sir, but what is out there. I felt it stalking me, but I never saw the creature." For a creature it surely was. "It can't be one of us, can it?" She deliberately made reference to her low state. Lady Steelhaugh could not be one such as she.

He eyed her, then shrugged. "Not a modified. A man? A beast? Something in between?" He looked towards the two guards. "Follow it if you can and report to me later. But be careful. Something killed

Boney Bea last night." The guards blanched but went quickly about their business. At the third confessional to the left, always locked against regular petitioners, one inserted the half cog 'coin' of St. Drogo. Inside was an emergency arsenal from which they armed themselves. In no more than a minute they slipped through a side door.

Lord Stillingfleet watched with approval. "They're good lads. May find some information tonight." He slid a glance toward Ella. "Unless you'd like to try."

"I-uh-I—"

"She will do no such thing," said the priest.

Stillingfleet inclined his head to Ella. "My lady." Then he followed Proximus and Mr. Wright down the secret stair.

The priest drew Ella away from the door. "The last few years have brought numerous changes to the residents of London, particularly those exposed to chemical attacks."

Ella nodded. "Yes. The rages, the peculiars like the Valkyrie. But London has always been infested with odd folk." They gave the city its particular character.

"True enough. But it seems of late these 'things' have moved beyond the expected. Men are turning into beasts, killing. Dying in horrible ways."

"The gases?"

"I don't think so. Something else," mused the priest, his voice pitched low as they passed a petitioner.

"An illness?"

"Perhaps. It appears to strike when the gases are strongest." He turned to face her. "You must stay away on these nights, Cinder. You," he glanced down, a tear appearing in his eye, "you give people hope. If anything were to happen…"

"I'll be careful," she promised. Though she couldn't imagine how someone like her could give anyone hope. Her mother caused the disaster now playing out on London's streets.

"C-I-N-D-E-R H-E-L-P."

She whirled. "Valkyrie! You frightened me."

The Birdman stood with his pigeon cuddled gently in his large hands. The bird had regained its health and become quite the pet of the hospital, though it did lose its leg.

Despite the fright, Ella smiled. "Yes, I'll help. I have just the thing."

She led him towards the tinker's room. Judith's thievery could wait, she had a bird to fit with a prosthesis.

*****

Aerysleigh paused at the sound of the howl and removed his gas mask to better hear. The two police officers accompanying him shuddered and looked around, sticks held at the ready. Doors slammed. The deep fog took on a green tinge, Aerysleigh replaced his mask and continued on, one hand gripping the hilt of his sword, the other checking the pistol strapped to his thigh.

Though the pants and holsters, along with the heavy great coat were not the attire of a gentleman, the weeks of walking the streets had taught Aerysleigh one thing—be prepared. Underneath he wore bandoliers of extra ammunition and as many weapons as he once wore as a captain.

After a moment, one of his companions, Grigsby, straightened, glancing around with quick head jerks. "Just another bloke gone mad, from the sound of it."

Violet, a slim girl made bulky with the amount of equipment padding her frame, chuckled. "Sure."

But to Aerysleigh the night felt wrong—premonition ticked up his spine and raised the hair on the back of his neck. A feeling similar to the the feeling he got before an ambush. *This* was the type of darkness Basil warned him about, the kind were the prostitutes kept their business inside rather than on the street. The kind of night when thieves and murderers plotted instead of acted. He tried to put a finger on the difference but could not.

The howl summed up the feeling completely.

Aerysleigh let his feet take him in the direction of the cathedral. The area around Saint Drogo bustled with an activity felt rather than seen. Nothing stirred on the streets, but the cobbles thrummed with the rumble of engines and the pumping of bellows. No matter the time or the pressing dangers, the priests cared for the destitute of London. Working all shifts to alleviate the suffering of the forgotten poor.

Passing by the steps, he wondered if *she* were there. Metal *snicked* when he paused in the street, debating whether or not to go in. He looked closely at the door. Spikes protruded from the bolts and several shone in the weak light from the gas lanterns decorating the pillars of the cathedral. He climbed the steps and touched one with a finger and held to the light.

Blood.

Fresh by the looks of it.

He stepped away, his senses sharp now as he studied the darkness. The shadows seemed to jump and twist, drawing his eye only to find it deceived.

"Let's move on," Grigsby suggested.

Violet nodded. "Yes, lets."

A shiver ran up Aerysleigh's spine similar to those he got before battle. "How about the station on Bacon Street?" he suggested. "We could take a cup a tea before moving out?"

The other two agreed vigorously and hurried down the cobbled street.

Aerysleigh paused, looking back towards the doors, wondering what could have happened here but knowing enough to realise the people inside would never tell.

Would she? He tried to pry his mind away from the golden-haired Tinker.

Movement caught his eye and he leaped to the ready.

The Valkyrie walked from the alley next to St. Drogo. Come to think of it, whenever Aerysleigh came this way quite a bit of traffic moved in and out of that narrow lane. Maskless and barefoot despite the obvious rise of the mists, the skeletal bloke hunched over something tucked in his tattered coat.

"What are you doing there?" Aerysleigh demanded, his question harsher than he intended.

Valkyrie snapped his beak, but did not act surprised, carefully tucking whatever he hid further out of sight.

Could this be the thief plaguing London?

The birdman moved about with ease and used ways known only by rats and birds. Aerysleigh narrowed his gaze. Basil mentioned trained mice when speaking of the Cinder burglaries.

"Here now, show me what you have," Aerysleigh said, breaking his rapier from its sheath. The Valkyrie was known to rages, as were many of the chemically altered.

The chap hunched away, eyes downcast, unwilling to show his hands, but also unwilling to fight. Aerysleigh clicked his sword back into rest and held up his hands.

"I won't hurt you. I'm curious as to what you have." *Not a trait encouraged in St. Drogo* he remembered a soft voice telling him. He let a breath out, and with it his tension.

The Valkyrie eyed him but did not move. Realising the mask made him look suspicious to one that would not wear one, Aerysleigh removed it.

The fellow instantly relaxed. "C-I-N-D-E-R F-R-I-E-N-D," he

clacked.

At least, Aerysleigh thought it was what he said in Morse code, but it made no sense. He started to shake his head, then stopped. If the fellow knew Cinder, thought him a friend, perhaps he could help track the thief down. Before he could deny or affirm the charge, The Valkryrie opened his coat and brought out his treasure.

Aerysleigh let out his breath. "A bird?"

"P-R-E-T-T-Y C-I-N-D-E-R F-I-X L-E-G-." He clacked.

Definitely misunderstanding the bloke.

Either that or his Morse Code had rusted over completely. Still, he leaned over the proffered pigeon. The avian lay quietly in the Birdman's large hands, completely trusting some may call a monster. It arched its neck into the caressing fingers. The Valkyrie allowed Aerysleigh to lean close and view the metal prosthesis attached just below the bird's knee. At the end of the artificial leg was a perfect foot. It did not open and close but would provide balance and support. Aerysleigh shifted his body so the gaslight's illumination revealed more. Though crafted for a bird, the workmanship was exquisite, down to the little claws etched into the edge of the metal toes. After spending a night pouring over this lady's work, he knew exactly who made this.

"You mean Miss Ella did this for you?" Her kindness astounded him. Not only did she work all night with humans needing attention, she took the time to care for a bird who most likely wouldn't live the year out. *Could the woman be more saintly?*

"P-R-E-T-T-Y L-A-D-Y" The Valkryie agreed. "N-O B-I-T-E"

"I should think not," Aerysleigh agreed, but then his attention was already diverted to the doors of St. Drogo.

She is *here.*

Perhaps he should step in after all. Ask her about the Valkyrie and his garbled Morse code.

He looked towards the disappearing back of his partners. He could make a quick visit, just to make sure all was well in the cathedral.

At that moment the alarm sounded at the station three blocks away on Bacon Street calling nearby constables to come to the aid.

A Cinder strike!

Aerysleigh took one more glance at the cathedral, then replaced his mask and hurried away. No sense letting Basil think him a shirker. Still, a little part of him wanted to stay at St. Drogo and find the 'pretty lady' who mended broken birds.

Chapter Twenty-Five

The Crime

Aerysleigh tossed down the reports with a growl and stared across the room where Basil worked behind his desk.

"No luck?" his friend asked.

"'Tis the same at every crime scene. Unexplained escapes. Impossible entries. The sophisticated equipment required that would take a bloke over six feet tall and twelve stone to pack. However, judging on the small spaces utilised by the thief, there is no way he could be that size."

He leaped to his feet and paced to and fro. "Then there are the mouse prints. Mouse prints! Does he employ a trained army of the rodents to do his bidding?"

"Perhaps an animal charmer," offered Basil dryly.

Aerysleigh ignored him. "This is someone who knows their way in and out, and yet, all they pilfer are specific jewels, sometimes leaving those more valuable as though constrained by a list of some sort. Besides the occasional papers, of course." He glanced up at Basil's continued silence and wry expression. "With the deaths and disappearances, I can't see why we are even focusing on this case."

Basil set his pen in the inkwell and sat back, eyeing his friend curiously. "Well, for one, because you asked. Remember? You thought it sounded diverting. Is this no longer true?"

"It is, but I knew it was the only one you would let me pursue.

Safe. As if I need safe," he grumbled. "But there were other things you mentioned that day too. The blood in the streets, strange occurrences. I felt it last night. Something is out there."

"Yes," Basil agreed. "and those instances pile up higher and higher, most with even less clues than the Cinder files. However, the incidents appear to strike the darkest parts of town, Dorset street and the like."

"You mean the places that the police are loathe to go?" St. Drogo seemed to be the edge of some invisible line.

Basil shuffled his papers without seeing them. "It is a dangerous place, but we go where we are needed." He looked up sharply. "You haven't been this prickly in a long time. What is it, old chap? Your mother after you again?"

Aerysleigh sighed and threw himself back into the chair, glaring sullenly at his own stack of reports. "I met a girl."

Basil grinned. "Ahhh."

"What is 'ah' supposed to mean? It's not some romantic interest." *No, just smelled of sunshine and smoke.* Made him look around every corner, poke around in the mustiest corners of the older museums looking for her. He'd frightened a few of the curators when he came from a dark corner, hoping one of the fusty old men to be someone much younger and blonder.

"No?"

Lost in his thoughts he nearly forgot the conversation. "No! I thought I'd impress her, talk about working on the Cinder case, and she upbraided me for my lack of sight into the true travesties happening under Scotland Yard's very nose."

"Sounds like a shrew. Did you meet her at one of your mother's required functions? An activist of sorts? Perhaps she was trying to impress *you*?"

"Yes. No. I mean. I *did* meet her at the garden party at the museum." *And at St. Drogo* "But I sneaked off and she did too."

"Followed you?"

"No. I frightened her. She had no idea of my presence. But we got to talking, she chastised me, and then she took off."

"As in ran away?"

"Yes. That is what I said. Why are you acting as though I am speaking gibberish?"

Basil raised an eyebrow at him and Aerysleigh threw up his hands. "Alright. So maybe it is a bit odd. But I've never met anyone like her, and I didn't even get her whole name."

Except the one from St. Drogo, Ella, which struck him as only part of a name. He didn't know why he refrained from mentioning to his friend that this intriguing lady could be found at a modified sanctuary and the only Catholic church in town. He rubbed the ear with a slight hearing loss. "You know how it goes." He caught Basil's smile. "My curiosity is not romantic in nature, you cad. Can one not be intrigued by a girl without everyone trying to marry me off?"

"If I were your mother, I'd say no."

"But you're not, you're my friend."

Basil stood abruptly. "Well then, as your friend I say let's get some fresh air and go look at the latest Cinder strike." He shook his head sadly. "For as much as I hate to say it, the peerage is raising a ruckus and demanding all commissioners to focus every bit of manpower on solving these crimes. The others will have to be done in our spare time."

Aerysleigh snorted. From working closely with Basil the last few months, he learned time was in short supply for all of the police organization.

"Besides, I have two of my best on it. You remember Quin Kerney and Meares Roorke?"

Aerysleigh nodded, reaching for his coat. "Very well then. But I think more resources should be focused on the heinous crimes you mentioned."

Basil stared at him strangely as they walked out of the door. "What is it?"

"You *are* the crown prince, Aerysleigh."

Aerysleigh paused. To admit to such a thing would be to make it real. To stop playing this game he had immersed himself in and seize the reins of power, to make a difference. But no, that is what his brother had done. He would not give in to the pressure to be the next Prince Robby. He growled and pushed past his friend. He wished he could speak to his father as he once had. In fact, he determined to try.

But first... "Let's go inspect that crime scene."

*****

Aerysleigh examined the boot prints discovered by an observant gardener a few hours after the burglary of the city home of the Marquis Rothmundath. The mysterious tracks puzzled him but revealed more information than ever found at any other site. He squatted to take a closer look—if only he could unravel them. The footprints, two side by side in the hedge insinuated the burglar stood and waited.

For what? A ride up?

The muddy impressions faced the stone wall which led the detectives to assume some sort of apparatus lifted him from the ground. The thief seemed to have a gift for gadgets. However, an inexplicable gut feeling made Aerysleigh focus his attention. Something odd about them.

He rubbed his face. Perhaps he *was* going barmy over a girl after all. Even now he saw her in the slim outline of the print. So much for the theory this was a tall fellow. He traced the outline. One was creased precisely at the ball of the foot, the left impression deeper and more pronounced.

"Ho there, Aerysleigh," called Basil from the roof. "The stone here is disturbed. I'll wager supper at the club our thief used a grappling hook."

"From this angle?" Aerysleigh demanded. "To get a good arc on the throw the bloke must have stood further away."

"Supper, eh?"

"Prove it first."

"Come up then."

"One moment." He turned back to his examination. Cinder stood here and threw—no fired a hook—for he never really doubted Basil's deduction. Though he worked a desk job, his department led the force in solved crimes. Basil visited and worked the cases as though they were personal, following the progress of his detectives and making his own observations. The fellow was brilliant when it came to making deductions.

Aerysleigh followed the path to the back door, knowing the prints weren't going to explain themselves. About half way to the roof a thought struck him, and he ran the rest of the way, climbing through an attic window to join Basil at the false parapet.

"His foot!" he blurted, leaning on the stone to catch his breath.

Basil nodded and pointed at the stone and the marks of a hook. "See there. You owe me lunch, old man."

Aerysleigh waved his words away. "Of course, I knew you were right all along. But his foot, it sits deeper in the mud and creases at an unexpected point because it is heavier, perhaps special made boots?"

Basil stroked his chin. "Fair enough, but there are boot makers on every corner."

"But few specialise in this type of work and would be well known to those needing this type of expertise."

"True. I'll have the men look into it." Basil eyed him. "So, did the case take your mind off the girl as you hoped?"

"No, blast it."

Basil laughed. "Come then, and we will worry about it over a good rack of lamb. Surely, she can't be that difficult to find. You say she is educated? Outspoken? and a lady? There cannot be many such creatures in London."

Aerysleigh nodded in agreement, but Cinder was also a unique individual and look at the difficulty they had finding him. He didn't hold out much hope for tracking down the girl either unless she wanted to be found.

Chapter Twenty-Six

An Idea

Ella set her bag of baubles in front of Judith and stepped away. Her eyes downcast, features carefully arranged into bland submission. The last thing she needed was to betray her true thoughts of disgust and anger. She shuddered to think this was now her life—servant to a traitor, spy, and mad scientist—but there it was.

Judith hefted the velvet purse, then spilled the glittering contents onto the small table. "Good. You were unseen?"

"Of course." A shiver of fear raced up her spine at the memory of running through the dark from the unknown beast.

Judith glanced at her sharply. "There were troubles?"

"No," Ella said. "It is just becoming more difficult," she paused. "More dangerous."

Judith expression twisted into one of dark amusement. "Yes, I can see where the body snatchers from the medical schools would consider you quite the prize." At Ella's look of surprise, she chuckled. "You think that I do not stay abreast of the news?"

"Well, no. There are...monsters." She finally managed to say.

Her stepmother waved her concerns away, but the smile lingered. "Poppycock. No more now than before."

Why hadn't she seen it before? If her stepmother, a German

agent, could walk in society and conduct her experiments under the very noses of the aristocracy, what would keep others of her ilk from doing the same?

"Next on your list—" Judith continued.

Blame it on her exhaustion and fear from the previous night, but all manners deserted her, and Ella blurted. "So soon?"

Judith stroked her pocket where Ella assumed she imprisoned Philippe until her successful return—the threat clear. "Do you have a difficulty?" Her stepmother asked in a sugar sweet tone.

Ella clenched her fists. "No, ma'am." If not for her friends...the thought died before she could fully form it. But she had friends, and though few, they were her life line to sanity, and she could not afford to lose another. Her arm trembled. She reached across her body to hold it still, unwilling to fumble for the nerve rejuvenator and betray her upset.

"Good. Prince Aerysleigh's secretary is Alfred Peeny—tight fisted, closed mouthed individual unwilling to take reasonable bribes. I want you to obtain a copy of the prince's social engagements."

Like every mention of the prince all thoughts in Ella's head came to a screeching halt. "Pardon?"

"I want to know where he is going to be. Besides the usual soirees and times at the gentleman's club, I want to know the very streets he walks down."

Once again, a chill raced down Ella's spine, but it had nothing to do with the evil in the streets. No. Evil sat right in front of her. With that sort of information, Judith could have Prince Aerysleigh kidnapped—assassinated—anything. Her stepmother continued to talk though Ella's mind remained on the prince. "Places where it would be likely for a young lady to run into the man. It is time for my daughters to earn the years invested in their education." Ella's silence must have continued too long, for Judith glanced up sharply. "Do you understand?"

Ella swallowed hard. "Yes, ma'am. But—"

Judith lifted an eyebrow. "Yes?"

"Princes don't marry commoners," she burst out, more from her own pain than anything else. She hated this attraction for the prince, but by Judith's expression she could see she stumbled horribly. Her stepmother took great pride in the beauty and training of her daughters and worked very hard at presenting them in society as one of the aristocracy, from the continent to be sure. But Ella knew Judith's background, as well as her father's penchant for marrying outside of the peerage.

However, Judith seemed to be in a forgiving mood. She dismissed Ella's protest with a superior sigh. "The king himself married a commoner, the daughter of a plantation owner and a half blood at that."

"Had he been crown prince at the time," Ella said slowly, "or even remotely in line to the throne, he never would have been allowed to marry for love. The complete annihilation of Queen Victoria's line elevated him suddenly, and after he had married."

"Do you presume to give me a history lesson, Ella."

Ella ducked her head. "No, ma'am."

"Then enough. Return to your duties. And get me that calender."

Ella exited swiftly to hide the sudden burn of anger in her cheeks. Her position prevented her from doing much, but at the very least she would not be the one to hand the prince to the enemy.

*****

"Father?" Aerysleigh took the skeletal hand in his own and leaned close. The limb trembled in his grip. He glanced at the Princess Ursula. "Has he spoken?"

"No, not today. Not for a long time," his widowed sister-in-law responded.

Even from the last time Aerysleigh visited his father, he could tell his condition worsened. The king's chest was wrapped in an iron box which pulled at his lungs to make breathing easier.

He raised his gaze to the royal surgeon, but the bearded man just shook his head. Queen Constantina had requested the presence of this esteemed doctor, long retired to his country manor, after everyone else gave up. He was known the world over for his wizardly with herbs. Even without a knighthood the patents on his medicinal concoctions guaranteed an income for his heir in perpetuity.

Sir Litton's muttonchops twitched at Aerysleigh's unspoken question. "No change, your highness."

Aerysleigh eyed the four centurion automatons around the room, the harsh smell of oil a nauseating blend with everything medicinal. Something had changed. Not only these new guards, but he had passed several human ones, most in the halls to his father's rooms.

The surgeon laid a hand on the princess' shoulder. "Perhaps you should retire, your highness."

Princess Ursula nodded and rose, the rustle of her black day dress competing with the background hiss of the breathing apparatus. Sir Litton watched her exit and then took Aerysleigh's arm and led him to a dark corner. "She comes daily, poor soul, to check on His Majesty and bring him tea."

"Why the guards?"

Sir Litton stared at him a long moment. "I have requested them. No natural malady keeps your father in this condition."

"What does then? What have you discovered?"

"Nothing substantial, but I suspect poison. A nerve agent of some sort. The King is fully cognisant, but the symptoms of paralysis, nausea, and the weakening of the muscles is not indicative of a fever as originally thought." The man stroked his moustache, rheumy eyes wandering as he contemplated. "No, I am almost positive both he and His Royal Highness Prince Robert have suffered an attack of the most dastardly type."

"Poison?" Aerysleigh echoed. "Who? How?"

Sir Litton motioned to the automatons. "I trust the guard to ferret out the assassin. Only the most trusted servants and guards are admitted. My job is to aid the king. Unfortunately, I fear I am running out of time. Though he fights to hold on, his majesty's symptoms worsen. Nothing I have tried has inhibited the deterioration."

Aerysleigh returned to his father's side and once again took his hand. "I am sorry, Father." He whispered. Here he was chasing Cinder and worried about his mother's marriage traps, when so much more was happening right under his nose. He needed to be more attentive to everything. His father stared straight ahead, unblinking.

Sir Litton stooped and used a dropper to moisten the king's eyes.

"What am I to do?" Aerysleigh whispered after the Royal Surgeon retreated to the corner. Even the most dismal battle never dismayed him as the situation he faced now. Almost imperceptibly his father's fingers tightened on his own. Joy ricocheted through him. "Sir Litton! He squeezed my fingers!"

The old man sitting in an overstuffed chair jumped from where he had nodded off. "Yes, your highness," he said. "Involuntary reflex, I believe."

Aerysleigh collapsed on his stool, deflated. But then the squeeze came again, and again. The pattern seemed to repeat in a way which suggested his father sought to communicate. He held his breath and counted. Squeeze-squeeze-squeeze. Pause. Squeeze-squeeze. Pause. Squeeze-squeeze.

"Sis?" He whispered, once against finding himself misunderstanding Morse Code. He never thought himself so deficient. However, he failed to interpret the Valkryie in front of St. Drogo correctly and now his father.

Maybe the twitches *were* involuntary. He sighed and began to extricate himself from his father's fingers. The king gripped him hard and fast. Aerysleigh gaze flew to his father's face but saw no change in the frozen expression.

Squeeze-squeeze-long hold-squeeze-squeeze.

No. Most definitely not involuntary.

"F." He said.

The squeezes continued.

"I-N-D. Find?" His father neither confirmed nor denied Aerysleigh's interpretation but continued.

"Find sister?"

He leaned back in the chair and passed his free hand over his patched eye. Once he had a sister. Perhaps his father lost track of time, back to when he had three children instead of two.

He rose to leave.

His father must be locked in a dream he sometimes wished he could join. However, the lurking automatons did give him an idea.

Chapter Twenty-Seven

The Dance

Though the armistice celebration was subdued by the king's lingering illness, fireworks bloomed above the fog and soot cover. The newspapers proclaimed the news, a welcome change from the redundancy of the stories to this point. Advertisements on every available post and wall shouted out— 'Prussia is finished!' 'Napoleon Sues for Peace!'

Though, as Proximus pointed out one night at The Fence, when one read the complete article, the headlines didn't tell the whole story. Prussia did not concede defeat, and most likely never would. The countries of Europe were taking a breather. And the only good news was Napoleon could not threaten Britain if allied with Britain in facing the Confederation of German States.

If the activity at Iron Crest could be believed, Prussia had not powered down—merely changed tactics.

Cinder shook her head, both at the naivety of her countrymen, and at the fact just a few months ago she might have believed the news herself. Was this victory all the gossips in the tea houses and gentleman's club proclaimed? No!

Ella closed her eyes to conjure the faces of her parents. *Would Mama and Papa had celebrated so prematurely?*

Having discovered what she knew of them, she doubted it. They would have known, as she did now, that the war was not over, just buried. She hated to admit her stepmother had been right. The aristocracy were blind to reality. Missing a few baubles became the subject of more animated conversation than the true dangers a foot.

Despite the armistice retiring Britain from several conflicts abroad, Judith continued her work, experimenting on her daughters and others behind closed doors. Ella saw little evidence of the sinister experiments her stepmother described in the past. However, couriers came at odd hours with deliveries from airships. More often than not, she found herself confined to the forge, Judith trusting only Myrtle to wait upon her and the girls.

Still, Judith required a great deal of money and sent Ella away when not locked in her room. Each robbery became increasingly difficult as the aristocracy took measures to protect their wealth. However, tonight may prove easier than the last.

Dr. Bon Hamlet also had favours to ask, the influx of destitute souls to St. Drogo continued unending. With an eye to relieving coughs suffered by so many, Ella, no Cinder, made stealthy visits to the opium dens. This took her to the docks, seedier and more dangerous areas, and not only from the mists. Each time her heart raced, and she jumped at shadows, but the beast did not give chase again. When the surgeon made her tincture from the stolen opiates and gave it to a child racked by a cough, it made it all worthwhile.

One evening, Dr. Bon Hamlet caught her arm. "I know this is much to ask of you, Ella."

Ella laid her palm on the lady's hand. The physician's face was drawn and tired, but as always, a fire burned behind those spectacles. "You know I will do anything to help," she said. Anything to atone for her mother's mistake.

"There is talk that the merchants will side with the Lords on the next vote before the Lower House." Dr. Bon Hamlet hesitated, something Ella found disconcerting and somewhat insulting.

She regularly stole for this woman, her freedom and loved ones at stake each and every time. What could her friend feel she not be told?

"I know you do not concern yourself with politics, but we must know where the merchants stand."

"Who needs to know?" Ella asked, curiosity getting the better of her.

Several people approached them in the hall, Dr. Bon Hamlet pulled Ella into an alcove under a Madonna statue. "You've heard of SPAMM? They champion the rights of modifieds."

Ella nodded. She knew this, even suspected it to be based within the halls of St. Drogo. She never enquired, in fact went out of her way not to discover any of the cathedral's numerous secrets beyond those necessary to complete her tasks. Best for everyone not to. What would happen if she knew sensitive information and Judith threatened her friends? She shuddered to think. Myrtle and the mice may not be considered human, but they were all she had.

"Find out, Ella, please. Your skills are unique, you can move in both society and poor—"

Ella shook her head. "Not society."

Dr. Bon Hamlet's face fell.

"But I will do what I can," Ella quickly added.

The surgeon hugged her. "Thank you."

*****

A few enquiries at the market confirmed a public dance at an assembly hall the following night. Borrowing a dress from The Fence, Ella prepared to masquerade as a merchant's daughter, a disguise she employed occasionally. However, it made her nervous to venture so audaciously into the public eye.

Tindale House was not a large affair, only holding a hundred people or so, but it was rowdy. The approaching season, the time when the land owners returned to their townhouses and brought an influx employment and business, made the merchant class inclined to celebrate.

Ella tugged at the bodice of her dress, lower cut than any she had ever worn, and adjusted the long velvet cloak to ensure it covered the set of straps supporting her modification. Even so the frock gaped unbecomingly. No doubt it fit more modestly the woman who pawned the gown, one with more generous assets than Ella possessed. Still, it could not be helped. She doubted anyone of a mind to notice an ill-fitting gown. It wasn't like she planned to dance.

People, carriages, and even an airship hovered over the assembly hall. She paused on the raised portico, listening and watching as though waiting for someone. She sensed a disquiet further down the winding streets, an occasional yell. Papers, hastily plastered to both lampposts and building facades, proclaimed a protest scheduled for this very night. Ella wavered in her decision to attend this dance.

Upon closer inspection the crowd pushing into the Tindale showed no worry. Eager faces glowed in the lamp light and voices rose and fell with excitement—not fear. Mind made up, Ella pulled the vial of her mother's perfume from her chatelaine and daubed a drop at her neck and wrist. *For luck.* Then she wove through the throng without touching, listening to the snippets of conversation.

The band played a lively two-step, and the floor vibrated with the footsteps of the enthusiastic dancers. She recognised several people from St. Drogo acting as servants tonight.

In hastily cobbled uniforms to hide modifications, they rushed food, but most often drink, to dancers already feeling the heat and close press of bodies. She did her best to avoid them, lingering on the outskirts of groups while eavesdropping. When someone gave her a curious look, she waved at no one in particular across the room and then moved away.

Often congregates of older men talked politics while their ladies and daughters danced with the younger men. Ella stood back to elbow with a few, as though watching the dancers, and gleaned as much information as possible. Tonight was no exception, though not in the way she planned.

Every third group seemed enamoured with the story of a merchant who distrusted the banks to the extent of keeping his fortune under his mistress' bed. The topic fascinated the oldest of gentleman to the youngest maid. Not the marches in the street for modified rights. Not the armistice. Not even a mention of the last sighting of Prince Aerysleigh, something Ella found particularly interesting for reasons she did not want to admit to herself.

"Right under his mattress?" a young lady shrieked with laughter, covering her mouth quickly at a rebuking glance from her mother.

Ella moved on.

"A veritable treasure, right in his own home. Hasn't he heard about Cinder? It's like an open invitation," said a moustached elder with a monocle. "Now, the Bank of England is where every intelligent man needs to deposit his funds. That Cinder thief will never break into their vault..."

Ella shook her head. It seemed everyone could be diverted with the smallest gossip. The whole affair made no sense.

After a few rounds, Ella noticed someone else moving in a fashion much like her own—only much more visible. Instead of on the outskirts of the knots of gossips, he positioned himself in the middle.

Ella paused at a pillar and watched for a moment. The fellow was tall with dark hair too long to be fashionable and tied back neatly. His dusky skin reminded her of someone. Too many hats and feathers blocked her eye line to get a clear view, so she moved, listening and watching. He talked to one or two people in one group, more people, especially young ladies, rushing to cluster around, but he did not tarry long nor ask anyone to dance. The ebb of the story dogged his path.

Ella crept along the edges of the room, keeping him in sight. She did not, however, keep close enough watch of her own position. A harried servant with a large tray rammed into her shoulder. She tripped on the overlong skirt and would have fallen if not for strong hands setting her to rights. She pulled away, afraid whoever touched her would feel the steel prosthesis. Though merchants were more open to the modifieds—in fact the store keepers, captains, and goods dealers were their biggest employers—Ella would rather not be identified by her limb in public.

When she turned to apologise, a burning dark eyed gazed and amused grin froze the words on her lips.

"Tinker Maybelle," he teased. Ella straightened and prepared to curtsy, nearly falling when her boot caught the hem again.

"Your highness—"

He caught her arm. "Not here. I am incognito tonight."

She winced at his touch and eyed his supposed costume. True— he did not appear as he often had of late. The dreadlocks were gone, his hair smooth. He wore a charcoal coloured coat, though not the usual grade for a dandy, it was of the latest fashion with wide velvet lapels and a string tie. Though well cut, it was obviously not his— perhaps borrowed for the evening's festivities. Despite the attempt at anonymity, eyes still watched his every move from behind fans and raised cups.

She touched her temple. "You took your eye patch off."

The prince grinned, his brown eye flashing with humour while the other stayed a determined milky white. "It actually dissuades people from looking directly at me." He spread his hands, "thus the incognito part."

She sniffed. Some modifieds used their disability to their advantage in begging or working, others hid it, she doubted few, even the prince himself, could go incognito with one. She caught the curious looks flashed not so subtly their way. "I think people may be humouring you." With was why she needed to move, her position at Prince Aerysleigh's side drew too much attention. She pulled her cloak over her shoulders to hide her dreadful frock and wished it weren't mud brown before she caught herself.

"You were the one spreading the gossip," she said with a sudden burst of insight. "But why?"

The prince arched an eyebrow at her, but the cavalier expression didn't quite work. "Gossip? No, merely an entertaining story to pass a tedious time."

Ella cocked her head. "But you are not required to be here..." Just because she did not procure the calendar for Judith didn't mean she hadn't taken a peek when the prince's secretary put his portfolio down at a private club. It helped to know a good many of the servants about London. Unless, of course, he had come for his own amusement. She wouldn't put it past him. This was the crown prince who liked to spend his spare time chasing Cinder after all.

He bowed to ask her to dance. "Would you—?"

"No," she interrupted, the sharp outburst getting even more attention. She quickly added, "I was just leaving."

"But most people come to a dance to, well, dance," reasoned Prince Aerysleigh.

He did have a point. It would look odd for her not dance, now that she had drawn some attention that is. She almost put her hand in his.

A commotion near the door turned heads away. The arrival of some lordling perhaps, but it brought her back to her right mind. Hopefully it would distract the prince as well. It did not, but when she looked up, it certainly drew hers. Her breath left her lungs in a rush.

"Judith," she whispered.

Chapter Twenty-Eight

The Riot

Why is she here?
The secretary. Ella's stepmother must have used her own information network to obtain the prince's schedule and somehow read between the lines and figured him to be at the Tindale House. By the way her hungry eyes scanned the crowd, Ella knew Judith was hunting.

Nothing would stop her stepmother's quest to throw at least one of her daughters at a royal marriage, and Ella stood right next to Judith's quarry. Flanking her stepmother were Isabeau and Aurelia. Both girls dressed well beyond what a local dance called for.

Their whale bone corsets nipped in their waists to tiny proportions made even smaller by flared skirts of sapphire and emerald silk. The sisters looked like jewels among stones. Despite their beauty, Ella detected their unhappiness at being put on display in the way they refused to meet the curious gazes and hid behind their mother. The Steelhaugh family jewels burned like fire in their hair, at their throats and ears.

Ella dropped her gaze.

I need to get away before she sees me.

Isabeau's dark head lifted as though scenting the air. In no time her uncanny ability to find Ella would home in on her position. If Judith spied her as well, mingling above the servant station she had imposed—or worse, if she saw Ella with the prince—the consequences would be dear.

Ella shifted her weight, leaning towards the shadows of the wall. "I have to leave now."

"By all means let me escort—"

For the second time in the matter of minutes she cut Aerysleigh off. "No." She cringed at her lack of manners.

Isabeau's gaze snapped her direction as though she heard that single word, the sudden movement gaining Aurelia's attention as well. The older sister jerked her chin towards the back entrance. Ella needed no more prodding. She turned and bolted into the kitchen.

Pots clattered behind her as she pushed past the staff. "Sorry. So sorry. Excuse me, please." At last, she burst from the servant's door into a wide alley.

The stench of chamber pots, grease, and horse droppings filled her nostrils and brought blinding tears.

A shoulder rammed against hers out of the dark. Unable to stop her forward momentum, she sprawled into the source of the pungent odours.

"Beg your par—" she snapped. But no one paid her any mind— not the fellow who had bowled her over, nor the rest of the mob pushing past. Torches lit the alley to display men and women carrying placards and marching shoulder to shoulder with grim expressions. Some brazenly displayed their prosthetics. Automatons of all sorts accompanied the marchers. Night boys with their steam powered offal bins. A tea cart clattered over the cobbles and a soup pot on stilted legs from one of the boarding houses. Even a decommissioned enforcer.

But Ella had no more time to gawk.

A knee knocked against her head, and she rolled to avoid the dozens of tromping boots, thoroughly soaking the frock in more refuse.

A low chant swelled above the music leaking through the windows of the dance hall— 'Representation for all'. Ella pressed her back against the wall opposite and attempted to regain her feet. A familiar strong hand appeared to help her stand.

"The cads," the prince hissed, "Are you all right?"

Ella brushed at the borrowed gown. Proximus would not be pleased about the state of his wares. "I'm fine." She tried to push him towards the door of the kitchen. She knew these people. An aristocrat, even one incognito in a borrowed coat, would not be welcome. Besides, she could not be anywhere near the man with her stepmother on the prowl.

Her good intentions came to nought. The stubborn man did not budge. The wave of people grew thicker. Caught up in the throng, Ella and Aerysleigh were pushed inexorably along. Several elbows dug into her side as she fought against the current. She stumbled again, falling into the prince. He wrapped an arm around her and hefted her upright.

Ella couldn't help but put her arm around his waist and move in closer. She tried to blame it on the crowd. However, somewhere in her steadfast denial she wanted nothing more than to be right where she was.

The borrowed slippers sank into something she was loathe to identify, although it probably already decorated her gown. They turned the corner onto main street and marched toward the front of Tindale House with purpose.

Some of the younger fellows in the assembly hall dashed to the portico to observe the commotion. Horses neighed at the sudden push of humanity and one unruly colt reared in its traces. Both men and drivers hollered at the chanting crowd, pushing the rally participants away from their vehicles.

Ella tried to worm her way to the back of the crowd, determined to get away. But the press of bodies came to a standstill, placards lifted high, and the chant growing. They reached their destination, determined to sway the vote of the merchants with their rally.

"Hey, metal face, come give us a kiss," a young swell jeered from the safety of his friends.

Elders peered from the windows with disapproving eyes. Ella kept her head lowered and turned sideways to keep her face out of the light. *What if Judith spied her here?* Ella searched for the carriage bearing the Steelhaugh coat of arms but found the crowd too dense.

The prince, obviously of like mind about escape, pushed against a fellow behind them. "Move aside," he ordered in a voice she was sure he used to command his airship. He prodded a dock worker with his cane. The big man turned slowly, and Ella swallowed a sudden premonition of fear.

Drax.

And he looked like he just came from an opium den.

He focused on the smaller chap with the cane, but Aerysleigh did not back down. Ella grabbed the dock worker's arm. "Drax," she said. "Please let us through."

Her soft words drew the big man's attention and his expression cleared. "Mistress?"

"Yes," she said in a low voice, "could you make room?"

With an effort the mountainous fellow took one step, then

another, clearing a path only big enough for Ella. She slipped by, but he put out an arm to stop Aerysleigh from following.

"Not you."

"Drax, please." Once again, he blinked, slow to understand, and then lifted his arm. Ella grabbed the prince's hand before his pride demanded satisfaction and made her way to a brick edifice at the rear of the crowd. She braced against the rough wall to catch her breath and assessed her surroundings.

"Merchants and Modifieds unite!" The crowd continued to chant. Hoisted signs called for 'equal rights for modifieds' and simply 'metal against 648'. The curious and the bored alike clogged the street. Some joined in the chant, others jeered. There was no way out. Gradually Ella became aware of the warmth in her palm and realised she still clenched the prince's hand. She tried to let go.

He held on tightly. "Stay close," he said. "We need to find a way out of this mess. It's not safe for you here."

Wings fluttered above and every person, modified or not, looked up. The Valkyrie floated from one building to the next with arms outstretched, a diaphanous material connected from leg to arm like wings.

He clacked out a code with his beak. "B-E-W-A-R-E."

Both crowds cringed. A feather bedecked lady highlighted by the lantern light screamed at the sight, falling against a loose knot of her friends closest the door. Those of the rally found their courage and cheered the frightening modified, embracing his insanity.

One brave fellow from the dance, well into his cups, raised a tankard. "Go home, freaks."

The crowd chanted, still peaceful, then the drunkard threw his mug. It bounced on the cobbles, showering the boots and dresses of those on the front lines.

The marchers surged and jostled, the determined chant turning into something ugly and low. Elbows and backs pushed the prince against Ella, pinning her against the wall. Pressed in close by the crowd, she wondered if he could feel the racing of her heart. She looked up to find him staring bemusedly down at her.

"You smell of jasmine and ash," he said slowly.

Ella swallowed. *Better than offal and vegetable parings.*

He leaned closer, taking a deep breath where her pulse thundered above the gaping bodice of the borrowed frock. She wanted to push away, truly she did, but found herself leaning closer.

Though feeling dazed herself, Ella regained her wits quickly. She pulled at the fabric and found the strength to sidle away.

The marchers produced staves, a few onlookers hefted bottles, while the merchants appeared ready to barricade themselves in the Tindale House and fight.

This was so wrong. The modifieds and the merchants need each other.

A fight would cause bad feelings that would allow the passage of the damaging laws Dr. Bon Hamlet feared.

"Do you have a pistol?" she asked Aerysleigh without preamble.

He nodded. "Just a derringer, its—"

She forced her hand from his, the distance adding clarity to her thoughts. "Fire it into the air. Stop this nonsense."

The downtrodden servant was gone, the quick-thinking Cinder now in her place. She fumbled at the chatelaine—why couldn't women of fashion simply wear belts? —until her fingers found a folded knife, she removed a black shirttail from the bloke in front of her, working quickly while the prince raised his derringer.

It misfired with a sputtered pop.

"Jammed," he growled. Lowering the weapon, he strained to see the mechanics in the dark. "Wish I had my goggles right about now."

Cinder tossed the bit of cloth at him. "Here, put this on." She took the tiny firearm. "These things are useless. I'm surprised a soldier bothers to carry such an ineffective weapon."

"It's a specialised design. Besides, I can't very well carry a rifle, now could I?" he teased. He held up the scrap of cloth. "What is this?"

Her fingers moved smoothly, clearing the jam and checking the load. "An eye patch, of course. The people need their prince to stop this before the situation becomes irretrievable." She paused and glanced up. "Go on, put it on."

With the hint of a smile, Aerysleigh obeyed. She shoved the pistol at him. "Here. Make some noise."

*****

Aerysleigh found himself taking orders from the cheeky maid. A long time had passed since anyone bossed him about in such a manner. Amused despite the situation, he tied on the foul-smelling patch and accepted the weapon. Bottles broke, cabbages and potatoes from nearby carts pelted the Tindale House. Sword canes flashed in the gas lamps from the pillared portico.

Battle.

It had been a while, but the intensity filled his limbs with a liveliness missing of late.

"Stay here," he said to Ella. "You should be safe."

She scorched him with a look which told him she would do no such thing and fiddled with something in the sleeve of that deplorable frock. These people were hers and she did not fear them. *But she should.* Crowds were unpredictable things, as the tumble in the alley already proved.

"Please," he added, suspicious of her frown. As much as he wanted to put the world on hold, to parry words and discover more about this intriguing maid—the scent she wore, where she came from, and so much more—he could not. The crowd surged forward.

He drew in a deep breath, raised the pistol and fired. The crowd ignored the pop, though a few heads turned his way. However, this modified pistol had a few surprises. He fired again, and again, and again.

Finally, the majority of people quieted and turned.

"Enough," he roared. The crowd parted and he strode through the gap between the two sides. Despite the intensity of the situation, he risked a glance backwards.

The maid had disappeared.

*****

The wall groaned under Cinder's weight, the moorings responsible for securing the edifice to the rest of the structure threatening to fail. Crumbling mortar and bits of stone fell into her eyes. The spring-loaded grappling hook, a light one kept in reserve in a compartment in her prosthesis, slipped in its grasp. More stone showered down.

How did this tenement harbour residents as rickety as it was?

A sideways glance revealed broken panes through which wafted mildew scented air. Maybe the building didn't do such a good job after all. Ella gave the rope a quick jerk to speed the spring mechanism along. The thin rope whirred, and she rose quickly. Near the roof, she ducked a sagging clothesline, unbleached trousers still smelling of sheep and raining sooty water, brushed along the front of her frock.

I am never going to get this dress clean enough to return.

At last, she pulled herself over a squat wall. With little wind this night, factory smoke draped the shoulders of nearby buildings like a funeral veil. Wishing for a mask, she turned and peered through irritated eyes at the raucous crowd below.

The prince strode through the seething mass, a bright flame

among the darkness. His dusky face, half covered by the makeshift eye patch and alive with the thrill of the moment, revealed the blood of slaves and field hands from the sugar plantation.

Ella marvelled at the fact that he walked as a prince among these people. An event made possible by the sudden demise of Queen Victoria just days after her coronation. One of the first coordinated chemical attacks from the continent also removed all those in obvious line for the throne.

Desperate searches ultimately unearthed a royal cousin eligible to rule. He lived in obscurity running a sugar plantation and had married a woman of mixed blood. The new king immediately pressed a law before the houses to free all slaves. Ironically, the inevitable ebb and flow of politics and life, produced a new class of slaves—the modifieds.

It seemed only right that Aerysleigh would be the one to champion them. It occurred to Cinder that keeping her head down and doing as told for the protection of herself and her friends, may not be the right path. Perhaps she should do more.

She couldn't help but compare her lurking and thieving to the courageous mien of Prince Aerysleigh shouldering his way through the angry crowd as though on the deck of an airship. He held his shoulders square, his very demeanour demanding and holding the attention of all. Compared to his forthright actions, her small penance of working at St. Drogo seemed mild.

As the prince reached the steps and raised his hands for silence, the angry shouts dissipated, Cinder realised this is what the people needed. Someone to boldly take their side. Somebody they could follow and love.

When the barrage of rotten vegetables waned, the prince spoke. "Please," he implored, "this is not the way to accomplish anything. Are we like the Colonies in their Civil War that we would rise up against our own? Take to fighting in the streets? Turn our beloved city into a battleground? We are a nation of laws and just representation."

"There are no laws for us," yelled a soot-faced miner with shoulders protected by metal. Protective eye wear wrinkled his brow, a candle encased in glass at the centre.

The crowd rumbled.

"The merchants treat us like slaves," cried a woman,

The government takes our children and sends them to war or worse…"

"The medical school," supplied someone else.

"Or the mines. We have no way to protect them—or ourselves."

The prince's dark eyes moved over the people, silencing the murmurs with a look. "I will represent you," he yelled.

Cinder's heart swelled with pride and though he continued to speak the thumping in her chest filled her ears. Few aristocrats could claim his particular position, having both been served and served himself in the military. Along with the support of Lord Stillingfleet, she felt assured the modifieds would be heard.

A bright colour from the doorway of Tindale House caught her attention. Judith pushed through the crowd dragging Aurelia behind her. The Prince's words soothed the mob, the people relaxed and meandered away.

Judith touched his arm and he turned with a bow. Cinder's stepmother pulled the younger daughter forward, motioning for Isabeau. Despite their slightly unhappy expressions, her sisters' severe beauty was enough to turn anyone's head. By the way Aerysleigh nodded and smiled it was obvious he was not oblivious to their elegant appeal.

The girls curtsied, all charm and grace, if not somewhat cool. Judith motioned towards the Tindale House where the music began once more—no doubt encouraging Prince Aerysleigh to choose a daughter for a dance.

Ella found she could watch no longer and determined to head to St. Drogo where she could be of use. Still, something made her hesitate, to pause in those noxious clouds of factory smoke.

The prince made a courtly gesture for the women to proceed him and then looked as though he would follow. He paused and turned back, peering towards the wall where he left her. A faint smile quirked his lips.

He raised his gaze upwards and she fervently wished he could pierce the gloom, to see her watching above the crowd—to know she had not abandoned him. But the sooty fog bounced the light back to the street and though she could see him, he could not see beyond the first story. Finally, he turned and followed her stepmother.

Cinder dashed a tear from her cheek and blamed it on the foul smoke. How she yearned to drop all pretence, to be like of her stepsisters in their beautiful gowns and artfully arranged hair. To clasp his hand once more. She looked at the mud brown frock made obscene with grease drippings and offal, the straps of her prosthesis clearly showing now. Metal glinted through several rips in her sleeve.

She removed her gloves, revealing the metal hand. This was her reality. No prince, not even one with one eye, who had fought beside and for people like her, would voluntarily hold these hands. Not flesh and blood, but metal and bone.

She sighed, wanting to thump her head against the brick. She was Cinder, a thief.

Nothing more.

Chapter Twenty-Nine

A Trap

Cinder moved carefully on the widow's walk of the older home, grimacing every time a pebble stirred. A rickety airship dock rose above the flat roof. At her touch, the whole structure groaned. Whoever built the thing once had wealth, but no more. The house fairly wilted with neglect. The gardens grew wild and fierce, the gravel drive to the front entrance choked with weeds. Still a twist of smoke curled from the kitchen chimney and a few candles glowed in the servant's quarters. Perhaps care takers for a family gone abroad?

It did not fit the narrative of a rich man with money under a mattress—unless, of course, his thrifty ways sacrificed his home. Although doubtful, it mattered not. Even though she suspected a trap, even voiced her objections to her stepmother, the avaricious fiend insisted. Simple enquiries led Cinder to this declining estate near May Hill.

She sent Flora to investigate the rooms down one of the inactive flues and settled back to wait. She pulled the vial with her mother's perfume from her belt and dabbed a drop on her flesh wrist. Her fingers trembled a mite, so she took an injection of nerve rejuvenator, adjusting her equipment and generally fiddling while she waited.

Time passed slowly, the little mouse taking longer than any time before. When the metal body finally slipped into sight, Cinder let out a breath of relief.

"What took so long?" she asked.

The mouse twitched her metal whiskers and ran a paw down one to remove a wisp of cobweb.

Cinder caught it on a finger and looked closer. A heavy pall of smoke covered the moon making the night crypt dark, so she held the webbing to the light cast by the eyes of the two mice. "Is this from the chimney or the rooms?"

Flora stopped her grooming and regarded Cinder with bright eyes. Phillipe rasped a metal squeak from the widow's walk and disappeared down the east side of the house.

A small balcony jutted over a wild hedge garden once groomed to a classical pattern. Cinder rappelled down and peered through the window. One small candle rested on a night table, wick nearly spent. A fire burned down to coals cast the room in a scarlet glow. Cinder tried the door and found it unlocked.

So easy. Too easy.

She eased inside, straining her ear to catch any sounds of life, and tried the bed first. She ran her hand between the chain spring mattress and the horsehair covering then under the spread.

Nothing.

Lighting a match, she checked the mildew smelling wardrobe, only to find moths and an old rat's nest. She studied the chamber's panelling—straight forward wood with no artwork covering the plain walls. *Perhaps I needed to try another room.* Mousey activity under the bed drew her attention before she could make a decision.

Flora and Phillipe tugged at a small trunk hidden in the shadows behind the large foot, attempting to pull it into the open.

Cinder reached out a hand. "Stop."

Too late. Wires attached to the back of the trunk thrummed and alarm bells tinkled in the far-off recesses of the house.

Footsteps thumped in the distance, hollow and wooden sounding as though someone hurried up the servant's stair.

"The bell, Basil, hurry," said a voice Cinder recognised.

"I think you have Cinder on the brain, your highness. In this house, it could very well have been a rodent."

"It was a small chime to be sure, but a chime all the same. A thief wouldn't just pull the thing as hard as they could, would they?"

That was exactly what they had done.

"Aerysleigh, you are too impatient. A good constable does not chase down every shadow." Basil's voice sounded far away, but Prince Aerysleigh seemed to be moving swiftly.

With no time to escape, Cinder hurried to the drapes covering the balcony door and had just enough time to duck behind them as the bedroom door flew open.

Through a small crack she could see the prince standing in the centre of the room, arms akimbo. His friend, the police commissioner, limped in behind, much of his weight supported on a cane. "See there," he said. "Nothing." But his sharp eyes peered into every corner with the wariness of a soldier.

Prince Aerysleigh walked to the bed. "Do you smell that?"

"You mean the noxious bay?"

A loud sniff near the closet made Cinder cringe. "No, more like...a recently struck match. Something else as well. Ash?" The comment made her want to smell her clothes. She had made her customary exit from Iron Crest through the chimney to retrieve the heliobike, however, she never thought such a manoeuvre might give her away.

Phillipe chose that minute to make a dash towards the open door, perhaps thinking himself abandoned. The prince's gaze followed the movement. "What is that? A mouse? We've seen mouse prints at all the other burglarised locations, did we not?"

"Indeed, we did."

Prince Aerysleigh cut off the mouse's escape route with a quick stomp, so Phillipe skittered towards the bed instead. With the men's attention on the metal creature, Cinder scooped Flora up and slipped out the door, wincing as her satchel thudded on the jamb with a sullen thud.

"Hurry, the balcony!" Basil yelled.

Cinder grabbed the dangling rope, gave it a quick jerk to activate the spring-loaded mechanism, and floated towards the roof. A whoosh of air warned her to look down. The face of the startled prince stared up after her.

"Quick," he called. "You catch the mouse. I'm headed to the roof."

Knowing each second mattered now, Cinder snapped out her vaulting pole. The stable roof was a good distance away, the landing likely to hurt, but it did have a nice slope to help the takeoff of her heliobike. It lay ready and beckoning on the shingled ridge, but she paused. She couldn't leave without Phillipe.

As though conjured, the wayward mouse appeared on the ledge and squeaked.

"You naughty rascal," she scolded, and scooped him into the bag with the Flora. Positioning the satchel on her back, she hurried to the far side of the flat roof. The trap door burst open so close to her feet she nearly stepped on the head of the prince poking out.

"Halt, thief!"

Did he honestly think that she would stop? She needed to buy some time. *I can't afford a chase over London.* A heliobike was too easy to track and the cover provided by smoggy night would make negotiating chimneys and rooftops difficult. And of course, she couldn't fly straight towards Iron Crest.

Vaulting was out as well.

Though this particular roof was flat with a lovely atrium, the lawns and a stone wall separated the estate from its neighbours. Even if she managed to gain those roof tops, several had sharply pitched angles covered with treacherous slate. Each footstep needed be considered carefully.

Counting down the seconds it would take him to reach her, Cinder pulled extra twine from her pocket and gave it to Flora. "Tie it off, trip and bind him," she whispered into the copper ear.

The orders were succinct and simple, but there was no way to know if they would be carried out as she envisioned. She set the mouse in the shadows and drew her rapier to taunt her pursuer into thinking he had her cornered, rolling her pole towards the edge she planned to depart from.

Without apparent hesitation, Aerysleigh drew his own weapon and approached without taking the time to assess his surroundings. Not that he would have seen the tiny mouse waiting to trap him, but still, an ex-soldier ought to be more wary of a thief actually stopping when ordered.

The conversation of weapons began with a clank and a spark. Cinder grunted as she slid the weight of his blow aside. He held nothing back from the match and was incredibly strong and fast. Despite her extensive training, she knew in an instant if she did not do something quickly, she would lose this match.

Her fencing tutor had been a master, however, she only ever practised with him. A slight, wiry fellow, he was a good match for her. But Prince Aerysleigh was tall, his reach long and his arms strong from years on the airships. How well she remembered the feeling of safety under his protective arm in the raucous just a few nights before. His tightly braided hair was tied back into businesslike braids, a patch over his injured eye. He smiled with the assurance of victory.

The cad knows I'm struggling! The realisation added a quickness to her feet and mechanical hand not there before.

Once his blade glazed down hers and past her guard, slicing her glove and striking the metal forearm. He paused in his attack as though perturbed at the rasping sound. "Reconstructed?" he asked, "I would not have guessed."

Cinder took the advantage and lunged with a hard thrust which could have skewered him had he not jerked aside. "Too fast for you?" she asked.

"The flexibly of the prosthetic wrist allows you a fine manoeuvrability. It merely took me by surprise," he rejoined, "how does it work?"

Of course, he would be taken by her modification. It seemed his curiosity never ended.

She smiled as she spied another surprise waiting for him. Flora's copper ears winked in her blue glow where she waited with the twine. "Trade secret, but I will be sure to give the smith your compliments," she said to keep his eye on her.

"You do that," he said.

Just a few more steps and he would be in position. However, at the moment she thought to make her move, Aerysleigh leaped forward, reversing their positions, and nearly forcing her into her own trap.

She swished her rapier down and took a high step over the rope. Pain blossomed in her shoulder as the move allowed her opponent to score a grazing hit. A warm stickiness slid down her sleeve.

"Though it may have to be from prison that you write your note," Prince Aerysleigh added.

"You spar well, but your inflated ego which thinks this match a foregone conclusion is mistaken."

The prince paused to take a deep breath. It pleased her to know the fight winded him. It made the ache in her own side lessen somewhat. But soon Commissioner Traverson would be making his way up the stairs and she doubted she could best two such men.

"As much as I would love to stay—" Her words died when he rapped a quick beat against the middle of her epee, twitching it away and stepping close in the half beat of her heart it took her to recover. Their blades locked at the hilt. She stood face to chest, gazing up into the long-lashed eye through the lit green lens of a unique set of goggles. Her heart thundered in her ears—blocking out his next words. She only knew he leaned close—too close—to press his advantage, his mouth tickling her ear.

He jerked back. "What the devil, you smell...you feel like...You're a woman!"

Time to go.

His surprise was all she needed. A quick spin, a hard push, and his heels caught the rope. He reeled back. Both of them dropped their swords. He clutched at her, wrapping his arms tight around her and pulling her over with him to keep her from escaping. However, with his hands busy, his head struck the stone of the rooftop with a crack.

Cinder tucked her head into his shoulder and rolled through the tangle of limbs, finding her feet while Flora made fast his hands and feet.

"Hurry." she urged. The mouse jumped into her satchel. Cinder took up her pole and prepared to vault to the stable.

Something made her look back. He lay blinking up at the smoggy night, not yet struggling against his bonds.

She sighed and returned to her fallen opponent. With a jerk she tore the dangling sleeve covering her prosthesis the rest of the way off, then lifted Aerysleigh's head and placed the scrap of material underneath. "There."

"Stop, thief." Basil pushed through the atrium's door and headed for the opposite door shouting what must be a favourite constable phrase.

Cinder let her hand linger for just a moment on the prince's chest, just to assure herself his rhythmic breathing had not faltered—or so she told herself—then turned and vaulted into the night.

Chapter Thirty

The Club

Aerysleigh settled into the horse-hair chair of his favourite West End gentlemen's club, White's, and swirled the cane sugar in his Old Fashioned. He stared into the muddied whiskey, took a swallow, and sighed as he waited for the bitters to soothe the throbbing in his head. He shifted so the cloth wrapped ice cooled the rising goose egg, then looked across to Basil with a definite challenge.

"I'm telling you the truth. And don't tell me the knock on my skull addled my brain. I've been hit harder and you know it. I know what I saw, and if I dare say, felt." *And smelled* he added silently. Certainly, no bloke he ever encountered smelled as intoxicating as the thief on the roof.

Basil chuckled, took a sip on his own drink and held it up to the light. "Ahh. I enjoy the simpler mix of this drink for certain."

Aerysleigh cocked an eyebrow at his friend.

"A woman you say? I would never have thought it?" Basil continued at the prompt to get back to business.

"Because she has eluded you for so long? Or because of the feats of strength and dexterity displayed at the burgled sites?" he ribbed the commissioner.

Basil did not take the bait but smiled wryly. "Both, I suppose.

Though she seems quite taken with you. Even took the time to pad that hard skull of yours."

Aerysleigh nodded. He had mused over the actions of the thief—her return to place the scrap of material under his head, the lingering touch on his chest. Did she consider picking his pocket? But no, his wallet was where he left it, as was his watch and utility belt.

He tore his thoughts away from the softness of her touch, onto the arm from which she removed the sleeve. "But her modification, Basil. I have never seen the like." He believed Cinder thought him more dazed than he actually was. He could see her, at least her arm, very well in the darkness, for just before their little repartee of weapons he donned his light enhancing goggles. "It was the most unique piece of metal I have ever seen. A functional wrist joint and movable fingers. She even fought with her prosthesis when I struck her other arm, and nearly beat me to boot." He paused and adjusted the ice. "She could have left me..."

Basil's eyes sharpened at the description of the lady's prosthesis and leaned forward, but then he sat back with a grimace. How much pain was his old friend in? Was he considering joining the modifieds to escape it?

"You *are* a handsome devil, not to mention the most eligible bachelor in England. Perhaps she was trying for your hand," said Basil, completely changing the topic.

Aerysleigh scoffed and let him have his way. Basil didn't talk about the war wound that nearly crippled him. A waitress, a new one he figured as he had not seen a woman server in White's before, ran a hand across his shoulders. "Is there anything I can get you?"

He shrugged her hand away as delicately as he could. Once he might have welcomed the advances of a pretty lass, but lately he only craved both the company and the touches of a certain lady from St. Drogo. "No, thank you, I am fine."

"I didn't know the club added women servers." Basil lifted his glass, "I could do with another—"

A commotion at the door cut him off. "Stop that woman," cried the director, pointing to the disappearing waitress.

Basil shook his head. "I should have figured. Not only are the thieves stopping to romance you, women are breaking into the inner sanctum of the gentleman's club to draw your attention."

Aerysleigh groaned. "It's getting worse," but then again, he also didn't mind Cinder's soft touch and he wondered at his tendency to vacillate. "How could Cinder have even known who I was? It was dark. I had my goggles on."

"If you were close enough to feel *her,* she was certainly close enough to recognise *you.*"

"Well, that takes out the theory that our thief might be one of the aristocracy just having a bit of fun. A young male, yes. A well-bred lady? I don't think so." He frowned as a thought of his sister intruded. She would have performed the acts of Cinder well enough and with impunity. A sense of melancholy threatened him.

Many times, since his father charged him to find his sister, the deceased princess preyed much on his mind. He straightened. "It doesn't add up. Cinder spoke like a gentlewoman. She handled the blade as though trained by a master, even with a mechanical arm."

"And now we are back to the modified. No gentleman, and certainly no lady, would submit to the indignity of a metal alteration. The only aristocrat with any sort of metal would be Lord Stillingfleet who wears a mask and is mostly a hermit. No, it must be as we deduced before—a member of the working class sympathetic to modifieds, and now we at least know why."

"St. Drogo would be the place to find those answers," Aerysleigh said.

Basil brushed his comment aside. "There is no penetrating St. Drogo. The Marquess of Wheelfell has it well in hand. And besides, you have tried already—several times from what I understand. In addition, they police their own kind fairly well."

"What do you mean?"

Basil shifted as though uncomfortable. "I mean, they are not just going to give up one of their own. Especially if this is a RobinHoodesque type of burglary where our thief gives the loot to the poor." Basil leaned forward, suddenly intent. "And I must remind you, Aerysleigh, in light of the recent debates before Parliament, if this mechanical arm is the wonder you say, she may technically be considered an automaton—not human."

Aerysleigh stared at his drink morosely, attempting to think past the throbbing in his skull. His surprise at Cinder being a woman had cost him the chance to apprehend her. Though he did not want to disappoint his friend, he found his admiration of Cinder growing. Especially now that he knew her to be of the gentler sex—modification notwithstanding.

He snorted. *Gentler indeed.* She had bested him after all. Though he did suspect her tiny accomplices to be part of the victory.

What wonderful gadgets this woman possessed.

He straightened. "She has to be an engineer and machinist."

"So, we surmised," Basil said dryly.

"But not an ordinary metal pounder. Think on it. The unexplained appearance of prosthesis for veterans and poor."

"All can be explained by the charity workers at St. Drogo."

"Yes." Aerysleigh leaned forward in his excitement. "But it's more than that. She is inventive and talented, surely someone has seen her, or knows of her shop."

"Maybe, but none of the tools or prosthesis made for the poor have the level of sophistication you speak of. A wrist that turns? Fingers that loosen and grip?"

"Yes, connected to the nerves, I would suppose. I had a first mate with a hand somewhat like that, but he would never tell where it came from."

"Of course, he wouldn't. That takes the expertise of a very special kind of doctor, one willing to break our laws against mechanising humans. Someone off continent?"

"Exactly so, a cross between a witch doctor, a scientist, and a physician."

The commissioner chuckled and pretended to think. "I can rightly tell you, not the name of a single possibility leaps to mind."

"Rumours on the street then?"

"You set too much store on snitches. Most will tell you anything for a shilling. We can't chase every rumour of a physician operating in the backrooms of the slums. We'd be interviewing every midwife with a bit of the supernatural and crooked doctor from here to Michaelmas."

Aerysleigh leaned back and took another drink. "True. Then we set a trap."

"Do you honestly think she will fall for another?"

"She fell for the first. We will just have to make the bait something she cannot refuse."

"And what in all of England would temp Cinder to risk herself twice?"

Aerysleigh grinned. "My mother's jewels of course." He stood and paced around the two chairs. They purposely chose a secluded corner of the club, but Aerysleigh felt restless in its confines. Besides, he always did his best thinking on his feet. "We will have a ball, open it to all the women in the land. And on display will be the queen's jewels."

"Did you just say *all* of the women? What a security nightmare! Not only for your mother's jewels—she would have my head if her dowry took a walk—but for you as well."

Still, Basil's eyes glowed with the possibilities as he

contemplated the idea. "'Tis a risk. Surely, she would sense a trap? Criminy, what if something happened?"

"We wouldn't allow Cinder to get to the jewels, just close enough. After all, she didn't make off with our last bait."

"No, she just knocked out the prince."

Aerysleigh glared at his friend. "We will make a big deal of moving the jewels from the vault at the bank and hide them in the palace, replacing those on display with paste replicas. My mother has had several made over the years as not to risk the real set."

"And what if your mother does not agree to such a scheme. Opening the palace to a horde of commoners? She would have a seizure."

"True. True," Aerysleigh agreed. "I will have to give her an incentive as well as Cinder."

Basil leaned forward and observed him through slitted eyes as though he had lost his mind. "What in the Kingdom would convince your mother to do what would surely be considered the height of madness?"

"What is it that my mother wants above all else in the Kingdom?"

"Why that's easy. She wants you to marry..."

Aerysleigh chuckled as Basil's words trailed off and gaped at him open mouthed. "Precisely. I will tell mother I am looking for a bride and will choose one from the ladies at the ball. How could she refuse."

Basil's jaw snapped shut. "Oh bravo, your highness. Bravo."

CHAPTER THIRTY-ONE

THE KING

"Mother," Aerysleigh announced. "I need to have a ba—"

"There you are." Queen Constantina rose from her desk. "Everyone has been looking all over for you. Where have you been?"

She held out trembling hands and Aerysleigh took them, expecting the worst. "I have been at White's, Mother. What is wrong?"

With a rustle of skirts his mother drew him to a settee and settled back down as though she could stand no longer. "Your father is calling for you."

This set Aerysleigh back. Just 24 hours earlier, King Redmond still languished in the clutches of the iron lung—speech of any sort beyond him. "Calling?"

"Yes. Somehow he communicated to Sir Litton something about Ursula."

"Ursula?" Though it made him sound like a simpleton, Aerysleigh could not help but parrot his mother's words. Nothing made sense. "My sister?"

The queen shot him a sharp glance. "Yes. Robert's wife. After Sir Litton restrained her, your father improved enough to come out of the lung."

"This is wonderful news."

She put a hand across her eyes to hide the shimmer of tears. "She was poisoning him, Aerysleigh."

Of all the conniving, dastardly acts! His father loved Ursula. Doted on her like a daughter. Despite the urge to hit something repeatedly, he put an arm around his mother's shoulders and gave a gentle squeeze. "There now. Everything is going to be alright. I will go see him right away. But where is she? What happened?"

"She went back to her rooms the guards said, then simply disappeared. How could she? She meant to kill him, but she has been a part of our family for years."

Aerysleigh bit his tongue. He had pointed out numerous times how his mother severely underestimated the resolve of the confederated German states to expand their territory. But he would not rub alcohol into this open wound.

Once, his mother and father hoped the marriage to Robert's Austrian Princess would bring peace to the continent. Instead it allowed a spy and assassin into the palace. He nearly lost his father and Britain her monarch in this high-stakes gamble. However, when the king regained his strength, he could end this foolish peace treaty responsible for turning airships into mail carriers and soldiers onto the street.

He rose to hurry to his father and remembered his mission in searching her out.

First things first.

"Mother. I want to have a ball and I want all the eligible maidens of the land invited."

Her hand fluttered to her chest again and her eyes glowed. "Oh, Aerysleigh. You are finally—"

"Going to catch Cinder," Aerysleigh finished for her.

"What?"

"Oh, and your best paste jewels to catch the thief." He paced the length of the room. *Yes. The trap would be set and sprung.* With his father well he could return to his proper place at the front and—

"Stop your pacing. It is undignified. This thing with you chasing this common criminal as though you are actually a common footpad must end," his mother said from the settee.

"The end will come when I catch her."

"Aerysleigh."

At his mother's tone, he looked up sharply.

"Lord Stillingfleet has spoken to me about this chase you are leading. It seems you are upsetting his charity work at that Catholic cathedral. What is this about you at a near riot at the Tindale House the other night?"

"Lord Stillingfleet? He came here?"

"Of course not. He is a veritable recluse after that accident. He dabbles at alchemy, you know. He sent a letter by."

"Did he?"

"Yes. He intimated that you may be making a nuisance of yourself and he would consider it a personal favor if I would speak to you."

"Why would you owe Lord Stillingfleet a favour that would stop me from apprehending a criminal?"

Queen Constantina touched her unlined cheek. "Well, his alchemy does have some uses. He makes the most wonderful skin creams, you know."

Lord Stillingfleet himself just confirmed his suspicions that Cinder was somehow connected to St. Drogo. For some reason the cathedral sheltered the thief. Aerysleigh smiled to himself. However, he held the key to getting his way.

"A ball, Mother."

The queen's frown softened, and he knew his victory certain. "We did have an understanding. Six months wasn't it?" she said.

He grimaced and nodded.

"Well, yes. *If* your father stabilises, a celebration would be most appropriate. The highest families will be invited..."

Before she disappeared into her formidable world of party planning, Aerysleigh had another request. "Not the wealthiest maidens, Mother. All of them."

"What do you mean?"

"I want all the ladies of the land invited." He hoped that not only would Cinder make an appearance, he dearly wished a certain tinker would as well.

His mother lifted a brow. "All of them?" her voice dripped disdain. He met her gaze unflinching. A long time had passed since he looked at his mother, he realised. Despite her years, she still possessed enviable beauty and elegance. The planter's wife turned regal. He shook his head. How quickly one forgot one's roots.

"All. Lady's maids and shop girls, I will dance with them all." *And look terribly busy while Basil springs our trap.* At his mother's horrified expression, he grinned. "And modifieds. Send a special courier to St. Drogo for me."

His mother rose. "No! I must draw the line at this latest madness."

He plunged on. "I will choose a wife as agreed." Not that he intended to stay around for the reading of any bans. No. His father had proof of Germany's perfidy and they would work to crush them once and for all.

His mother interrupted his daydreams. "You already have someone in mind then? A respectable girl from the Peerage?"

He shrugged. "A masque ball." That would encourage Cinder's appearance. He bet Basil another dinner that with Modifieds, masks, and jewels involved, the thief could hardly stay away. He kissed his mother's cheek. "Thank you, Mother."

"But you haven't answered any of my questions."

He headed for the door. "Gold embossed invitations would be nice, don't you think? Airship may work as a method of distribution, but you know best, of course."

"Aerysleigh."

He feigned deafness. "I will go see Father now. I know you have it well in hand." He waved and shut the door firmly behind him, pausing just briefly to take a deep breath.

*****

It did his heart good to see his father sitting up in bed. He still looked one step away from the grave, with skeletal fingers gripping a tea cup and pallid complexion, but he was alive. That is all that mattered.

Sentry automatons stood at the ready, no longer slumbering against the walls, and before them sprawled a body. At first glance Aerysleigh could not determine whether it be human or automaton. No blood stained the carpet, but upon closer inspection he realised it was both. A modified human of which he had never seen the like.

But he had heard of them.

Just before the armistice news had come from the front of yet another soldier created by the Germans. Metal and bone fused with nerves and muscles, but the light had gone from this one's eyes and face was blank.

Aerysleigh knelt by the machine and pushed back the hair. *Ursula.*

"Mother said she disappeared," he said.

"It was easier," said a gentleman of the guard. "For the queen."

He nodded and sighed. "It makes no sense. Father showed her nothing but kindness." He looked up sharply, meeting the gaze of the sympathetic bodyguard. "And Robert?"

The fellow nodded. "I'm afraid so, your highness." Aerysleigh closed his eyes, pushing down the burning pain and rage at the mention of his brother. "What kind of person poisons her own husband?"

"Son."

Aerysleigh rearranged his features and hurried to his father's side. His sudden movement caused the automatons along the sides of the room to jerk to attention.

"Settle down," Sir Litton rasped from his chair. He looked so exhausted even his great moustache drooped. The smile he gave Aerysleigh showed the weight of his years but also joy. The automatons creaked back into a parade rest at the command.

Aerysleigh touched his father's hand. "Father, you look better"

"Liar," the king wheezed.

Aerysleigh slid his gaze to Sir Litton.

"Whatever was in the tea the traitorous princess concocted was some sort of nerve agent," said the doctor.

Aerysleigh nodded. "One of the Germen's favourite methods of attack. They have no honour."

Sir Litton glanced at King Redmond and his father returned the gaze for a long moment then nodded. "I fear it may be irreversible," he said. He took a deep breath. "And the symptoms may worsen with time if we cannot find a treatment. I have enquired of Lord Stillingfleet and he is researching the problem. His preliminary tests point to a mutated form of puffer fish poison."

"The Marquess of Wheelfell seems to have been busy here at the palace lately," Aerysleigh remarked dryly. "Don't worry, Father, I believe he may possess contacts that will help."

His father leaned against his pillows, his face as mask of concentration as he struggled to breath. Aerysleigh hated the helplessness that overwhelmed him watching the monarch struggle.

He whirled on the doctor. "What is being done? Did she act alone?" For some reason his mind jumped to Cinder. Could she be part of this foul scheme?

"We are attempting to recreate exactly when Ursula was replaced with the automaton," the doctor continued from his corner. "Scotland Yard is investigating as well as the King's guard. We believe that the real princess has not been with us since Robert died. She's worn a veil ever since."

It would be easy too. A doting princess, laid low by the death of her husband, wanting nothing more than to nurse her father-in-law. And kill him.

King Redmond opened his eyes suddenly and looked at his old friend. "Sir Litton. Everyone. Leave us," he ordered in a voice as strong and powerful as before he grew ill.

Without a word, the faithful doctor cleared the room.

His father motioned for Aerysleigh to come near and he leaned in until the king's breath brushed his face.

Bony fingers dug into Aerysleigh's arm. "Did you find your sister?"

Of all the things his father might have said, Aerysleigh did not expect those words. Now that he actually voiced the question, Aerysleigh could not deny it was the same order given in Morse Code a week hence. He could not find the words to reply.

His father released his grip. A rattle sounded low in his lungs.

"Father," Aerysleigh said as gently as he could, "Rosalind is dead."

"No," his father barked.

He wanted to argue but his father grabbed the back of his neck and held him fast. "The explosion maimed her. She *nearly* died. Your mother..." He shook his head. "She couldn't handle the news. I sent Rosalind to St. Drogo."

Aerysleigh felt his blood run cold and he trembled under his father's ruthless grasp.

"Lord Stillingfleet said you were at St. Drogo," prompted the king. "I assumed it was for your sister."

"I went to find news of this Cinder person."

"Never mind Cinder. He is of St. Drogo. Find your sister." He hacked. When he wiped his mouth, blood stained the handkerchief. "She is next in line and you must work this out before I—" Coughs shuddered through his father's body, sapping the last of his strength.

"Sir Litton," Aerysleigh cried.

The faithful doctor pushed through the door and limped quickly to the bedside.

"Bring the lung," Sir Litton snapped at the nearest automaton. He pulled frantically at the bell above the king's head. Nurses and doctors, aids and apothecaries rushed in. Aerysleigh stepped away, his mind in a turmoil. He could at this very moment lose his father—and at the same time, somewhere, he regained a sister.

CHAPTER THIRTY-TWO

THE IMPOSTER

Lady Harrington switched on the tiny apparatus to fan her corseted bulk with the force of a hurricane.

Despite the cool air, the corpulent lady looked ready to swoon at any moment. Ella pitied her poor servant girl already loaded down with satchels of vials and apparatus to serve her mistress. She doubted the slight thing could handle even a fly's weight more.

"Broomsticks and dust pans," Ella muttered under her breath, then looked up guiltily so see if anyone noticed her lack of decorum. Isabeau's lips twitched, but no one else seemed aware of the antics of servant with such juicy gossip at hand.

"The invitation came embossed with gold," Lady Harrington said, her voice trembly with giddiness. Whether from the excitement of the bespoken invitation or from the amount of sugar she just consumed, Ella was hard pressed to tell. The ladies in the tea room came with the express purpose of examining the latest book by Boggs and Tuckman on the evils of the modified society. Instead they met more for gossip and Lady Harrington had the choicest tidbit today.

Judith Steelhaugh, in attendance to find a new mark for Cinder, instead found her attention focused on this incredible news.

"From Queen Constantina herself," Lady Harrington continued. "There is to be a ball in honour of the prince." She leaned towards the table, though her substantial bosom allowed only the briefest inclination of her double chin.

Judith took a sip of tea, then returned it to the saucer and added a tiny bit of sugar. Lady Harrington's gaze followed her every movement, as if waiting for the questions to pour forth from her companion. Judith did not give her the pleasure.

"But why?" demanded Miss Mayskirt, a governess sent on behalf of Lady Gosset and no doubt charged not to miss a thing.

Lady Harrington opened her mouth to reply, but Judith's cold, low voice cut in. "To find a bride for the damaged prince, of course. I heard the invitation went out to every household in London. How...low." Each word spoke in a succinct cultured tone that made the other ladies sit back and reassess their eagerness to attend this ball. Ella shook her head. How well her stepmother manipulated people.

She just wants less of the peerage at the ball to compete with her own daughters.

"It's been ever so long since there has been a proper ball at the palace," squeaked Eurania Eventine. Nearly twenty-three and considered to have been on the marriage market too long, she added, "and everyone gets to dance with him."

"In poor taste, if you ask me," replied Judith, but her gaze slid to Isabeau and Aurelia sitting at a nearby table. Obviously, she wanted one of her daughters to marry Prince Aerysleigh, why couldn't everyone see her game?

"Why ever would the queen agree to such a thing?" Miss Mayskirt asked quietly.

Back in her element with the renewed attention, Lady Harrington smiled like a cat locked in a larder. "Well, now, that's just it. You know how cagey Prince Aerysleigh has been about settling down."

The young ladies in the room voiced a collective groan. Mothers nodded their frustration.

"I have it on good authority that he will attempt to make a love match at the ball."

Dertha and Hatty, Lady Harrington's daughters, sat with the quiet Isabeau and Aurelia at their own table. They chattered on about meaningless subjects, blissfully unaware of any lack of reaction on the part of the two sisters.

"I plan to exhibit my knowledge of fencing," Dertha exclaimed.

"It is said Prince Aerysleigh enjoys physical exertion, particularly a 'argument of weapons' and a 'battle of wits'."

Aurelia's speared the girl with an exasperated look. "I think you mean a conversation of weapons."

Ella was sure Isabeau kicked her sister under the table, but the comment sailed over Dertha's head. "I think my mask shall be a fencing helmet."

Ella coughed and proffered Aurelia her kerchief to distract the girl. Her stepsister gave a strained but thankful smile, and Ella turned her attention back to Lady Harrington.

"The best news is this. The queen's jewels will be on display during the ball."

Judith lifted her head. "Really?"

"Indeed, and not only that, the lucky lady chosen by the prince will wear a tiara and parure from the collection throughout the evening." Lady Harrington settled back into her chair, satisfied the gossip bomb detonated as planned. The whole menagerie of London's Zoo could have stampeded through the room and no one would have noticed while the ladies digested the information. Then the dam broke and the chattering began all at once.

Hatty went on to describe a monstrous taffeta creation in cream and peach she commissioned just this morning.

Judith asked very pointed questions about which jewels would be on display.

After a moment, Ella's stepmother set down her tea cup. "For the chance to catch the eye of the prince, to marry him, I *suppose* it may be worth attending the same ball as the low born. My daughters will, of course, outshine them." Her grin was more tiger-like than that of a sophisticated lady, but Ella doubted anyone noticed besides her. Judith hid her true colours well.

"Of course," said Lady Harrington, though now she eyed Judith's daughters as though contemplating their demise. Ella couldn't quite squash her own jealousy. The effort caused her nerves to jump and she dropped the gas masks. Her arm trembled noticeably and no matter how she tried to grab the masks with her left hand, the fingers refused to work. She waited too long for the rejuvenator injection.

"Oh my," said one of the ladies at the sideshow Ella created, "is she a modified person?"

Judith eyes narrowed. "Take care of that."

Ella retreated to the kitchen where Miss Bee created her delectable pastries. She caught the eye of the curious cook. The woman had her sleeves rolled up past her elbows while she kneaded a lump of dough, metal modifications giving her extra strength to punch it down with just the right amount of force.

"Mistress?" the cook looked around. "Cinder?"

"Never mind me," Ella said. She opened the throat of her dress and gave herself a quick injection to settle her nerves. *When would she ever learn to control her emotions?* She shook her head. Whenever the prince's name came up, it seemed more difficult to contain herself than any other time.

Once again, Ella took her place against the wall in the large outer room. Judith ignored her while everyone else forgot she was even there.

She checked the watch pinned to her sleeve and felt her temper rise. *How much longer could these cackling hens talk?* By the look on Judith's face, Ella suspected her next order would be to find out more about this ball. More specifically, the queen's jewels. Though now unattainable at the bank, they only left the vault on rare occasions, such as a museum loan, the moving of the jewels would offer an opportunity seldom seen.

Perhaps this theft would be Cinder's last. The one that would get her nicked for sure. What a welcomed thought! The only thing about that would be the prince's disappointment—that and she would never see him again. Locked away in Newgate as she would be.

A lamp lighter stomped along with his gas automation, the pale flickers of the newly lit string of street lamps giving off a yellow glow in the gloom of another foggy London afternoon. The air lacked the scent of sulphur, a clue of the poisonous gases, yet someone screamed from somewhere outside.

Instantly, all attention turned to the large window fronting the street. Police whistles blew, a sound becoming more common of late. However, the following cry of 'stop thief' brought a smile to Ella's lips. She ducked her head away from Judith's sharp look and stepped closer to the door.

The door flew open, smashing Ella against the wall, hat skewing over her eyes.

"I am Cinder!" yelled a fellow dressed head to toe in black with a hump on his back. He held out a bag with a pincher while the other hand fired a derringer into the ceiling. "All of you give me your purses."

Harcourt!

The thief tossed her a saucy salute when she glared his way. On a good day Harcourt may be called interesting-looking, if clean—a condition Ella had never witnessed—and sober. Today, dressed in burglar's clothes that emphasised his skeletal frame, slight hunchback, and pincher, he looked like a caricature from a nightmare. Instead of the meekly proffered purses he demanded, the ladies in the tea room screamed like a room of cannonballs flying overhead and scattered.

Harcourt, shocked to stillness with the screams and the flurry of skirts, froze in the doorway—the only escape for the frightened women. Finally, Lady Harrington, spying the open door with dusk beyond and police on the way, charged. The rest, screaming and yelling like flustered geese, followed. One struck the thief's shoulder with a well-aimed parasol and he spun into Ella, knocking her flat on her back with the sot on top of her.

One whiff and she knew the bloke to be stinking drunk as well as pretending to be her.

"When you recover your footing, see to the matter discussed this hour," said Judith. She picked up her skirts and stepped over her and Harcourt.

The door slapped shut behind her.

Ella pushed the thief off and leaped to her feet. "You fool. What are you doing?"

Harcourt stared up at her, "Oh, hellu there, Mistress Cinder," he burped. "Cinder Ella." He frowned. "Ella Cinder."

She took a quick look around then reached down and shook the bony shoulder. "Pigeons and poppycock, stop this foolishness. What are you trying to do? Get me and everyone here in trouble?"

The cleaning automaton buzzed into action, however, no one else remained in the room.

"Just doing what I'm told. The coppers been all over St. Drogo and got a snitch to talk about monsters running a secret pawn shop an' all. So, when they came a sniffing Lord Stillingfleet had me dress up like Cinder and take a little run while they turned the Fence into a proper store room."

Ella rubbed her temples. Harcourt dressing as Cinder and using her code name in public, in broad daylight, compromised her alias on too many levels to count. She could practically feel the heat breathing down her neck. A peek out the window confirmed this.

The footpads approached the door cautiously, peering into adjacent shops and following fingers pointed towards the tea house. They held clubs at the ready, all seriousness despite Harcourt's drunken playacting. In but a moment they would be in the shop and wondering why she stayed.

She swallowed hard when a tall figure strode around the corner. *Why is it* he *always appears at the most awkward times?* However, she took a moment to look him over and make sure the knock on the head hadn't damaged him.

He looks just as good as ever.

Harcourt cackled. "See sumthin' you like?"

She whirled. "Hit me."

Harcourt reeled a bit. "Wha-? No!"

"You have to give me a floorer and get out of here. They will stop and tend to me so you can get away."

"Ahh, Miss CinderElla—I can't do that."

"Just pretend, but you have to leave some sort of mark. With that derringer, quickly."

The hunchback heaved himself to his feet, glanced out the window. "But, Miss, this ain't what Stillingfleet tol' me. I'm to get caught, don't you see? It takes the heat off of you."

"You can and you will." She never asked for anyone to go to jail for her and could not fathom why Stillingfleet would want to protect her.

"Here, your highness," someone yelled, "In Miss Bee's. We don't think he came out."

"Be careful," Aerysleigh's measured voice called back. "He could have accomplices or hostages."

Harcourt seemed hurt by that last phrase. "I don't take hostages. And I don't hit women. They'd string me up for sure."

Ella snapped her fingers in front of his face. "Forget about that. I won't see you pay for being me, no matter who put you up to it. Hopefully, they didn't get a good look at you." *Or smelled him. A blind dog could track him by scent alone at this point.*

Harcourt snapped his pincher in agitation. "Sorry about this, Miss."

The world spun then darkened to shades of grey and black.

Chapter Thirty-Three

The Invitation

erysleigh followed the police officers into the tea room, thankful to be out and about. His mind felt musty and full near to bursting with the information relayed by his father.

The upheaval of the royal family with the disappearance and evident guilt of his sister-in-law set his mother off. Factories roared with her orders for newer automatons. Human guards also increased.

However, the simple act of focusing on the Cinder investigation soothed him. Basil sensed his disquiet and did not pry, merely sent him out to an interview at a local pawn suspected of dealing with the thief. He jumped at the chance to explore the streets around St. Drogo and the workers of the East End. Just as he and the constables entered the Modfair Pawn, a fellow claiming to be Cinder broke from the back room and fled. Leaving a single constable to interview the Modfair proprietor, Mr. Wright, Aerysleigh and two others followed the thief.

The bloke led them on a merry chase, diving through occupied houses and stores, firing his weapon randomly. However, not once did Aerysleigh believe the chap to be the actual Cinder. Besides, he was certain the notorious burglar to be a woman. The man acted strangely as well. Namely, the thief's inability to pull away from the chase, like he wanted to be followed and his care to discharge his small calibre pistol where it did no damage.

The people on the streets made way for the runner. Pausing and watching him flee, subsequently blocking the path of Aerysleigh and his men. As though his prey was known to the locals.

An indication of Cinder? May*be.*

When Aerysleigh believed the impostor lost in the darkening streets, the thief made a commotion that drew their attention. Not once did he stand and fight or rely on the fascinating gadgets Cinder possessed.

Aerysleigh followed the trail of curses from the slums to Miss Bee's Tea Room, an establishment favoured by women of society. After a dizzying discharge of the brightly clothed occupants, Aerysleigh entered the room where one of his men knelt over a pile of skirts, a fall of blonde curls spilling across the hardwood floor.

At first glance, he believed one of the venerable ladies had swooned until he caught the copper scent of freshly spilled blood. *Not a smell one ever forgot.*

"What happened here?" he asked stepping closer. His breath hitched when he recognised the prone form of the mysterious tinker lady from St. Drogo.

"That hugger-mugger gave the poor miss quite a blow. She must have been going to scream, eh?" said the ginger-haired junior officer.

Aerysleigh waved the constable away. "Well, off with you. Bring him to justice. I will care for the lady." Though the fleeing man may not be Cinder it would be a clear day over the factories before he allowed the assailant to get away with striking a lady.

The officer picked up one of the lady's hands and attempted to pat it to bring her around but seemed flummoxed. "Wat's here?" He tugged at the well-made, yet worn, kid skin glove.

With a tap on the younger bloke's boot, Aerysleigh gave a significant look at Ella's helpless mien. "I may be old-fashioned, but I believe it proper to ask permission before mauling a lady."

His admonition came late. The woman jerked her hand away and whisked a small pen knife from her chatelaine. Even with her eyes closed the blade found the young constable's neck unerringly, stopping just before it nicked the skin.

"Leave my hand alone," she mumbled.

The officer flushed a radish red and leaped to his feet. His older partner guffawed while studying the automaton cleaning up broken pottery intently.

Aerysleigh hid his own grin and nodded towards the back door. "I believe our quarry has escaped. You may want to see to it."

The older constable grabbed his young partner by his collar and hauled him towards the door. "Yes, sir."

Removing his top hat and the eye patch, they itched horribly in the overheated tea room, Aerysleigh knelt by Ella's side, gently pushing her arm down.

"Let me just have a look," he said, bending to examine the cut behind her ear. Despite his concerns, little blood stained her high white collar.

Ella's eyelids fluttered, consciousness slowly returning.

What trained her reflexes to respond as they did? He witnessed such reactions—in battle. Still, he drew his handkerchief and pressed the linen gently to the wound. Despite his care, Ella moaned and attempted to sit up.

"Easy now," he said, "you've taken quite a blow."

Instead of soothing the confounded lady, she reacted exactly opposite of what he expected. Something he *should* expect by now. Cone flower-blue eyes popped open and she pushed his hand away. Jerking upright she looked wildly around. Once she confirmed the room deserted, she put her hand to her head with a sigh.

"I *did* say to take it slow," he admonished.

Ella shot him an evil glare. Before he could ponder further on her strange reactions, two more constables pushed their way through curious onlookers and a red-haired reporter asking questions.

Aerysleigh gestured at the gawkers gathering on the street. "Dispel this crowd and send the ladies home. Fetch a doctor, there's been an injury." He made sure to keep his back to the door to prevent anyone from recognising him. He was not in the mood for social niceties. Indeed, the only lady he wanted to talk to was in front of him. However, she seemed to spend her time trying to avoid him.

Insulting really.

"Metal and bone!" Ella grumbled. "That blasted crook—he actually hit me."

Finally, something verging on coherent if not a somewhat shocking language for society. It made him smile. "Please take my advice and rest a moment. You are bleeding."

She drew her hand away from her ear. "I see. However, I'm sure I've taken harder knocks from my fencing instructor."

He could not help but stare, fascinated. In this unguarded moment he may learn more about her than she might normally reveal.

"Harcourt just needs to learn where to hit someone. You can't go conking someone upside the ear when all that's needed is a well-aimed blow."

Aerysleigh kept that little gem of the fellow's name to himself. Evidently Ella knew her attacker. He decided to continue his ruse in believing Cinder to be a man. "Undoubtedly all thieves and attackers should be trained how to gently render someone unconscious. However, I do believe you to be one of the only people to have met the notorious outlaw Cinder."

She flushed a becoming pink and finally looked him in the eye. "Oh, it's you."

At least that is more of an expected reaction. He assumed his initial assessment that the blow dazed her and removed the usual wariness that kept her so tense must be correct.

He touched his hat. "Good evening. A doctor has been sent for—"

"No! No doctor. Please, just let me go." Ella's eyes grew wide and she arranged her skirts to rise.

He rocked back on his heels. *Did she plan to flee again as she had from St. Drogo, the party, and from the riot?* Though he did not blame her for leaving the scene of the mob. What was it which drove her away when another woman might have clung?

Yes, definitely insulting.

Well, if he could not stop her, this time he would join her. He held out his hand. She hesitated, and too late Aerysleigh remembered his eye patch. Annoyed with himself for such a social blunder. He turned away and lifted his hat. "Where did I put that thing?"

"What are you looking for?" Ella asked after a moment.

"My patch. I realise my eye makes people uncomfortable."

With a quick move she reached out and halted his search. "Your eye does not make me uncomfortable," she said. "You do."

He cocked a brow at her. "I am at a loss as to how to interpret that statement."

Ella smiled up at him. "As you will." She gripped the fingers of her glove, then slowly uncovered her prosthesis. "There. We are even." Aerysleigh grasped it and helped her to her feet.

The metal felt hard and rigid in his grip, the fingers unmoving. A word glinted in the lantern light with a half a cog underneath. He had seen this symbol—at St. Drogo. "Metal?" He asked.

"As you see," she retorted.

A cook appeared in the door to the kitchen. She frowned at him then looked with obvious concern at the lady. "Miss Ella? Do you need help?"

"No, thank you. If you don't mind, I'll use your kitchen to leave."

Ella shook her head and stood, swaying slightly.

When she rose, she over-balanced and Aerysleigh place his hand under her arm again. "Let me take you to your conveyance," he urged, "where is your maid or companion that I might call them?"

And give them a piece of my mind.

Ella shot him a slanted look from under her lashes then continued her progress to the door. He could swear he heard annoyance in her voice when she answered. "I have told you, your highness, I am not a lady. I *am* the companion."

Despite her insistence, he did not believe her. The cook pushed a coat and a gas mask into his free hand. "See her safe, your highness." The woman curtsied and hurried to open the door at the back side of the sweltering kitchen.

In the alley outside, Ella straightened and removed his hand from her arm. "Thank you for your concern, sir, but I can make my way on my own."

His pride definitely pricked, Aerysleigh decided to play her game. He straightened. "Very well then, by the sounds of the whistles I should be able to cut south and meet the men to apprehend Cinder at last."

Ella hesitated as predicted. *She definitely knows the reprobate leading the officers on a merry chase.*

"Very well, then, for a little way," she conceded.

Aerysleigh chuckled to himself as Ella made her way opposite the front of the tea room, weaving among the beggars and carts parked for the evening with practised skill.

Ella stopped and pressed something into the hand of a beggar child. The small girl instantly split it in two, shared it with a smaller child tucked under a rough wool blanket, and shoved it into her mouth. A biscuit from the tea room, evidently hid in the lady's skirt for just a moment to relieve someone's suffering.

The child held onto the metal hand for a moment, petting the shiny steel. Then a smile that rivalled the sun lit the urchin's face and she whispered something too low for Aerysleigh to hear. Ella placed a finger to her lips and moved on.

He studied his companion as they moved across a main street and into another alley, their general direction headed towards the East End.

Speaking of suspicious, a wraith-thin man, gave them a hard look. Aerysleigh moved to put himself between her and the fellow, but she gave the other a smile warm enough to melt an iceberg.

"Mr. Trigg. I see you have found work."

Instantly the miner touched his hard helmet, the candle perched there bobbing like a strange bird. "Thanks be to you, Miss Ella."

"Nonsense. Give Mrs.Trigg my regards."

They moved along, but several stopped Miss Ella, or she stopped for them. Always she had a kind word or something from the satchel she kept close. No one molested her, no pickpocket tried their luck. They received hard looks, but Aerysleigh realised they were for him, not the lady at his side.

Finally, when crossing into Scrubber Alley, his two companion officers caught up to him.

"'E gave us the slip, yer highness," said the older man. "Lost 'im in Whitechapel ways."

Aerysleigh dismissed the men.

Ella gave him a sideways look. "You don't have to worry about Harcourt," she said slowly. "He is innocent enough."

He hid a grin. *She's perfectly aware she slipped and gave the thief's name.*

"He claimed to be Cinder," Aerysleigh pointed out.

Ella covered her laugh. "He's no more Cinder than you are. His stench alone would give him away."

A truer phrase never spoken.

She paused at the twisted wrought iron of a small cemetery behind a church. Suspecting the head injury caused more pain than she let on, he decided to try one more time.

"Allow me to ease my mind and call a cab for you, at least until I am assured you are well."

For a long moment she gazed up at him. "Why?"

The direct question caught him off guard. "Pardon?"

She made a motion that took in the drab buildings and the falling night in one sweep. "You can see I am at home here. You have no idea where I might reside. You seem to have a fascination with the poor and the modified, beyond the self-centred concern of the rich where they assume such posturing makes them look good."

"I...I wouldn't call it a fascination." He thought over his actions since his recall. "Perhaps it is more that I miss the comradeship of the army. A comradeship I do not find among the Peerage."

"The affinity comes from being considered freaks and even not human by many." She cocked an eyebrow at him. "These people are a suspicious and proud lot, not to mention poor beyond your comprehension. The camaraderie you feel is one born of desperation, of watching children die of hunger or cold. Your fascination of them will come of no good unless you do something."

"You are speaking of the Tindale House and my promise to help."

"Yes."

"I am a man of my word. I will keep my promise; however, I do not agree to your deduction of an unhealthy fascination with the modifieds. I commanded several upon the *Sky Serpent.* I have nothing but the highest respect for men and woman willing to change their bodies in an effort to continue to serve."

Ella flashed him a wan look. "Said by a true aristocrat. Respect and admiration whilst you stare and visit St. Drogo and then allow laws to be passed which hurt those who make your life easier."

He snorted. "You judge my character very harshly."

She shrugged. "I have seen many of the rich come and go, but nothing changes. True advocates are few and morbid fascination common."

"Enough," he said, his voice so harsh it scraped the walls around them.

His companion did not cower, merely lifted her chin and studied him, examining his face as though searching for answers. Aerysleigh took her hand. It rested heavily in his, the metal hard yet warmer than he expected in the chill evening. He squeezed her fingers, both metal and bone, waiting for her to return the squeeze, knowing if she moved her fingers, she would confirm the dread suspicion growing in his heart.

Neither hand moved. He felt both an odd disappointment and then a giddiness this woman could not be Cinder, the prosthesis merely a metal reproduction and nothing out of the norm.

"My fascination is not with St. Drogo. It is not with the poor and the modifieds. Though I have found their plight to be despicable and swear to alleviate it as I may," he said.

"Then why?" she asked in a quiet voice. "Why are you here?"

"Because, Lady Ella, my fascination is with you."

*****

Ella's heart stopped for the span of several seconds. Finally, a single word stumbled from her lips. "Why?"

He smiled down at her, a slight quirk to his lips. "Because you, Ella, are a captivating person. Your commitment to the people of St. Drogo, your fascinating designs and skill at creating practical prosthesis. Your loyalty. You actually remind me of my sister a little."

"Princess Rosalind? She died when you were young, did she

not?" Ella asked, desperate to change the subject, even one so morbid as that.

The accident that took Rosalind's life and maimed Aerysleigh happened at a christening years before her own accident. Thinking of that led her thoughts to the day she met him. They were both leaving, he to join the Air Force, she sailing with her mother in *Lady Peril*, never to return the same.

The warm, breathless feeling deflated like airship envelope. She needed to get away. This close to the prince made her forget how dangerous he was.

What would he do if he realised she was the daughter of Lady Captain Steelhaugh? Ella tried to put some distance between them so she could think, but he held her hand fast. She fought to keep her prosthesis still.

"Rosalind was as caring and warm, if not a little unconventional—just like you." Something else seemed to be on the tip of his tongue and a shadow fell across his face. He freed her hand, she could have escaped, however, his pained expression kept her in rooted in place. She touched his face, drawn into the spell he wove.

It became so easy to forget, to be just a lady and her beau on a walk. "Your father?" she asked. "How is he?"

Aerysleigh frowned into the night, weaving his fingers through her metal ones. "Better. His nerves are damaged. Perhaps by the poison of a puffer fish."

"I'm sorry," she whispered, but her mind whirled. Instinctively she touched her belt and the vials there. Three left. Three nerve rejuvenators designed to reverse the effects of her dying nerves. However, her godmother once told her, by letter of course, that she found the formula by studying people stung by a mutated puffer fish and then working to counteract the poison.

She opened her mouth to say something but could not think of a way to explain why she would have such a serum. Why she carried it with her at all times.

The evening deepened. Long moments passed and then the sound of an airship above drew their attention upwards. Gold glittered from prow to stern, the sleek lines of the queen's personal airship unmistakable even in the fading light. Then it rained gold leaflets. Like burnished leaves of autumn, the papers drifted across London.

The prince smiled as the airship moved on. "She actually did it," he whispered.

Ella could barely tear her eyes from the ship, wanting to chase it, to get one of the coveted invitations for her own. She could never go. Her stepmother had other plans for her time that evening. But she could dream. She could pretend to be the girl of her memories, to join her mother and father dancing across the floor. But this time she would wear the sapphire dress and her partner would be the prince.

Tearing herself from the pleasant dream, she asked. "Did what?"

"She used the airship," he clarified. "I never thought my mother would." Prince Aerysleigh reached inside his vest and drew out one of those coveted invitations.

Ella's breath hitched and tears pricked her eyes.

"I would like you to come to the ball." He pressed the invitation into her right palm. "I have been carrying this around with me, hoping to find you. I wanted to give it to you personally, not—" He motioned at the airship, "that way. It will be quite the spectacle. Tell me you'll come...please!"

Ella dropped her eyes. He still wanted her to come even with the knowledge of her modification. *He said I'm captivating.*

"Please," he repeated. "Don't make me beg."

He wanted her though she told him time and again she was not the lady he thought. Her dream was an impossible one, destined to shatter in a million pieces.

She *would* come, but it would be for the queen's jewels, not to dance. She pulled herself together and tried not to imagine his arms around her while her skirts sang against the marble. Dreams were...dreams. Her stepmother, her modification, represented reality and the sooner she accepted that, the better.

"I..." she stuttered, unable to force the words past her lips.

An explosion reverberated through the alleys, rumbling through the cobbles at their feet. Ella blinked, confused. Fire gutted the sky above the wharfs. The gloom of evening brightened beyond the light of the sun's dying rays. The ships along the Thames raised the alarm, blowing their horns in desperate wails. But the cloud anvilling above the East End was not the Thames gases.

Fire bells joined the ruckus.

"The match factory," Ella breathed. She glanced at her watch. The factory would be full of match girls still working their fourteen-hour day. She shoved the invitation into her satchel. "I must go."

Ahead of her, the prince held open the cemetery gate. "I am coming with you."

She rushed down the alley and pushed past people milling in confusion.

"Cuthbert and Cox," she breathed. The miner she spoke to

earlier caught her eye, she plucked at his sleeve. "Go to St. Drogo, tell Dr. Bon Hamlet to prepare for the worst and send help."

The miner took off in the opposite direction. Ella dashed to a wider street partially blocked with the digging of new subterranean tunnels. She hiked her skirts and rushed to the ominous glow over the buildings.

She cursed her corset, longing for Cinder's breeches and coat. "Five explosions," she said when another explosion echoed over the shrill alarms.

Aerysleigh grabbed her shoulder and pulled her back as a fire carriage clattered past, horses knocking people and carts aside in their headlong rush. "Careful," he warned.

Ella hurried on, taking a moment to look into her satchel. She had packed for a boring day in the tea room with her stepmother and sisters, not for a medical emergency. At the bottom were a few herbs, useless in this situation, and only one rolled bandage. Extra nerve rejuvenators were in their padded case—but those were only good against the poison from a mutated puffer fish.

The prince again stopped her from crossing a street while her mind wandered. "Five?" he asked.

"If it is the match factory, there are cauldrons of potash and phosphorous which can explode when overheated."

"It could be boilers," offered Prince Aerysleigh.

Ella shrugged. "The smell." The prince sniffed the pungent air and nodded.

They closer they came to the East End factory, the more congested the traffic, and heavier the smell and heat. After a half-hour of winding through the congested streets to reach their destination, they were passed by no less than six fire carriages. Now, several concentrated water hoses concentrated on the bright flames. Ella covered her mouth.

Of the first two buildings, nothing remained but piles of rubble.

Chapter Thirty-Four

The Fire

Smoke and ash obscured the extensive grounds of Cuthbert and Cox. The match company maintained a large complex with a wide avenue stretching down the middle.

Usually the place teamed with waggons packed full of matchboxes destined for warehouses or ships on the wharf. Its airship dock allowed for the tethering of at least three cargo pallets, great platforms held aloft by rectangular envelopes. The detachable pallets were designed to drop onto steamers headed across the Atlantic to the Colonies or the channel to Europe.

Over one thousand girls from ages six and up worked in silence along the long tables in the stretching buildings under threat of a beating or a dock in pay. They patiently dipped and cut, dipped and cut. An industrious air usually hung about the place.

Tonight, chaos reigned.

Street vendors with wares from vegetables to oxygen tanks stared transfixed into the flames blossoming like deadly spring flowers. The choking smoke scoured Ella's throat. Thankfully she took the gas mask thrust into her hand by the prince and breathed deep of the filtered air.

"Smoke and ash," Ella breathed, forgetting her language in the shock of the moment. An emaciated girl staggered out of the opaque swirls, the scene back lit by orange fire Ella rushed forward and caught the paper-thin body as she collapsed.

The child's clothes clung to her in ragged tatters, charred flesh peeking lividly through the gaps. The nauseating mixture of burned hair and singed wool clung to her like another set of clothes.

"Miss Ella," the girl breathed. "There's fire everywhere. I can't find me ma."

Ella took off her mask and carefully placed it over the begrimed face. Other figures floundered through the gate, coughing and blinded by the thick smoke. Hands like claws reached for help. Another victim pushed past the others, skirts and hair flaming. Face a rictus of screams until she threw herself into the river.

"We need a place for the wounded," said the prince surveying the damage with a practised eye.

More firefighters appeared dragging thick hoses, but the small water tanks on their waggons had minimal effect on the blaze. Clumps of girls pressed out of the gate, their wounds now more severe. Prince Aerysleigh hurried to guide them away from the roaring inferno.

Ella caught sight of a familiar figure. "Drax!"

The big man turned her way. Next to him stood Harcourt who, having slipped past his pursuers, now looked markedly sober.

"Make a place for the wounded," she called then carried the match girl towards the nearest cart. A tanned farmer dumped his produce against a wall and hurried to help. Harcourt snapped his pincher for attention. Drax bellowed for the girls to make their way towards Ella. Aerysleigh lifted several who collapsed once they made the safety of the street.

Stalls and tables turned into a makeshift hospital filled with sobbing, soot faced girls. Several men also emerged, drivers, packers, managers, but more often than not they deposited a match girl to safety then turned back, grimly searching out the wounded.

After the fifth girl, Aerysleigh approached Ella, shaking his head. "What happened to their faces?"

Ella continued to tie a dirty rag around a weeping wound. She knew what he meant. Many of the girls and women that emerged from the smoke had jaws deformed in some way.

"Phossy jaw," she explained, motioning to another victim wandering in a daze.

Aerysleigh retrieved the girl. Ella offered her a dipper of water from one of the bucket brigades and wished she could do more.

"Phossy jaw?"

"Breathing in the phosphoric fumes gives the girls cancer. For pennies a day they receive a death sentence."

Screams echoed above the smoke, both turned back to the factory. Ella peered into the haze. The nearest workhouse lay in a pile of rubble and the one across the avenue from it missing its whole front. She squinted to see more but got side-tracked when Aerysleigh touched her shoulder.

"I am going in to see if I can help. It sounds like some of the girls may be trapped behind the fires."

She caught his fingers and stood. Fear for his safety caused her to act boldly, Ella leaned close. "The phosphorus will grow more unstable as the heat increases. It's nasty stuff. Be careful."

He smiled grimly. "Always." He held her hand and brushed a kiss across her glove. "Do you know how many of those explosive pots there are?"

Ella shook her head. She never visited the match factory but had covered several of the girls' incurable cancers with iron plates. "No. But there are at least four buildings where the match girls work. Each will have two or three cauldrons in a back room."

Prince Aerysleigh inclined his head toward the burning buildings. "I am more worried about the fire reaching the airships."

One of the air platforms above Cuthbert and Cox floated free and moved away at a sluggish pace. On a second, men scrambled frantically to escape the inferno. Fire cut off their escape below. Flames licked up the wood conveyor and stairs with nimble tongues. To save themselves, they had only one option—to cast off.

Another explosion drew screams from the crowd gathered on the street. Everyone paused and cringed. Aerysleigh ducked close, his shoulder sheltering Ella's head. Horses neighed and shouts came from the avenue where the first wave of firemen and bucket brigades fought the fires.

She leaned into his embrace. His muscles tensed as he prepared to head into the fray with the grim-faced firefighters. There was no stopping him. He was not the kind of man who directed from the sidelines.

She swallowed her fear and touched his cheek. "Go."

His smoldering gaze held her hypnotised. Then, he leaned down and kissed her fiercely. "Stay safe," he whispered hoarsely, then headed into the smoke with several other men.

More people arrived with handcarts and waggons.

Ella chose the most critically injured to be rushed to the nearest hospitals. Horse-drawn ambulances pushed through the congestion.

Lathered horses rolled their eyes in fear at the spurting flames and fought for space in the hard press of bodies. In the melee, Ella pulled from her satchel the three round spheres she never went without.

The three mice sat up without their usual whisker cleaning routines, noses twitching at the acrid smoke. "Follow the prince," Ella whispered. "Keep him safe." She knelt, the mice scampering from her palm and into the tangerine tinted night.

"Drax! Harcourt!" She called.

The two begrimed men approached, Drax carrying two small children, Harcourt ushering along a third.

"My lady," Harcourt bowed.

"Prince Aerysleigh went into the factory," she gripped Harcourt's arm so hard he winced. "Watch out for him."

Without a word the two men turned and disappeared into the swirling smoke. It took a moment for Ella to realise she had just sent everything she cared about in this world into the raging inferno.

Chapter Thirty-Five

The Mice

Aerysleigh stepped into the pit of Hell.

He picked his way over the scattered bricks and tried to pinpoint the source of the closest moans and screams.

Though the flames confined themselves to the back part of the factory, smoke billowed unrestrained. The facades of the first buildings had collapsed, reduced to gaping holes from the explosive chain reaction.

The tumbled walls mounded over waggons and the bodies of two horses, effectively blocking the progress of both horse and automaton drawn fire carts. A horse thrashed in its traces on the other side of the blockade while a lone man, eyes wide with determination, tried to calm and free the dray. The fellow cried for help, but there was no way around.

"Form a line!" Aerysleigh called. "Make a path." Two men who accompanied him on the climb of the tumbled blockage passed his order back. Volunteers bent their backs to the bricks, tossing the wreckage out of the way. However, it would take time. Time those trapped in the wreckage did not have.

A loosened air platform, mooring ropes trailing flames, drifted above, twisting to and fro in the wind. Aerysleigh judged the distance and direction then leaped for one of the few intact ropes. He lifted his feet above a burning waggon and dropped into a relatively clear area where the teamster had managed to free his horse and wrap his shirt around its eyes. Calmer now, the dray stood trembling and lathered.

Aerysleigh clapped the horseman on his shoulder. "They are working their way towards you."

The man nodded and pointed to the nearest workhouse. "There's girls in there, me thinks. Mr. Pinkle went in to 'elp, but 'e's not come out."

Aerysleigh nodded and headed for the open door, his path lit ominously by the orange tint of fire and blocked by wreckage and noxious vapours.

Movement on the right caught his attention and he turned to find the hulking bloke who challenged him at the riot. The brute muscled a dripping cart over the bricks. On the back, a hunchback with a pincher prosthesis manipulated the hose, bracing an unmodified hand against the pump and attempted to draw water.

Water sputtered.

Another man appeared and grabbed the handle, working the mechanism fiercely while the thief Aerysleigh chased just an hour before directed the stream along his path.

The cheeky fellow touched his hat in a clumsy salute. "Lady Eliana sends her compliments, your highness."

Aerysleigh shook a finger at him. "We will reconsider the earlier matter of striking a lady."

Harcourt had the grace to look chastised.

"Not to mention the merry chase you led the police on."

The thief laughed and tossed him a gas mask fished from under a pile of rope. "Lead on, sire."

Aerysleigh pressed the borrowed gas mask against his nose, seeking a sweeter air than the poisonous smoke swirling around him. He blinked away tears and rubbed the grime from the glass lenses to try and see the hellish scene. He climbed through the entrance of the nearest structure. Four lines of long tables lay splintered. Beyond those, an inner wall smoldered with the promise to burst into flame at any moment.

Spying a cowering shape under a table against one of the few standing walls, Aerysleigh hurried over. Water followed his path, drenching him, but clearing the clinging smoke.

Three children no larger than his hunting hounds huddled under the table filled with bundles of matchboxes. He took off his mask and offered it to the nearest tear streaked urchin. "Here you go, come with me."

He held out his hand. Another explosion elsewhere on the grounds rumbled through the floor, the wall above them swayed precariously.

The children screamed and clung to one another, Aerysleigh lunged and caught them all about the waist. He hauled them out from under the table. Under their coarse wool dresses they felt light as feathers—light enough for him to carry easily to the fire cart. He handed the children to Drax, a chain of men reached out to guide the girls to safety.

Another cry pulled Aerysleigh's attention back to the wall. The air platform on which he caught a ride earlier loomed close.

Another child, a mere shadow against the bricks, screamed as the bottom of the ship dragged across the top of the wall. Bricks tumbled, whole sections splintering the few remaining tables. He lunged over the blocks, linen breeches tearing on the sharp edges as he dove for the little girl. She scurried deeper into her hidey hole, just out of reach.

"Hurry, child, the wall is going to fall if you stay here." He looked up, the airship, envelope now ablaze, turned again as though driven by a determined child's hand to knock down the remaining walls.

"Get out of there, your highness," Harcourt yelled.

Aerysleigh glanced back. The thief lunged as though to come after him, but Drax grabbed him and pointed up. Aerysleigh's gaze followed the finger and knew he could never escape in time. He dove forward and joined the girl. The airship slammed into the wall and the bricks cascaded down around them.

*****

Aerysleigh coughed and groaned. Dust coated his throat, narrowing every gulping breath to a restricted wheeze. No limb obeyed his command to move. Bricks and timbers hemmed him in from all sides.

The child!

He struggled to shift his body weight, to free a hand to find the other occupant of the tomb but could not.

A draft touched his cheek and he turned to face it and sought the sweet air. Though it helped, each breath grew more difficult. The trickle of air was insufficient to support the needs of his lungs. He wasted precious oxygen with a curse, then lay still, breathing shallowly.

Shouts came from above where the stones arched over the table. To his right, where the match girl crouched moments earlier, the bricks formed a concave shape.

He smiled and dropped his head back to the stone.

The little thing knew what she was doing after all. She fled away from the fall of the wall instead of into it. He raised his chin again. The hazy light filtered through the hole, revealing table legs shattered with the impact of the collapse but the deep apron held fast.

I will have to compliment the carpenter.

It pinned him beneath, legs twisted to the side, hip jammed tight between floor and table top, arms by his side. Painful, true, but effectively saving his life. He managed to turn his shoulders right to alleviate the strain on his torso, but he could not stay that way for any length of time.

The light dimmed, and he realised someone crouched on the other side of the tunnel, now narrowed to only two bricks wide and one high. At one time it must have served as ventilation of a sort. Probably how the girl knew about it. Discovered, no doubt, during a shift when the draft of air would have been a welcome relief to the close confines of the factory.

Faint scratches told him people worked to remove the bricks covering him. The table groaned sinisterly as the weight shifted.

The pinprick of light blotted and changed. Yes, someone found the hole. He tried to get enough dust out of his throat to yell encouragement, but his breath died on his lips. He found himself nose to nose with a large rat.

Life on airships had inured him to the sight of these pests. Still, he hated the thieving rodents. To add insult to injury, he was certain Cinder's trained rats had been accomplices in his defeat in the duel on the roof.

But this rat was different, though large it was mouse-shaped. Its eyes glowed like twin blue lanterns, lighting up the small space like a beacon. Aerysleigh struggled under the pinning table, unable to defend himself. However, he found himself no match for the tons of brick atop him.

He jerked his chin left and right as the creature moved closer.

Frighten it. Show it I'm not as helpless as I look. He tucked his chin to make his only eye less of a target.

Undeterred by his struggles, the mouse proceeded toward him. It touched the table top and the bricks as though assessing his predicament. Halting near Aerysleigh's ear, the pest snuffled at his hair. Instead of soft whiskers, stiff bristles pulled at his braids.

Copper ears twitched, a tiny gem nose, possibly diamond, touched his own. Aerysleigh blinked to refocus. The mouse gleamed as though covered in armour. No, it *was* armour. A metal mouse put together so cunningly it looked real.

More disconcerting—it seemed to have a purpose in seeking him out.

The creature ran to his blind side. Little paws patted his patch, his braid, his cheek, then it scurried away. Aerysleigh relaxed until almost immediately the strange sound of metal paws running on the brick came again. This time the mouse returned dragging a long tube from which hissed the refreshing sound of oxygen. Immediately the freash air invigorated the atmosphere. He gulped for more. As though it understood his need, the mouse directed the stream towards his mouth. Aerysleigh wheezed.

Two other mice appeared.

Wonderful. That's all I need. Most pests.

Moving in complete silence but with perfect purpose, they brought a small tumbler of water to his lips. Though quite a bit dribbled down his neck, he eagerly accepted their offering. The sips cleared the dust in his throat. He hacked and spat, narrowly missing the first mouse. It jerked aside and glared—if a mechanical creature could glare.

"Sorry," he choked out.

"Your highness?" The high-pitched nasal tones of Harcourt called. Thief. Cinder impersonator. But seemingly at the beck of Ella.

"Yes," he yelled, "I am here." The oxygen cleared some of the dust from his brain and he found that thinking of kissing those upturned lips eased the pain in his knees and spine. Lady Eliana, Harcourt called her. Could it be the same as his tinker Ella? Had to be. Did the bloke misspeak? He thought not.

More yells. "Thank, God. Stay put, we'll 'ave you out in a jiff."

Aerysleigh couldn't help but chuckle. "Not going anywhere," he called. The mouse grabbed his face and pulled it towards her, surprisingly strong for its little size. He decided that judging by the slimmer shape and bossy attitude, the one holding the oxygen was female. She shoved the hose at him, whiskers twitching. He nodded, taking another breath.

"You are Cinder's beasts, aren't you?" he asked.

The mouse flicked her ears first his direction then back.

A soft voice drifted through the hole, the words unintelligible over the shouts of the men above, the voice unrecognisable. He didn't need to hear or understand. As the mice once more dribbled water on his lips, this time with a hint of cucumber. He fought for calm as his limbs cramped, allowing his thoughts to drift to pleasanter places.

In his mind Cinder, Ella, and this Lady Eliana merged into one.

Chapter Thirty-Six

The Child

Ella wiped blood from the face of a child handed to her through the smoke, then tried to determine the extent of her injuries. A drop landed on her nose and she looked up, breath fogging the air despite the heat. A light snow drifted from the sky. Girls sweating from the heat minutes ago now huddled shivering in threadbare garments. No doubt if they owned coats, they had been left behind in the hurry to survive. If the temperature continued to drop burns may be the least of their worries.

She took her coat off and wrapped it around the nearest child, but she only had one coat. Stumped, she stood and once again assessed the situation. A familiar figure in white coat and glasses leaped off a hand cart loaded with blankets.

"Ella."

Ella nearly collapsed with relief. "Dr. Bon Hamlet!" She hugged the woman tightly. "I am so glad you have come." She motioned to the cobbles littered with the wounded. Their moans filled the air. "There are so many and it's getting colder."

Dr. Bon Hamlet laid a hand on her shoulder. "We'll take care of them. The handcarts can ferry more wounded. You gave us a good start when you sent some of the wounded to St. Drogo. The priests are on the alert and are preparing the necessary space."

Immediately the doctor turned to direct the hand carts and ambulances to the most severely wounded. Ella sank down on a discarded pumpkin, thankful to have someone take over.

The mayhem turned into something more organized. For a moment she just watched, exhaustion and worry weights on her limbs. She dug in her satchel for a vial of the nerve rejuvenator, fingers nervously counting the remaining phials.

She used several in the last few days and had no idea when her godmother would send more—if she ever would. Ella turned away from the commotion.

She placed the vial in the syringe and injected herself in the bit of flesh showing above her glove. She looked around, feeling as though all eyes suddenly focused on her furtive movements.

No one paid her any mind.

Except for one.

A man leaned in the shadow a cordwainer's shop, not necessarily focused on her, but watching everything, especially the injured not yet moved. A chill skittered down her spine despite the warm night. The stories of body snatchers and Judith's medical experiments darkened her thoughts. When their eyes met, he touched his bowler brim, then turned and sauntered away. Ignoring the inferno just across the street as he calmly strolled away through the chaos.

P-R-E-T-T-Y C-I-N-D-E-R clacked a message at her elbow.

Ella jumped. "Valkyrie, you frightened me."

The birdman gazed past her to the place the mysterious fellow once occupied. Obviously, she was not the only one who found him disconcerting.

"Do you know what happened here?" she asked, hoping for a sensible reply.

Valkryie blinked then turned back to the fire. He did not look at the flames and instead examined the sky and the girls stretched out before him.

T-H-E-Y T-A-K-E T-H-E B-I-R-D-S T-O-O he clacked in one of the most comprehensive sentences she ever heard from him. When she tried to ask what this meant, he wandered after the strange man with a glint in his eye she did not like. She only hoped that if the bloke *were* a body snatcher, Valkyrie's dislike would keep him at bay.

Ella turned a worried gaze to the grounds of Cuthbert and Cox and caught her breath. A cargo platform drifted lazily through the smoke. Ropes trailed along the ground like ribbons from a maypole. Several were on fire. Like fuses they lead up to the abandoned craft.

Ella leaped to her feet, straining for a glimpse of Aerysleigh. Drax and Harcourt stood on a rubble pile silhouetted by the flames. Men pumped water into one of the buildings, but she saw no sign of the prince.

The airship turned, aiming directly for the wall which they sprayed. Now, Ella had no doubt as to the whereabouts of the prince. She rushed towards the avenue, a warning on her lips.

"Your highness, get out of there!" Harcourt yelled, springing past the firecart. Drax grabbed him by the shoulders and jerked him back. The low flying platform crashed into the wall and barrelled towards the back of the complex. Bricks showered down, the wall following.

"Aerysleigh," Ella screamed.

She fought her way through the lines of men, clambering up the bricks to Harcourt. "What happened? Where is he?"

Drax pointed wordlessly at the remains of a wall. Dust rose with the smoke, choking those without masks or filters. Ella coughed. Harcourt handed her a gas mask from the purloined fire cart. She darted down the other side, skirting smaller piles of bricks. She dropped beside an ominous pile of rubble and listened, unable to call for the fear clutching her throat. Harcourt, Drax, and the other men followed her.

"'E was right there." Harcourt pointed. "'E saw another child, I think."

Of course, he would not leave someone behind.

"Hurry," she said. She grabbed a brick and flung it to the side. For a long moment she tried to clear the rubbish alone, then the others dove in. Once they realized it may be Prince Aerysleigh under the pile, they began to dig with frantic abandon.

Drax moved back, using his great strength to clear whole section of intact wall to make way for more men. Immune to the heat and sharp edges of the bricks, Ella used her left hand to throw the bricks far away. Even so the work progressed slowly.

"Mistress?"

Ella turned at the soft voice. A dust covered child stood near the end of the wall's foundation. "Euda?" she hurried over. "What are you doing here? This is a dangerous place."

The little girl sniffed and coughed, rubbing at her ear, the metal one missing yet again. "I was workin'. Me ma got me a job as a match girl."

Ella's stomach dropped dropped, already imagining the girl's fate.

"I found a hidey hole," she motioned to the brick. "'E wanted to help me."

Ella knelt in front of the girl. "Who did?"

"Yer man."

Ella grasped the stick thin arms. "Where? How did you get out?"

Flora and her brothers scampered onto the brick next to Euda's shoulder, all staring at her intently.

"This way," said Euda. She and the mice scurried to a small alleyway between a standing wall and the foundation. The girl pointed to archway of bricks, now filled in except for a mouse sized hole. "I like to stand there when I work. The hole was bigger, and I could breath."

Ella knelt and peered into the darkness, when Flora's soft metal brushed her chin, she patted her little helper.

"Go look, Flora. See...see if he's alive."

*****

Ella peered across the Kensington Palace courtyard from her shadowed perch next to a chimney. Closed since Prince Robert's death, someone must have deemed it the most suitable place to install the wounded Aerysleigh once the work crew pulled him from the debris of the match factory. Barely had she laid an ear on his chest to determine if he lived, before a handful of royal guard pushed everyone aside and carried the prince off. Quietly she withdrew the tube of oxygen Flora took in earlier and followed.

Other palaces were closer. Homes of high-ranking friends who could have been imposed upon, happy, no doubt, to take in the prostrate prince—especially if said home contained unmarried daughters. Ella suspected Aerysleigh might have come to his senses once exposed to fresh air and ordered his bearers to his home.

I hope.

Ella watched carefully, noting where the lights came to life and the bustle concentrated. She listened for sounds which indicated Aerysleigh's health had turned. Finally, the activity on the first floor centralised.

I should leave, Ella chastised herself. No doubt Judith wanted an update on the queen's jewels, a subject so far from Ella's thoughts she barely remembered anything beyond sitting on the freezing roofing tiles. Snow coated everything with a light dusting, dulling sounds and making her skirts heavy. Her nose and ears were numb with the cold and shivers ran up and down her limbs. It would be a long walk back to Iron Crest.

Choosing a chimney radiating heat, she settled down to wait, smoothing the dirty skirts of her town dress over her boots. The left boot showed much wear, the damage beyond her expertise and she dared not take it to a cobbler. The sleeves of her coat, retrieved after the child in it was transported, once of a heavy material, now looked frayed at the edges. She pulled the lapels closer. When she did so, her fingers brushed the invitation Aerysleigh gave her.

She pulled it out into the weak moonlight and smoothed the wrinkles. She could not see the writing, but she traced the engraving. *The Lord Chamberlain is commanded by the Queen to invite...all women of London to a masque ball a Kensington Palace.* She smiled and tucked the invitation away.

All women, even modifieds. How had he managed to convince his mother of that one? It was well known Queen Constantina embraced neither her roots, or a love for commoners.

Though she knew Judith coveted these invitations, Ella determined she would not give over this one. She would gather others if a courier had not yet found the overgrown looking gates of Iron Crest, but she *could not* have the one Aerysleigh gave her himself.

She longed to attend the ball despite the peril. The dangers of attending as a guest were almost as high as those for her to go as Cinder intent of stealing the queen's jewels. Though Aerysleigh knew her to be a modified, he could never dream at how far. She stared at the metal hand and wiggled the fingers by tensing her muscles. Using the hand used to be difficult. Everything had to be relearned-how to move her arm, rotate her wrist, wiggle her fingers. It took a great deal of concentration to command the correct wires running from her back to work. Now it came naturally.

No. No one could imagine, let alone know the extent to which Dr. Bihari changed me.

She rested her chin on her knees and stared down at the first-floor window with a smile. *But if I could go, what would I wear?*

It didn't hurt to dream about something that would never come true. Her mother's sapphire dress most certainly, altered to cover her arm and the straps that held it on, of course. She would have to wear her boots. Few of her shoes contained the special block that cradled her half foot and balanced her steps.

Ella plucked at the laces. To dance she must wear the boots. Heaven forbid she waddle like a Christmas goose.

In the wee night hours, the queen's carriage crunched through the ice into the courtyard and Queen Constantina herself descended. Ella couldn't imagine the state of the monarch's thoughts—losing two children, being pulled from the side of an ill husband to attend another son. She hurt for her pain and prayed for her peace. The queen mother did not stay long, however, which caused Ella to hope the news must be good.

Even after the frenetic activity subsided, Ella waited until a single light glowed in the kitchen and the horses settled in the stable before making her move. Only a single automaton directed by a night boy to clean up the horse droppings stirred when she stood and shook the cold from her limbs.

She dabbed a bit of her mother's perfume on her wrist for luck and scaled the ivy to the ground floor.

I just have to know.

Chapter Thirty-Seven

The Intruders

Aerysleigh came out of a restless sleep into instant awareness by a change in the room. He lay still, reaching out with his senses to find the reason he woke. A breeze from an open window brushed across his face bringing with it the earthy smell of gardens freshly turned and hedges trimmed. A fire popped in the grate. Drapes rustled. But none of these things warranted the disturbance of his rest.

He ran over the schematics of the bedchamber in his mind's eye. Fireplace and bed dominated the room. Heavy drapes surrounded him on four sides, though he kept one pulled back to enjoy the crisp air from a cracked window fighting the stifling heat of the fire. The gilded wall paper would reflect the dim firelight, casting silent shadows to cavort across desk, large chairs, and the WAR45 automaton standing at attention by the door.

Then he realised what woke him. The absence of ticking. A grandfather clock flanked a wardrobe just to his left, its subtle and constant noise a pleasant tune to lure one to sleep—was quiet. The automaton, also a usual source of background noise, made not a sound. Even the mantle clock sat hushed.

The doctors and servants were long gone, dismissed by himself somewhat testily after being poked and even bled at his mother's command. The excitement concerning his extraction from the match factory and his subsequent speedy removal from the scene, sat ill with him. Though unconscious for a time, his faculties quickly returned en route, and he found himself relatively uninjured. The few cuts and lingering soreness from lying in an uncomfortable position was nothing compared to what others suffered.

Still, despite repeated demands to return to the factory, the ambulance conveyed him to Kensington where servants put him to bed like an invalid. They promptly sent for Dr. Edleton, a man of dubious medical expertise who catered to the anxiety and bunions of the aristocracy, and worse—his mother.

He sensed rather than heard a movement. Somewhere by the window. Her scent floated to him heat, ash, and the faintest scent of jasmine.

Ella.

He kept his eyes closed, breathing even, willing her to come closer.

Then, from the other side of the room, the door brushed against the carpet as it opened. However, what followed was not the soft footfalls of a servant. Instead came the near silent sound of turning wheels, such as on a cart. Resisting the urge to turn and look, he tried to puzzle out who else could have entered his chamber.

Even the night seemed to hold its breath when a log dropped in the grate and the fire flared briefly while he pondered. Thoughts leaped to his mind of his father's poisoning, the terrible crimes, body snatchers, and the overwhelming sense of apprehension he felt outside St. Drogo not long ago. *Had an assassin found him?* He tensed, preparing to fight for his life with the only weapons he had on hand—pillows.

"Come, Ella," said a woman's voice he did not recognise but lilted across his memory like a dream. "Determine for the both of us that he is well."

A life time later, a soft touch fluttered on his chest, a cold hand which took the measure of each breath. A pause, and then another featherlight touch on his forehead and then—a sigh of relief.

"He lives," said Ella in a low tone.

"Thanks to you, I understand."

He could imagine her blushing even in the dark. The difficult lady found the smallest compliment disconcerting, he could not imagine her taking credit for saving his life so easily.

"The mice—"

"Were directed by you," interrupted the low voice of the unknown woman.

He longed to take a peek but dared not shift lest they both fly. At first, he thought the other speaker must be Cinder, but if the mice were not hers, it had to be someone else.

"Who are you?" Ella whispered.

Yes, Aerysleigh agreed. *Tell us.*

"Someone who cares a great deal about him. And you."

"What do you mean?" Ella asked.

"Surely you do not think your godmother left you totally bereft of friends in her absence. SPAMM takes care of its own, you know, as does MCCD.

"I don't know the MCCD."

"It does not matter. Harcourt and Drax are not the most unobtrusive guardians, however they have performed satisfactorily, I think. But now I will take my leave. Like you, I just wanted visual proof of his health and to thank you for saving his life."

"You knew I would be here?"

"I suspected. Good evening, Lady Steelhaugh."

"But I'm not..." Ella's voice died away.

Hoping Ella was as flummoxed by the visitor as he, Aerysleigh turned his head and peered from under his lashes at the retreating figure. In the gloom, he made out a straight back and dark hair twisted in the usual high dressed woman's knot. A large bonnet hid everything else. Most noteworthy was the fact the lady used an invalid's wheeled chair.

The dark-hair gentlewoman paused with her hand on the door. "You can open your eye now, Airy. But don't try to follow me. I had a servant put a little something in your tea and the WAR is disabled for a time."

Shock kept him tied to the bed and his tongue stuck to the top of his mouth. Only his twin sister ever called him that. He tried to move more and found his limbs heavy and unresponsive.

Rosalind!

Where had she come from? How did she contrive to come to Kensington in the middle of the night without alerting a bevy of servants? She entered by the door—in a chair no less. Where were his attendants? Why was she not announced or detained?

How the devil did a gaggle of women manage to invade his bedchamber in the middle of the night, hold a conversation over his head, and no one seemed the wiser?

A rustling of the bed drapes and the movement of the comforter alerted him to the fact that Ella prepared to leave while he pondered his security problems. He forced his arm to reach out in her direction and caught her prosthesis. He held it as delicately as he would a butterfly.

"Stay."

Ella drew in a sharp breath and whirled. "You *were* awake," she accused.

He grinned at her consternation. "I was. It's hard to get any sleep around here with strangers coming in and out and a whole conversation going on over my head."

She had the grace to look chagrined, staring through the shadows at the now closed door as he had just moments before.

"Who was that?" he demanded.

Ella shrugged. "I am not sure."

Stone walled there.

"Quit lurking. Come here. I am not going to bite." He doubted he could, though the thought was tempting. *What had that woman put in his tea?*

"I should go. I shouldn't be here."

"But you are, and I am glad of it." He fought the effects of whatever drug his sister managed to get into his tea and held out his other hand.

Ella came swiftly to the bedside and slipped her palm into his. However, she perched on the bedside, ready to fly at any moment. The light of the fire revealed smudges across her cheeks and the bridge of her nose. She dropped her gaze and pushed away a long winding tendril of blonde hair leaving another smudge.

"What is Spam?" he asked, hoping to get a few answers to the questions whirling through his mind.

"S-P-A-M-M," she spelled. "It is an acronym for the Society for the Protection of Automatons, Mutants, and Modifieds."

He nodded. "Based at St. Drogo no doubt."

Ella shrugged. "Maybe. I stay out of such matters."

And yet she has a protection detail. Interesting. Who is this woman exactly?

Ella acted so cagey about the smallest details of her life, he dared not mention he'd overheard—his sister?—call her Lady Steelhaugh.

Thinking of his sister made him want to leap from the bed and follow her. Obviously, she too had secrets. *First of which, how was she even alive?*

"You came directly from the fire? How did it end up? No one will tell me much, or they don't know, I can't tell. What of the girls? Did someone find the little one hiding in the building with me?"

Ella settled somewhat, her mind distracted by the horrors of the evening and his questions. "Euda is fine. She led me to the hole on the side of the wall."

Three little heads popped up over the side of the bed and he smiled at the mechanical marvels. They looked so very life-like. "You brought my little friends." He patted the blankets. "Come then. There is no one about to impugn your mistress' reputation." The smallest mouse twitched her whiskers. In four bounds she perched on his shoulder and peered into his eye with a question.

He chuckled. "I promise to sit here like the perfect gentleman." Satisfied, the mouse leaped to the pillow at his shoulder and preceded to clean her whiskers.

Ella smiled at her mechanical pet. "She likes you."

He nodded. "I definitely like her. She saved my life. However, I suspect we have met before." He glanced up sharply. "How is it you have the pets of the notorious thief Cinder?"

Startled, she asked. "Wh—what do you mean?"

"Mouse footprints have been found at the site of of all her escapades. Are you a friend? Perhaps you met her at St. Drogo? Is that how you have her mechanical contraptions?"

"I know of her," Ella conceded. "From St. Drogo and other places."

"People there do not seem to see her as the thief she is."

Ella waved away his observation with an impatient gesture. "Sometimes people are trapped by their circumstances to do things others do not understand."

Aerysleigh scoffed. "To thieve?"

Ella looked him straight in the face now, her dander up. "Yes. And other things. Tonight, you saw hundreds of girls working in a match factory despite the dangers. Even though many of them will get a cancer that will first disfigure then kill them." She looked away. "Sometimes there are only hard choices."

Images of the match girls' emaciated forms draped in threadbare garments and wearing cancer disfigured faces appeared in his mind. Aerysleigh sighed and leaned back into the pillows. "Yes. Will St. Drogo take them in? Will they alert the Ladies Aid Societies?"

"Several hospitals are available. The injured were transported throughout London. They will all have at least some aspect of care. I don't know the number killed, a score at least. They were still digging out bodies when I left, but it could have been worse. Much worse."

He nodded, a grim silence falling between them.

Suddenly Ella softened and her hand found his again. He loved how it fit his perfectly. "How are *you* doing?" she asked softly.

He twined their fingers and squeezed gently. "I am perfectly fine. Besides feeling drugged, that is. A compromise had to be reached with my mother and the surgeons, however, so I am to stay in this bed until morning." He glowered at the fire. "But come the dawn I plan to go to Cuthbert and Cox and see the damage for myself. Then it is on to the hospitals to enquire after the wounded."

And lay a trap for Cinder at the upcoming ball. And find his sister whether she wanted to be found or not.

He regretted doubting his father's sanity now.

Ella stroked his arm. "Your thoughtfulness will be appreciated." She tried unsuccessfully to stifle a yawn. "Excuse me, it has been a long day."

"I have been a boar. I received my rest, yet I keep you from yours."

"I must leave. The servants will rouse soon."

"There are hours yet. Stay. Take a rest, then go."

He tugged her back against his shoulder. She offered little resistance and relaxed into his side. "Maybe just a short nap. I feel like I couldn't make it out the window if I wanted."

"Perhaps you should try the door. Evidently the other lady found no impedance that way." The WAR remained silent as did the clocks.

She grimaced at the bed, pristine white even in the limited light. "I look a fright. I will smudge the pillows," she murmured.

"Smudge away," he breathed into the tangle of hair at his chin. Ignoring the twinge of soreness in his ribs and shoulder, he tightened his arm around her.

"It's been so long," she murmured so low he nearly missed it.

"What has?" he demanded, a surge of jealously gripped him at the thought of her in of the arms of another man. "Since someone held you?"

She pushed her shoulder into his ribs. "No, silly, a proper bed."

"Kiss me," he said suddenly remembering heat of the kiss at the match factory, "before you sleep." Soft lips touched his and he let her feel the heat of his desire.

Her chin dropped away, her breathing grew regular, exhaustion overcoming her desire to leave at last.

Aerysleigh chuckled. Always the unexpected with her. He

relaxed into the pillows, enjoying the feel of her body resting against his. His arm tingled, a warning it would ache in time, but he didn't care. He would let his whole body go turn to ice just to hold her like this.

What would it be like to hold her every night?

He determined he would...no matter what. No ruse to fool his mother into thinking he'd marry. He *would* choose a bride the night of the ball.

If only she would come.

CHAPTER THIRTY-EIGHT

THE MORNING AFTER

"Psst. Psst."

Ella rubbed her face into the soft sheet at the insistent intrusion of the dream of a proper bed and down pillows. She reached for the thin blanket Judith allowed her to cover her pallet in the forge. Instead her fingers sank in a fluffy coverlet.

Ahh, such a sweet dream.

She pulled the down bolster to her shoulders and snuggled into the warmth pressed against her face. An unfamiliar combination of scents flooded her senses. Leather and smoke, scotch and lineament. Something soft tickled her nose. "Go away, Flora," she said.

"Psst."

She batted at the persistent tickle. A soft chuckle rumbled under her cheek and her eyes flew open and her chin jerked up.

Aerysleigh smiled down at her, his braids brushing her cheek. "Good morning."

Not a dream at all.

With a wild push she flung herself off the side of the bed and promptly fell in the tangled bed linens onto the floor. "*Ommph.*"

Aerysleigh leaned over the side of the mattress, his grin growing. "Do you always wake so violently?"

"I slept with you," heat burned up her neck at the memory of his hard chest. She remembered the feeling of exhaustion, but that tired? *Really, Ella!* "I mean..." The cool breeze from the window sent shivers up her arm. She clasp the neck of her threadbare gown. "My coat!"

"On the chair," he said evenly.

"You took it off?!"

"I did. It was quite damp, and you looked very uncomfortable."

"Psst." The annoying interruption of her dreams now saved her. She scooted backwards, bumped her head on a writing table, and then used it to rise.

All the while Aerysleigh watched her without moving, his cocoa coloured eye dancing with a merriment he tried to hide. Sometime during the night, he donned his eye patch. He nodded towards the window. "I do believe your erstwhile guardian is trying to rouse you."

Ella frowned and limped to the window. "Harcourt," she whispered. "What are you doing here?"

"The cocks are crowing, Lady Elia—"

"I told you not to call me that."

"But Drax and me got worried about ye."

Ella sighed. "How the devil...?" She glanced back at Aerysleigh. He stared hard at the watercolour of *Sky Serpent* over the fireplace, but his lips twitched as he fought his amusement.

She took a deep breath. "I have to go. I'm sorry..." she trailed off. What exactly did one say when a woman spent the night in a man's room? She flushed again.

His expression changed quickly from amusement to one of wariness. The impact of her waking in the prince's room, his bed, sunk in. *What he must think of her!* He seemed aloof of a sudden. Did he expect her to raise a ruckus? Trap him into marriage? Her heart sank.

Rumours of indiscretions among those who pretended to be above such things were common, though honestly the gossip did not seem to touch Aerysleigh. However, more than one young lady had been ruined by rumours and more than one rake trapped into marriage. She placed her hands on her cheeks, unable to confront his questioning gaze.

Just leave. Yes, go quietly. You never have to see him again. The ball is in a week. He will choose a bride and stay where he belongs, far away from St. Drogo and you.

She turned towards the window for her escape. *So much for using the door.* If Harcourt managed to rouse himself from his usual alcohol soused slumber, the responsible palace servant must be awake. She entered by the window, she must leave by it. *As quickly as possible.*

Suddenly he stood beside her and pulled her into his arms. "Ahh, Ella. I can see the cogs turning in that amazing brain of yours."

She hid her face in his night shirt, wanting to run and stay both. "I..."

"I don't think I've known you to be at a loss of words before. I think I like it."

She lifted her chin to glare at him and realised he was smiling again, her wariness disappeared. Their eyes searched each other's faces.

Did he see what he wanted? That I wouldn't hold this against him? Ruin his life? That he is safe from me?

"Please stay." He stroked his thumb across her cheek. "Stay and talk to me."

When she opened her mouth to protest, Aerysleigh kissed her hard enough to take her breath away. She wrapped her arms around him and tugged him closer. His lips trailed fire down her neck. She lost herself in the feeling, tangling her hands in his braids to find his lips again.

A cock crowed.

"My lady," an insistent voice hissed. "People be waking."

Ella pulled as far away as he let her. "You have to let me go," she whispered.

He pressed his forehead to hers. "What if I don't want to? Ever?"

Her heart leaped. If it were only true. *What if he knew of my modification? Would his reaction remain the same?* How she wanted to tell him, she just couldn't push the words past her lips. "It can't be," she said instead.

"Stay," Aerysleigh whispered against her lips. "Talk to me. Tell me why it is you run away. Trust me."

"I don't think this is talking," she observed, leaning in for more.

The three mice leaped to the windowsill. Flora tugged on his sleeve. One of the largest mice ran back and forth, peering down at Harcourt, and then at Ella, clearly agitated by her dallying. Aerysleigh brushed the loose blonde tendrils of hair from her face. "Is it your *friend*—Cinder?"

Ella jerked back, but his arms held her fast. "What?"

"Is it Cinder? Is she blackmailing you somehow?"

Ella stared at him. "Why would you say that?"

"She's a thief, obviously comfortable on the other side of the law and protected by St. Drogo."

"And you take that to mean she has some sort of hold over the people there? Including me?" This time she shoved him away with the force of metal. He stood firm. "You know nothing," she hissed. "And you assume too much."

"Lady Eliana!" Harcourt called outside, nearly loud enough to bring a guard. Reality set in and Ella slapped both hands against the wonderfully warm chest, putting space between her and his intoxicating body so she could think.

Aerysleigh let her go, but his hands lingered on her arms, warm against metal and cloth. He took her hand in his and kissed the knuckles gently. Ella wanted to cry at his gentleness. "Forgive me. I only want to understand you."

She bit her lip, wanting to tell him everything. But so much was at stake. "I—I can't."

He nodded, but she felt the distance grow between them as he straightened. "I understand."

No, you don't.

"Come back then," he whispered.

She nearly melted right then and there.

*****

Ella paused, silhouette framed by the dawn in rivalry of the finest art. He hoped to outlast her, let his silence do the speaking, willing her to trust him. For a split second it seemed as though he would win. Ella took a deep breath and pressed something into his hand.

He looked down at the small vial and back at her in askance.

"It is a nerve rejuvenator, specifically designed to reverse the damage of the mutated puffer fish," she explained, "for your father."

Holding the vial up he peered at the pink liquid. "How...?" Looking back up he found she had disappeared. At her exit, the WAR45 jerked up, its head swivelling as though looking for an intruder.

"Stand down, War, everything is fine."

The automaton regarded him a long moment. "Password," it demanded.

Aerysleigh shook his head, of all the times for his security to go regimental on him. "Seventeen seventy."

The WAR45 paced the room in a predetermined pattern, then went out the door on its regular rounds.

Doubting the efficacy of the automatons, Aerysleigh walked to the window and looked out. Ella had disappeared, but either Harcourt moved slower, or he stayed behind to make certain no one followed his lady. Aerysleigh motioned the interesting-looking fellow over. The Cinder impersonator and Ella guard hesitated. Aerysleigh straightened, making his gesture commanding. He may be in his nightshirt, but he expected orders to be obeyed—few resisted, especially those who served in the military as he suspected Harcourt once did.

The fellow approached, his pincher snapping by his side with impatience. He touched his cap then bowed. "Yer Highness?'

"Thank you for saving me yesterday."

Harcourt's eyes slanted away, gazing at the windows and doors for servants rousing. He shrugged. "Weren't my doing. The lady asked. I obeyed." He pulled at his disreputable jacket as though he had any hope at making it presentable. "Me and Drax keep her safe."

"Indeed. You do a good job. Who orders it so?"

Harcourt gave him a sharp look. "Why, Lord Stillingfleet, of course. He watches out for us all."

"You all?"

"The modifieds, yer highness. Or did ye not know Ella be one of us?" the chap said with a scoffing snort.

"I know. It doesn't matter."

The short fellow swung his gaze back. "No, it don't. But most people can't see that now, can they?" The man touched his cap then like a shadow slipped away as quietly as Ella had.

Did they teach such things at St. Drogo?

Aerysleigh clenched his hands by his side at a sudden surge of jealously. Lord Stillingfleet seemed to be meddling quite a bit in his affairs with both Cinder and Ella. He resolved to have a word with the bloke.

He sat quickly at his desk and set the vial before him. Choosing a paper monogrammed in gold, he penned a letter summoning The Marquess of Wheelfell, recluse that he was, to the ball. Aerysleigh hoped to at last get the truth about his connection between Cinder and Ella. He clutched the pen so tightly the nib broke and splattered the paper with ink.

Grumbling, Aerysleigh reached for another and set the blotter on the spill. He tapped his chin, eyes narrowing at the doorway. St. Drogo and its surprisingly large network of people could also be the only place that Rosalind could have remained hidden all these years. He pushed back the questions that crowded his mind.

Yes, Lord Stillingfleet seemed to have the keys to many of the mysteries stumping him at the moment. He pulled the cord for a messenger boy to find the whereabouts of the Marquess of Wheelfell. Aerysleigh planned to deliver both vial and message to the meddling Lord.

Brilliant scientist or not. Protector of the modifieds or not—if the man has designs on Ella, I will put a stop to that. From here on out, Ella needs no protection but my own.

Chapter Thirty-Nine

The Plots

Judith kept Ella busy for the following week. Even if Ella wanted to go to London, she could not. Her stepmother hired a local boy to run errands to town and back—for dressmakers, several because the selection of fabrics offered by the first two were not up to her standards, and for ribbons and slippers.

With Myrtle's help Ella toiled from the early morning hours into the night. Together they filled the shoes of cook and scullery, laundress, stable help, as well as secretaries, slop maid, lady's maid, hall boy, and gardener.

Despite the work, however, Ella's mind whirled at a fast pace. She vacillated between sudden euphoria and the deepest depression of spirits she had not felt since her father's death. She dreamed of arriving at the ball, only this time she had not modified the sapphire dress to cover her modification. The prosthesis shown in all its ugly, metal glory, and the prince walked towards her and took her hand and then they danced, sweeping across the floor before the entire world.

Then reality would set in, usually while scooping manure or tossing out the night jars. She should not even think of dancing with

Aerysleigh, let alone marry him—despite his sweet words in the heat of a moment.

I'll just go and watch and stay in the shadows where he can't see me. At least, until he chooses his bride, then I'll leave.

Myrtle asked her what the matter was. When Ella looked at her in askance at the aberration the automaton opened her hands and shrugged her shoulders. "Yer acting strangely. It makes me ask strange questions."

Ella frowned. "That doesn't make any sense." But then, so much did not make sense about Dr. Bihari's creations.

"Neither does the way yer actin'." Myrtle motioned to the contraption Ella dragged from a cobwebbed corner of the forge and was currently cleaning. It stood on three legs with eight arms sticking out from a large ball. Each arm was armed with a brush, comb, or dispensed hair pins. "What *are* ye doing now?"

Ella stopped her work and stood back. "It is my mother's hair dresser." She studied the options. The hair styles in the machine were a decade old.

Myrtle nodded knowingly. "Exactly."

Ella snapped her dust cloth at the contraption and went back to her assigned duties. What need would she have of an intricate hair style? A simple chignon with a dustcover was good enough for the likes of her.

Even Judith took notice of Ella's preoccupation. When a request for coffee in the sitting room never came, she stormed into the kitchen where Ella polished the silver. "What seems to be occupying your mental capacity to its utmost?"

Ella looked up. "I'm sorry, did you say something."

Judith's face turned a bright red. Myrtle turned away quickly with an audible snort.

"I asked for coffee an hour ago?"

"Oh. Did you?" Ella rose heavily. "Alright."

Ella looked at her stepmother dully and tried to tear her mind from the sweet dilemma keeping her occupied. "I am attempting to puzzle out how to retrieve the queen's jewels." Ella lied with the first thing that popped into her mind. She was exhausted and hungry. Nowhere on the Judith's extensive lists were meal times for herself, only her stepmother and sisters. She added. "I don't have the time to make my usual reconnaissance and plans."

Judith bared her teeth in a smile reminiscent of a starving lone wolf. "You will have to work faster then, my dear."

Ella dropped a spoon into the tray. "Impossible," she muttered.

Judith stalked over and slapped Ella across the cheek. She tumbled from her stool and into the ashes of the fire. Myrtle's quick reflexes grabbed Ella's dress and pulled her back, saving her from a severe burn. Even so, the thin material parted and ripped along the sleeve seams.

The automaton froze, but Ella had gained her balance and stood, clutching at the fabric.

Judith's lips curled at the blue light illuminating the dark chimney corner from Ella's back. She leaned in close. "I will have those jewels, or you will not have a home." Spittle flew with the force of her words. She looked pointedly at Myrtle. "Or help. The house must be extra clean by tomorrow. I have a guest arriving."

Ella clutched her cheek and glared at the woman's straight back. On a whim, she stuck her tongue out. She really longed to throw something. At the continued silence in the room, Ella turned to Myrtle. The automaton stood frozen, hand still reaching out to help Ella, face twisted in a rictus of shock.

"She hit you," Myrtle said. "Again."

Ella sighed. "It's alright, Myrtle."

"No. It's not. She can strike me. I'm a machine. You're not. Yer the Lady Steelhaugh."

Ella stepped quickly to her friend and put her fingers to her lips. "Please Myrtle. Don't talk like that. You will get us both into trouble."

"'On your life, Myrtle, keep the lady safe,'" Myrtle parroted suddenly, her voice tinny with a memory. Some leftover programming, Ella guessed, but it seemed to happen more and more. Myrtle never did act like machine. She leaned in close and examined the automaton's metal casing. It was scored and stained.

"Bunions and boilers! What has she been doing to you when I am gone?"

Myrtle stared right through her. "She asks me to do things. Sometimes I obey. Sometimes I don't. No matter. She likes t' damage things. People."

"What people, Myrtle? What are you talking about?"

Myrtle turned back to her cooking. "You. Isabeau. Aurelia. The mice. She hurts things."

"And you?"

"I'm a machine. I don't hurt."

That Ella did not believe. She well remembered how Judith could incapacitate Myrtle. The memory of her friend laying on the floor blackened Ella's vision with impotent rage for a long moment.

Ella laid her prosthesis on Myrtle's shoulder—metal on metal.

Her friend had been used badly while Ella spent so much time in the city the preceding weeks and desperately needed maintenance. The automaton creaked when she moved and occasionally got a hitch in her speech.

"Come, Myrtle. Let's get some oil into those old joints of yours."

Myrtle took the kettle from the fire. "But the lady's coffee."

Ella waved it away. "It can wait some more."

*****

"Ella, Ella. Come here."

Ella turned from lighting the hall lanterns at Isabeau's insistent call. "What is it?"

Her stepsister put a finger to her lips. "*Shh.*" She motioned into the girls' bed chamber and closed the door without a sound. Despite their pact, Ella's schedule was such she did not see her stepsisters much.

The room had changed drastically. The curtains were closed against the dying sun and on top of those hung heavy tapestries and comforters that turned the room into the deepest night.

Two candles burned, one on a desk littered with papers. Ella stepped closer. The pages were filled with chemical formulae in a neat script, none of which she could make out. They seemed to revolve around working with blood, but Isabeau hissed at her and scraped the papers together with a quiet rustle.

Aurelia lay on a bed in the furthest corner, hands folded on her breast and pale hair loose and flowing. Add a lily and a letter and she would have been a replica for Elaine of Astolat. The girl did not move at all.

Ella approached the bed. Her stepsister didn't even appear to breath. "Is Aurelia well?" she asked.

Isabeau dropped the papers she snatched from Ella and hurried over. "Don't wake her, she is sleeping."

Ella put her hands on her hips, too tired for games. "What are you about? I have chores I must attend to." She raised her voice at the end of her questions. Isabeau lunged at her and slapped a hand across her mouth.

The bruise left by Judith just that morning stung sharply, and Ella tried to break the elder stepsister's grasp. She jerked and grabbed the hand with her metal arm and exerted all the force of her powerful fingers, but she could not break her sister's effective grip.

Isabeau grunted. "Be still," she whispered in Ella's ear.

When Ella quit struggling, Isabeau let go. She motioned her towards the fireplace where a new brass pipe snaked out of the chimney. Through it came the sounds of voices.

She looked at Isabeau in askance.

Isabeau covered the pipe. "Mother and her guest," she whispered. "We don't know his name, but he is pretty high up in the chain of command. He gives Mother her orders."

Ella shrugged. A name meant nothing but reminded her of the night she listened at the window. She shivered, convinced Judith and her cohorts personified evil. Ella moved her left ear closer to listen.

"If you have made no progress, Jutta, it is time to terminate your experiments and move on."

"But, Herr, I have Cinder supplying us with ready cash, my daughters show promising signs of *stable* changes—"

"You are months behind what Strobble is doing in London. With the fresh bodies from among the poor, he has created more powerful monsters than anything you have shown me. What, one of your girls sleeps all day? The other can smell things? Bah, these are not the attributes of the great soldiers we need. If Isabeau or Aurelia do not catch the eye of Prince Aerysleigh at the ball tomorrow evening, you will go back to the continent."

"And my daughters?" Judith's voice sounded strange, even through the pipe.

"They will be recruited into other aspects of the organisation. I should have known not to let a woman raise children out of the creche. You become too attached. Just like you did to your natural son. Women grow weak and unfocused over children."

Suddenly, Ella remembered Judith's story about her son and husband dying while they chased Ella's mother into a storm and the rage Judith displayed. She shot a look at Isabeau. *What did she think of not being called a natural daughter?*

But her stepsister was nodding her head as though it all made sense. She caught Ella's look. "I knew it all along," she said.

"I have moved on, *Herr*. I never shirked my duty," Judith continued her protests.

"Shirked? *Nein*. But your work is subpar. Your experiments are not working. The progress is too slow, besides. This is your last warning. Octavia's daughter is to get the jewels. The *werwolf* or *blutsauger* will marry the prince or we will find another way."

In the corner Aurelia jerked awake with a start. Isabeau quickly stuffed a rag down the pipe and hurried to her sister. The blonde girl looked around. "Where am I?" she asked.

"Home. You are in your room," Isabeau replied.

Aurelia shook her head, looking around sadly. "This is not home. Home is where you are safe. We are not safe here. We are not safe anywhere."

Isabeau put her arms around Aurelia's shoulders. The younger sister seemed thinner, more ethereal. Her translucent skin glowed in the weak light. However, when she looked up the blue irises disappeared leaving her black pupils to consume her entire eye. She sank into her sister's arms as though exhausted.

"I am hungry," Aurelia said.

Thinking the words directed at her, Ella turned the door. "I will get you some cold—"

Aurelia opened her mouth and lunged for Isabeau's wrist. Isabeau grabbed her sister's chin in a brutal grip. They struggled silently, Isabeau blowing out a breath as she fought to hold her sister. "Don't you bite me. Get control of yourself. Now."

"Hungry," Aurelia hissed. She strained to get at her sister.

Ella flew to Isabeau's aid. Something told her she must not get her flesh close to Aurelia, so she reached in with metal and pried Aurelia's face from Isabeau's wrist. Though slight of build, Aurelia fought with the strength of a draft horse. They wrestled for a long moment. Even with the two of them fighting to restrain Aurelia she nearly overcame them. Then, just as suddenly as she attacked, she collapsed back onto Isabeau. All three girls tumbled to the bed.

They lay panting in a heap until Aurelia stirred. "I'm alright now. I'm sorry."

Isabeau picked herself up from the mattress and hugged her sister. "It's alright, dolly. I know you didn't mean it. We will work on having something for you to eat when you wake."

Aurelia sighed, every movement languid. When her black-eyed gaze settled on Ella, Ella pushed herself out of range quickly.

The pale sister smiled, her elongated canines flashed. "What is *she* doing here?"

"Mother's handler is downstairs." Isabeau answered. "Aurelia. Your teeth."

"You know I can't control them when I am hungry. What does he want?" said Aurelia with a delicate shrug.

Isabeau took a deep breath. "Our time is up. We are considered failures."

Ella looked between the two. "But you aren't, are you? Are you modified like me? Or something else entirely?"

Aurelia grinned. Ella retreated further. "No," said the pale sister.

"But yes."

"What she means is that we are not monsters such as the creatures other scientists are breeding," Isabeau interjected. "Mother decided the best route for creating the soldiers Prussia needs to win over the world, is to raise them from children. Slowly altering their blood and temperament. We have been changed, very slowly mind you, since we were babes."

"You have been keeping things from Judith." Ella stated, knitting her brows. She didn't blame them at all but didn't fully understand why they would do so or even what Judith had done to them.

Isabeau walked to the desk and flipped through the stack of papers. She held up a sheet covered in fine script. "Aurelia has mastered forging Mother's writing. We falsify records and results when we can, keeping anything that she might consider an advancement from her. Unfortunately, she has a great memory. We have to be careful."

"But you give her enough to give her hope," Ella looked from sister to sister.

Isabeau nodded.

"Smart."

"Or not," said Aurelia.

"If one of us does not capture the prince's hand, we will be reassigned," said Isabeau.

Aurelia shivered. Ella could only guess what that would mean for the two girls. She bit her lip. They were all trapped.

"What if *I* married the prince?" Ella asked suddenly.

Isabeau stood. "What do you mean?"

"What if I married Prince Aerysleigh? What if I revealed what Judith is? Protected you?"

Would he do that? He did not mind her prosthesis. At Saint Drogo he promised to stand up for the modifieds. What if she took that step and believed him?

"Without Judith, Cinder could disappear." *Along with Aerysleigh's obsession with capturing her.* Ella knew he wanted her, but Cinder stood between them.

"Can you?" Isabeau leaned towards her and took a deep breath. Ella braced for some sort of attack. Her stepsister pulled back suddenly. "You can!" she exclaimed in a hope-filled voice and looked over her shoulder. "She smells like him, Aurelia. You have been with him."

Ella frowned and sniffed her sleeve. "How do you do that? That was days ago." All she could smell was horses and polish, kerosene and the lamb she served for supper.

Isabeau brushed off Ella's observation. "It is faint, but it is there. Once I learn the smells of people and things, I do not forget them."

"What an amazing talent," Ella said.

"No," Isabeau snapped. "It is not. Not when it comes with other baggage."

"You are very strong," Ella stated.

Again, her elder stepsister nodded. "Yes, among other things." She glanced towards the tapestry covered window. "Unfortunately, it will be a full moon tomorrow night."

"How do you know?"

Isabeau grinned. "It is just one of those things."

"So, what does that mean?"

Isabeau sighed and shook her head. "It means we will be little help if you get in trouble. It will be all we can do to keep ourselves under control."

Aurelia flung her sheets off her lap and rose with fluid grace. "Speak for yourself, Isabeau." She lifted her arms. "I like the night." She glided towards Ella, her feet barely touching the floor. Once again, Ella found herself retreating and wishing for a weapon.

Against your own stepsister, Ella, don't be ridiculous.

Maybe, but Aurelia seems very dangerous at the moment.

"What I want to know is, if she can do this thing. Will Prince Aerysleigh protect us? Why should he?" Aurelia's iris-less eyes searched Ella's face, and if possible, her teeth grew even longer, resting on her bottom lip—ivory on scarlet.

Ella stopped backing and reached out with her metal hand, palm down. "Because I will ask him. Because we are sisters." She swallowed hard. "He said he would stand for the right of modifieds and mutants and was angry at the way they are being treated."

"Bah. People say things they don't mean all the time," said Aurelia. "Things like, *'You are my child'. 'I love you'. 'Take this poison like a good girl.'*"

"Aurelia!" Isabeau snapped.

Ella nodded. "I agree. We will hold him to his word. But I need your help."

Isabeau walked over and put her hand on Ella's. "The gown?"

Ella nodded. "I need it modified to fit..." she motioned to her arm. "This."

Aurelia sighed and put her hand on Isabeau's. "We can, but I don't have much faith this will work."

Ella looked between her stepsisters. Isabeau with her dark-haired beauty and canine-like eyes. Aurelia, so pale and still, and so very dangerous. "As I see it, we don't have a choice." She nearly cringed remembering her conversation with Aerysleigh. *Choices.* Sometimes there just weren't any good choices. And tonight, he was hers.

She prayed he didn't betray her faith.

*****

"Ella, come into the library," said Judith through a crack in the door.

Ella paused her weary trudge to the forge where she longed for a small rest. At some point she planned to make a drawing or two of more realistic cheek covers for the phossy jaw girls, but she had to be able to see straight first.

She pushed into the library. "What?"

Judith sat in front of a large fire Ella built earlier. "Throw a log on for me," said her stepmother. Which reminded Ella the wood chopper sprang a fuel leak this morning and she forgot to procure a new line. She bent to the fire with a sigh and leaned towards the heat.

A hand suddenly gripped the back of her neck, holding her face to the orange flames with an iron grip. Fingers dug into the pressure points below her ears and spots swam in front of her eyes.

"I am tired of your attitude, girl. It will stop now, or my use for you is finished. Do you understand?"

"Yes, my lady." The words eeked out between gritted teeth. Still, it satisfied her stepmother and the hold loosened. When Ella turned, Judith sat in her chair again, her mother's chair, arranging a shawl about her shoulders.

"Good. On another note," her stepmother continued in a conversational tone. "I have thought about you not having enough time, so I have planned for a distraction at the ball to occur at midnight."

"That is rather early, don't you think?" Balls went into full swing much later. Ella herself preferred the quiet times of the early morning to make a visit to a target. Little stirred in the wee hours before the cock crowed, and exhausted aristocrats sought their beds. Still, procuring the protection of Aerysleigh would negate the necessity of pinching the queen's jewels so she must not argue too vehemently about anything her stepmother planned.

"Never mind. The distraction should allow you to get close to some of the jewels."

Ella cocked her head at Judith's strange choice of words. "Close?"

Judith chuckled. "Close enough. Those jewels will set me up for a very long time. Especially when one of the girls marries the prince." She gave Ella a calculating look. "I might even need a servant or two *less.*"

Ella shivered at the implication, but Judith ignored her.

"Yes, I think the distraction will do just fine for you. A fitting end to the career of Cinder, don't you think?"

"End?" Ella echoed.

"Yes," Judith stared into the fire, her mind far away. "I think it will work nicely." She glanced up suddenly and Ella looked quickly away. Madness seemed to lurk in the woman's taunt expression. "Go about your chores then."

Ella quickly left the room, cold fingers of a dread crept up her modified spine.

Chapter Forty

The Marquess

It took a large breakfast before the surgeon even considered allowing Aerysleigh to venture forth. Then, because his valet had become empowered with marching orders from the butler who received them from Queen Constantina, he was bathed, shaved, trimmed, and turned out properly. However, before Aerysleigh completed his escape, the butler insisted on one last change to his routine.

"Really, Mr. Ward, don't you think that is a bit excessive?" Aerysleigh nodded towards assigned personal protection automaton. "I had no need of one of those while I captained an airship," he reminded the butler.

Mr. Ward sniffed. "Your Highness was not throwing himself under falling buildings and being dragged home insensible either."

"I was not unconscious when I arrived," Aerysleigh argued, though he sensed a losing battle.

The butler cleared his throat and played his trump. "The queen specifically asked that the machine be assigned."

Aerysleigh sighed. "Alright, then. If it will get me out of here the faster."

"Your carriage is ready, sire."

"I did not request a carriage. I distinctly remember asking for a horse."

"The queen's orders," said Mr. Ward.

Aerysleigh took the carriage. Then left it and the driver at a stable with the command the fellow return to the palace in three hours after a good supper—with or without him.

He could not shake the WAR as easily and it stomped along beside him at a steady pace. Consequently, the hands on his waistcoat watch approached high noon before he made his way to the gates of Cuthburt and Cox.

Here a flurry of activity greeted his amazed eyes.

Protesters marched through the churned snow down main street in front of the factory. Mostly women and girls, they carried hastily made banners calling for the use of red phosphorus. Others called for fair pay and a strike of all the match girls of London. Almost all the girls wore coats too thin for the weather or no coat at all. If not disfigured by cancers, their faces reflected their lives, with even the young girls looking like drawn old women rather than children.

WARs walked alongside the column of women. Aerysleigh could not determine if they were to clear the way for the girls, or to keep them in line. However, no one molested the marchers, besides several reporters firing general questions to anyone who would answer. One particular journalist spied him, an auburn-haired woman with a quick gaze, but he nipped through a store before she could catch him.

Never had he witnessed so many protests and near riots in the city. London's growing pains were spilling out onto the street where all could see. From what he remembered as a boy unrest in the lower classes was quickly handled out of sight. This time, however, the seething anger against low pay, starvation, and unfair treatment, refused to be covered up. London was changing, just as the world changed.

The grounds of Cuthbert and Cox seethed as well, but this was of a different sort of activity, more mechanical in nature. Men and automatons swarmed over the rubble like bees on sugar. They sifted through the debris, stacking bricks onto pallets and loading them onto carts which were pulled away by teams of four drays. Lumber lined the streets and allies for loading and reuse. With one man directing three of four machines, the work progressed smoothly and quickly.

Overseeing the activity like a feudal king was Lord Stillingfleet, Marquess of Wheelfell. He worked from a waggon transformed into a simple office. As per rumour, Aerysleigh recognised him not from his clothes, for despite the weather and well made, he had thrown his coat aside. His cravat hung loose, and his waistcoat sported soot, as though he had lent a hand in the dirty work around him. Nor by the subtle clink of glass from each of his movements indicating an apothecary belt somewhere on his person. He knew it to be the Lord Stillingfleet by his metal mask. It covered his forehead, nose, left cheek, and most of his mouth.

Aerysleigh could not remember the incident that caused the man to don his mask, however he was known for his work as an apothecary as well as making chemical weapons for the war effort.

A few girls, several obviously badly injured, waited at the foot of a ladder leading up to the platform. Aerysleigh couldn't put his finger on it—he never met the man before—but something about the man's overbearing attitude, albeit from afar, rubbed him worse than rough wool body linen.

Aerysleigh headed straight for him.

The man did not acknowledge his approach. Aerysleigh stood like a schoolboy before a master waiting his turn. The man handed envelopes down to the waiting girls. "This should get you by until the match factory reopens," he said to a tall woman who seemed to shepherd the other girls. She clutched an over-sized man's coat about her spare frame despite the fires burning off debris and heat radiating from the bricks.

"How long?" she croaked.

Lord Stillingfleet's metal mask seemed to soften. He crouched to look her in the eye. "We will get it opened as soon as possible, but there will be some changes here."

The woman nodded. "Good. Me girls are thinkin' about striking."

Lord Stillingfleet nodded. "Do it. But get yourselves organised first. You have the power to bring the red phosphorus to the industry." The woman and girls seemed to take courage under his speech and when they went away determination straightened their spines.

Still, Lord Stillingfleet paid no attention to Aerysleigh. Instead, he waited while the gentleman finished a letter and handed it to a waiting errand boy before looking up.

The marquess appeared distinctly annoyed. "What are you doing here?"

Aerysleigh narrowed his eyes but allowed the lack of decorum to slip. By all accounts the man was a veritable hermit with little occasion to practice niceties. Besides, after a morning rife with setbacks, Aerysleigh struggled with his own impatience. He bowed. "Lord Stillingfleet."

The man gave an impatient wave of his hand. "Call me Phineas, I don't have the time or patience for the whole song and dance of society. Do you have a reason for being here, your highness?"

A few months had passed since anyone had treated him with such disregard. In fact, it may have been when he was just getting is air legs as a cabin boy in the military. "Did you just encourage those women to strike?" He enquired, not sure which outrage to address first—his honour or those of his peers.

Phineas shrugged. "Of course. I can't do everything."

"But why?" To encourage a strike was against his class. "The peerage will—"

"What? Ostracise me?" The marquess chuckled. "That is the least of my worries. The match industry needs to change, and it needs to change now before more match girls are condemned to a suffering death." He sounded like Ella and a flash of jealously again stirred under Aerysleigh's waistcoat.

A man hurried to the platform. His fine coat and fastidious manner indicated he may be the marquess' manservant. "M'Lord, Mr. Cox has arrived."

Stillingfleet waved him off. "He can wait. He is responsible for this mess even after repeated warnings. I will see him later." He glanced at his watch. "Six o'clock at the Savile. Remind him he is to bring a plan to convert to the red or the girls will strike and shut him down longer."

The man touched his hat. "Yes, M'Lord." He paused and cast a look Aerysleigh's way, bowing awkwardly. "Your highness."

At least someone has some manners.

Once again, a social faux pas. Aerysleigh wondered how Phineas ranked above a prince but shrugged it away. Several other passing workers touched their caps, some bowing quickly before continuing about their tasks. He turned back to the marquess who eyed him thoughtfully.

"It seems your near-death experience has endeared you to the workers here."

Aerysleigh dismissed the idea that loyalty could be bought. "I did not do it for their respect."

"Indeed, that is the very reason why they respect you. It appears your style of leadership follows you from the airship. Rumours were that you often risked yourself for the common man. Yesterday it was a modified girl."

"We are all human."

Again, the marquess gave him a strange look. "Few see the situation in that light."

"Times are changing," Aerysleigh said slowly, musing over his thoughts on his walk to the match factory. "London is changing. Attitudes must adapt as well. What is the red? And how is it you can demand this of the owner of the largest match factory in London. Are you a partner?"

"So many questions, your highness."

"You have no idea. And I am beyond asking them and getting no answers."

Instead of reacting with anger at Aerysleigh's temper, this seemed to put Phineas at his ease. He motioned to a rickety chair across from the desk and lowered himself into his own, moving slowly as though in pain.

The WAR attempted to negotiate the small ladder attached to the waggon platform to fulfil the butlers spacial commands. The first rung broke under his excessive weight, stupefying its endeavour. "You may release your WAR," said Phineas with a condescending grin. "There is no danger here."

Aerysleigh ground his teeth. "I am afraid I cannot. It is assigned by Queen Constantina and pulling its card will cause an alarm."

Lord Stillingfleet nodded. "I see. Mr. Middleton," he called to a man overseeing the destruction of a nearby wall. The man stomped over. By his walk, Aerysleigh suspected both legs to be metal prosthesis. "Would you mind reassigning His Highness' automaton to a more useful function than destroying my stairs."

In five minutes, the fellow had the back off the machine while it tried to avoid him, wires pulled, reconnected, and a new mission laid out. The WAR began picking up stray bricks and stacking them with the others.

"Useful man," Aerysleigh observed.

Phineas shrugged. "I like to employ useful men. Now let me see if I can answer a few of your questions. The red refers to red phosphorus. A safer means for match production than the white. While white phosphorus is still generated when the match is struck, the process of actually making the match is much less dangerous. I asked Mr. Cox to change months ago. Placed a petition to the Director of Imports for a ban on the importation of white to put more pressure on for moving to the red. All to no avail. This is the result. I demand it because I am the Marquess of Wheelfell. Does that explain sufficiently?"

Aerysleigh felt rebuked somehow. He watched the activity around him for a long moment, waiting for for Lord Stillingfleet to try and dismiss him.

Instead, Phineas cocked a single eyebrow at him. Aerysleigh stifled a grin. Here sat two one-eyed men trying to stare each other down. Though to be fair, the other man managed to study him through a slit in his iron mask. "How are you after lying under a wall for an hour?" The marquess asked as though finally finding his manners.

Aerysleigh remembered the night before with a smile and a frown both. "I am perplexed. Evidently that WAR is the only properly working automaton in all of Kensington, and most likely because he arrived this morning by order of the queen. All of the clocks in the palace have lost three hours and evidently I was drugged."

Phineas seemed amused at these pronouncements. "Ah, you have received a visit from your sister." Even more questions leaped to Aerysleigh lips, but Lord Stillingfleet stood abruptly with palm upraised. "I believe this conversation to be more sensitive than should be carried out a top a waggon." He looked around him and nodded. "All is well in hand here. Mr. Middleton, I am for home. Have the men take dinner in an hour then continue the clearing."

He donned his coat and turned to Aerysleigh. "Join me for tea, your highness?"

*****

The ride in the blue velvet interior of the carriage bearing the Wheelfell crest was silent. When Aerysleigh tried to speak, the confounded man across from him sent a warning look Aerysleigh felt compelled to obey.

They were deposited before a brick and pillared town home on Park Lane. Once inside, a butler took their overcoats and Phineas showed Aerysleigh to a library where he poured two drinks from a crystal decanter. Still facing away, he removed his mask, tossed his shot back quickly, then poured another before replacing his mask and turning back to Aerysleigh.

"I apologise for the abruptness of our leaving."

Aerysleigh lifted his brow.

Phineas handed him a beverage. "As well as my rudeness in the carriage. Mr. Davey is a new driver. I do not have faith in him yet." He motioned for Aerysleigh to drink. "Especially when speaking of such a sensitive matter as the princess." He sipped his drink carefully from the corner of his mouth and Aerysleigh followed suit, waiting for the man to talk at last. He did not disappoint.

"So, Rosalind has visited you?"

Aerysleigh bristled at the familiar address of his sister by this man. He had just learned her to be alive. So many others knew more of her than he.

"How do you know?"

The marquess settled back into his chair, but Aerysleigh sensed a tension about him. "Only she has the ability to do the things you have described. However, there has been no news of her for several months."

"You know her well?"

"No one knows her well." Phineas touched his mask absently. "We have unfinished business she and I." He straightened. "Did she say anything? Indicate what she was doing?"

"She thought me insensible and talked to the tinker, Ella."

"Tinker Ella?" Phineas shook his head. "You mean...ah, yes. The blonde from St. Drogo. That woman has attachments everywhere." Aerysleigh could not determine whether he talked of Rosalind or Ella, but once again he took offence to the fact that this man seemed to know more about both than he did.

Aerysleigh leaned forward. "My father has charged me with finding my sister. My mother with finding a wife. You seem to be the man with the knowledge of both."

The marquess swirled the liquid in his drink and stared at it as though it may have the answers. He looked up sharply. "Some information is not mine to give. Rosalind was turned over to St. Drogo over ten years ago, maimed and disabled from the boiler incident that took your eye."

"But why?"

"Those are questions for the king, though I believe it stemmed from concern about your mother's reaction to Rosalind's disability."

"What happened to her?"

"Shrapnel from the boiler lodged in her back, cutting her spine. The surgeons did what they could, but she remained confined to a chair. Once she recovered, your father set her up in a house with servants, her identity kept a secret from all. She became my ward. I over saw her education. She is a brilliant woman with a gift for organising and motivating men." Phineas fell into a contemplative reverie as though he would not speak again.

Aerysleigh's curiosity, however, was not satisfied. "Where is she now?"

Lord Stillingfleet shrugged. "I do not know. We had a disagreement and she went her own way these past years."

"A disagreement? On what?"

Stillingfleet looked at him sharply. "Over many things." He stood. "However, I cannot tell you where she is now. I am sorry. If there is nothing more, I must get back to work."

He dismisses me like a common errand boy!

Still, questions beat around in Aerysleigh's brain like bats in a belfry. And this man may have the answers.

Once again, he swallowed his pride and reached into the inner pocket of his coat. He withdrew a vial and held it up to the sun filtering through the translucent lace draperies. The pink liquid inside shone as though with a light of its own. "There is this."

Lord Stillingfleet paused in his effort to show Aerysleigh the door and took the vial from his hand carefully. "This is the work of Dr. Bihari." Phineas said with a reverence one saved for church. "But it is rumoured she died months ago in Egypt."

"I was told it is from a mutated puffer fish."

"Where did you get this?" The marquess demanded.

Aerysleigh pretended nonchalance and leaned back in his chair, fighting not to show surprise at Stillingfleet's intensity. "I was given it by a friend."

"Both you and I know there is only one woman in all of London that carries this concoction, and she needs it. Why give it to you?" A cool breeze seemed to swirl from the empty fireplace and chill the room considerably. He prayed Ella had not given him her last vial. That she was not suffering for it somewhere.

"She said it would help my father. You are the man charged with counter acting the poison that laid him low, I thought it would be of interest to you." He stood, "but if not." He reached for the vial.

Phineas pulled it out of his reach. "I will analyse this, of course. However, many have tried to duplicate the work of Dr. Bihari. None have succeeded. Did this have to do with your cryptic summons for me to attend your ball a week hence?"

"Partly. I want to warn you not to interfere with my plans to choose Ella for my bride. To renounce any claims you may think you have on her through St. Drogo—or elsewhere."

Lord Stilllingfleet pocketed the vial. "Claims?" He threw back his head and laughed.

"You think me humorous, sir?" Aerysleigh ground out.

Phineas grew suddenly serious. "No, your highness, I think you naive. Despite your fascination with the modifieds and the common man, the peerage will resist the changes you have in mind. Including marrying one."

Why does everyone think me fascinated with the modifieds?

He was simply out and out in love with one. He waited for Lord Stillingfleet's next blow. "You're one to talk, lord and master behind the scenes of St. Drogo."

Stillingfleet snorted at this. "I am hardly behind the scenes, your highness. But I have heard the talk of your gadding about town with one of my volunteers there."

"And you take a great fascination in the lives of the workers there, do you?"

"I do," Lord Stillingfleet said, calm in the face of Aerysleigh's anger. "And how does Queen Constantina feel about the rumours?"

Aerysleigh leaped to his feet. "You should know. You wrote a letter to her and father both, it seems, but despite opposition, I swear I will have her."

Phineas regarded him a long moment. "Yes, I see you are quite serious. And the peers would oppose you. Yes, I think I will help you, this should be very amusing. Sit down, your highness." Aerysleigh sat, though he felt like recalcitrant schoolboy. "There may be a solution, a way to smooth some feathers before they are ruffled."

Relief swarmed through Aerysleigh, though he hadn't realised he felt such trepidation at revealing his plans. The peerage didn't worry him. His mother was a whole other matter.

"How?"

"By informing every one of the fact that your Tinker Ella, talented smith and budding engineer. More, I'd warrant if she spent more time with her studies at St. Drogo. Besides that, she's also the Lady Eliana Steelhaugh, Baroness of Iron Crest."

Aerysleigh leaped to his feet again. "Ah ha. I knew her to be a lady. But why the subterfuge? Why does she insist on no affiliation to a house?"

"Far be it from me to discern the mind of a lady," said Lord Stillingfleet derisively. "She lives quietly, volunteering at St. Drogo quite a bit until the baron remarried a year ago just before her majority. He then conveniently died six months later, leaving the barony to his new wife with no provisions for Lady Eliana. This left her completely dependent on the goodwill of the new lady."

Aerysleigh nodded. "Much of that would explain her actions. Though not all."

"I bid you luck on finding all about any woman," Lord Stillingfleet chuckled. "They can be as slippery as pickled herring."

Aerysleigh thoughts were miles away. "Thank you for your assistance, sir." He showed himself to the door but paused at the threshold. He turned back and watched Phineas hold the vial to the light. "One more thing."

"Yes, your highness?"

"I mean to capture your Cinder."

Instead of fear or denial or a reaction that indicated unease at the closeness of Aerysleigh's deduction of Cinder being part of St. Drogo, Lord Stillingfleet let loose a deep belly laugh that rivalled the one from before.

"Not if she captures you first, your highness."

Chapter Forty-One

The Dream

Isabeau wove the last sapphire ribbon through Ella's hair and stood back. "You look beautiful."

Ella stared at the stranger in the mirror and touched one of the curls trailing across her shoulder. While she ironed ribbons, polished the carriage, curried the horses, hired a driver, served breakfast, supper, washed gloves, and finally helped the girls into their under garments and dresses—her stepsisters sewed a translucent addition to the bodice of her mother's ball gown.

The new augmentation covered well the straps of her prosthesis. Two long sleeves of the same material drifted down over her upper arms while long white gloves completed the ensemble. Though not of the latest fashion, it was beyond a doubt the most beautiful garment Ella ever wore.

She twirled around the room, so light on her feet she neatly avoided the writing table, the desk littered with glassware, and the beds. Her work boots were noiseless on the thick Persian carpet and carried her with a grace she didn't know she possessed.

Aurelia wound up a music box. A quartet of metal birds popped up and chirped out a piece by Mozart. With a giggle, she joined Ella's dance. The bells and and flute sounds drifted through the room. Aurelia beckoned to Isabeau. With a worried glance at the door, the elder sister took their hands and joined in.

Ella gazed at her beautiful sisters. Isabeau was resplendent in a topaz gown. Her ebony hair, swept away from her high forehead in waves and curls, was adorned with ribbons and pearls. Aurelia wore an emerald green gown with a pink roses along the bodice and skirt. Blonde ringlets bounced on her shoulder as she danced with wild abandon, a tint of red in her azure eyes.

A surge of love for her stepsisters overwhelmed Ella. When the music stopped, she hugged them both. "Thank you. I don't know how you did it but thank you."

Isabeau touched her cheek. "You do so much for us, it was the least we could do." She motioned towards the three mice who sniffed curiously at the now silent birds. "Besides, we had help. The little one in particular has some very nimble fingers and sews a fine stitch. They are marvels."

"My wee miracles," agreed Ella, though she never thought to ask the creatures to help in darning socks.

"Just be sure to do what you said." Aurelia turned and flung open the blue and gold curtains. The sun had set, but ruby and tangerine rays still panted the sky above the dense fog settling over London proper.

The barometer attached to the sash caught Ella's attention. "The air pressure is dropping."

Her eldest stepsister walked to the window and sniffed. "A storm?"

"Maybe. It could indicate the Thames gases may be troublesome tonight," said Ella, worried about her friends who lived in ramshackle shelters.

"Not an auspicious night for a ball," giggled Aurelia. "And a full moon as well."

"Will you be alright?" Ella asked. They did not explain the significance of the moon phase and she felt uncomfortable asking.

Isabeau took Ella's hand. "We will be fine. More so if you gain us protection to continue our work." She glanced at Aurelia who took to dancing again by herself. "To find a cure."

"I will do my best," Ella promised. She lifted her skirt and stuck out one of her worn boots. "I should have brushed up on my dancing skills. If I trod on Aerysleigh's foot, I may have no chance in convincing him of anything."

"Using first names, are we?" asked Isabeau with a sly look. "Either way, he'd be a fool to make a decision based on your dancing. Come we will work on it." She held out her arms, but as Ella reached for her, the bell in the hall rang.

"Ella," Judith screeched from the first floor. "Where are you?"

All three girls froze at the shrill tone. Ella shuddered. Judith's fits of rage were no longer controlled cruelty. She yelled more and struck out more at all of them. No one could please her fast enough. Ella's neck still bore the marks of her grip from the night before.

Isabeau laid a finger on her lips and placed her ear on the door. "Don't let her see you. Mother's been angry too often." She opened the door and called out. "She's not up here, Mother. Perhaps she went to the stable after the carriage and driver. It is past time to leave."

"I know that," Judith snapped from the foot of the stairs. She said something under her breath Ella did not catch and the sound of her footsteps receded.

At the door Isabeau breathed a sigh of relief. "She grows more unpredictable each day," she said, rubbing at her arm. Before the dark-haired sister put on her gloves earlier, Ella noticed fresh syringe marks on the alabaster arms.

Ella hugged her older sister. One way or the other, they had to escape Judith. *All of them.* Aurelia stopped her giddy dance, cheeks flushed with blood red roses.

"I gave you too much blood," said Isabeau.

Aurelia laughed again. "I like it. I feel wonderful."

"Will she be alright?" asked Ella, praying her stepsister did not attack anyone at the ball.

Isabeau must have sensed her concern. "Her red corpuscles grow strangely thin over time. Aurelia must have fresh infusions to replenish her blood. But too much...?" Isabeau shrugged. "She acts like this. Aurelia, you must not draw attention to yourself tonight. We are under enough scrutiny. Any aberration will be reported and may disrupt all our plans."

Aurelia bit her lip, elongated canines gleaming, but her gaiety spilt over and she continued to twirl. "What harm will it do? It is a ball, and I want to dance. We will be the least conspicuous there, if any modifieds appear, that is. I may find a young baron to—"

Isabeau grabbed Aurelia's arm. "Because mother will notice, and she will want to do more tests. You are past the stage of hiding it."

Aurelia tried to adopt a serious face, but she touched the tip of Isabeau's ear hidden beneath eaves of thick, ebony hair. "As are you, my sister, as are you."

Ella joined Isabeau's pleading. "Please, just let me speak to Aerysleigh, gain his protection. I gave him something at our last meeting that I hope will give him some faith in me."

Both girls turned curious eyes her way. "What did you give him, Ella?" asked Isabeau.

Ella touched the last vial of nerve rejuvenator hidden in the folds of her skirt.

Isabeau's gaze followed her movement. "Oh, Ella. How many do you have left?"

"One."

"But no shipment has arrived from Dr. Bihari since your father died," Aurelia squeaked. "Mother said—" She put a hand over her mouth.

Isabeau continued, "Mother heard that Dr. Bihari had been killed in Egypt. Some sort of virus released from one of the Pharaoh's tombs she was excavating."

"Prussian spies are watching her too?" Ella asked. *How many spies could they possibly have?*

"They try," Isabeau confirmed. "Prussia hopes to convince her to join the German Confederacy. The doctor *is* the greatest chemist and surgeon ever. Mother hoped her people could recover some of the ground they lost when your mother bombed their European labs by capturing Dr. Bihari. She eludes them every time. Until this last report they did not even know where she was."

Ella felt a weight settle on her. One rejuvenator left. Depending on her activity she may need it sooner than later. *Then what? The loss of my arm?* She shuddered. "It will be alright. If she escaped them before, she will again. It could be just a rumour."

The girls nodded but did not look convinced.

"Besides. I am almost certain Aerysleigh took the vial to Lord Stillingfleet. If anyone can decipher the chemical formula, it would be he."

I hope.

"Isabeau. Aurelia." Judith called. "The carriage is here, and I still see no sign of your lazy stepsister."

"Coming, Mother," Isabeau called. She squeezed Ella's hand. "Good luck tonight."

Ella returned the tight grip.

I'm going to need it.

Chapter Forty-Two

A Mistake

Ella dabbed a bit of her mother's jasmine perfume on the pulse just below her ears and took courage from the familiar smell. She blotted nostalgic tears with a kerchief. *I miss them so much.* She longed to speak to them, to feel their comforting presence. All she had now were memories and a bit of perfume. She took a deep breath and fastened a string of pearls around her neck.

"That should do it."

The sounds of hurried departure rose from the lower hall. Even at this distance and muffled by carpet and walls, Judith's strident voice echoed above the soft murmurs of her daughters. Gravel grated from the drive as the coachman brought the carriage around, the restless jingle of harness from fresh horses carried through the open window. Ella shivered and went to close it.

Why does Aurelia insist on the window being open?

She paused and stared the rising moon resting above the factory haze settling on the shoulders of the city proper. Again, she looked at the barometer hung on the sash.

There may not be a storm tonight, but the gases will be particularly dangerous. She sighed and turned back to the room.

Best get on my way.

Her journey to Kensington would be quicker, but more work. She just hoped she could get her father's personal airship floating.

She looked down at her gown. With Myrtle's help and a good oil cloth to cover the dress she hoped to arrive in at least acceptable condition.

Then she spied a pile of white items on the dressing table.

Aurelia's gloves!

She flew across the room and snatched up the white silk. No lady went anywhere without her gloves. What was the girl thinking? But Ella knew. Somehow the full moon brought about changes in her stepsisters—the wildness about Isabeau's eyes and Aurelia's perturbing levity.

Ella raced from the bedchamber and down the stairs.

"Wait," she called holding up the gloves.

Ella became aware of several things at once—Aurelia's sly smile, Myrtle gaping at her from the kitchen door, the frozen figures of Judith and Isabeau.

"Ella, no," Isabeau cried.

Too late Ella realised she was not dressed as Cinder as Judith expected. She had been missing for several hours and unresponsive when her stepmother called. However, she could not check her headlong flight or pretend that she planned to go to the ball as Cinder any longer. She arrived at the bottom of the stairs, breathless from the constricting corset and her own stupidity.

Judith's expression twisted in rage, all painted beauty gone, the whites of her eyes red with broken vessels and revealing the insanity Ella always suspected lurked beneath the polished, controlled exterior.

"Octavia!" Judith screeched.

Ella stumbled to a stop nearly looking around for her mother at Judith's scream. But the mad eyes fastened on nobody but herself.

Her stepmother ripped off her gloves and advanced with arms outstretched, fingers curved into claws. Like a maddened dog, Judith attacked. She slapped at Ella, a windmill gone mad. Ella closed her eyes and covered her face from the gouging fingers. The delicate stitches binding the overlay covering Ella's prosthesis straps ripped from the bodice.

"How dare you," she yelled into Ella's face. "HOW DARE YOU?!" Spittle spewed from her twisted mouth. Too shocked to respond, Ella fell to the ground, barely registering the rending of her dress. The over skirt flew off, the pearls bounced like rain drops on the polished marble floor. She snatched the ribbons from Ella's hair, yanking out tufts of Ella's long tresses.

Ella landed on her hands and knees. "Stop," she cried. "Why are you doing this?"

Judith heaved above her like a horse run to ground, hair in disarray and green apple dress skewed across her bosom. She paced to a spindle legged receiving table and pulled out her shock mechanism. It whirred menacingly in her hand. Ella cringed back in memory of the pain, wanting to fight back to defend herself, but knew she could not. Myrtle's and the mice's lives were at stake.

She would endure—even if her stepmother killed her this time.

Judith jabbed. Electricity sung through Ella's body, arching every nerve into high tension. She screamed. Judith jabbed again and again. Ella tried to climb back up the stairs, but her body twisted and jerked uncontrollably. Myrtle clanked in the hallway stomping to her aid.

Judith pointed the arcing weapon at her faithful friend. "Don't come any closer or I will use this one you." A WAR should feel no emotion, should not be able to reason out the consequences of actions beyond their programming, but Myrtle stopped.

"No, Myrtle." Ella said to reinforce the servant's hesitation. "Please stay."

Myrtle's human like face twisted in indecision with the lamp she had been cleaning held tightly to her chest. Ella tried to smile in reassurance.

Her stepmother struck her again, enraged by the expression. "I hate the sight of you. You took everything from me. The favor of the emperor, the love of everyone. Even when you threw it in their faces and betrayed the fatherland, they loved and respected you. Spoke of you in awed whispers."

When the device whined and died, Judith drew a letter knife from her chatelaine, sharp and wicked looking, and sliced at the straps holding Ella's arm to her body. Pain burned along Ella's shoulders, preventing from lifting her hands to protect herself any more.

Her prosthesis jerked and compartments opened. Tools tumbled out and with them the precious invitation. She reached for the fluttering paper, but Judith beat her to it. With a vicious stomp, she crushed Ella's fingers and kicked her arm away. She tore to invitation into tiny pieces and threw them at Ella.

"You lied to me. You have always lied to me. Just like your traitorous mother."

Ella rolled to her metal side and screamed.

The straps finally gave way, allowing the heavy metal to slip. She whimpered as she tried to twist back but found no relief. Wires pulled inside her arm. Weight tugged all the way to her back where the wires fused into her spine. It felt like she was being turned inside out.

Judith waited until Ella lay still and nearly insensible from pain, then buried the blade in the folds of the sapphire dress. Only the old corset made of bone and metal saved Ella from taking a mortal wound. The small blade snapped. Judith threw it aside.

Flora and her brothers swarmed down the railing. They leaped to the ground then climbed Judith's dress, sharp claws shredding the delicate fabric. Judith flailed her arms as razor sharp teeth chomped down on her wrists and fingers. She slapped Dane to the floor and crushed him. His metal body trembled. Blue eyes winked closed.

"Stop. Please, don't hurt them." Ella cried.

But Judith was beyond hearing. She tossed Flora against the wall. She grabbed Phillipe by the tail and smacked him into the iron railing until his head separated from his body and flew to the ground. Judith tossed the mechanical mouse at Ella with a sneer.

She leaned down into Ella's face. "You left me nothing," she raged. "You even took my husband. My son. Made me sacrifice my girls to get back into their graces." She stood back and watched Ella puke and jerk with a cruel gaze. "But no more," she whispered. "No more."

She arranged her dress and disappeared into the library.

"It wasn't me," Ella sobbed into the carpet. "I didn't do anything."

Isabeau and Aurelia gasped. Ella forced her eyes open, trying to make sense of the blurred images through the tears and the pain.

Judith stalked to the stairs and levelled a revolver at Ella's head. "You will plague me no longer," she whispered. She palmed the hammer and pushed it back.

"No," screeched Myrtle. She lunged from the side entrance as though freed from her fear. The glass whale oil lamp raised high.

Ella twitched in an effort stop her, *deja vu* from the first time Judith punished the servant ricocheting through her mind. "Myrtle. Not Myrtle."

Judith switched targets and fired in one smooth motion.

Red and blue liquids oozed from the round hole that appeared in the middle of Myrtle's forehead. She crumpled with a gasping wheeze like the forge bellow at the end of a press. The lantern thumped on the carpet, the curved oil tank separating. Thick liquid oozed from the top, the smell of the wharfs and fish mongers filling the front hall.

Ella attempted to crawl towards her faithful friend. Agony shot up her arm, only her human hand worked, the fingers digging into the soiled carpet. She froze at the sound of the pistol's hammer again being cocked and the clicking of the cylinder lining up the next bullet.

The one intended for her.

Ella closed her eyes and waited. *Perhaps this was for the best.*

"Mother," said Isabeau in a soft voice.

Judith whirled towards her daughters. They huddled against the far wall, hands clasped tightly, faces pale blurs in the shadows.

"The carriage is waiting, you must compose yourself," Isabeau continued in a voice devoid of emotion.

Ella rolled on her side and stared up at the dark-haired stepsister. *How could she be so calm?*

Isabeau did not look at her. "We must hurry if we are to be presented to the prince." In that statement Ella comprehended all they had lost. She would never be able to approach Aerysleigh for his protection now, let alone think about her lofty ideal of actually marrying him. They gambled, and in an instant of inattention, she failed them all.

Judith stood as though undecided, the hand gun's muzzle wavered uncertainly between the girls, Ella, and the floor. A silence of a tomb filled the entry broken only by the tick of the great clock further down the hall.

Aurelia stepped forward and took the gun from her mother's hand. "Besides, Mother, you said that if you killed Ella the solicitors will take away everything."

No. Let her shoot me. Let this be done.

Judith calmed suddenly, her chin lifted, and she straightened her bodice. "You are right. But we are done here. The insurance money from this monstrosity of a house will see us through until the jewels are delivered by my associates."

She grabbed a lamp from a wall sconce and tossed it at Myrtle's slumped form. The fire took with a whoosh, licking hungrily at the whale oil and catching Myrtle's threadbare day dress.

Judith turned to the door. "Come, girls, we will be late."

Through the haze of orange and heavy smoke filling her senses, Ella saw Isabeau and Aurelia follow their mother out the door.

Isabeau paused. "Run away, CinderElla," she whispered. "Run away where she can never find you."

Then she closed the door.

Chapter Forty-Three

A Ladder

The world constricted to a narrow tunnel filled with Myrtle's discarded husk and stifling fumes. Despite Isabeau's urging, Ella found no strength to remove herself from the fiery threat.

The fire crept closer and smoldered through the carpet like creeping black rot, yet it did not ignite. Heat warmed her boots and melted the glue while it bit at the stitches. Flames flared around Myrtle's form. The smolders reached the oil leaking from joints twisted by her collapse. The thread-bare wool dress caught, reminding Ella of the poor girl from the match factory who threw herself into the Thames.

Emboldened, the flames grew. Tongues of orange tested the wallpaper, found it palatable, then crawled up the wall. Smoke roiled thick and black, coating the lower hall. Ella closed her eyes but failed to stop the tears no matter how she tried. She waited for the noxious fumes to overcome her and end the pain forever.

A tiny paw caressed her tender cheek. Ella's eyes snapped open. Flora stood nose to nose, blue eyes begging.

"I can't, Flora, not any more. Go away, get out of the house."

Flora scampered to the straps of Ella's prosthesis and she groaned at the pain even the minuscule weight of the mechanical mouse caused.

The mouse balanced on her shoulder stump, straps in her paws.

Ella's stomach heaved. Smoke clogged her throat and nostrils. She tried to brush the mouse off, but Flora scurried out of reach. She patted a spark threatening her mistress then scratched at the carpet in a futile attempt to keep the seething fire away—her efforts endearing.

Flora would stay with Ella and die too if she chose that path. Determination returned. She would not be responsible for yet another death. Ella's arm buckled, landing her face first into the carpet.

Fetid smoke crept across the floor and wrapped her in its suffocating embrace. The fire consumed the wainscot and paper of the front hall now, licking along the walls.

If I'm to escape, it has to be now.

Sobs escaped with every jerk on her nerves from the wires when she attempted to stand. She leaned against the lower step and cradled the prosthesis close with her human hand, hugging it against her body. She tried again to move.

Nerves shrieked. Fingers twitched. Finally, she made it to her feet. Flora darted toward the kitchen. Ella followed a less direct route, pushing her back against the wall and skirting the foyer. Her body ached, still in the painful throes of her stepmother's attack, but Flora's bright, blue eyes shone beseechingly from the dim hall, and spurred her on.

The fire found a lamp and roared up. It gave Ella the final impetus and strength to run.

She rushed through the kitchen. Flora dogging her heels. Both escaped into the drab herb garden flanking the entrance. The bright orange flames lit their path as the fire found more fuel in the furniture.

Windows popped. The second floor now alive with the capering flames. Ella hurried to the corner of the garden where a memorial to her mother spun *ad infinitum*. Her father built it while Ella recovered from the accident, but she never visited—the rush of painful memories too great. Now she threw herself to the ground in front of the spinning wheels which turned a tiny replica of *Lady Peril* above a pond clogged with weeds.

"Why?" she demanded. Ella dug a loose stone from the pond wall and chucked it at the airship. "You promised me you would be here when I needed you, but you lied. Both of you. Now you're gone. All that remains is that venomous fiend. She's ruined everything. Taken everything."

Ella collapsed onto the wall. Her last bit of strength gone up with the ravaging flames.

You've won, Judith. You took your arch rival's husband and killed him. You destroyed her daughter, burned her home. As a coupe d'etat you'll see my heart's desire married to one of your daughters.

Ribbons tangled with tendrils of blonde trailed across her shoulders. Nothing remained of the beautiful upsweep created by Isabeau. Ella picked at the once iridescent gown now clinging to her in shreds. This sent into in a fresh torrent of tears.

Flora jumped to the wall and stroked Ella's dishevelled hair. With a tiny paw, she wiped a tear from Ella's cheek.

Ella held out her hand for Flora to jump onto and spoke softly. "You are all I have left. Judith would have taken you too if she knew you survived."

Thoughts of Dane and Phillipe's crushed bodies again sapped her, but thoughts of Aerysleigh intruded on her grief.

"He will make a good king no matter who he marries. He doesn't mind strong opinions." She traced the half cog on the metal arm hanging by wires from her stump. "Or monsters. His good heart won't be corrupted by Judith."

But Ella knew that if he remained stalwart, her stepmother would plot to kill him. It was no use. She no longer believed there was an inkling of hope.

This dream must be given up entirely if I am to survive.

Ella surveyed the damage. Fire now engulfed the house and sent waves of heat into the garden which curled the winter brown vegetation. The forge glistened as the flames licked at the door, to her right the east wing also burned. Only the little kitchen gate remained open for escape. Still she hesitated while Iron Crest burned. But it had not truly existed since her mother's death.

"Good riddance," she muttered. Recent events in her ancestral home seemed to erase all the years of good. Besides, Judith would have to find a new base of operations.

"I pray she doesn't find them in the palace," Ella whispered.

"Ahoy there, little fool."

Ella stared at Flora. "Did you say something?"

The mouse cocked her head and looked up.

"Up here, you silly girl. Grab the ladder and let's get out of here before those flames light this old lady up."

A ladder dropped from the sky.

Chapter Forty-Four

A Fairy Godmother

Ella squinted upwards through the heat and haze. The bulk of an airship hid the moon, but the silhouette of a head surrounded by a wealth of midnight hair peered over the side and down at Ella.

Indecision froze her thoughts.

Stay and burn. Stay and wait for Judith to remember she didn't shoot me and return to finish the job.

Neither option looked attractive.

Flora hopped on her shoulder as Ella struggled again to her feet. Slowly she released her metal hand to seize the rope ladder but groaned as the weight pulled on the dangling wires.

Ella fell against the wall. "I can't climb," she called up.

The heat gusted suddenly, curling dangerously close to the airship.

The face disappeared. "Drax, where are you, *dummkopf*? I pay you for protection, not eating."

A large, familiar form slid down the rope moments later. Tears leaked down her cheeks at the welcome sight of a friend. Drax touched his cap then turned. "Get on my back, Mistress."

Ella wrapped her good arm around Drax's thick neck and stabilised the prosthesis against his back. They rose quickly through the heat until Drax set her down gently on the swaying deck. She stumbled, but two strong hands steadied her.

"Get *The Asp* out of here, Captain, before we light up the whole county," yelled a commanding voice at Ella's elbow. Ella couldn't help but stare at the diminutive Roma woman. Dressed in a belled skirt, over-sized peasant blouse with no corset or stays, the lady's flamboyant manner was out of fashion. Her voice was low, loud, and grating. The woman's expectant gaze promoted Ella to remember her, but she couldn't quite grasp the elusive memory. Something about the Kohl lined eyes and the bright vest seemed familiar. A face from long ago dream. However, this woman was much younger than she should be if she were a contemporary of her mother.

"Who are you?" Ella asked.

The ship lurched away from the fire, nearly sending her tumbling head over toes again. Rock solid, the petite lady steadied her once again.

"Fancy you not remembering your own godmother," she sniffed, smooth face scrunched with disappointment.

Then Ella remembered those feverish nights after the accident. Those eyes staring at her with clinical detachment. In protection of her sanity through the pain, Ella turned the surgeon into a fairy.

"You were my fairy godmother," Ella blurted.

The woman snorted. "I *am* your godmother, not a fairy. And a doctor, not a witch as some people get carried away and call me. Dr. Theodosia Fifka Bihari at your service. Though, we have met many times before." The doctor peered up into Ella's eyes. "Though you may not recollect."

"I recall some. I mean, in my dreams. You took care of my arm. You made me..." Ella took a deep breath. "This."

The woman's face softened. "I suppose I did. But you should be proud of your arm. Some of my best work. Techniques pulled right off the walls of the ancient Egyptian tombs. Your father and I decided it best if I operate while you were completely under to lessen the trauma. Seems like we may not have succeeded entirely."

"Come now. To my cabin." She stalked towards the stern of the ship. "Imagine, passing laws against people just because they are a little different," she muttered.

Ella followed somewhat slower, cradling her arm, her thoughts awhirl.

"Don't' dawdle, child, come along."

"My arm," Ella said, "I don't think it will last."

Dr. Bihari nodded. "I see. Can't do anything out here. Let us get into the light where I can see you. She dug in a vest pocket. "Where are my spectacles?"

A fellow coiling a rope paused and pointed at the silver chain hanging around the doctor's neck.

"Oh right, of course. Come, Ella. We have a lot of work ahead of us to get you to the ball so you can snatch up that charming prince right from under Jutta's nose." She chuckled. "Oh, and bring modifieds such as yourself into the light."

Ella stumbled after the doctor's quick march step. "You know?"

"I know everything about you. And I know Jutta, or Judith as you know her. The Society has been searching for her for years, ever since your mother took out the confederation lab experimenting on humans. I never did expect to find her here, hiding under our very noses."

Ella wanted to interject a question, but her godmother never slowed.

"However, like I said, I am your godmother and though the zombies might have slowed me down some—did I mention I might have released a virus when I unsealed a hidden tomb?"

Ella shook her head.

Dr. Bihari shrugged a shoulder. "No matter. I honestly did mean to be back as soon as I heard your father set off in that great airship in the sky..."

She glanced back and grimaced at Ella's bewildered gaze and then the doctor continued, "You know...*died*. After all, I figured you'd be running low on nerve rejuvenator."

Ella nodded. "Yes."

"No matter. I am here now. We have a knees up to get you to." She wrinkled her nose. "You can't go anywhere looking like that. No, you need to be the dog's dinner to outshine all those peacocks. And I have just the thing. Of course, it helps you already caught his eye..."

The doctor chattered non-stop through a small door, down a thin corridor, and into a room at the stern of the ship.

Ella froze and stared through the large glass windows at the burning Iron Crest. She took a deep breath before stepping into the sumptuous room. The last time she had been in a captain's cabin she lost an arm.

Dr. Bihari sensed her hesitation and turned. "Don't stand there like a daft cow. We'll have a chin wag whilst I dress your hair, so it all makes sense. But first," she pinched her nose.

"A bath."

*****

While Ella relaxed in a bath, Dr. Bihari told the captain to circle London a few times and then set to work on Ella's arm.

"Keep your face turned away," the doctor advised. "People tend to get faint over their own blood."

"I have seen plenty of blood," Ella said sharply. "I work at the hospital."

"That may be, but when it comes to one's own fluids, the game changes." She popped a panel off the shoulder casing and exposed the blue glowing wires. Ella's stomach lurched. She turned her face away to study the room.

Tapestries and maps covered the wall, all with weavings and etchings that reminded Ella of hieroglyphs. Shelves and cupboards secured navigational equipment, excavation tools, and other things Ella could not identify. Glassware and surgical tools on a tray by the tub clanked with the rocking of the ship.

Her godmother introduced the two cabin girls busy about the room. "This is Portia and the tall one there is Saphi."

Saphi fetched for Dr. Bihari, sometimes anticipating her needs before she asked. Portia brought a silk robe for Ella and lay it over a chair.

"Portia will accompany you to the ball."

"I'll be alright," said Ella.

Portia brought towels and then untangled, brushed and washed Ella's waist length hair. "Think of me as a lady's companion," she said. "For propriety's sake." Ella sniffed and blushed both. *A little late for that.*

When the cabin girl reached for a brush, her profile revealed a sort of deformity on her back. Like everyone else on this airship, the girl had a mutation or modification. In her short walk to the cabin, Ella noticed everything from intriguing gadgets to prosthesis. Instead of being unnerved, Ella felt at home.

Her arm jumped when Dr. Bihari touched a nerve. Ella's metal fingers flexed and grabbed the side of the tub. "There you go." The little woman snapped a panel closed and stood. "Any more damage and you would have been in real trouble." Ella felt a pinch "And you are ready to go. Now. Out of the tub. Gracious, you like to dawdle, and into the chair so Saphi can dress your hair."

As though in a dream Ella rose. Portia wrapped her in a thick towel. Saphi held the robe. She limped across the floor to the small dressing table bolted to the wall. It was filled with tools not made for a lady's toilette. Dr. Bihari swept her instruments aside while Saphi laid out brushes, ribbons, powder, pearls, and set to work.

A soft knock on the door and a man whose lower half ended in an apparatus of spider legs, delivered a large tray of food. Ella's stomach rumbled. Portia placed the platter within reach. A variety of meats and fruits Ella hadn't seen in years were artistically arranged. With a sigh, her godmother plated a piece of meat pie then tossed herself into a chair, and threw a leg over the side, watching Saphi carefully.

Portia gathered the scraps of Ella's old dress and removed them from the room. Flora uncurled from her dormant state and leaped to the floor. Immediately a metal cat sitting in the large stern window, turned its head and blinked. Emerald eyes glowed. Flora stood on her hind legs and studied the creature then scampered up the drapes. Metal chimed as the mouse jumped into the paws of the cat. The cat stroked the mouses head.

"They act as though they know one another."

"As well they should," Bihari confirmed. "I found them in the same pyramid. Selfish sort of Pharaoh had all his servants and creatures killed. The mice and Thoth just sat in the dark until the light of my lantern revived them. Those old Egyptian doctors knew so many medical treatments and methods that have been lost—one of the reasons I am studying them. But come, that is not what you really want to ask, now is it?"

Ella shook her head, only to be caught and held by Saphi's strong hand. "Stay still, please, miss."

Bihari chuckled. "I used to arrange your mother's hair back when we were in the creche." She shrugged. "Never was very good at it though. Probably a good thing she became the lady and not me, eh?"

Bihari leaned out of her chair. "She had hair like yours, long and curly, like sunlight on a cloud." She winked. "The Prince will never be able to resist you when Saphi is done. She knows her trade."

Ella winced as Saphi tightened a coil. "Hair dresser?"

"No, not exactly. She, like everyone else on the ship, have talents to complement my work. Saphi knows Ancient Egyptian coiffure and microscopic hair analysis."

"But, Godmother—"

"Theo, please."

"I have so many questions. You explained why you didn't come before, but why now? Why send me to the ball when Judith will be there, and she will do anything in her power to stop me?" Ella took a deep breath, no doubt if she paused too long Theo would start talking again. "And you're so young!"

"The age thing, I'll explain later. Maybe. It's complicated. Lower that one flower to just above her ear," advised Theo.

Saphi adjusted the mirror so Ella could see her profile. The front was combed back and fluffed. The hair above her ear and down her back was twisted into large roses by wrapping and pinning the golden tresses into a pinwheel. Pearls glinted from the waves. Ella blinked. She had never seen such a beautiful pattern woven into hair.

"Judith's activities have only just come to the Society's attention. Though Lord Stillingfleet was aware of your clandestine activities, and even directed some through Dr. Bon Hamlet, no one had any idea that you were being blackmailed by a Prussian agent. Why didn't you tell anyone?"

Ella dropped her gaze. "She threatened Myrtle and the mice. Their lives for my silence." *What did the secrecy gain me? Everyone but Flora dead.*

She closed her eyes and leaned into Saphi's hands, the pain rising like bile in her throat.

Theo rose and placed her hand on Ella's shoulder. "You should have trusted us, my dear."

"But what does the Society want with me? Why are they watching me?"

"It is on my request. Your mother and I started SPAMM, left it in Lord Stillingfleet's capable hands. However, I knew I would not be around like a proper godmother, so I asked them to watch over you."

She bent her lips into a severe frown. "And the society didn't do a very good job of it. Stealing to fund the enemy? Disgraceful."

Ella stared at her godmother in the low light, trying to read her expression, but feeling the sting of her own guilt. "I'm sorry."

"Not you, my dear," said Theo with a wave. "SPAMM."

Portia stuck her head in the door. "Captain says we circled London enough that the WARs are being alerted."

Theo waved her away. "Very well. Time to get you dressed." She pulled Ella towards the centre of the cabin. "As I was saying, the Society has been hunting Jutta ever since we learned she escaped from the lab. Then came the reports that the homeless and poor were disappearing here in London, usually a sign of illegal experimentation—Prussian, French, English—it could be any or all. It has become apparent we grossly under-estimated her. After the throne is she—planning to put one of those experiments in the prince's bed to finish the job the German's started."

Ella tried not to think about Aerysleigh suffering the same fate as his brother and father. Saphi slipped the robe from her shoulders and began to dress her in the softest under garments. Ella ran her hands over the pantaloons.

"From China," said Theo then opened the wardrobe and withdrew a stunning creation of silk. It sparkled with the brilliance of sapphire and diamond embellishments sewn on the sweeping skirt. Tiny jewels danced from the hem to the neckline of the gown where lace delicately covered the near scandalous bodice. The back dipped to a tightly laced corset where onyx panels trimmed with ribbons peeked from the sapphire over skirt. The gown begged to dance.

Ella stepped into the skirt and held her breath as Saphi tugged the laces tight. She tried not to look in the mirror. *I don't dare look in the mirror. The last gown ended in tatters.*

However, she couldn't help but notice Theo sneaking sly glances at her. Finally, she took a peek and gasped at her refined appearance. Golden hair piled high and trailing down the open back in ringlets and roses, eyes reflected the dim light of the hurricane lamps with the brilliance of star fire.

Who is this seductress in the mirror? Certainly not the soot streaked Cinder abseiling down ash hazed walls, or the beaten down hostage of a mad German scientist, not even the girl who laughed up at Aerysleigh as they walked arm in arm for that brief moment of peace before the Cuthbert and Cox fire. *No, the creature in the mirror was beautiful, strong, powerful. Somehow a mixture of all three.*

"But my arm." Even in the dim light it glowed harshly. A beautiful implement to be sure, but one that marked her.

Theodosia spun. "What of it?"

"Shouldn't I hide it?"

Theodosia's face turned dusky rose under her tan and for a moment she seemed at a loss for words. "Hide it?" she demanded. "Hide it? Whatever for? Be proud of that thing—it is a part of you and a marvel. Why would I want you to hide some of my best work?" She put her hands on her hips. "Take a moment and get a gander at your arm. Take a good look."

Ella lifted her chin. "I know what it looks like."

"Do you?"

Ella's gaze drifted to the prosthesis she had lived with the last ten years. Once large and heavy, it now fit her perfectly, the use of it intuitive—a natural extension like her bone arm. She added flourishes over time, the scroll work, changing out and refilling the compartments, even creating different hands to fit the detachable one with movable fingers.

But the magic was in the hidden parts. The faint glow. The special wires reaching under her skin to her spine. The attachment at just the right places to command the tiniest movement. It chaffed sometimes. She hated it sometimes, but it had saved her many times over.

Theodosia watched her for a long moment. "Do you know I have not been able to recreate that process? Lord knows I've tried. Seems like there's people a plenty getting their arms and hands blown off. I even went back to the proverbial drawing board, but an earthquake buried the city where I found the instructions. Got nothing but a bunch of cock ups for my trouble. Was it because you were so young? The cut so clean? I don't know. But be proud of it. You are one of a kind."

Ella had no idea Theodosia could not replicate the process. "And Myrtle?"

Theodosia's expression turned pensive. "Myrtle too. She was not a WAR, but a woman who saved your mother's life. Octavia could not bear to lose her. Just as your father could not bear to part with you. Perhaps that is the key, but if so, it is undefinable. I had your father destroy the machine I made to put you two together. Regretted it ever since."

The clock on the wall gonged the eight o'clock hour. Her godmother pulled herself from her reverie. "But you are lacking your gloves and mask. Come, Captain Mahulda thinks of everything."

"Mahulda?"

"My captain. French aristocracy before they went and beheaded everyone." Theo held out a pair of sapphire gloves and slid them up Ella's arms to her elbows.

Theodosia snapped a diamond bracelet onto her wrist. "There you go. Let them look at that. Real, you know, not some paste and glass many of those women will be wearing. And a necklace. Turn around. A neck so lovely barely needs anything at all, but a little something, positioned just so, will draw the prince's eye nicely. No one will even notice a strap or two."

Heat rose in Ella's cheeks at her godmother's bold words.

"Don't be such a prude." The lady peered around her image. "If only your mother could see you now. So! Enough sentimentality for one night. Here is your mask. Off to the boat. Portia is waiting, so is Flora. They will go as your spies and Judith alarms."

Ella took a halting step forward. Bare feet, forgotten in her haste to dress, made themselves known. Instead of the smooth glide she wished to make in the beautiful dress, she limped instead. Despair washed through her. Her boots were ruined and stank of fire of smoke. Walking in unmodified shoes of any worth would be impossible. "It is all for nought," she cried. "I can't even walk, let alone dance."

Theodosia turned and studied Ella, then her eyes widened. "Amazing." She hurried to the wardrobe and withdrew a package. "This came to me by way of your father. It was as though he sensed you would need them one day soon and his time was short." She thrust the box at Ella. "Here, open it quickly."

Ella obeyed and gasped. "Metal slippers?" She stroked the burnished leather overlaid with cooper dancing shoes, fingers drifted over the tiny chains decorating the juncture of sole and metal. Cogs and wheels, miniatures of tiny forge implements, all entwined with flowers. "They are so beautiful," she whispered.

Theodosia wiped a tear. "Just as they should be. The finest copper from Cornwall. Your father made them just for you. See there on the sole? There is his mark."

Ella touched the hammer crowned by a laurel wreath with a lump on her throat. Only Alsanger Victor Steelhaugh used this symbol. All of his work bore it. It took her back to the times when he wrapped his arms around her and guided her hands to strike the impression for him.

Theodosia cleared her throat. "The left is special, feel inside."

Ella slipped her hand into the shoe, knowing what she would find—a wad of leather. It was fashioned just so and as supple as the other, the inside soft and form fitting. Saphi took the slipper and kneeling, placed it on Ella's foot. Now, when Ella took a step, she floated.

Ella hugged Theodosia tightly. "You *are* a fairy godmother after all."

The petite woman hugged her back. "Doctor. Scientist. Egyptologist. Even witch would be better than this fairy godmother appellation." She sniffed and gave Ella another tight squeeze.

Saphi cleared her throat. "The life boat, ma'am," she reminded them.

Theodosia pushed away. "There you be. Off to the ball. Claim the prince for the modifieds."

"What?" Ella's stomach clenched. The realisation set in that once again she was not a girl going off to a ball to flirt and to dance.

People wanted something of her.

Her godmother's expression hardened into a look reminiscent of Judith's calculating gaze. Goose flesh tickled up Ella's arm despite the stifling heat of the cabin. Theodosia, Judith, and her mother grew up together, trained from the youngest age to be weapons for the great machine taking over Europe. Though two escaped and used their training for the greater good, her godmother seemed prepared to use every tool to her advantage.

Even Ella.

Does no one want me just for me? Who doesn't want to use me? Every step in her life seemed to have been controlled by people with ulterior motives.

"You have been raised and watched over by SPAMM since your accident. A medical marvel who makes friends both high and low. It is time now to use that to help those less fortunate than yourself. As queen you could do so much."

Tears crowded at Ella's eyes. *A tool. That's all I am.*

Theodosia shook her arm. "No crying now. You will turn your peaches and cream complexion blotchy."

How could she not cry? She wanted to rant and rail against the unfairness of the world like a child. However, if anything, this night showed it would do no good.

Ella lifted her chin.

She would go to the ball. She would have the most wonderful time in her whole life, and she would talk to the prince and if he could not love her as the flawed woman she was, perhaps his kind heart would secure protection for herself and her sisters. She would not rely on SPAMM, the society only wanted to use her just as Judith did.

Theodosia tightened the grip on her arm as though sensing her thoughts. "You have until midnight, then you must come out of the ball. Let Judith follow you. We will take care of the rest."

"Let me set this out. You want me to steal the prince's heart in," she glanced at the clock, "four hours so Modifies can have an ear to the throne. Then you wish for me to lure Judith away from any WARs, of which there will most likely be many considering the queen's jewels are on display, so you can take her."

Who cared what Ella wanted—no needed?

Aerysleigh her heart cried.

Theodosia nodded as though closing a business deal.

"In a word—yes."

Chapter Forty-Five

The Arrival

Ella floated through the sky towards the glowing palace on hopes and prayers, most of them not hers. The extensive gardens were lit with hundreds of lanterns, illuminating paths of white gravel filled with the moving dots of people.

Tents sprouted along the paths and across the lawns and the smell of roasted fowl, spices, and sweets wafted by on the updraughts. The air seemed to hold its breath, a pause before the arrival of a storm, which made the evening perfect for the planned festivities.

Still, the Thames gleamed green. The insidious gases crept maliciously from the water and up the banks like some primordial organism. Boats clanged their bells, warning the riverfront workers to don masks and the nearby populace to take what shelter they may.

And tonight, that shelter was Kensington Palace.

Never had a monarch opened his home in such a way. Anyone who received a golden invitation on the fickle wind could walk through the normally barred gates unchallenged. The streets to the vast estate thronged with people. The hum of conversation joined the background cacophony of the street and the factories to create an exciting orchestra of sound. Instead of the riots and protests that set the tone the past few months, the voices crackled with joyous energy. Even from the sky, Ella sensed the excitement.

Automatons of all sorts stalked along with the modifieds and humans. Some held aloft great lights that chased shadows into the gutters. There would be no skulking of monsters tonight.

Enshrouded in light from below and darkness from above gave Ella the feeling of being surrounded by magic and beyond mortal care.

She searched and found the large landing pad where airships jostled for position. Jewelled ladies and debonair men from country estates disembarked for the first time in London for the start of the season.

And what a start this would be.

Portia aimed their little craft away from the crowded aeroport. Instead, tacking towards the roof of the horse stables designed for delivery craft. A long ramp wrapped around the top side of the two-story building, ending in the back with a direct route to a side gate of the palace proper. Though busy with the bustle of servants, a few footmen waited to help those arriving by this route.

One helped Ella from the life boat with a deep bow. "My Lady."

Ella nodded, waiting for Portia to follow as her companion for the evening. The girl, though dressed in a beautiful gown and the evening mild for the early spring, wore a shawl wrapped tight about her shoulders. Together they made their way into the three-sided square of Kensington where she spent the night just a week ago.

At the thought of Aerysleigh's passionate kisses she dropped her eyes and smiled. Imaginary butterflies tickled under her corset. She pulled a fan from her reticule and fanned at the warmth in her cheeks.

Windows stood open, brimming with light, music, and people. Reporters moved about, asking questions of the attendees and taking copious notes. At every portal servants checked the filigree invitations. Her dream world vanished as Ella remembered Judith ripping hers to shreds. She turned back to her companion. Portia waited with a sly grin and held up two invitations.

"Dr. Bihari thought we might need these." She passed them to the man servant, and they stepped into magic.

People pressed in on all sides, hats, masks, and hair pieces undulating wave-like as the excited populace moved to and fro. Doors to all the rooms had been opened or removed to allow ample space for the merriment.

Even so, it was not enough.

Every bit of floor held innumerable people. She could not imagine the aristocracy keeping themselves aloof from anyone in this maze.

Ella's heart hesitated a beat. *How will I find Aerysleigh in such a throng?*

She made her way towards the music and stepped into a gilded chamber lined with ladies and gentlemen. She caught the glint of metal here and there and let out a breath of relief at the number of others like her. Even without obvious modifications, she easily recognised those from the lower boroughs, not by the quality of their linens, but by the embellishments of their gown and breeches.

The men sported watches and leather, springs and gauntlets—items she prayed did not contain weapons. There were belts packed with necessities of trade—tools, vials, and tanks of oxygen for those with damaged lungs. Some sported ornate gadgets designed to tell time, read barometric pressure, or give early warning to the rise of the gases.

The women's corsets were metal, leather, and bone and worn atop their dresses. More than one woman wore the Phossy jaw covering. Even masks could not hide the marks of a hard life in the lines of their faces and expressions.

Ella's arm felt exposed. Never had she been so bold as to bare it to the world. She vacillated between the urge to hide it and longing to throw a shawl over it. But the smiles of those around her and their own pride in their beings gave her courage. The confidence she found in the guise of Cinder rose.

She lifted her chin, anonymous behind her mask.

Tonight, her people came out of hiding the laws of the land and the general mistrust by the aristocracy forced them into. They had a prince to champion their cause. Though some seemed uneasy, it could be the luxury and wealth displayed in every corner of the palace that made them so.

Servants proffered fluted glasses rimmed with gold to commoner and peer alike. Chocolate fountains, ice cream sculptures, and fantastical delicacies from the most illustrious confectioners were on display, consumed, and replaced at a never-ending rate. Automated carts chugged through the crowds, mechanical arms filling the top tray from lower cabinets drawers.

Shop assistants stood shoulder to shoulder with scullery maids, both agog at the spectacle. Members of the aristocracy preened by, however, the jewel encrusted dresses were the least of the wonders.

Ella passed through each room, admiration turning to astonishment at the tables groaning under sugar plums and marzipan, candies, and pies. Multi-tiered cakes rose above the other offerings topped with flamboyant peacocks made of icing, long feathers drooping down the lower cakes. Another chamber held supper foods, meats and vegetables, and still another contained beverages around a centrepiece of an iced unicorn.

Guard automatons were present in the corner of every chamber with one in every hall, but they remained silent, the mood of the people around them too gay to trigger their defencive mechanisms. However, it did make her wonder where the jewels were on display. She quickly turned her thoughts elsewhere. No one could make her steal any longer. A rush of emotions nearly toppled her.

Dead. My reasons for keeping silent are all dead.

Portia rushed to her side and steadied her. "My Lady?"

For a blind moment Ella looked around unseeing. *What if I run into Judith and she tries to finish the job?*

She patted her companion's hand. "I'm fine," she finally managed to say. Surely in this multitude of people, her stepmother would never find her. Not that it mattered any more. She straightened.

Only one thing in all of England left to steal—*the prince's heart.* But not for anyone else.

Just for me.

She pushed on, drinking in the beauty, the smells, and sounds. Music seeped from every corner, small quartets of strings spaced just far enough apart their playing did not interfere with the others.

She followed the lilting call of a waltz through several rooms, her slippered feet gliding across carpet and hardwood like a whisper. The crowds opened before her, people she recognised, and many she did not, bowing and curtsying. She dipped and smiled and nodded, but she never ceased her search for the tall, dark prince with the dazzling smile.

Would he wear his hair in braids tonight in defiance of fashion? Would he don his eye patch or leave it off in solidarity with others maimed by the war?

Harcourt nodded from beside an elephant shaped topiary. When she passed, he pushed off the wall and shadowed her.

Greetings of: "Lady Ella.", "Mistress Ella," followed her along with the occasional "Cinder". Finally, she found the ball room where couples whirled in the intricate dances Ella only half remembered. Gowns—borrowed and new made—of silk, cotton, and wool, embellished the sounds of the orchestra at the far end of the room.

The gilded walls blazed, all the scones and chandeliers sending showers of light on the whirling couples below. Dr. Bon Hamlet, minus her blood speckled lab coat and resplendent in a violet gown, danced by on the arm of another doctor from St. Drogo. They smiled at her.

Then time stopped.

Aerysleigh approached her from the centre of the room. Had he been dancing? She couldn't tell. Did he recognise her under the mask? By his direct route toward her, he must.

She drank in the sight of his tall figure, an island of stillness while the dancers swung around him. From his black jacket to his cerulean silk waist coat to his perfectly pressed trousers and unfashionably long hair brushed to a high shine to match a raven's wing—he looked every inch the prince.

She barely knew the actions of her own feet as they took her to meet him. As though realising the force of the attraction at opposite ends of the hall, the dancers halted, dresses twirling to silence, every eye on Prince Aerysleigh as he found his lady.

The orchestra wound to a halt with the whine of strings. Whispers rustled like paper, but Ella only saw her prince. He filled her vision completely. So handsome her heart nearly ceased beating. She couldn't have refrained from approaching him if she tried, the pull towards him stronger than any magnet.

They stopped together, just a hand span between them. His breath touched her hair, her skirts his legs. She sank into a curtsy, onyx and sapphire gown billowing. Aerysleigh placed a hand on his chest and bowed.

For a long moment he stared, face impassive. The longer he stared, the louder the voices around them became. She dropped her gaze to the floor, confounded by his silence.

"Say something," she whispered.

"You are..." he took a deep breath. The sound of his voice sent shivers cascading down her spine.

Did he notice the metal of my arm? Did it change his mind?

Ella closed her eyes and waited.

"Magnificent," he finished.

Chapter Forty-Six

The Mad Woman

Before Ella could formulate a reply, Aerysleigh offered his hand. "Will you dance with me, my lady?"

Now she did become aware of all the staring faces.

Though several people offered friendly smiles, there were enough disapproving looks to eat away at her confidence. She put her left hand on his, but even the metal trembled with fear. "But there is no music, my prince," she teased to hide her response.

Aerysleigh squeezed her hard metal fingers and looked around him as though noticing for the first time the absence of music and dancing. He grinned. "I guarantee if you dance with me, the music will begin."

Automatically she curled her fingers around his and gathered her skirts in her right. He gave her an odd look, then spun her into the first steps of a waltz. With a crash of discordant notes, the orchestra hurried to catch up. By the time the strings caught the woodwinds and settled into the rhythm of the song, Ella was beyond hearing anything but the disjointed cadence of her own heart.

Half-remembered dance steps guided her feet, but even if the memories would not cooperate, Aerysleigh led so well it required no real thought on her part. Other couples joined in, but it made no matter to her. She gazed up into his striking face, mesmerised by the bemused smile which quirked his lips and the reflection of the chandeliers on his dusky skin.

She couldn't tell how long they danced.

Time managed to stand still and fly by in an instant. No words passed between them, but she hoped he could see every emotion flooding her heart on her face. Occasionally a small thought niggled at the back of her mind. Like a grain of sand in a slipper, thoughts persisted that time meant something important—that there were other things that should be on her mind besides the feel of Aerysleigh's hand on the small of her back. The press of their gloves. The warmth of the room. The world narrowed to just these sensations and nothing more.

The crowd along the wall undulated. Aerysleigh spun her to the side of the dance floor. "Come, meet my mother."

Ella pulled back. "The *queen*?"

With a chuckle Aerysleigh pulled her in to an adjacent drawing room. "Yes, also known as my mother."

People around them formed a column and bowed or curtsied. Above their heads, Queen Constantina walked with her attendants. She smiled and nodded to everyone, high and low born alike, but her onyx eyes scanned the crowd restlessly. When she spied her son standing at the opposite end of the room, the queen turned abruptly their way. Ella's pulse raced and she longed to turn and run.

Suddenly her ancestral heritage took charge and she lifted her chin. *I am the daughter of Baron and Lady Steelhaugh of Iron Crest. You are also a thief* her conscience interjected. Aerysleigh's hand in hers gave her strength as well, she would not be intimidated, though the gaze the queen bent her way could not be called friendly.

Queen Constantina was even more breathtaking than the ink sketches in the papers allowed—a pretty youth transformed into a beautiful lady. A shade darker than her son, her skin glowed in the lights. Dewberry dark eyes seemed to take up the majority of a face with pronounced cheekbones, full lips, and wide nostrils.

The weight of a million eyes helped Ella into a low curtsy.

"Mother," Aerysleigh announced, the pride evident in his voice. "May I present Lady Eliana Graceling Steelhaugh of Iron Crest."

Queen Constantina lifted a brow. "Steelhaugh? Of Iron Crest? I don't recall the name. Who are your parents, child? Have you been presented?" the queen's voice was cold enough to freeze blood.

Aerysleigh tightened his fingers around her hand.

Ella rose from her curtsy and opened her mouth to answer, but the prince cut in. "You know perfectly well the names," he ground out. Another slight curtsy and Ella interrupted the prince.

I don't need Aerysleigh to fight my battles.

She removed her mask. "My parents are Baron Alsanger Victor Steelhaugh and Lady Captain Octavia Kendall Steelhaugh, your majesty, and no, I was never presented."

The queen put a hand to her breast and looked to her son. "Never presented? How odd. The best families always present their daughters, but then..." she gave a significant look to the exposed metal appendage. Ella resisted the temptation to cover her arm with her other hand.

"Mother," Aerysleigh said, his voice low in warning. "Mind your manners."

His mother turned her full attention to her son. "Aerysleigh. You can't be serious."

Aerysleigh did not quail under the weight of his mother's black-eyed gaze, but returned it pound for pound. "Never more so."

Before the prince and queen could start a family feud at the ball, a couple jostled Ella into Aerysleigh. Her metal hand clamped on his for support. He knit his brows and stared at their hands. "Ella?" he asked.

She had no answer but looked around for the cause of the commotion which had every head turning away from the royal drama.

"Fools!" a familiar voice screeched from the doorway. Ella spun, knowing the face of the woman she would find.

For the second time that evening a collective gasp rustled around the room. Judith stood near a collection of chaises, even more dishevelled than earlier. Her hair hung in wispy tendrils, feathers drooping. With bodice askew, hem muddied, and a bit of chiffon torn, Judith's gown looked as though she just finished savaging Ella and killing Myrtle. All at once the events of the evening caught up with Ella, the pain ricocheting through her. She searched among the crowd for sign of her stepsisters, but they were nowhere to be seen.

"Fools," Judith screeched again, wide blood-shot eyes focused on Ella. "Can't you see the monster in front of you? The one weaselling her way into your very midst, into the heart of your prince?"

Aerysleigh stepped forward, Ella's hand clenched tightly in his. "You forget yourself, Madam. WARs, attend me."

Metal clanked as the four automatons from each corner of the room switched from dormant to active. People pushed to move from their path, but Judith stood her ground.

She pointed a shaking finger at Aerysleigh. "You have been

duped, your highness," she cackled. "All this time you are chasing the thief Cinder, but the whole time she is right in front of you. Not only is she a monster. She is a thief. The lowest of all. One who sneaks into your home at night and takes your precious possessions."

Judith choked on her laughter, bending over double to draw a tight breath. She jerked her head up and gazed at Ella. "It's all true, isn't it? Tell them."

Aerysleigh fairly shook with rage. He pointed at Judith. "Arrest this mad woman."

Judith slid out of the arm reach of nearest WAR. She paced towards Ella with deadly intent. Ella lifted her chin and stepped beside the prince.

I must be brave.

"You are the evil one here, Judith. You work for England's enemies and experiment on your own daughters."

Aerysleigh put a hand out. "Stop, madam."

Judith sniffed, only ten feet away. Aerysleigh moved to step in front of Ella. Her love deepened at his attempts to protect her. "Be careful," he warned. "She's mad."

"Mad? Mad, am I?"

Judith circled around them forcing Ella and Aerysleigh to turn with her. A knife gleamed in her hand. The WARs tried to pinpoint the culprit and though people moved out of their way, it only confused them more.

One automation grabbed an older matron by the shoulder. The buxom lady screamed and collapsed. Judith chose that moment to strike. With the quickness of a cat she leaped in, feinting towards the prostate by-stander.

Aerysleigh tried to block her, but the woman suddenly revived and gripped his leg. Judith's blade caught the shoulder of his coat. Before she could land another blow on her love, Ella stepped in front of the attack, turning her back and lifting her prosthesis to protect the prince.

The weapon caught at the sapphire and onyx gown where it fastened in back, slicing the lacing and allowing it to gape open and fall to the ground.

Judith stabbed again and again. The thick prosthesis strapping and corset metal once again acting as armour though her stepmother aimed for the body, intent to kill.

Aerysleigh shook off the woman clutching his boot and grabbed Judith's arm. He forced her away from Ella and pushed Judith towards the only coherent WAR. It wrapped its metal arms around the mad woman, but she seemed not to care.

"There! There is your Cinder. How does she do the things she does? She is a monster!"

Covered now only by the Chinese chemise and pantaloons, the blue glow Ella shared with the mice, the cat Thoth, and Myrtle showed through. Her hands, both metal and bone, opened and closed in agitation and in the sudden quiet the clicking of the metal sounded freight train loud.

In the ruckus Aerysleigh dropped her hand. Ella's heart shattered like exploding glass at the gaze he levelled her way. The shards lodged throughout her body and each breath became agony.

"Is this true?" he demanded. The condemnation in his voice broke the remnants of her strength.

"I wanted to tell you, I really did, but she threatened…"

The queen would not listen, without hesitation she pointed at Ella. "Arrest this woman too," she demanded.

The ball attendees pulled away to allow another WAR to do its work. Then the crowd shifted.

"No," Portia removed her shawl and stepped forward, spreading a pair of vestigial wings. Several women, and some men, swooned at the sight. Harcourt, Drax, and many others stepped into the open space and formed a loose ring around Ella.

"Watch out," yelled a gentleman near the large open doors fronting the wide gardens. A dark figure swooped in from the night. Valkyrie settled on his feet, beak clacking in agitation.

"N-O B-I-T-E C-I-N-D-E-R. C-I-N-D-E-R G-O-O-D."

Aerysleigh's eyes widened as Valkyrie's coded message sunk in.

"It's true," the prince whispered, betrayal written in every feature. Every word.

Another man pushed to the front. Lord Stillingfleet, metal mask in place. His gaze met Ella's.

"Go," he said.

Chapter Forty-Seven

The Supporters

The sudden, angry mutter of the members of Ella's protective circle caused Aerysleigh to realise he made a terrible mistake.

"Follow her," ordered Queen Constantina. "Can't you see she's a monster?"

"No," murmured Aerysleigh, reality sinking in. "She is beautiful inside and out."

With no thought to the disarray of the ball, he started after Ella.

A hand grabbed his arm.

Lord Stillingfleet. Ever the meddler—sticking his metal mask where it least belonged.

"Sire," said the marquess's low voice. "Perhaps you need to attend to this."

At that moment he became aware of several things. A phalanx of WAR protection units surrounded his mother. Another restrained Ella's unknown accuser while the room cleared of people and filled with more automatons and royal guards.

"Queen's protection detail, please remove the queen to safety," he ordered. The guards turned and marched from the room.

He nodded to the human King's Men. "You may return to your posts. Everything is alright. Please keep watch for any other disturbances."

Five minutes ago, he would have been on the lookout for Cinder, but the issue didn't concern him any longer.

Unless the captured woman had lied.

No, Ella's face revealed all. She is *Cinder.*

Questions pounded at his mind. He just wanted to chase after her, to demand answers, but he could not.

He turned to matters commanding his attention. "Palace Protection Squad, return to observation mode."

Immediately, the other sentinels returned to their unobtrusive posts in corners and halls. A screech drew his gaze to the struggling woman.

If only there were a dungeon in Kensington.

Basil approached and stood quietly at his shoulder. Ever the faithful friend.

"All that time planning our trap," Aerysleigh said, unable to keep the bitterness from his tone. "The elaborate ruse of moving the jewels, setting up passwords and alarms throughout the viewing room. Everything for nought."

Basil cleared his throat. "We do have a secure room where we planned to hold Cinder."

Aerysleigh nodded. "Do it."

His friend motioned to the automaton. "Follow me."

The remaining crowd seemed to sigh. Although a long time had passed since the last automaton beserker, people still seemed more at ease when they were gone.

Music started up again. Voices returned to normal, even though the flurry of movement attracted some attention, there were over fifty rooms filled with people. There would be talk, especially since some of the commotion happened in the presence of Queen Constantina, however the relative few who witnessed the event were inconsequential compared to the sheer number of visitors this night.

I hope.

He turned to the array of people before him.

Valkyrie stood nearest. He regarded Aerysleigh steadily. The metal contraption on his jaw hung open. Aerysleigh recalled meeting the birdman before. He always seemed barmy while snapping out strange bits of Morse code, cradling his birds. But tonight, Valkyrie appeared extremely sane. His soft brown eyes questioning.

Something clicked in Aerysleigh's brain from a year ago. "She was the lady on the bridge." The lady that smelled of jasmine and smoke—Ella. A woman dressed in breeches and good with a grappling hook—Cinder.

However, it was the expressions of betrayal and anger around him that shocked him. *Wasn't I the one deceived?*

He had been led on a merry chase these last few months, piecing together clues to which he'd been so blind, and now the sanctity of his home breeched. To top everything, his mother had been endangered by a mad woman somehow connected to Cinder.

Why should anyone be upset with me?

He glared at the mob which surrounded him. But it was his own blindness that angered him most. Although upset with the secrets kept from him, his pride smarted with the knowledge he missed all the clues.

Besides Harcourt and Drax, whom Aerysleigh had come to recognise as some sort of protection detail, those surrounding him ranged from merchants and their wives, and tradesman to marines and aeronaughts with war scarred faces.

There were match girls, several with iron facial coverings. All the metal, from prosthesis to masks displayed the half of a cog he'd noticed on Ella's own hand.

There were painted ladies, shop girls, factory and dock workers. It seemed nearly every occupation had a representative protecting Cinder. A few, the younger set, were mutants. A fellow who breathed through his neck, a lady with wings.

"You knew," he accused them all.

"Of course, we knew," said the hunchback, Harcourt.

"Where is your honour? You protected a thief. An illegal modified," said Aerysleigh.

But does that really matter?

No, it was more that she didn't trust him.

Would I have listened?

The conversation in his bedroom haunted him.

She tried to tell me.

"It don't matter what she is," said a merchant's wife bedecked in a fine wool Sunday dress. "She made my boy a scooter on the account he can't walk. And she didn't ask for nothing."

A thick fingered fellow thumped his thigh and it echoed hollowly. "She fixed me up a leg after the sawbones cut it off."

"She nursed my babe back to health at St. Drogo like he were her own."

"She repaired the furnace in our Notingdale Tenement when no one else would."

"Cinder had Proximus give me a hay penny for my hat pin when he didn't want to give me nothing."

Accolades rose. Each clamouring for attention to tell Aerysleigh of the things CinderElla, thief, smith, and nurse, did for them.

"But I don't understand," he exclaimed when the commotion ebbed. "Why steal?"

A lady in a violet gown stepped forward. A doctor he recognised from St. Drogo. "That was our fault, I believe."

"Mine," muttered Harcourt with a clank of his pincher hand.

"We assumed her safe at Iron Crest, though it seems she was not," said the doctor. "Facts have only recently come to light that her new stepmother, Judith Steelhaugh, also known as Jutta Linberg, is a Prussian agent that may have killed the Baron Steelhaugh."

Harcourt grumbled and started off after the WAR that had taken the mad woman captive. "I should just kill her now. Where did they take the witch?"

Drax grabbed him by the shoulder. "No killing.

Chapter Forty-Eight

In the Garden

Ella fled into the dark, pushing through the crowds.

Where to go? What to do?

The palace lawns beckoned her, a grove of trees and a small lake black smudges against shades of silver.

Even here she found parties and couples of all classes taking the air in the magical gardens. Ella wove her way among the throng, clutching her dress, trying to hide the modification and the blue glow. With so much to occupy their senses, very few eyes followed her. Spying a willow, Ella hurried into the security of the long branches and found a bench hidden beneath the boughs.

Despite the early season, the beginning of buds and multiple branches were the perfect hiding place. Light from the garden torches penetrated the Stygian darkness, turning it to a grey dusk.

She collapsed on the seat and buried her face into her hands, reserves of courage and strength depleted. Aches and pains wracked her body. The magic cloud which carried her feet to Aerysleigh now turned to quicksand which sucked at her heels and her soul.

His face. The betrayal on his face.

Such a colossal mistake.

He would have loved me with the arm. The extent of her modification may have taken him by surprise, but Ella sensed it would not have been an issue. However, the revelation that she was Cinder, the one blamed for diverting the peerage's attention, and the thief he had been hunting all along, seemed too much.

Branches rustled above. To her surprise a young lady in a ball gown dropped from where the tree forked into a large branch with limbs trailing in the water. Or at least tried to. Just before her feet hit the ground, her dress caught, and she tumbled the rest of the way. Ella jumped to her feet to help the lady. A mass of red hair tumbled over a pert nose and askew glasses.

"Are you alright?" Ella asked.

"Oh yes," she said. "It wouldn't be the first time I fell out of a tree."

"But what were you doing up there?"

"Getting a feel for the lay of the land and the party." The lady brushed off a velvet green ball gown. With leaves and sticks stuck in the rosettes and the generally crumpled appearance, the gown looked as though it had seen better days and hard use.

"You're welcome inside," said Ella. "Everyone is, you know."

"I know," the woman stuck out her hand. "Molly Mayhem. I'm a reporter. When covering parties, I like to get a sense of the atmosphere both inside and out. This is a gay time is it not? Modifieds and aristocrats rubbing shoulders like one is not about to make the other illegal." She paused for a breath and squinted at Ella. "Oh my. I think you are in even worse state than I."

The lady's breathless talk and unaffected ways made Ella laugh. "You are right. I'm Ella."

"I know. What happened to your dress?"

"My stepmother."

Molly blinked. "Oh."

Ella sat again. Molly perched beside her. "She revealed to everyone I have an advanced, illegal modification and that I am the thief Cinder. She did this in front of Queen Constantina and then threatened the prince with a knife."

"Oh my."

"It looks like my stepsisters have taken advantage of the pandemonium to abscond. Good for them, I say. But it leaves me in a quandary."

Molly picked at a leaf on her dress. "Indeed."

Ella searched Molly's face. "You don't seem surprised by any of this."

"On the contrary. I think you have left me speechless. And that doesn't happen very often, let me tell you." She paused. "Well, maybe not completely speechless. But I have been following Cinder for quite some time and knew it to be you. Anyone who is consistently around St. Drogo would at least suspect. But few are."

"Except you."

"I have a nose for news." Silence fell between them, soft notes of music drifted from the palace and Ella closed her eyes, fighting off recent memories.

Molly took her hand. "I am sorry. I thought you and Prince Aerysleigh were the perfect couple."

Ella shook her head. "Not when everything is based on lies."

"Not lies," said Molly. She patted Ella's hand. "Everyone saw how he looked at you. He loves you, all of you, Cinder and Ella, he just needs to come around. Men are like that, you know."

"Like what?"

"Slow."

Ella stifled a hysterical giggle. "Thank you."

The draped foliage parted, and Ella clutched at her tattered garment. Valkyrie hobbled in, his putrid stench filling the enclosed space. D-A-N-G-E-R C-I-N-D-E-R

Ella hurried to the branches and peered out at the crowd, but nothing seemed to have changed.

She turned back to Valkyrie. "What do you mean?"

"Oh," said Molly. She clapped her hands delightedly and slipped a pencil and pad from a reticule belted at her waist. "You speak Morse Code. How lovely. May I have an interview, Mr. Valkyrie?"

Valkyrie snapped at her. Shrugging off Ella's repeated questions, he climbed the tree and sat on the same bough from which Molly fell.

"You, old bird," Ella said without rancour. Despite his biting her, he meant well. Perhaps the aid rendered to his pigeon softened something in him—at least towards her. But his cryptic message meant nothing.

Three miles away at Westminster Palace, Big Ben gonged the midnight hour. At first it was simply the background noise of London, the chimes blending in with the noise of the ball and the ships on the Thames.

Then it struck her.

Midnight.

Alarms and fog horns sounded from the river.

"The gases are rising," said Molly.

The air thumped with the unmistakable ignition of helium. An airship near the stables burst into flames. Once again Ella thrust her head through the screen and gasped.

The sky brightened with the false sunrise of yellow and orange. *A distraction.*

Ella whirled to Molly. "The queen's jewels."

While the reporter frowned, Ella tried to tie her dress on. No doubt while all eyes focused on the fire, thieves were moving into position to take the jewels. Judith mentioned a distraction and a way to get rid of Ella.

A trap her intuition screamed. *But I won't let Judith take one more thing that did not belong to her. She stole everything from me, but no more.*

"Here, take mine." Molly thrust a satchel into Ella's fumbling fingers.

Light flared as an airship on fire drifted towards the lake. Inside Molly's satchel were dark breeches, shirt, and coat, along with an emergency gas mask and goggles. Ella looked at the journalist in wonder.

Molly shrugged. "I always try to be prepared, and not climb trees in my ball gown."

Overhead Valkyrie clacked something Ella didn't quit catch.

Molly turned towards the tree. "I was simply trying to get a look at the bird with a prosthesis," she called. "I just happened to be in my day dress at the time."

"He bit you too?" asked Ella with a grimace.

Molly put her hands on her hips. "Pushed me right out of a tree, he did. I'd never seen a bird with a peg leg before."

Ella dropped the shredded dress. It didn't cover much anyway. Molly held the blouse for her to slip in. "The foot turned out alright, didn't it?"

Molly quickly did up the buttons on the back and danced around in front of Ella while she slipped on the pants. "I knew it. You made it, didn't you?"

"I did." Ella stared down at her feet. Though Molly had a pair of boots in the satchel, there was no possibility of them fitting Ella's stump, not with any sort of stability. "I guess it's slippers tonight. Not very good for running or fighting if it comes to that."

"Why would it?"

"Another stepmother trick," said Ella. "She hopes to distract everyone with a fire and steal the jewels. The plan was to get rid of me as well, but until thirty minutes ago she thought she killed me at Iron Crest."

"But she didn't kill you," said Molly softly.

Ella lifted her chin.

Judith might have crushed me for a time, destroyed my reputation, damaged my pride, perhaps may still get me arrested, but I'm not dead.

The confidence she knew as Cinder welled in her chest, but it felt different. A combination of the two personalities—CinderElla.

"No," she said. "No, she did not."

Chapter Forty-Nine

The Theives

Aerysleigh handed a fire brigade WAR a bucket of water and directed it towards the pile of straw threatened by blowing sparks. The engine kept on Kensington grounds pumped its load of water on the stables. Just about every able-bodied man from the ball lent their aid to putting out the fire.

The blaze was a small thing, the airship that mysteriously caught fire drifting over the lawn and alighting in the lake. However, several small fires sprang up and threatened the haycock.

He was thankful for the amount of common folk on the grounds who took off their Sunday best and lent their strength to the servants and automatons. It could have been worse. He turned back to the palace, his home away from home for so long and an important piece of history.

"Your Highness," Basil called from the portico. One look at his friend's face made Aerysleigh hurry to his side.

"What is it?"

Basil limped close to be heard above the sounds of the workers and the gossipping onlookers. "During the confusion, Lady Steelhaugh escaped, but I suspect this," he motioned to the fire, "to be a ruse."

Aerysleigh's mind made the jump and anger consumed him. "Cinder's after the jewels," he snarled.

"Wait," Basil yelled.

Aerysleigh would hear none of it. He sprinted towards the upstairs rooms set up to display his mother's jewels. Paste copies though they be, it was the thought that she would do this, even now after being exposed.

How cold could the woman be?

To rip out his heart in one instant, then steal from him, Him! In the next.

He grabbed a medieval sword from one of the old suits of armour guarding the servant's stair and raced up the risers two at a time. With the night in shambles, nothing ending as it should, not to mention the seething burn of his injured pride and the black hole where his heart used to be, he would not allow anything else to be taken from him.

At a sconce on the first landing, something alighted on his shoulder. He turned and found his nose inches from Ella's mouse. Anger made his first impulse to smash the creature, throw it against the wall and jump on it like a child in a tantrum. But he didn't. She'd saved his life once.

"Well come along then," he growled.

The mouse twitched her whiskers at him then swarmed down his lapels into his inside breast pocket. He sprinted on ahead.

Sounds of metal striking metal slowed his headlong rush. No soldiers. No WARs lined the walls.

Where is everyone?

He cautiously cracked open the hidden door into the large room they had chosen for the exhibition. Glass cases filled with tiaras and accompanying parure lined the walls. Sprinkled about the floor were several more cases displaying the jewelry Queen Constantina favoured, along with the most valuable.

In front of the centre most case, two figures fought. Aerysleigh had no trouble recognising Ella whose blonde hair shone forge fire bright. Her movements were not those of the accomplished fencer who met him on the rooftop for she fought in delicate ball slippers rather than proper footwear.

Three more black clad combatants approached from all sides, eager to join their companion in defeating the lady.

"Ella, behind you," Aerysleigh called before she could back into the trap.

She struck hard at the bloke in front of her and whirled to protect her flank. She stumbled and took a knee, narrowly avoiding a lunge passing overhead.

"Just put her down," snapped one of the men.

"But don't kill her," rejoined another, a woman.

Aerysleigh jumped into the fray.

He jammed his shoulder into the nearest attacker then engaged the one across from him. Ella snapped her adversary on the face with the blade. As he stumbled, she conked him over the head with her metal arm. He sank soundlessly to the tile.

Now, they stood back to back, blades threatening the remaining three.

"Two for the price of one," said the female attacker through her cloth mask. "The prince is a prize greater than all the queen's jewels. Take him."

Aerysleigh stepped left and found Ella matched his move, keeping her back to his. He reached back and found her hand, squeezing it. He prayed she understood the message. On the third squeeze he feinted towards the woman.

At the same time Ella lunged forward, blocked a strike, and crunched another fellow upside the head. He joined his mate on the floor. Odds more even now, Aerysleigh turned his attention to the last male attacker. Ella struck at the female with swift, sure strokes.

The big man pulled a pistol and levelled it at Aerysleigh's chest. Aerysleigh dropped his foil and slapped at the wrist with both hands in opposite directions. The weapon fell, discharging, the echoing pop not loud enough to cover the satisfying snap of the bloke's wrist.

Glass shattered and someone screamed.

Without hesitation, Aerysleigh swept up his medieval weapon and held it at the man's throat. The downed man glared up at him through tinted goggles and bared his teeth. Before Aerysleigh could stop him, he popped something into his mouth and bit down. Green smoke roiled from his mouth. Aerysleigh leaped back. The man convulsed violently, once, twice, and lay still. With no time to ponder the thief's willingness to kill himself, Aerysleigh turned to help Ella.

Ella and her adversary exchanged hard blows. Ella's heavy sword, evidently nicked from a suit of armour as well, moved slower and slower against the last attacker's wicked machete.

Just when it looked as though she reached the end of her strength, she switched hands and fought with the remarkable prosthesis. It moved just as well, if not faster and stronger than her other arm. Aerysleigh looked for a chance to jump into the fray, but one of the men on the floor stirred and pulled a pistol from his long, dark coat. He aimed it at Ella's unprotected back.

"No," Aerysleigh yelled.

The pistol cracked.

Ella tumbled over the body of the first fellow she felled with a sharp cry. Aerysleigh leaped on the back of the pistol wielding thief and beat him on the head with the hilt of his sword until he quit struggling. He sank down with a moan. Looking up, Aerysleigh spied the female adversary advancing on Ella who lay prone.

The last thief drew a pistol from a hip holster with a smirk.

"You've been a worthy adversary, Cinder, just as promised," said the woman. "But now, you must stay and pay for your crimes." She pushed the hammer back.

Aerysleigh grabbed the pistol in the lax grip of his downed man, then leaped in front of Ella.

Pistols fired as one.

He grunted as the ball slapped his shoulder. The woman sank to her knees, red blossoming on her chest like a gay posy. She looked down at it then at him and sank to the ground with a burbling sigh.

Aerysleigh dropped to his haunches then lay down and closed his eyes.

Chapter Fifty

The Shoe

Ella fought the dizziness caused by her skull meeting the black and white marble tile and rolled to where Aerysleigh lay with his eyes closed. Panic constricted her throat, but she managed to squeak out his name.

"Aerysleigh," she cried, grabbing his shoulders. "You foolish, foolish man, why did you jump in front of that crazy woman?"

Even in her dazed state she recognised the danger he put himself in. *For me.* Someone who had deceived him, taunted him as Cinder, who hid things from him. His gallant heart just would not rest. Even for a criminal. And that made her angry. She gave him a hard shake.

The prince groaned. "Leave off, woman. I'm fine."

He opened his eyes, his patch long gone in the scuffle, and looked up at her. She patted his chest. "But you got shot. I heard it. I saw it." Still, no blood appeared on his jacket. In fact, he seemed in remarkably good shape. She rocked back on her heels. "Did she miss?"

Aerysleigh sighed and sat up, rubbing at his shoulder where a small round hole smoked in his jacket. "She didn't miss. I had a guardian angel." He reached inside his breast pocket and pulled out the crumpled form of a metal mouse.

"Flora," Ella cried, taking the still body into her palm. She stroked the copper ears and the sleek body. "Oh, Flora." Tears spilled from Ella's eyes. "Not you too."

Aerysleigh cupped his palm under hers. "Is she...?" He trailed off. She understood his dilemma.

Do machines die? She sniffed.

They certainly did. When that incredible blue light went out of her dear little friends, she felt their death as surely as she felt the deaths of her mother and father. They may be metal, but these mice filled her heart like family. She bit back a sob, but that only made her pain worse.

My very last friend.

"Is she dead?" Aerysleigh repeated.

Ella turned the mouse over on her back, seeking the blue glow of the heartstone that separated the mice from any other automaton. Flora opened one sapphire eye and released her claws, dropping a round pellet into Ella's hand.

"She's alive," Ella cried, cuddling the mouse against her cheek. "Oh, you sweet creature." A glance at Aerysleigh found him mirroring her own delighted grin.

He touched the tip of a copper ear. "Thank you, Flora, for saving my life—again." The mouse rose to her feet somewhat stiffly and sat back on her haunches. She pulled Aerysleigh's face towards her and rubbed her stiff whiskers against his cheek then turned and crawled into a pocket in Ella's ill-fitting breeches.

"I believe she just said, 'you're welcome'," said Ella.

The prince pulled back with a thunderstruck expression. "Amazing."

Their gazes met and held a few scant inches apart. Ella felt her sudden joy falter. "Aerysleigh," she began.

"Ella," he said at the same time. The wonder in his voice slipped away, replaced by something harder. "Did you come to take the jewels?"

The apology trembling on her lips slipped away. "*What?!* Is that why you think I'm here?" She drew away from his mesmerising closeness and pushed herself to her feet. He followed suit, his expression wary.

You did that. You put that distrust there. And you deserve it all.

He motioned to the room littered with bodies and shattered glass. "All I know is that when I got here *you* were here."

"Fighting for my life," she reminded him.

"Maybe," he said stiffly. "Maybe not. These could have been

accomplices in a burglary gone bad, could it not?"

"You can't believe that?" she gasped.

"Why shouldn't I?" he demanded. For every pace she retreated, he followed with one of his own. She tread on the heel of her ball slipper and the short one slipped off. She hobbled back another step, but Aerysleigh did not notice her handicap.

"Look around you, Ella. Here you are, dressed like *that*. Where did you even get those clothes? Did you hide them beforehand at Kensington? Were you planning the heist the night you came to 'check on me'? Did you leave your clothes? Were you planning the burglary even when you—" his voice rose, strident with righteous indignation, "—even when you kissed me?"

"No," Ella sobbed. "No and again no. You don't understand! She said she would kill Myrtle. She said—"

Yells resounded on all the stairs accompanied by the unmistakable clomp of WARs. Above all rose the stentorian call of Commissioner Traverson.

"You should have trusted me, Ella," Aerysleigh pressed.

"I know," she tried again, her back pressed against an open window sash evidently used by the bandits. "I wanted to. I even tried, but—"

"I would have listened, Ella."

She dropped her head. "No. I don't think you would have. Just like you aren't listening now."

Aerysleigh opened his mouth, then bit down hard and closed his eyes.

Ella took that moment to switch out her hand with the grappling hook. She leaned out and fired it towards the roof.

His eyes snapped open at the sound. "Ella, wait."

She jerked the spring and disappeared into the night.

*****

All four portals suddenly thronged with king's men, police, and automatons, all led by Basil. Aerysleigh lunged for the window and looked up, but once again her speed surprised him.

"Aerysleigh!" Basil yelled, crunching across the glass shards. WARs picked up the bodies of the bandits and one groaned.

"Be careful of a cyanide pill," Aerysleigh called over his shoulder. *At least one of the thieves needs to talk.*

He glanced once more at the night sky, knowing he would find nothing. Ella had ways of escape he could never fathom. He turned back to the room, now completely swarmed with people, and something caught his eye. He bent and picked up the delicate ball slipper.

What cunning workmanship.

He ran his hand along the gears and chains. Inside it, he felt her warmth. He frowned as his fingertips hit a cushioned block inside.

Despite the turmoil around him-the questions fired at him from all directions plus the destruction of the room—he laughed. The activity in the chamber ceased.

Basil gave him an odd look, then motioned to the men.

"Take the prisoners to Scotland Yard immediately," Basil said to the automaton holding a wriggling man, "And those to the morgue. Bently, Connie, Mortimer. Go with the WAR, and don't you dare lose another prisoner, you hear me?" The detectives nodded. "Everyone else out. Now."

Slowly people filed from the room. Not a few cast anxious glances over their shoulder at the prince laughing over a lady's slipper.

Aerysleigh ignored them.

Basil approached. "Your highness?"

He held up the shoe. "A specially made slipper. See?"

Basil reached for it, but he snatched it back. "I see. Cinder's, I presume?"

He nodded. "We talked about the unique boots she wore. It's because she only has half a foot." He closed his eyes, remembering her hobbling step. Mortification overcame him. He just would not listen. He knew the moment he came upon the scene in the jewel chamber she was not there to steal the jewels, no matter how it appeared. Ella was not that sort of person. Not with the removal of her stepmother's threats.

"We did investigate several boot makers," Basil said.

"We never would've found them. Something like this, this is made with utmost care." He turned it over and spied the maker's mark. "A hammer and laurel?" He looked at his friend.

"Baron Steelhaugh's mark," supplied Basil.

Aerysleigh nodded grimly. "Her father."

Silenced stretched between them.

"I just made the worst mistake of my life," Aerysleigh announced. "I drove her away and with her skills what are the chances of me tracking her down when I failed so miserably the first time? With her right in front of me even?"

"What do you want to do?" Basil asked finally. "She can't be far."

He motioned to the slipper. "Not shoeless."

Aerysleigh chuckled. "We thought her escape impossible many a time in this chase, have we not?"

Basil dropped his gaze and looked abashed.

"Somehow, some way I need to find her.

Even if I have to try this damned shoe on every woman in the kingdom to prove it's her, I will."

Chapter Fifty-One

The Search

T wo months later, Aerysleigh paced the short open space in Basil's Scotland Yard office. *Five steps. Turn. Five Steps. Turn.* He glared at his friend who reclined on the chair behind his desk. Hands linked around his neck, the commissioner ignored the mounds of papers surrounding him and watched Aerysleigh with a grim look.

Lines around Basil's face attested to a painful night with his leg and the scent of opium clung to his jacket. Still, like clockwork, the young detective arrived at his cramped office every day as if to do nothing but watch over Aerysleigh's search for CinderElla.

"You shouldn't be at work this morning." Aerysleigh ground out, attempting to mask his frustration with concern.

"And you shouldn't be here at all," Basil rejoined. "Don't you have a kingdom to run?"

Aerysleigh snorted. "My father is well enough for that now." *Thanks to the potion Ella gave me.*

He ground his teeth at the reminder she still eluded the ever-widening search.

How does she do it? We practically have the entire city on the look out for her.

"Any forward movement in your search?" Basil prodded.

"Not at all. Lord Stillingfleet insists he hasn't seen her. The homeless and poor might as well have their lips welded shut for all the information they offer."

Aerysleigh pounded a fist into his palm. Their wary gazes shone with accusation and he felt keenly the withdrawal of their love and support.

"The crux of it all, is that I failed everyone. Cinder made them believe I was different. She gave them hope that I cared and would champion their cause against oppression."

He picked up the newspaper on the corner of the desk and tossed it within Basil's reach. "However, according to a certain Molly 'Mayhem' Carter with the Modified Post, I was proved false at the first test." Not that he denied the accusation. "If it weren't for my damned, stiff-necked pride which allowed her stepmother to reveal Cinder at the ball this search wouldn't be unnecessary. Why didn't I listen?"

"According to this paper, you were sighted at the Hungerford Bridge."

"Yes, I attempted to communicate with the Valkyrie."

"How did that end up?" By Basil's smile, Aerysleigh suspected the commissioner already knew.

"Fool bird tried to bite me, then flew away in a sulk."

"Well, from what you told me about rescuing Cinder from his bridge, he even bites his friends."

Aerysleigh sighed. "No word from her in two months. No robberies. No charitable activities at St. Drogo. I get glared at where ever I go—I can't fathom if it's because I rejected their princess or proved unworthy of her."

Papers rustled as Basil as he flipped through the pages. "Though these are old accounts, I keep them due to the interesting reading. Here you're getting blasted for your lack of respect for the modifieds—another piece by Molly Mayhem."

"That's not the worst of it. Even *London's Weekly*, the paper known for defending the upper class, cites my numerous failings as a host and claim me to be more for the common man than the Peerage. I can't win on any count."

Snapping the papers closed, Basil pulled a file towards him. "The investigation at the burned out estate of Iron Crest reveals little. The identity of the mechanised woman is still unknown. Interviews with servants got us nowhere. Most were dismissed over ten years ago, a few only hired on occasion after the new baroness took over the estate."

Basil flipped through the file's contents. "There's talk, of course, speculation, but nothing substantial. Most everyone thought Eliana Steelhaugh died with her mother aboard *Lady Peril*."

He handed the folder to Aerysleigh who scanned through it impatiently. "I've seen it all before. What's most frustrating," he exclaimed, "is no one can tell me what became of Ella through those months after her father passed. It's all tied together, the sudden change in stealing classified documents to jewels and the rise in crime. Yet, without her, no definite conclusion can be drawn." He leaned against the desk and studied the map pinned to the opposite wall.

So here he was, in Basil's office every single day, going over the reports of the four inspectors travelling the length and breadth of London with the cursed slipper. He often went with them, giving directions to places she frequented. He hoped to surprise her in disguise, to have the shoe fit suddenly.

Nil.

Therefore, he searched.

Once walking down the street, a whiff of that particular jasmine scent she favored reached his nostrils. His heart sped up as he examined every passerby—any moment expecting to find her brilliant blue eyes and saucy smile shining up at him from beneath a large bonnet. Besides nearly getting slapped by an enraged matron, she never appeared.

Then, a change in the wind blew the scent away.

Aerysleigh lifted the slipper from the desk. This represented his last hope. Basil chuckled at him when he believed Aerysleigh in a lighter mood. Sometimes, his friend wondered aloud why someone as wily as Cinder would allow herself to be cornered and a shoe fit to her foot. Aerysleigh gave several reasons, but it was only one he cared about.

If Ella allows the inspectors to find her, to try the shoe, then she forgives me. Pure and simple.

Inspector third class, Tamera Jenkins, a fresh-faced recruit with large, brown eyes and gold braids hanging down her back, stepped into the office with a knock. "Your highness. Sir. Begging your pardon, but there be two girls here who insist they see you." Her gaze bounced between the commissioner and prince as though indecisive of whom to address.

Basil straightened and adjusted his tie. "Who do they want to see?"

"The prince, sir. And you."

"Well, show them in," said Aerysleigh.

"Yes, your highness."

"I suppose you want them to try the slipper," said Basil.

Aerysleigh snorted. "As if there are two in all the land that have not yet tried it."

Basil nodded in agreement. "Even so. Why meet with them?"

Aersyleigh shrugged.

Two striking women stepped into the office. The taller wore a wary expression. Her hair shown a deep blue-black and brows arched high over wide green eyes that glinted with a hint of gold. Beautiful indeed, but the least of Aerysleigh's concerns, though he could tell Basil's head had been turned. The blonde surveyed the small room with avid curiosity and a sort of disconcerting winter wolf hunger.

He bowed then ignored other pleasantries. An odd feeling itched between his shoulder blades, he knew these women from somewhere. "Your servant, ladies. How can we help you?"

"I am Isabeau Linberg Steelhaugh and this is my sister Aurelia."

Aerysleigh nerves jumped at their names. "You're her stepsisters!"

"Yes, we've come about Ella," Isabeau said.

"What of her?" Aerysleigh demanded.

"Please, your highness, you have to understand," said Aurelia, "Very few events in her life were of her own free will. She's not half as bad as some of the newspapers imply." She nodded towards *London's Weekly.*

Aerysleigh grit his teeth. "Do you know where she is?"

The two looked at each other then nodded. "We do," said the first. "But before we tell you anything, we need assurances you will not hurt her...or us."

Basil cleared his throat. "That remains to be seen, Miss Steelhaugh. Her legal status is somewhat," he glanced at Aersyleigh, "up in the air."

"But, Mother made her do all those things," exclaimed Aurelia. "She told her she'd kill Myrtle and then she did, but that was after she poisoned Baron Steelhaugh and..."

The dark-haired beauty squeezed her sister's hand, stopping her in mid-sentence.

"Just tell me where she is," said Aerysleigh, "that's all I care about."

Basil came around the desk, put a hand on Aerysleigh's shoulder, then gripped hard. "Please have a seat." He motioned graciously.

"Tell us what you came to tell us."

The blonde bared her teeth in a smile at Aerysleigh and flounced to the single seat in front of the desk. Her sister fidgeted with her gloves. "It's such a very long story. I'm not sure where to begin."

"Where you met Ella would be good," said Basil. Aerysleigh took a deep breath but Basil snapped a hand in the air. "Just tell us everything."

Aerysleigh rubbed his neck and leaned against the wall then adjusted his eye patch.

This could take a very long time.

Chapter Fifty-Two

The Change of Heart

A cloud of dust rose from the drape covered sofa as Ella
pounded its back on her way past. On the chair next to her,
Dr. Bihari coughed, tightened the screw on a patient kitchen
automaton, and glared at Ella across the top of her high
magnification glasses.

"Ella, go practice your swordsmanship. Go bedevil Portia for
some dinner. Something. Anything. But if you continue that infernal
pacing and sighing, I will tear off your other arm."

Life with Theodosia the past two months taught Ella two
things—her godmother had a no-nonsense, somewhat volatile
temper, and she never bluffed. Ella sat with a *whoosh*. She missed the
swish of skirts to emphasise her point. Breeches just did not have the
same effect, but it would have been lost on Theo, anyway.

Her godmother turned another screw and switched the
automaton on. "There you go." The doctor pulled out her lists,
pouring over them for the millionth time.

"Two months gathering supplies, men and women, weapons,
and research tools," her godmother muttered. "Two months lost
when I should be solving the small problem of a plague turning
humans into zombie-like creatures."

"Pardon?" asked Ella, almost afraid to ask. She vacillated
between eagerness to be off and explore new worlds, and sadness at
leaving the old behind. She did admit to herself, in the darkest of
night, in the tiniest bit of her heart, that most of her sadness was due
to Aerysleigh. She could not get him out of her mind.

"Nothing," came Theo's answer. "Though I wish you'd stop

mooning over that milk sop."

Ella knew exactly who she meant. "I saw him the other day."

Dr. Bihari sighed and leaned back in her chair, arranging her features into an expression of extreme interest. "Do tell."

Ella ignored her sarcasm. "He was just below on the street with a bunch of those inspectors going door to door."

"They missed this door," grumbled her godmother.

"A matron nearly took his head off when he detained her daughter." She stifled a giggle at the memory. "Of course, when it became clear to all who he was, everyone went their separate ways. That was the last I saw of him."

Theodosia visibly tried to rein in her exasperation. Ella was onto her godmother's game of keeping her distracted, however. Every day, Theo assigned her books to read until the piles filled her chambers.

"Have you read you biology selection for the day?"

Ella shifted uncomfortably. "Musty old tomes," she muttered. Reading remained laborious though the situation grew worse when her godmother discovered Ella's difficulty. The good doctor expounded for long hours on all manner of subjects. She also devised an intense physical regime that included fencing with members of the crew who did not fight with any sort of honour.

A class on gymnastics and meditation called Yoga was also a part of the daily regime. Several others of the crew also participated, including Theo whose muffled curses made meditation difficult.

Ella also learned gun smithing and tinkering, along with mathematics and engineering. Classes she enjoyed immensely. Lessons in surgery came to an immediate halt when she watched an operation and fainted dead away. That reaction was better, however, than the one before when she lost her dinner.

Nights were the worst.

No matter how tired her body, her mind raced like an airship before the wind. Always she dreamed of dancing with Aerysleigh, reliving the memory of the ball and the feel of weightlessness as he swung her around the floor. However, the dream invariably ended in bloodshed and revulsion, of course.

She stared out the window at the perfect spring. "When do we leave?" she asked.

Theo closed her notebook with a slap. "Within the hour."

Ella straightened. "So soon?"

Her godmother gave her an amused look and nodded. "We are ready. Captain Mahulda has given the go on the *Royal Asp* and we've found five modifieds to join the crew."

Adding crew took the most time due to the secrecy surrounding Theo's life as well as the added complication of concealing the now infamous CinderElla—a name beginning to grow on her. It fit this dual personality that seemed to be her now.

Theodosia stood. "Right then, pack your trunk. Pack light, mind you, and only what we discussed. No frivolous gowns and whatnots. There will be no balls where we are going."

"As if I have any," Ella replied. She suppressed a grin at the thought of Theodosia's sumptuous quarters on the *Asp.*

Her godmother shook the papers at Ella's expression. "Off with you—"

Shouts of warning echoed in the hall. Doors slammed.

Drax burst into the room. "The prince be here," he warned.

Theo wasted no time. "Quick girl, the balcony. My men know what to do. Look for the ladder." The smile she flashed at Ella seemed incongruous to the urgency of the moment. The little woman left Ella alone, pushing Drax into a tiny escape portal behind a painting of a behemoth lady on a small horse.

Ella ran to the double-doors leading to the balcony over the street. Outside, a ladder lead to the roof and the dock above where the *Royal Asp* waited.

She grasped the rungs.

"Wait."

She turned.

Aerysleigh stood just outside the door, his hand held up. He looked so handsome it made her chest ache. She ran her gaze over his braids, and eye patch, frozen as though hypnotised while hungrily trying to memorise every minute detail before she left forever.

How did he find me? Why? Will he arrest me?

"What?" she demanded, finding her tongue. "No *'stop thief'*?"

He hunched his shoulder somewhat. "Just wait," he said in a softer voice. "Please."

She paused, though she could not pinpoint why. *I don't think I can stand it, if he reviled me again.*

Worse, he said nothing.

Another ladder dropped from the sky, hanging just within reach. She glanced up.

Theodosia leaned over the rail. "Climb aboard, girl," she called, impatience in every gesture. She would not stall long. Her godmother had important work to continue while others hunted Judith again.

One small leap and Ella would be climbing aboard the *Asp*, making a new life.

Theodosia offered her a place on the front lines of research where she would have the opportunity to supply her government with precious knowledge gleaned from ancient civilisations. She would be with like-minded people, those who knew the outside of a person did not make their heart.

"Why?" she demanded. "I thought you different. Hoped you were. Instead, I fell in love with a shadow of a dream."

Aerysleigh looked stricken with apoplexy. "You love me?"

His dumbfounded expression was all the answer she needed. The longer the silence stretched, the more obvious it became what she needed to do. She reached for the rung that would take her from this place of hurt. Away from *him* forever. She grabbed the rope ladder like a life line.

As though he sensed the direction of her thoughts, Aerysleigh lunged forward and said the only words capable of giving her pause. "Forgive me."

Her heart stopped. She knew it would never start again. If she had not already given it to him of her own free will, he would have torn it right from her chest. Of all things, of all words, she never anticipated those.

"Ella. Cinder. Whatever name you go by, I don't care. I want only that you come and be my CinderElla."

The fickle breeze made her decision for her. The *Royal Asp* bucked in the rising wind and strained to be free of her moorings. The ladder swung out from the balcony, taking Ella with it. She grabbed the rungs and then climbed with a speed to the ship where hands hauled her over the edge. Panting and sobbing, she collapsed to the deck, unable to look back.

"The sod," said Theodosia. "What did he say to you? Give me the word and I'll lay waste to the whole house. No, bugger that," she raised her voice. "Ready port side cannons and blast that house back to the Stone Age."

Without a mention of the fact their crown prince happened to be inside said house, the crew jumped to obey. "No. Stop. Please, don't," Ella cried.

Theo tapped her foot impatiently. "Dolly, you need to learn that men who make you cry aren't worth a brass farthing, let alone allowed to live. I don't care what you think he means to you. There's plenty where he came from." The *Asp* rumbled as the canons shifted into position.

Ella got to her feet and grabbed her godmother's arm. "No! He apologised."

"Belay my last order," Theo yelled. "What do you mean, he apologised? Why are you crying then? By Horus, why are you even on my ship? You don't belong here."

Too true! Ella leaned over the side. "Take me back."

Theo twisted an upraised finger in a circular motion. "Return to the dock. The lady's had a change of heart. Finally."

Ella hugged her godmother. "Thank you."

"Don't thank me. I ought to put a bullet between his eyes for as long as he took to find you."

"What do you mean?" Ella demanded.

"For two bloody months I've dithered about, waiting for the bloke to have a stroke of genius and put it all together. Never did. *I* had to hunt up your stepsisters, sweet girls by the way, but mighty strange, to give him my address. Though you'd think the airship called the *Royal Asp* would be a dead giveaway but no—"

"You found Aurelia and Isabeau?"

"Not brain surgery, my dear. They're living in a boarding house east of St. Drogo. Took a bit of convincing. That blonde's wilder than a hatter and twice as feral as a wolf."

"But you told *him* where I was?"

Theo planted her hands on her hips. "Of course, I did. Besides, your mooning, his stirring up London with that blasted slipper was too much. If this country's going to get on the right track, we need the Prince General he was, and we weren't going to get there with his head in the clouds." She raised a fist. "Stop it right here and let her down." Theo kissed Ella on the cheek. "Now off with you. I'm months behind in my research."

Ella wrapped her arms around Theodosia and lifted her in a crushing hug. "Thank you, fairy godmother. You're magic, you know that, right?"

Theo sniffed.

"I am a *scientist*, my dear, nothing magic about it."

Chapter Fifty-Three

The Proposal

Aerysleigh raced up the ladder attached to the building to the docks above, unable to believe his incompetence.

The woman left him. *Again.*

The ship turned and opened its cannon ports. So *that* was her answer. He didn't blame her. Not really.

He dropped his probing gaze and sneaked a hand to his pocket where he stashed the slipper. After all this time, after rehearsing what to her over and over again, in the heat of the moment he had been all but incomprehensible. No wonder she ran. He couldn't even get her name right.

What did she want to be called anyway? Ella? Cinder? The mix of the two? No matter. All he wanted was her by his side again. He would never think straight until he had her.

"Call me CinderElla," said a sweet voice behind him. "I like it."

He spun. In his inattention *the Asp* had circled. His lady dropped lightly to the dock from the rope ladder.

Enough talk.

He strode towards her. She stood her ground with a wary expression. He meant to spend the rest of his life making up for that horrible moment at the ball up to her.

Aerysleigh wrapped Ella in his arms, holding her so tightly she squirmed. "Can't breathe," she whispered.

He released some, but not all the way, afraid she would find a way to escape. "I am never letting you run again."

She chuckled, actually laughed at him. "I have no intention of even trying."

"Good then," he knelt, keeping fast her hands in his. "Make it official and marry me."

"Is that a question?"

"It is. Mostly. I love you. Every time you run away, the joy gets sucked out of my life. Say you will stop this misery and promise never to leave me again."

Ella stroked his cheek with her prosthesis. "And this?" she asked.

He grasped it, holding on for dear life. Then turned his face to her palm and kissed the hard metal.

Her eyes widened.

"As long as it's a part of you, I don't care. I do have to warn you, however, if you say yes, I may never let you out of my sight again."

Tears trembled on her golden lashes. "Then yes, a thousand times, yes."

He kissed her fiercely, then felt a movement in his pocket. He glanced down. Flora climbed from Ella to his breast pocket and pushed at the object there. "Oh, I almost forgot."

She froze as though expecting him to say something terrible, to take back the words he just said. He withdrew her slipper. "A token of my love."

The crew above erupted in cheers.

Chapter Fifty-Four

The End

CinderElla fidgeted with her gloves as she stood just inside the doors preparing to enter the balcony where she would greet her countrymen as their princess. She dared a peek from behind the curtain and gasped at the assembled throng.

"*Breathe. Breathe. Breathe*," Ella chanted. "People are going to stare, but no one has actually ruled your modifications inhuman. You can do this."

"A nice confidence talk, my dear" quipped Aerysleigh. He strode into the chamber, shaking off his attendants. "But completely unnecessary."

Ella's tenseness drained away when she gazed at her love, resplendent in his formal uniform and fur lined cape. "You testified before the House of Lords and Commons and gained us a special dispensation to marry. After all, it was your nerve rejuvenator that saved my father."

"Dr. Bihari's," corrected Ella.

Aerysleigh shrugged. "Details." He stopped just a hand's breadth away and leaned to her ear. "Though I would have married you regardless of what those old stuffed shirts declared."

He may have, but Ella couldn't help the relief brought by sanction.

"And married we are," she reminded him. Walking down the long aisle in the church towards her love allowed the many people and possible sour looks to dissipate into a blur. Today was different.

She was their princess. One day to be queen. She touched her hair, hoping it looked alright.

"Stop it," Aerysleigh took her metal hand in his and raised it to his lips. Her heart leaped every time he did that as though she could actually feel the touch of his kiss. "You look perfect," he said.

"What if they don't like me?"

He gave her a curious look. "They already love you. Besides, it's too late to run," he teased, tugging her close.

She melted into his arms. "I would never. I promised."

"So, you did. Come then, meet your people."

Two Personal Protection units pulled back the curtain and the couple stepped out into the sunlight hand in hand.

The herald stamped his staff.

"His Royal Highness the Prince of Wales Aerysleigh Cole Highridge and Her Royal Highness, Duchess of Cornwall." He paused and looked back.

Ella nodded.

"Cinder Eliana Graceling Steelhaugh Highridge."

THE END

Metal and Bone

Turn the page for a sneak peek into the next book in the world of
Metal and Bone

Cogs and Fur

By

C.I. Chevron

Chapter One

Taken

The hand holding the pipette over the beaker trembled, knocking the glass pieces together with a high-pitched chime that hurt her ears. Entranced by the swirl of blood, Isabeau Steelhaugh ignored the tremor and continued to stir the mixture with the rod in her left hand. *Could this be it? Would the corpuscles react?*

"Just do it," advised Aurelia from the string and wood bed perched under the tiny window. "What is this? The millionth time?" The sigh accompanied by the peevish tone told Isabeau her sister harboured little hope for the success of this round of research.

She didn't take her eyes from the mesmerising dance of red corpuscles in green reagent. "Get away from the window," she said out of habit, knowing full well where her sister sat. Her younger sibling always took too many risks. "It will be dark soon and it's a full moon tonight," Isabeau added.

"There are clouds. And smoke. And other things," Aurelia answered without moving.

"Regardless, the danger is there."

"You may see the night and the moon as dangers," Aurelia's dress rustled as she rose with a slowness the epitome of defiance. "However, I do not," she finished.

Remember, she's the youngest. Though only two years older, sometimes Isabeau feel ancient compared to her fey, pale sister. *She's becoming more uncontrollable with each passing night.*

Isabeau finally looked across the three-step distance separating her from the most important person in her life. The only one she trusted explicitly, the one who endured...and survived alongside her. She opened her mouth to argue and Aurelia lifted her chin, ready for the challenge. Instead, Isabeau cocked her head towards the street. "Did you hear that?"

Above the usual clatter of carriages, the last ditch offers from vendors to potential customers, and workers moving to and from the docks and factories, came the grind and rub of metal on metal. The sound continued rhythmically, teasing the edges of her hearing.

"What?" asked Aurelia, her voice now a whisper and all challenge gone. "Is it her?"

Isabeau waved for silence with the pipette. She closed her eyes and let her mind drift with the sound, reaching beyond the realm of human hearing, sifting through the noises until she focused exclusively on the metallic rasp.

"It's a modified and it's coming this way," she concluded.

Aurelia shrank into the corner with a hiss. Her needle-sharp canines gleamed ivory in the onyx shadows.

Discarding her tools, Isabeau hurried to her sister's side and waited. A human modified with metal, wood, or leather posed little threat. In fact, a good many an honest citizen found themselves missing a limb from accident or war, her own stepsister, Princess CinderElla, being one of them.

However, when one was hunted as they were, everyone became suspect, particularly the modifieds and those mutated by the chemical poisons in the air. These were the very people her mother would use to run them to ground. The laws of the land allowed for eight percent of the body to be modified, a hand, a foot, half of a limb. In the age of discovery, however, many people went above and beyond the law. Illegal experiments, such as those of the wanted German double agent, Jutta Linberg-Steelhaugh, tended to produce monsters—like her.

And Jutta would stop at nothing to get her rogue experiments, or daughters as some people thought them, back under her thumb.

The tiny window of the basement room faced Tinman Alley, a broken, cobbled thoroughfare in the Whitechapel area of the East London slums. A dangerous place to hide, but a free zone where few questions were asked. Other noises competed with the one she strained to follow, and she lost the brittle sound.

"Lower the lamp?" Aurelia breathed into her ear.

Isabeau eyed the paraffin device lighting her work. "Too obvious, it would just act as a signal. Be still." As always in the face of danger, little sister bowed to her wisdom and remained silent. Still, Isabeau second guessed her decision. Should she dim the light? *If we are observed, I don't want to give evidence we suspect anything.*

She released her breath. "Whatever made the noise is gone. Maybe I am being too sensitive. The sounds could be a dock worker or even a soldier." She gave her trembling sister a squeeze and stroked the golden tresses resting on her shoulder. "I'm sorry. I did not mean to upset you needlessly."

"You never do anything without cause. Many a time your remarkable hearing has saved us from capture." Aurelia flashed her a smile, the canines gone, "Though I do think it a perfectly rotten way to call me from the window." They shared an uneasy laugh. "Go, test the blood...if it is not already too late?"

Isabeau rushed back to the table. "I nearly forgot." She held the beaker against the tiny flame and bit back her disappointment. Black sludge coated the bottom of the glass, the antidote from the pipette staining the rough wooden surface. "I'm going to have to start over. Our blood is just so...reactive. Maybe I should try the process in the daylight."

"You already tried that," reminded Aurelia leaning over to peer at the contents. "It takes you a full turn of the hourglass to prepare the chemicals, and me just as long to set the apparatus. Besides, you know my blood behaves even more vigorously during the daylight."

Isabeau stirred a bit of water into the beaker and tossed the ruined experiment into the night jar. "I know. I just wish I could figure this out. If only we had Mother's notes, or even the notations of our changes over the years." She slapped her hand on the splintered wood, an action that only served to drive a splinter into her thumb. "Anything would be better than this blind experimentation."

Aurelia sank onto the bed, suddenly listless and if possible, even more pale. "But we don't. So why fight it?"

"How are you feeling?" asked Isabeau, touching Aurelia's forehead. So cold.

"Good. I'm hungry and little weak."

"Bread?" If that is what one dared call the hard loaf balanced atop a small apothecary chest.

"Not that kind of hungry."

"How many days have passed since your last injection?"

Her sister waved a negligent hand. "I don't know. Two. Three."

"Aurelia, you need to help me keep track of these things. I can't do everything, you know. We won't have a prayer of finding a cure if you do not collect every bit of scientific evidence possible."

"A prayer. Funny. I don't think God hears creatures like us."

In three very unladylike strides, Isabeau crossed to the trunk by the door. "Don't mock God, Aurelia. At the very least I would like to escape His notice, though a little help would not be unwelcome. Now where is my notebook?"

She flipped open the lid and pawed through the meagre contents. Two simple dresses, nightdresses, unmentionables, and corsets—a far cry from just six months ago when she and Aurelia were presented as marriage candidates at Prince Aerysleigh's Kensington Palace ball. Though the whole fiasco ended happily for her stepsister, now the Duchess of York, Isabeau and Aurelia found it safer to hide—from everyone.

She hissed as her fingers came in contact with the mirror and brush.

"Watch the silver..." warned her sister.

"Couldn't you put them a little lower or between layers?" Isabeau blew on her stinging digits. The scientist in her noted how her silver allergy seemed to wax and wane with the moon's phases.

"I tried, but your constant rummaging doesn't make it easy. You always find them. And why do you put the hypodermics and notebooks at the bottom of the trunk? You know I need them."

"I don't want anyone to find a record of my experiments," Isabeau snapped, the fear from moments before and now frustration getting the better of her. She attempted to rein in her temper. "It would help if you tried to jot down a few notations on your physical state." But now that she concentrated on the problem, Isabeau sensed the time between Aurelia's infusions grew shorter.

She removed a belt lined with sliders from under the sought for notebook. She checked the hypodermic snug in its leather compartment and the assortment of glass vials in their slings. "Now, we just need a healthy donor."

Aurelia groaned. "I hate that part."

"I know, but if we are ever going to find a cure..."

"I know, I know. We have to do a few unsavoury things."

Isabeau frowned. "That's right. You are nothing but at odds with me at every turn tonight. Grab your travelling coat and let's go before you become too weak to move. I am not carrying you."

Aurelia remained on the bed. "I know you could. You're getting stronger all the time."

Isabeau froze at the reminder of her own changes. Sometimes, by focusing on curing Aurelia, she could forget such things.

Aurelia motioned toward the flickering amber light of the gas lights in the street. "But if I just embrace the moon...I could be strong—like you."

"No!" Isabeau attempted to rise then sank back down with a moan.

Metal rubbed metal as the sound that plagued her hearing five minutes before screeched to a crippling frequency. She huddled beside the trunk and gripped her ears. The door burst inward, slamming Isabeau against the wall. The belt flew from her grasp.

We've been found!

"Aurelia!" Isabeau cried.

The lamp sputtered and dimmed, but she required no light to see the mammoth shadow which filled her swimming vision. It carried one shoulder hunched higher than the other, torso twisting sideways with each forward step. Metal encased his face, goggles tight against a bare skull in the back, as though to hide some horrible disfigurement. Attached to his chest was a contraption with bellows that produced the shrill noise.

Isabeau clutched her temple, incapacitated by the sudden ache from the assault on her ears and the blow. Aurelia stood, a fiery-eyed angel. She looked so small and thin. Only Isabeau and Ella knew how dangerous she truly was. But Aurelia's limbs trembled in her threadbare gown as though against a terrible gale. She needed help, and Isabeau was the only one who could protect her.

"Where is the other girl?" demanded the intruder, unaware of Isabeau crouched behind him. His head rotated back and forth above a metal collar. Ape-like, his arms hung low, protected by iron vambraces sporting spikes. Nostrils flared as he snuffled.

Isabeau gathered her skirts and collected her knees under her. She pulled the belt closer and slipped the hypodermic from its case. With shaking fingers, she chose the second vial which contained the potent cyanide, all the while gauging the slow progress of the monster toward her sister.

At three paces, Aurelia drew her lips back from razor sharp teeth in a snarl. Fingers formed claws ending in wicked nails. She leaped, slashing at the reaching arms. Any other time her attack would have been effective, but now her body betrayed her. She stumbled into his grasping embrace. A taloned hand wrapped around her fragile neck, lifting her from the ground. "Ahh, yer the weak one. Ere's the other?"

"Right here," Isabeau growled, a rumbling sound wrenched from the monster she concealed inside. However, with her sister in trouble, she did not hesitate to use those special abilities she fought hard to restrain. She leapt, hypodermic poised to strike. The monster spun faster than she anticipated, striking her with Aurelia's ragdoll limp body. Arms flailing uselessly, she crashed into the table. Glass splintered, digging into her skin. Blood slicked her palms, the copper scent strong to her sensitive senses. The lamp shattered. Oil and fire escaped in a muted explosion. The dry table caught and burned, the light in the dull room sudden and intense.

Isabeau tucked her elbows under her body and rolled away. The plunger of the hypodermic bent then broke under her weight, the cyanide staining her dress. No matter where anyone stood, the size of the room prevented true escape from the flames. The monster yelled for help. A bearded fellow with a canvas sack and a rat-faced bloke covered in a strong chemical smell pushed through the door.

Chloroform!

Beard-man immediately took his canvas bag to the flames. "Put it out!" he screamed. "All of Whitechapel will burn."

"Let it," grunted the fiend. "Get th' girl, Flint. She wants 'em both and 'ill pay 'andsomely."

Rat-face, Flint, tried to dance around the growing conflagration to trap Isabeau, waving a scented cloth with an evil grin. She jerked the scissors from her chatelaine just before he caught her arm and tried to get the chloroform close to her nose. She plunged the small implement into his neck, aiming for his jugular.

Besides the fact Isabeau had never stabbed a man—she was no Princess Ella—her senses reeled from the assault of sound and smell. Both her aim and use of force was off and the scissors skidded across her attacker's coat collar. A narrow cut gleamed scarlet on the dingy white of his shirt. She pulled back for a second attempt, but Flint pushed her away, screaming and clutching a wound much too shallow for Isabeau's liking.

She faced the monster now, ignoring the other fellow who leapt about the fire. "Let go of my sister."

"How 'bout you come with me? She's missed ye," the twisted man replied in a conversational tone.

Isabeau grit her teeth. *How had her mother found them?* They had been so careful. They never did the same thing twice, never took the same route, or shopped at the same vendors. Even when Aurelia's hunger forced them to find a donor, they never used the same location. Despite the anonymity offered by the crushing humanity of the slum, someone recognised them. "Tell my mother she can rot in whatever hell she's found to take her. She doesn't own us anymore."

A miner's coal-dark visage peered through the window. Bushy eyebrows shot up as he took in the scene. "Fire!" He screeched at a pitch high enough to shatter windows. The yell was taken up through the slums, like a wave rippling away, growing stronger and more urgent as the word passed. Next to cholera and smallpox, fire was the third greatest fear held by the denizens of the slums. A single tipped candle could destroy blocks and leave hundreds homeless.

Isabeau cringed back as more people looked in the window and footsteps pounded on the stairs.

The brute motioned to Isabeau. "Get her," he ordered the bearded fellow who now held only smoldering remnants of his sack. The charred smell competed with the lung searing smoke filling the room. The big bloke dragged Aurelia toward the door, shoving past a gaping couple holding small pitchers of water.

"No," Isabeau shouted. She sprang to grab her sister, using all her strength and covering the ten feet in a single bound. The rat-faced Flint grabbed her ankle. Isabeau slapped against the hard floor, her skirts tangling about her boots. Kicking violently, she tried to fight free.

She turned to pry at the grasping fingers, but the other bloke abandoned the fire and kicked her in the back. She tumbled onto the chest of the fallen fellow, her face inches from the source of putrid onion breath and flapping lips yelling for help. His eyes begged. The wound grew larger by the second, covering them both in hot, sticky blood. She slapped at the spasming fingers which kept her from her goal. She needed to help Aurelia.

The bearded fellow pushed the gigantic fiend through the door though he moved at his own speed. "Get outta here. The bobbies will be on the way. Go, we'll get the other girl later."

Feeling as though she had been hit by a steam engine, Isabeau dragged her body after the disappearing duo then leaned against the door sobbing.

"Aurelia," she screamed, desperate for a reply.

But even her acute hearing caught no answer.

Chapter Two

The Commissioner

Basil Traverson stepped carefully over the cobbles of North Umberland Avenue. Silently he cursed the need for the cane with each painful step while attempting the stoic and dignified expression of a gentleman turned war hero. By the reactions of the people he passed, he failed miserably.

He lingered at a corner costermonger to buy a meat pie. The distraction gave him the opportunity to surreptitiously rest his leg and consider the mounds of reports waiting on his desk. With the Cinder case solved, or at least quietly made to disappear by the love addled prince, Basil had the time to turn his attention to crimes of a more serious bent.

Missing persons reports abounded, a fact easily attributed to Body Snatchers intent on making a quick profit, no doubt. While death was common in the stacked, overcrowded slums, reports of murders had risen precipitously—each one more fantastical than the one before.

Rumours tickled his ears of creatures stalking the street, walking barefaced though the poisonous Thames mists. None of it made sense, but all seemed to point to illegal scientific research, perhaps by the missing German infiltrator and spy Judith Linberg-Steelhaugh.

And her daughters, Isabeau and Aurelia, were the keys to finding her.

Unfortunately, they too remained in hiding. All reports suggested the pair remained in London and despite their lady-like upbringing, they seemed to know how to blend in. There could also be more to them that casual observation missed for the modifieds sheltered the pair for some inexplicable reason. Still, the sisters, especially the eldest, stood apart and should be easily identifiable.

He remembered well his first and only meeting with Isabeau Linberg-Steelhaugh. During the massive manhunt conducted for her stepsister, a modified human now lovingly called CinderElla, she appeared at Scotland Yard. The information she gave allowed the prince to stop his love from fleeing the country and secure his happily-ever-after. *Bully for him.*

But it was the raven-haired beauty that took Basil's breath away. Not only did she have the height and figure to capture a man's attention, the flashing green eyes challenged everything. Her gaze showed a canny intelligence beneath the canvas of the demure lady. Her willingness to potentially sacrifice herself for the love match of two people whose interests ran contrary to her own, moved Basil more than a woman had in a long time. It recalled his war days when the soldiers of his unit died so he might live.

Foolish romantic notions.

Shaking off his melancholy, he straightened to continue his progress to the metro police headquarters. Despite the evening hour, the street remained packed with sellers hawking their wares.

His eyes roamed the crowd.

Years on the continent taught him how awareness of his surroundings could save a life. Most of the people seemed normal enough, intent on their daily activities rather than nefarious deeds. The glint of metal was obvious and prevalent. Many of the men and women were war veterans turned civilians and most bore scars or limbs replaced with prostheses. Others possessed a difference about them a little harder to detect, mutation from the chemical weapons used on the continent and the effects of the poisonous mists that rose from the Thames.

He caught the devious gaze of an iron-jawed man loitering in the doorway of the Trotter public house. Carefully the fellow turned his head away as though looking for a friend. Basil knew better but left it alone. He snorted. It wasn't as though he could stride across the street and interrogate the fellow. He would be long gone before Basil wove his way through the carts and horses. Most likely he'd be run over by a carriage.

"Evening, Commissioner." Basil jerked at the voice close to his shoulder, half drawing a blade from his cane.

The rude interrupter of his thoughts chuckled. "No need for that, sir, merely wishing you well on this fine night."

Basil straightened, all politeness, and bowed slightly. "Ms. Mayhem, how goes The Modified Observer? Still chasing Valkyrie sightings and touting the benefits of axle grease?"

The red-haired reporter frowned at his dig. She did have a reputation for being in the wrong place at the right time. Then she smiled and curtsied with the same exaggerated politeness. She was dressed as a respectable, if not practical, lady this evening, with modest dress and hat. Basil knew her to possess nearly as many disguises as the thief Cinder. Her clothes were obviously tailored to fit, though rumpled, and no doubt hid at least the implements of her trade. At least one of these being a lock pick kit.

"I am well enough, thank you. There is always plenty to report on as the crimes against modifieds rise," she said.

"As well as the crimes committed by them," Basil observed dryly.

The lady's smile brightened. "There are villainous characters of every sort in every walk of life. You of all people should know that, Commissioner."

"Indeed." He touched his hat to excuse himself and move on.

"Today I am quite interested in the movement of Isabeau Linberg-Steelhaugh from the Metro to Newgate Prison." Ms. Mayhem pulled a pad of paper from a hidden pocket along with the nub of a pencil. "Quite audacious considering she is the stepsister to Princess Eliana. A modified princess and member of the Society for the Protection and Advancement of Mutants and Modifieds."

Basil steeled his jaw from revealing any reaction to this bit of news. "Contrary to your practice of business, Ms. Mayhem, I do not discuss police business on street corners. I also need no reminder of the Princess' dubious affiliations."

As much as he suspected the nefarious plotting of S.P.A.M.M. and suspected Princess Eliana's loyalty with her involvement, she was the wife of his good friend and after only a brief stint of burglary, seemed to stay on the right side of the law. However, the news

Isabeau had been detained and subsequently moved was another matter entirely. One he should have been alerted to immediately.

He moved off down the street with renewed purpose.

"So, I'll be interviewing you later then," the lady called to his back, "after you have had a chance to catch up on the information."

Basil ignored the insinuation that he did not know the goings on in his department, despite the fact the charge in this particular case may be true.

A horn blared from the river, the call being picked up and trumpeted up and down the docks and warehouses by the city commissioned warning system and street vendors. The whole city froze. Not a horse snorted, not a vendor called, not even an infant fussed. For a heartbeat the only sound echoing across the slums and the manor houses alike was the wailing warning.

"The mists are rising!" called a sweeper boy pushing a broom in front of a young couple so they could cross the street with relative cleanliness.

At that instant the usual street pandemonium returned. Vendors tossed tarps over goods and barrowed away. Those with horses and donkeys vied for passage on the streets and pedestrians remained nimble or suffered the consequences.

Basil took the opportunity to escape. He hurried down the steet and stepped into the hall of Scotland Yard where a fleet of fresh-faced constables filed into a room and exited with gas masks.

"Give the stubborn ones thirty minutes," he advised Sergeant Palmer who checked seals and cannisters at the door, "then round them up and find a safe house."

"Yes, sir," she replied. "Orders came through today that Princess Eliana has designated the Canterlevel warehouse at the Wapping Dock as a refuge."

He gritted his teeth at the mention of the princess again, but this brought his mind back to the other problem, her stepsister.

"Fine. I've heard Isabeau Linberg-Steelhaugh may be in Newgate." The grey-haired sergeant adjusted the air on an oxygen canister and tapped the last young constable on the shoulder.

She waited with her reply until the fellow clomped down the stair. "Aye, sir, she was picked up this evening, not an hour ago, during an altercation in Whitechapel. Seems she tried to burn down the slums. Elan Doublestock made the apprehension."

"As in Baron Doublestock?"

"No. One of the sons—either the fourth or fifth. Seems he grew tired of the parlour parties and decided to go slumming."

"That particular hobby of some of the nobles is going to get someone hurt or killed."

"Yes, sir," the sergeant demurred. Once Basil carried that stigma. A third son of a Lord taking a police commission? Even now the men and women he worked with suspected his motives and drive.

"Have her brought to my office."

He had never seen the old Sergeant flustered. She had been around since the forming of the constabulary and had been a Bow Street runner, but now she looked quizzical. He marked the change of expression as a win on his part.

"Sir?"

"I want to interview the lady. Bring her to me."

Again, the sergeant paused.

"Didn't you hold her here?" He demanded.

"You were not in, sir, when she was detained, so I sent her to Newgate for holding."

He couldn't hide his horror. He met the lady once when she had revealed the whereabouts of her stepsister to Prince Aerysleigh, but her sophisticated manner and gentle speech proclaimed her a lady and she deserved to be treated as such.

"Get her now."

ABOUT THE AUTHOR

C.I. Chevron is an author known for her work in the world of *Metal and Bone* as well as sci-fi and fantasy short stories. She is a member and sometimes officer of North East Texas Writers Organization and active in a weekly critique group. She writes from a Texas hilltop where she lives with her husband, daughters, and too many animals to give an accurate count.

Want to learn more about C.I. Chevron and what's coming next?

https://www.cichevron.com/

https://www.facebook.com/cichevronauthor

Made in the USA
Middletown, DE
20 September 2021

48741241R00196